Re/L

Doms of the FBI #5

Michele Zurlo

www.michelezurloauthor.com

Re/Leased

Doms of the FBI: Re/Leased
Copyright © June 2016 by Michele Zurlo
ISBN: 978-1-942414-20-9

All rights reserved. This copy is intended for the original purchaser of this e-book ONLY. No part of this e-book may be reproduced, stored in or introduced into a retrieval system, or transmitted, in any form, or by any means (electronic, mechanical, photocopying, recording, or otherwise), without the prior written permission from the copyright owner and Lost Goddess Publishing LLC. Please do not participate in or encourage piracy of copyrighted materials in violation of the author's rights. Purchase only authorized editions.

Editor: Suzanne L. Spellicy
Cover Artist: Anne Kay

Published by
Lost Goddess Publishing LLC
www.michelezurloauthor.com

This e-book is a work of fiction. While reference might be made to actual historical events or existing locations, the names, characters, places and incidents are either the product of the author's imagination or are used fictitiously, and any resemblance to actual persons, living or dead, business establishments, events, or locales is entirely coincidental.

Warning: This e-book contains sexually explicit scenes and adult language and may be considered offensive to some readers. It is not meant for underage readers.

————

DISCLAIMER: Education and training are necessary in order to learn safe BDSM practices. Lost Goddess Publishing LLC is not responsible for any loss, harm, injury or death resulting from use of the information contained in any of its titles. This is a work of fiction, and license has been taken with regard to BDSM practices.

Michele Zurlo

Reading Order

Re/Bound

Re/Paired

Re/Claimed

Re/Defined

Re/Leased

Coming Soon: Re/Viewed

And keep an eye out for SAFE Security—a new BDSM series
from Michele Zurlo launching in 2017

Acknowledgements:

This novel would not exist without help from some key people. First I'd like to thank my editor/wife, who listened to me prattle on about David and Autumn for as long as I needed to talk and who helped me troubleshoot solutions to the many problems that came up.

I'd also like to thank Lea Ann Patton, the fan who won the chance to name the main characters of this novel. They fit the characters perfectly.

Chapter One

"CalderCo is hurting badly, David. There's nobody else I trust to straighten it out."

The message ended, leaving David staring at his phone. So many thoughts and fierce feelings pummeled his brain that he couldn't quite sort them out. Thirteen years had passed since he'd walked out on his father. Harsh words hadn't needed to flow between them because they'd already been said—whispered vehemently and shouted at the tops of their lungs—from the time David was old enough to rebel against the way his father insisted on controlling every aspect of his life.

His mother's death had sealed the deal. He'd packed his bags before the funeral, and he had been gone before his father had arrived home from the wake. Eighteen and freshly graduated, the world had been his for the taking. Eschewing his father's money and connections, he'd forged his own path just fine.

"You don't have to go." Dean Alloway pulled David from the darkness of his bitter memories.

David had met Dean in the Marines, and the duo had become fast friends. They'd saved each other's asses more times than either could count. He sighed heavily. "Yes, I do. I promised my mother on her deathbed that I'd come when he called—but only once." The feud between David and his father had been going on for as long as he could remember. His mother used to run interference. When she was around, David could breathe. He could be himself and not have to worry about the fallout. Once she fell ill, he and his father had taken steps to hide their hatred for one another.

But, of course, she hadn't been fooled. *"One day, your father is going to need you, David,"* she'd said, her voice raspy and weak. *"Be there for him. Do this for me. I love you."* She'd been too spent to say more, and she'd slipped away within the hour.

"Fine." Dean folded his hands on the table. He was a bigger guy than he seemed. The sweaters, vests, and dress pants went a long way toward disguising the bulky muscles earned during years of heavy physical labor, and the metrosexual haircut completed the image. Dean was all about understated power and surprising the enemy. And manicures. David had never met another man who got weekly manicures, yet could also neutralize a target with one well-placed blow. "Tell me what you need. Frankie, Jesse, and I are here for you, man. You're not alone. We'd never leave you hanging."

"I know you wouldn't, but this is something I have to do on my own."

"No, you don't." Frankie Sikara sauntered in, a wet towel draped over her shoulder. She kissed the top of his head before flopping down on the chair next to him. "Sell that bullshit elsewhere."

David hadn't known Frankie was in the building. From the black leggings and sports bra, he deduced that she'd spent the morning in the gym. "Jesse in the shower?"

"Yep. I kicked his ass, and now I'm leaving him alone to cry it out." She winked to let them know that Jesse didn't need medical attention. Frankie Sikara was one tough woman. Trained in six different martial arts, she was deadlier than any of them. "I heard part of the message. Let's hear the whole thing."

"We'll wait for Jesse," Dean countered. "You can go ahead and grab a shower."

They had one locker room in the facility, which wasn't the issue outsiders thought it would be. Once you'd been through hell and back with someone, little things like that ceased to matter. She was one of the guys. Frankie glared at Dean. "I already did, genius."

Dean frowned, which made him look all kinds of menacing and foreboding. Well, as foreboding as someone in a designer sweater could get. "You're not wearing a shirt."

"Another point for Captain Obvious." Frankie's dark eyes flashed, and David found himself smiling. The dress code was an ongoing point of contention between these two. "I'm waiting for my hair to dry so it doesn't get my shirt wet. If the sight of my bra offends you, I can take it off." Crossing her arms, she grasped the elastic band on the lower part of her sports bra.

Dean's expression didn't change, and that was a challenge Frankie wouldn't ignore.

As amusing as it was, David held up a hand. "How about you two parking lot the issue?"

"Dress code again?" Jesse Foraker came in, also missing a shirt. As he kept his hair high and tight, he didn't have Frankie's reason for going topless. "If you want us to wear shirts, then maybe you should stop stealing them from our lockers?"

The frown on Dean's face melted. He shrugged. "I left replacements."

"I'm not wearing that fucking shirt. It looks like I should be chugging a beer in a bowling alley." Jesse inclined his head toward the lone phone on the table. "What's going on?"

"David's dad called."

Jesse lifted a brow. "Damn. How long has it been?"

"Thirteen years." David hadn't thought about his father in so long that he'd stopped measuring the time. "I don't know how he got my number."

"I'm going to blame the Internet," Frankie said. "It's not like you're hiding."

"No, but I changed my name." He'd taken his mother's maiden name, Eastridge, when he'd cut ties. Accepting that his friends weren't going to let him handle this alone, David played the message again.

Three million dollars is missing from the company. This is going to break us if I can't find it, or at least find out who's responsible. I'm at a loss, David. The best guess I got is a woman, an employee named Autumn Sullivan. Something isn't right about her, and not just because she's into all that whips and chains crap. Anyway, I don't have hard evidence. CalderCo is hurting badly, David. There's nobody else I trust to straighten it out.

Jesse frowned. "Why doesn't he conduct an audit? He can turn the findings over to the FBI, and they'll prosecute. Insurance should cover the loss."

This was another point of contention between David and his father. "My dad's business is like an iceberg. Some stuff is above board, but there's a lot hidden under the water. There's no way he'll want law enforcement looking through his books."

Dean pressed his fingertips together. "How dirty are we talking? Mob connections?"

"Possibly. I've long suspected that he launders money. It could explain his desperation. If he's lost money belonging to the mob, they're not going to be patient while he goes looking for it." David had turned his back on the family business from a young age. It would only have given his father control over that part of his life too. "I'd love to see what the FBI has on him."

Frankie stood. "On it." She nailed Dean with a hard look. "I have extra shirts, but I would appreciate having back the one you took."

"It's in your office." Dean pointed to Jesse. "So is yours."

"Great. I'll dig up the dirt on Autumn Sullivan." Jesse followed Frankie out the door.

Left alone with Dean, David waited for his buddy to deliver his opinion. "You're not going in there alone. We'll research, do some recon, and then develop a plan."

These people were his family—always there to support him. Now they were going to help him honor his mother's memory. Before he choked on his emotions, David agreed to the plan. "Thanks."

―――――――――

"Hurry up. I hear the elevator." Chris Alcoa sputtered another vehement plea/threat, which Autumn ignored.

She listened carefully as she concentrated on moving the catches into the correct position. At last, her patience was rewarded with a soft click as the door unlocked. She turned the knob, grabbed her kit, and followed Chris into the room. This job would be a hell of a lot easier if he'd just given her the passwords and trusted her to do the job. But trust was at a premium between them. Autumn didn't take it personally. She didn't trust his ass either. This was a limited liability temporary partnership where neither was beholden to the other.

She tucked her tools into the soft leather holder and rolled it up. Her father had given her the kit for her seventh birthday, and she still took the top-of-the-line lock pick set everywhere. Now that he was gone, it was like having a piece of him always with her.

Chris settled into the office chair in front of the older-model desktop and booted up the machine. While she waited, Autumn scanned the office, looking for anything interesting. Given the fact that the computer wasn't even networked—it had slots for two different kinds of floppy disks—she didn't hold out much hope. Still, it was better to be safe than sorry. Listening and recording equipment could be networked elsewhere in the building.

Her search turned up nothing. She picked up a paperweight and sighed. This wasn't the life she'd envisioned for herself, especially not after the accident. Pissing off powerful people never led anywhere good—as her father had proved once and for all. Autumn considered that last incident an unintentional farewell gift, and the scar on her shoulder functioned as a constant reminder.

"Don't touch anything." Chris hissed again. He really was a snake. Either that, or he'd sprung a leak.

"You're the idiot not wearing gloves." From an early age, Autumn had mastered the art of speaking clearly at a low volume—another lesson from Dad.

Ignoring Chris, she studied the picture frames, looking for likely candidates. She didn't know what he was after, and she couldn't resist looking to see what other kinds of secrets were hiding in the office. The owner of this place didn't seem innovative, so she figured the safe was probably behind a framed piece of art. However, the one over the bookshelf only concealed the bad paint job behind.

"What are you doing? Stop touching stuff." Now he sounded worried.

Autumn smiled. Amateur. "Sixteen minutes until the security comes by. We have plenty of time." It might have been a two-man job, but that was only because a series of locked doors and an antiquated security system stymied the original man. Enter Autumn, the mistress of breaking and entering, skills she hired out when she needed extra cash.

None of the pictures—no paintings here—proved fruitful. She was about to give up when she noticed that a section of books were less dusty than those surrounding them. One by one, she flipped through them. The books were inconsequential, nothing more than hardcover garage sale finds. Someone had collected them in an effort to give the cheap office décor and its owner a sense of literary style. Nothing except literature. Knocking on the wood panel in the rear, however, produced a hollow sound.

"Damn it, Jenna. I didn't hire you to sit there and read. Be the lookout." Chris tapped the computer's keys harder to show just how mad he was.

"Simmer down. They'll never know I was here." The novice, on the other hand, was leaving too many clues. Hair from his clothes—cat, most likely, mixed with shavings from his lunchtime visit to the Kwickie Cut Hut—was shedding all over the place. Her hair was tightly coiled, and her clothes were freshly cleaned. She knew how to not leave a trace. And when to use an alias.

Feeling along the back of the bookcase, she found the spring that released a panel. She'd found the safe—good thing she'd brought her state-of-the-art mini stethoscope, this one a hand-me-down from Dad. She set to work, listening for those tumblers to lock into place. It wasn't on the cutting edge of safe technology. Judging from the location, the owner was relying on the hiding place doing most of the security work. She could crack this without graphing the clicks.

Autumn had it open inside twenty seconds. "How are you doing over there?" She wasn't in his field of vision unless he turned around, but she could see him just fine.

"I'm downloading the files I need right now."

"Fantastic. Right on schedule." She didn't give a rip about those files. Recipes for barbeque sauce bored her. There were thousands on the Internet, and millions more if you changed out some of the ingredients for things you liked better. The contents of a safe, though, that was the stuff! Cracking a safe was better than tearing off wrapping paper, and opening her first one had ruined the whole idea of getting presents that were easy to open. Her father, bless his generous and thoughtful heart, had begun hiding her gifts in increasingly difficult safes. Her eighteenth birthday present had taken seven months to open.

Her breath caught as she swung the door out. Inside, she found some of the usual items—passports, a couple hundred in cash, personal papers—and some of the unusual—a plastic container with assorted baby teeth, a worn dog collar, and a pair of dolls. Autumn had never caught the Barbie bug. She hadn't cared one whit about the plastic blonde doll with the lifeless, painted eyes. Her sister had a small collection, and they'd mostly used them to plan heists. Of course, Summer had also spent hours dressing her dolls, fixing their hair, and imagining them in all sorts of glamorous situations.

Thinking of Summer made Autumn's heart thump painfully. The accident three years ago that had led to six surgeries on her shoulder had put her older sister in a coma. She took one of the dolls and stared at it. The hair was super long and dark, like Autumn's, and the outfit was unlike anything she'd seen on a children's doll. Hand sewn with tiny silver sequins, the ostentatious dress screamed at her. She grabbed the other doll.

Fuck me. These were real Sonny and Cher dolls. Summer had been obsessed with watching reruns of the variety show one summer when they'd rented a cabin that had a VHS collection. They weren't all that valuable now, not really, but Summer would have loved them. Autumn left the cash and tucked the dolls into her satchel.

"Almost ready." Chris really needed a patch kit, one that covered his whole mouth.

She closed the safe and replaced the books. Perfect. Then she glanced at the desk. "Put everything back exactly as you found it."

He scooted the chair closer to the desk.

Autumn rolled her eyes. The son of a bitch was going to get caught because he'd eventually brag to the wrong person. Of course, he worked for a competing firm, so the bragging might net him a promotion. She adjusted the chair lower, moved the keyboard closer to the monitor, and lined up the pencils next to the keyboard. A meticulously neat office meant the owner would notice if his pencils weren't perfect.

In the parking garage, before they separated, Chris grabbed her arm. "Find anything good to read?"

"The Adventures of Huckleberry Finn." If he hadn't noticed her robbing a safe, then she wasn't going to say anything about also taking the book. He handed her an envelope. She thumbed through the bills to count them and make sure they were real. "Pleasure, Chris."

With that, she left the garage. He didn't need to see her getaway car, or Poco, as she affectionately termed the Piece-O Crap-O. She waited in the shadows until his car drove way, and then she strolled to where she'd hidden Poco. They'd made good time, and she shouldn't be too late getting to Sunshine Acres.

"Hey there, young lady." Lorne shuffled across the hall as soon as Autumn came into the lobby. "I don't think we've met. I'm Lorne."

"Hi, Lorne." She shook his hand as she did every day. He'd lived a long and exciting life that began when he'd run away from home at sixteen to join the army during World War II. He was one of the many residents she'd come to know during her regular visits. "It's great to meet a handsome devil like you. How are they treating you?"

"The nurses are dutiful and efficient." He maintained a somber demeanor. "But I think the lady in 3B might have taken a shine to me. She pinched my bottom."

"It was an accident." The lady in 3B, Edith to her friends, zoomed from behind a tall potted plant. She screeched her wheelchair to a halt inches from Autumn. The cosmetology school must have just left because Edith had her hair done, and she wore full makeup. "If I wanted to make a pass at you, I'd ask you to dinner."

As Autumn watched, Edith pinched Lorne's bottom. He winked at her.

"Yoga starts in three minutes." Edith patted her lap. "Want a ride?"

Lorne sat down, and the pair took off. Autumn smiled as she navigated the maze of hallways that took her to the Vegetable Patch, as they affectionately and unofficially termed the ward housing long-term coma patients. She paused in the kitchen long enough to give Sonny and Cher a washing—who knew where they'd been?—and when she made it to Summer's room, she found that her sister had a visitor already.

"Julianne, I didn't know you were coming today." Autumn hugged her sister's best friend and the woman who'd helped her get a job. A real job, not one where she had to have an entrance and exit strategy ready ahead of time—and a contingency plan in case things went sideways.

The plucky redhead grinned, her hazel eyes green in the soft light. "You're twenty minutes late."

"For me, that's early." Autumn had a problem with being on time for anything legal. If she were to focus on the positives, she was punctual when it really mattered.

"True. The nurse said she woke up today."

Ever since the accident, Summer would wake up for a couple of minutes every few weeks. Sometimes she spoke, but most of the time she stared at her surroundings, lost and bewildered. Autumn liked to be around when that happened to help soothe her sister. She hated to think of the stress Summer suffered when she wasn't around. She peered closer at Summer, hoping lightning would strike twice in the same day. "When?"

"Ten twenty-seven this morning. She was up for ninety seconds. I already reamed them for not calling."

Autumn sighed. She understood the staff's reluctance—she and Julianne dropped everything to rush here every time it happened only to find that Summer had slipped back into the coma before they could make it. However, it was their job to make that call immediately. She grasped her sister's hand. "Summer, I'm so sorry I wasn't here. I hope you weren't too scared. It's the same room as last time, and I have your favorite things on the dresser where you can see them."

People thought she was crazy, talking to Summer the way she did, but Autumn paid them no mind. Her sister was trapped in there, and there was no way Autumn was going to leave her alone.

"I was telling her about my date last night," Julianne said. "It was pretty bad. The guy, Brad, told me he wasn't a smoker, but every time he came back from the bathroom—how many times do you need to pee during dinner?—he smelled like cigar smoke. Seriously, how can people stand those things? They smell like unwashed ass."

Julianne's father and grandfather had died from lung cancer, and so she'd sworn never to kiss a smoker. Autumn didn't comment. She sometimes sneaked a cigarette every now and again to calm her nerves. The smell reminded her of her father. "Was that it, or did he do other gross stuff like pick his nose or lean to the side to make it easier to fart?"

"You laugh, but I wasn't exaggerating about those guys." Julianne sighed. "I suck at finding men to date. Every one of them is somehow a loser. You know what I need?"

"Someone to vet your dates before you go out with them?" Autumn was a great judge of character. The moment she met Julianne, she knew that Summer had made a true friend. All these years later, Julianne was the only one who visited Summer.

"Yeah. I'm not going to go on another date that you don't meet first and approve." Julianne frowned. "I have a date Friday night. What are you doing after work?"

Autumn had a meeting with a friend to whom she owed a favor. "I have a little time. When and where?"

"My favorite coffee shop at five-thirty?"

Autumn put the details into the calendar on her phone so that she wouldn't forget.

Later, after Julianne left, Autumn dimmed the lights and closed the door. She never told Summer everything just in case the nursing staff was listening, but she told her enough. Her sister would understand the oblique references.

"I had a job today, which means I can pay for this month's PT. Yay! Anyway, I got you something." She pulled the dolls out of her bag and held them up for Summer to see. "Cher is wearing a Bob Mackie original, and Sonny is dressed to match her, but not to outdo her. She was always the star of the show. Remember when you spent a month sewing all those sequins onto your nightgown? She's wearing silver sequins. I'm going to put these on the dresser so you can see them when you wake up."

She chattered on for a while longer, and by the time the nurse came by to tell her that visiting hours were over, she'd finished reading a few chapters of Huck Finn aloud.

Chapter Two

"Autumn Sullivan didn't exist before six years ago. She was born with a credit score, checking account, birth certificate, and Facebook page full of kitten memes, but nothing I've been able to find is more than six years old." Jesse pressed another button on the remote, and an image of Autumn Sullivan came up.

Brilliant green eyes shone with hidden laughter, and dark brown hair framed a perfect, oval face. Freckles dotted the bridge of her nose, cute little spots on her sun-kissed skin. The other images showed parts of her face, but never a full-on frontal shot. "She's beautiful." David hadn't meant to say that out loud, but he did, and with this group, there was no covering that up. "She probably uses that to distract people while she's up to no good."

Frankie chuckled. "You're presuming guilt?"

"My dad had to have a good reason for singling her out."

"He said he wasn't sure, that something about it wasn't right," she reminded him.

"Yeah," he agreed. "Something isn't right about a thirty-year-old person who didn't exist until six years ago."

"If she's in witness protection, her history would look like this," Dean suggested. "Frankie, what did you find out from your friends in the FBI?"

"Brandy Lockmeyer said she wasn't in their database. However, CalderCo is on their watchlist. They're suspected of money laundering, which is what David thought they were doing." She gestured to Jesse to advance to the next slide. "They also suspect insider trading and fraud, but they don't have proof. If CalderCo is doing anything illegal, they're doing a great job of keeping it under wraps. The Feds don't have anything approaching a reason to get a warrant. There is no active investigation at this time."

Documents flashed across the screen, quarterly reports juxtaposed with pictures of empty warehouses. David wasn't surprised to hear these things about his father's company. Bill Calder had been secretive about his work and controlling when it came to his family. He'd shut David out of the business right up until he decided it was time for David to learn the ropes. By that time, David had discerned enough to know he didn't want to follow that path in life, and he for damn sure didn't want his father to have a say in anything he did. "Are they going to get in my way?"

"No, but they won't turn their noses up at your findings if you chose to share them."

Jesse clicked the next slide, and an image of a man with shoulder-length dark hair and black eyes came up. He looked sinister and forbidding, exactly the kind of man his father would hire as a bodyguard. "This is SSA Jordan Monaghan. You'll recognize him as the man Frankie and I were called in to help. We guarded his girlfriend while he worked with a team to catch the perp."

"Who turned out to be the ASAC of the Detroit field office." Dean's dry tone communicated his lack of surprise. "I don't know Lockmeyer or Monaghan like Frankie and Jesse do, so I'm not as inclined to blindly trust her or her agents."

"I've arranged a meet-and-greet with Monaghan at a play party." Frankie sneaked that gem into the debrief.

"What? Why?" David hadn't been to a play party in years.

"It's time for you to get back on the wagon." Frankie patted his hand. "You've played the moody, pouty, heartbroken slob long enough."

David hadn't played anything. His last relationship had disintegrated. After four years of bliss, she'd left him for another man. He could still hear her impatient response to his request for an explanation. She'd tossed it over her shoulder as she carried her suitcases out the door. *It just wasn't meant to be, okay? You're married to your work, and I'm tired of having a Master only when you have free time.* That had been three years ago. He'd moved on emotionally, and he'd abandoned the D/s lifestyle. Vanilla dating and casual encounters were much easier to walk away from. "I'm not any of those things. To begin with, I'm impeccably dressed."

"Yeah, that suit is a nice way to plant your nose in Dean's ass," Jesse chimed in. "Anyway, I've arranged a meeting with a mutual friend. She'll set you up with your date. You'll get a chance to vet Autumn Sullivan and get to know Jordan Monaghan. I've included a dossier in your folder that lists the likely players you'll find at the party and members of Monaghan's unit. Dustin Brandt and his sub are on the guest list, as is Keith Rossetti and his sub. Malcolm Legato and his wife plan to attend. She's a masochist, so perhaps you should pack your whips, and he recently quit the FBI."

"Spend some time with Legato," Dean interjected. "I hear he's good with technology. We can always use another geek, and if he's looking to freelance, maybe we can help him out."

"You want me to hire him to work undercover at CalderCo?" David frowned. He didn't want law enforcement, even if it was in the past, involved at all. "I'd rather have Jesse go in undercover and spend some time in the geek tank." At least he knew anything Jesse found would be kept confidential.

"Do what you need to do." Dean paged through his folder. "Who is the mutual friend?"

"Beatrice DePau knows Sullivan. Two years ago, we extracted her grandson from a compound in Mexico run by a drug cartel. He had been kidnapped from a local university and held for ransom. Beatrice said she'd rather pay us to get him out and do some damage than give money to terrorists and drug dealers. We blew up the compound." Jesse advanced three slides, stopping on an image of an elderly woman. "She runs Elite Solutions Modeling Agency."

"Sounds like an escort service," Dean said.

"It is." Jesse grinned. "Autumn Sullivan occasionally works there as a Domina. Beatrice knows more about Sullivan that she'll ever admit, but she's not talking. However, she did guarantee that Sullivan would attend the party as David's sub. Apparently she sometimes switches if the pay and circumstances are right. I made it worth her while. David is going to need to fly up tonight to meet with her. I've made the arrangements." Jesse slid an envelope across the table. Inside, David found round-trip tickets to Michigan. "You'll be back home by midnight."

"What's the plan for infiltrating CalderCo?" Dean asked. "I mean, aside from having Jesse get a job in tech support?"

David had talked to his father, treating him as a potential client instead of the man who sat on the sidelines of his Little League games yelling at him every time he missed a ball. "I'm representing a firm that does external audits. That'll give me access to people and systems." His father had wanted to introduce him as the prodigal son returning to take over the company, but David had nixed that, telling his father that no one could know they were related. With his Nordic coloring, David had always favored his mother's side of the family. His father's Mediterranean heritage only showed up in David's rich, brown eyes.

Dean nodded. "Great idea. You'll call if you need reinforcements? Frankie and I will be working a job, but we can drop it and pick it up later if need be."

David nodded. "Sounds like everything is in place." He gathered the folder of intel and the plane tickets. "I'll debrief with Jesse tomorrow."

Frankie followed him out the door. "I'm going to want details about the play party."

"Anyone in particular I should look out for?" David knew Frankie too well to think she wasn't fishing for a specific piece of information.

"Yeah. Autumn Sullivan."

"How are you this fine evening, Mr. Eastridge?"

David studied Beatrice DePau. The elderly woman had a slight build that made her seem frail. A closer look exposed the lie. The eighty-three-year-old's body was fit, honed through a lifetime commitment to healthy eating and tae kwon do. Her blue eyes shone with shrewdness, and her titian hair was the same color it had been for at least sixty years. Neither David nor the rest of his crew at SAFE Security had been able to find color photographs older than that.

He met her gaze and returned the friendly smile. "I'm doing fine, ma'am. Thank you for helping me on such short notice."

She took his hands in her petite ones. "I owe you guys quite a debt after you helped with my grandson. It's my pleasure to take care of you."

David wondered exactly what Autumn Sullivan expected would happen at a play party. "I'm not looking for a *date* date. I just need an escort who knows what she's doing."

Patting one of his hands, she grinned, and her eyes sparkled with mischief. "Jesse explained already. You'll like Bree."

Her use of the alias Autumn used for her work as a Domina threw him off for a microsecond. He scanned the empty office. "Where is she?"

Beatrice's expression briefly wrinkled, the closest she came to a frown. "She's later than usual. This is her one fault. I asked her to be here by six-thirty, so it shouldn't be long now."

"It's after seven." Working in private security had taught David the art of patience, but this was different. Sullivan was under the impression that he was a client, and it was unprofessional to keep a client waiting.

"Why don't you go ahead and have a seat?" Beatrice indicated the sofa in her office. "I can get you another model, if that's what you want."

"No. That's all right. I'll wait."

Just then, the door burst open. Autumn Sullivan—in a pantsuit suitable for a day at the office—hurried inside. He knew she worked at CalderCo, but he'd expected her to change into something a little more appropriate for a model meeting a potential date. "Sorry I'm late. Traffic." She kissed Beatrice's proffered cheek before turning her attention to David. She offered her hand. "I'm Mistress Bree. You must be David."

The same stunning green eyes regarded him with friendly firmness, and her smile brightened the room. David drank in her features, noting her almond-shaped eyes, high cheek bones, and the gentle curve of her chin. The pictures hadn't done her justice. They lacked the palpable force of her presence. Her full, bow-shaped lips made him long for a taste. The entire time he stared, she waited with amused patience, and the moment he realized that fact, he remembered his manners.

He mustered his most charming smile and shook her hand. "David Eastridge."

She gestured to the sofa. "Sit." Though she said it with a smile, there was no mistaking the authority in her voice. "We have plenty of time to talk."

Complications registered, and David frowned at Beatrice. "Beatrice, I think there's been a misunderstanding. I need a submissive, and Bree is clearly a dominant." Perhaps she didn't know she was to bottom for him?

Beatrice set a glass of water and a cup of coffee on the low table in front of the sofa. "She switches occasionally." She reached up to set a hand on Bree's shoulder. "David is new in town, and he needs a submissive. He's trustworthy, or else I wouldn't have sanctioned this meeting."

A slight frown creased between Bree's eyebrows, vanishing so quickly that he questioned whether it had been there at all. "It's very nice to meet you, David." The air of authority had left her tone, leaving it neutral. He liked that she wasn't automatically submissive. True submission was earned, and though he didn't need it for this, he appreciated her modulated, respectful response.

He gestured to the sofa, indicating where she should sit. "Please."

As she sat, she flashed a quirky little grin at his stolen move and the entreaty issued as a command. He sat on the other end of the sofa, and she angled her body to face him.

Beatrice took a seat on a chair opposite them. "David, you'll find Bree able to meet most of your requirements. For the record, please note that Solutions Elite Escort Service does not condone sexual activity. Our escorts provide companionship and conversation—nothing more. Is that understood?"

Her speech was straight from the liability disclaimer he'd signed, but her tone left no doubt that she expected them both to play by the rules. Watching the way Beatrice and Bree interacted, it was clear that Bree was special to the elderly businesswoman. David wondered if they'd known one another for more than six years.

"Yes, Ms. B." Bree nailed David with a steady look. "I don't sleep with clients. Ever. There will be no kissing, no contact with my breasts, ass, or private areas, and the same goes for you. My clothes will remain on my body, and your clothes will remain on yours."

David pursed his mouth. His mind had snapped firmly into business mode, and that meant negotiation. She'd laid out some stringent hard limits. He needed to see how firm they were. "I need you to pretend to be my sometimes-girlfriend. There will need to be occasional kissing. It's a play party. We won't be alone."

She didn't look thrilled by the idea of kissing him, and that ruffled his ego feathers. "Your friends haven't met me. It can be a first date, and not kissing on a first date is understandable." Obviously an experienced negotiator, she neither flinched nor fidgeted, and where many women might try to appease him, she made no attempt.

He liked her chutzpah. She had spunk. Perhaps that's what didn't sit right with his father—she seemed too honest and self-assured to have stolen three million dollars. "True," he conceded. "But when things go well on a date, kissing happens."

She studied him, and he wondered what thoughts zinged through her head as she took his measure. By most standards, he was passably handsome. Many women found his athletic physique attractive. Combined with an above-average height, blond hair that he let grow almost long enough to fall over his rich brown eyes, David didn't have a problem with the fairer sex.

But the way she regarded him left no doubt she was looking beneath the surface. A sub needed to be able to read her Dom, so he let her study him for as long as she needed. Finally she responded. "Unaccompanied Doms—especially males—are not allowed at reputable play parties. You need me in order to get in. What is the real reason you need to be there?"

She was definitely experienced, and that fit his needs perfectly. He turned his hand over, sending a subtle signal that he was being open with her by exposing his palm. "Though I grew up here, I've been gone a long time. The friend I was supposed to take to the party is unable to attend for reasons related to her job."

For several seconds, nobody said anything. Bree lifted a brow. "And so?"

And so this woman was smart. She saw right through his non-answer. David found himself drawn to her even more. "I'm here on a job. I need to establish contacts in the BDSM community. A friend vouched for me, which is enough to get me on the guest list—provided I bring my own sub."

Understanding lit her irises. "They'll judge you by how you get along with your submissive. If they like you, then you're welcome to other events." She leaned closer. "Of course, you've been vouched for, so that's not the real reason, is it?"

"Some people there will make valuable contacts for future business opportunities."

That answer seemed more acceptable to her. She lifted a brow. "What is your business?"

"Analytics." It wasn't technically a lie. He analyzed a lot of information before taking action. "It's a referral-based business."

She spread her hands, a placating move. "You may kiss my cheek three times, but that's all, so you'd better make them count."

"Not good enough."

"Fine." She exhaled with a grace and civility that suggested he was lacking in those areas. "One French kiss."

"It's a start," he returned. "Depending on circumstances, there may be more."

"We'll see about that." A soft limit was probably the best for which he could hope under the circumstances. She rubbed her hands together. "Let's talk about what kind of play you do best."

He frowned. "The kind of play I do best?"

"Yes. If you're going there to impress other dominants, you'll need to bring your A game. What does that look like?

Are you awesome with a flogger? Perhaps you'd like to display how good you are with a double Florentine? Or maybe you're a great rigger, and you want to show off those skills?" She shifted and leaned closer, warming to the topic. "Don't you want the subs to beg for a turn with you?"

David knew the value of showing off, but he didn't necessarily need to hang out his shingle as a service top in order to gain the access he needed. "They're going to judge me by the way I treat you. They'll want to know you're happy and having fun, that I pay attention to your tells and respond accordingly. And that I keep you in line."

Her smile drooped. "Do you need me to misbehave?"

"No. As a matter of fact, I need a well-behaved sub. And don't forget, this is a first date. I thought that perhaps we'd try out a few things, which we'll discuss as we go along. I need to know your hard limits and preferences."

Her gaze slid to Beatrice, who opened a folder on the table. She extracted a form and handed it to him. "This is a list of Bree's limits and preferences. We utilize the standard stoplight system for safewords. Be aware that she's had surgery on her left shoulder, so be especially careful during bondage."

He studied the list. Most of her hard limits were his as well. He wasn't into bodily fluids or edge play, but she'd also nixed anything to do with sex play. Really she hadn't left much, but flogging and bondage, two of his favorites appeared on the preferences list. She'd specifically mentioned those. He folded the list and put it in his pocket, and then he faced Bree. "Do you agree to the plan?"

"Of course. I look forward to working with you."

The venue for the play party turned out to be someone's barn. Situated far back on a large parcel of acreage, light and music poured from doors that had been thrown wide open. Parking was indicated on either side of the gravel driveway, so Autumn, in her persona as Bree, turned sharply and came to a stop on the outskirts of the designated area. Poco didn't need to suffer the indignity of having to sit next to the other cars all night. She parked at the edge of the designated area and checked her hair one more time in the mirror. For this occasion, she'd wrangled her mane into a French braid that tracked diagonally across her head so that the rest of it would fall across her left shoulder. That left her upper back bare for flogging, and it provided some cover for the scars on her shoulder.

Not wanting to drive all this way in fetish wear—how awkward would it be to break down on the side of the road and have to explain that to someone?—she'd covered up with a white blouse and a simple skirt that fell to mid-calf. Despite her detour to a chain restaurant to scope out Julianne's date, she'd managed to arrive a few minutes early. Julianne's date hadn't set off any of Autumn's alarm bells. She'd told Julianne to have fun and not take the night too seriously, and then she'd lit out for this place. It wouldn't take long to get out of her mainstream outerwear. She unbuttoned her blouse.

The knock on her window scared the crap out of her. Heart racing, she looked up to see David, the man Ms. B. insisted she accompany "as a personal favor," regarding her with an amused grin. She rolled the window down an inch. "Hey there. We're both early."

He glanced at his watch. "I'm on time. You're a half hour late. According to Beatrice, that's as on-time as you get."

Frowning, Autumn checked the clock on her dashboard. It didn't match the time on his watch, so she compared it with her phone. The clock in her car was wrong. This happened far too often. She knew the cause—her battery kept dying, and that played havoc with the clock she often forgot to reset. "Oh, sorry, Sir. I hope I didn't keep you waiting. Let me slip out of this, and I'll be ready to go."

Without waiting for his permission, she shrugged out of the blouse and slipped out of the skirt. Underneath, she'd chosen a deep purple bustier with black lacing down the sides. It terminated in time to show off a small strip of her midsection. A matching skirt, appropriately short, covered her bottom. For shoes, she'd chosen black boots that came up to her knees. She'd found them at a thrift store for a dollar.

When she was ready to emerge, he opened the car door and helped her out. He held her hand as he looked her over. Autumn stood still, enduring his appraisal because he was the client. If he didn't like her outfit, he was within his rights to insist on changes. To that end, she'd brought a second pair of shoes and a longer skirt. The white blouse could be modified to tie beneath her breasts if he wanted her shoulders covered. Of course, once she presented those options, most clients went with the outfit she'd chosen. None of them had asked her to cover up more of her body.

"You look amazing." He looked at her face when he said it, not her body, and that earned him a point in his favor. "I like what you've done with your hair. And you've kept the makeup to a minimum."

That caveat had been in his instructions. "Thank you, Sir. You look..." She'd watched his face while he'd checked her out, noting his micro-expressions and looking for clues as to what he did and didn't like. Now she checked him out. He wore a jacket and tie over a dress shirt, and his slacks matched his jacket. "Like you're going to work."

Frowning, he surveyed his outfit.

"If I may be bold for a moment, Sir? You might be more comfortable without the jacket and tie." He was a very handsome man, and his body looked great in a suit, but this was a play party. Casual or fetish dress would be expected.

Now he was looking at her, staring with a firm, dominant expression that dared her to question his fashion choices further.

Autumn had never been one to back down when she knew she was right, and having played the Domina so often, she knew when "The Look" was mostly bluster. "You wouldn't happen to have brought a pair of jeans or leathers in your car?"

"Jeans." Implicit in the single word was the warning he hadn't yet articulated.

She lowered her gaze, acknowledging his dominance. "Sir, I know I'm a little out of line, but I have your best interests at heart. I'm here for you, and only you. Two nights ago, you told me that you're looking to fit in with a certain group of people. Though you look fantastic in a suit, it's more appropriate for an office setting. And it's going to get hot in there."

A glimmer of a smile cracked his hard façade, and he shook his head. "Come on, Bree." As he still had her hand, she had no choice but to follow him across the driveway and several cars closer to the barn. He clicked the button on his fob and the trunk of a black SUV opened. "Jeans. Lose the jacket and tie. Any other requests?"

"Do you have a short-sleeved shirt?"

He put his jacket on a hanger that he hung from a hook near the side window. A peek inside revealed three suitcases and a bunch of other shirts and jackets hanging in garment bags. She also assumed slacks were there somewhere. He unraveled his tie and tugged it off, which he somehow made into a sexy move without trying. Autumn forced her gaze elsewhere. This was a client. It didn't matter that she found him attractive or that she'd been sorely tempted to completely give in during the kiss negotiation.

"Watch out."

She stepped back as he closed the hatch. Though he hadn't changed, he'd found a pair of jeans in his luggage. She turned away from the car as he opened the door to the back seat. "I'll keep my back turned so you can have privacy."

"Thanks, but the windows are tinted so that you can't see inside. We could have sex in a crowded parking lot, and people would only know because I wouldn't gag you."

Though she didn't turn to see his face, she imagined him throwing a cheeky wink just before he closed the door. Most men would sound boastful or creepy saying something like that, but he managed it with understated confidence. Autumn liked understated confidence. She also liked tall blond men with sexy, athletic builds who took care of their clothes. Little things like that indicated someone to whom details mattered.

He emerged minutes later wearing jeans that hugged his thighs and ass. He'd also exchanged his dress shoes for tennis shoes. "How's this?"

"May I?" At his nod, she unbuttoned the top three buttons on his shirt. It didn't reveal much, but it went better with the casual air she was trying to help him affect. "I don't suppose you'll let me mess up your hair a little?"

"Nope. I have to draw the line somewhere, otherwise you may forget who's in charge." He was teasing her, and she found herself responding with a genuine smile.

"Understood, Sir. I'll wait until next time to ask you to untuck your shirt."

With a smile, he took her hand again, and he threaded it through his arm. "I prefer you on my left side. Keep your hand on me at all times. Give a little squeeze if you need to speak to me. Don't speak to anyone unless I give you permission. I do want you to have fun. Really have fun, not pretend to have fun. That's important."

She squeezed his arm. They were getting close to the barn. Light spilled over them, making his hair look even more yellow. "Sir? Can I talk to the other submissives during appropriate times?"

"Yes, but be discreet." He didn't have to elaborate further. She knew he didn't want people to know he'd paid for her services.

"Of course, Sir." Autumn was nervous. It had been a long time since she'd been to a play party. She hadn't been anywhere, really, since the accident. Though she looked forward to the evening, she didn't include this on her list of play parties. This was work, not pleasure. Through sheer determination, she steadied her nerves. David seemed like a nice guy, and he seemed to like her sense of humor. She'd managed to put him at ease. Now she just needed to keep him there.

He ran into someone he knew almost immediately. When he stopped, she made sure to stand a little behind him. And though she kept her gaze lowered, she had no trouble seeing the couple. He was exceptionally tall, with shaggy dark hair that fell to his shoulders, and like David, he wore jeans. Unlike David, this man's jeans were well worn, even torn in some places. His black cotton shirt looked new by comparison. His submissive was a woman with blue eyes and a voluptuous body poured into a pretty yellow sundress. She wore her hair in pigtails, and the stick of a sucker stuck from between her lips. The pair held hands like lovers, and they glowed like newlyweds.

"Jordan, it's good to finally meet you in person. Frankie and Jesse send their regards." David offered his hand.

The man let go of his submissive for a second while he shook David's hand. His smiled dimmed so that it was merely friendly, and Autumn glimpsed the air of danger surrounding this stranger. "Likewise. Welcome to Michigan. When did you get in?"

"An hour ago, though I came up earlier this week to meet with my next project."

"You must come to dinner. Are you busy tomorrow night?" The woman popped her sucker out to speak. Her friendly demeanor gushed with warmth. "I know you're probably unpacking, which means you won't have much food. I told Frankie we'd look after you. I'll make stuffed pork chops. You'll love them. Unless you don't eat pork. Please don't be afraid to tell me. I can make something else."

Jordan chuckled at his submissive's rambling. He kissed her cheek. "If you haven't already guessed, this is Amy. She's an excellent cook, and she's not going to let you get out of coming to dinner. If tomorrow doesn't work, let us know what night does. And if you'd prefer we brought dinner to your place, we can do that."

"I have plans with my father tomorrow, but I'm free on Sunday." David inclined his head in her direction. "This is Bree."

Amy leaped at the chance to talk to her. "Hi, Bree. It's nice to meet you. Did you come from Missouri with David?"

Most escorts chose a completely different name to give to clients. Autumn had been through plenty of names in her lifetime, and one more was no big deal. She looked to David for permission to address Amy. Really, Jordan should have been the first one to speak to her, but these two didn't seem all that interested in protocol.

David nodded, so Autumn smiled. "Hi, Amy. I'm from here. David and I met through a mutual acquaintance, so this is our first real date. And can I say that I love your dress? It's really cute."

She beamed, and that made Jordan happy. Happier. The man looked at his submissive as if he'd won the jackpot. "Thanks. This is one of Daddy's favorites."

Ahh—that explained the pigtails, the sucker, and Amy's almost childlike demeanor. She was a little.

Jordan put his arm around Amy and pulled her closer, but his polite smile remained directed at Autumn. "Welcome to our party, Bree. I hope you'll enjoy it. There are some play areas set up farther down. We'll have a couple of demonstrations later, and some fun games are supposed to happen every hour. I saw a piñata shaped like a dick, but I didn't want to ask what they're planning to do with it."

"Whack it off." Autumn pressed her lips together too late. She hoped David didn't mind too much. The comment kind of slipped out.

He laughed, which made her feel better. "I'm not sure I want to see that thing get beaten."

"The winners get little prizes, and the overall winners get a prize package," Amy supplied. "It has all sorts of cool stuff in it, like body butter, silk ropes, a handmade flogger, and a tiara. You don't have to play all the games. Points are added up at the end of the night."

David patted her hand where it wrapped around his bicep. "Maybe we'll play a few and see about getting Bree a tiara."

"Good luck with that." Jordan chuckled. "The competition is fierce."

Autumn studied David's reaction to see whether he wanted to participate, but she wasn't able to discern anything specific. She liked challenges, and she had a wicked competitive streak. If David wanted, she'd make sure they won. Perhaps, though, it would be better for his business prospects if they placed high instead of winning outright.

"We're going to walk around a bit, see the sights."

Jordan nodded. "Play spot the agents?"

"Already done. We'll see you around."

Autumn flashed a quick smile at Amy as she turned with David and entered the barn. It was a wide open space devoid of stalls or any signs animals may have at one time lived there. Bright lights, both white and colored, crisscrossed the high ceiling. Along one side, several areas were set up and roped off. In the far corner, tables and chairs were set up in rows in front of a huge display of food. She squeezed his arm, and when he inclined his head, she said, "Agents?"

"Yeah. Many of the Doms you'll meet tonight are FBI agents."

Autumn had an inborn skepticism when it came to law enforcement. She'd spent so much time learning how to evade their notice. Being at a play party full of them meant she needed to stay on her toes. And she admired David's audacity at bringing a paid escort to a party full of the people responsible for making sure Ms. B. wasn't running a high-priced hooker service. Which, of course, she wasn't. What those girls did off the clock was their business, and the more repeat business they got, the more Ms. B. could charge for a date. Autumn didn't play like that, so she didn't rake in the higher commissions. Sure, men liked to have her humiliate and flog them, but they often failed to come back when she didn't make sure the night had a happy ending.

They meandered to the back of the barn, and David stopped a few times to talk to people. She remained quiet, memorized names, and when he gave permission, she replied to greetings and questions. Whenever she spoke, she tried to work in some kind of positive statement, usually a compliment. If a Dominant was worthwhile, then his sub's opinion carried a lot of weight. It was her job to make sure they liked David.

Stopping next to the buffet, he said, "Are you hungry or thirsty?"

She'd grabbed an appetizer with Julianne and her date, so she wasn't starving. "Not yet. I tend to crave a snack around nine."

"Oh, yeah? What kind?"

"Whatever is around. I'm not picky. Almost all the food here looks scrumptious."

He laughed. "Almost all? What doesn't appeal to you?"

"The shrimp. For some reason, I never developed a liking for it." Her sister had loved it, and when shrimp had been on the dinner menu, Summer had always generously taken Autumn's portion.

"So if I take you out to dinner, you won't eat the shrimp off my plate?" The deep brown of his irises lightened when he was happy. Autumn found this tell appealing. It was something he couldn't control, a tell she could trust.

"I'd never eat off your plate. It's rude." Not to mention they wouldn't be going out to dinner or anywhere else. Autumn didn't date anymore. She didn't have time for relationships. Between work and Summer, she barely had time for sleep.

Before he could respond, a megaphone squeaked to life. "Hi, everybody."

The crowd had grown considerably since they'd arrived. They responded with a resounding, "Hi." Several whistled, and one petite blonde with a loud mouth shouted, "Darcy, show us your stripes!"

Darcy grinned. "Layla and I have put together some games for your enjoyment. The first one is about to start on the east side of the barn. If you're interested in playing, you need to get out there now. If you're just watching, give us about ten minutes. It'll be fun."

Autumn looked to David, silently asking if he wanted to play.

He frowned. "She didn't say what the game was. Maybe we should watch this first one."

Autumn snorted. "It's a game. The worst that can happen is we lose." She tugged on his arm. "Come on. I heard from a reliable source that it'll be fun."

"All right, but don't be surprised if it's a spanking contest."

It had been years since she'd been on the receiving end of a spanking. She remembered them fondly. At the time, she'd been going by Alicia Lowe. She and Summer had worked together to net almost sixty thousand in bonds. Good times. She winked at David. "I wore the right kind of underwear."

Interest sparked behind his eyes, but he didn't comment. "Shall we?"

The contest turned out to involve balloons and teams. She found herself in line with a string tied around her waist. The balloon was attached in the back. It flopped onto her ass. David stood behind her, similarly attired.

"I feel ridiculous."

She chuckled. "Wait until the woman behind you has to pop your balloon."

The woman behind him was a little shorter than Autumn, and she held herself with confidence and grace. The Italian beauty's grin matched Autumn's. "Don't worry. I won't be gentle."

The man behind her, a tall, handsome drink of water, laughed. "She's not kidding. I'm Keith, and this is Kat. I don't think we've met?"

David shook hands with the pair. "David Eastridge. I'm an associate of Frankie and Jesse's. This is Bree."

They exchanged pleasantries for a moment, and then the buzzer sounded. The goal was to pop as many balloons as they could in one minute. The first person in line ran to a chair situated about ten yards away. The second person ran after her. He rammed his pelvis into the balloon, but the contest proved deceptive in its simplicity. The balloon stretched and moved, fighting for life. The man pumped his pelvis harder, and eventually the balloon popped.

Autumn was up next. She calculated the height difference as she ran, and by the time she got to him, she'd worked out the physics. "Bend your knees more. Lower. That's it." She grabbed his hips and pressed forward. This was about accuracy and pressure, not speed. One determined thrust, and she popped the balloon.

She braced herself on the chair. David was taller, so she didn't bend her knees except to help with leverage. He grabbed her hips and thrust, but he didn't use enough force.

"Harder," she said. "Please, Sir!"

He laughed, so when he failed to pop the balloon a second time, she repeated herself really loudly. While she didn't mind winning, she kept his orders in mind—she was to have fun. In her head, that translated to making sure he had fun. "If you keep that up," he said, keeping his voice low, "I might think you're coming on to me."

She meant to do it again, but he surged forward and popped the balloon. Now she got to watch as Kat tried to pop David's balloon. She was laughing too hard and the balloon kept slipping to the side, so after a time, David helped out by pressing backward. Keith ran forward for his turn, and David returned to her at the back of the line. Together, they cheered their team. They came in third place out of eight teams, and she hugged David to celebrate their victory.

He kissed her on the cheek. "That's one."

A little later, they watched a man tie his sub into a corselet. If Autumn wasn't mistaken, it was the same woman who had announced the contest through the megaphone earlier. Up close, she looked a lot like Amy, only without the pigtails. Her Dominant had left her bra on, though he'd removed her shirt. He talked as he wove the ropes, and when he finished, he invited the onlookers to try their hand at it with their subs. "Jordan, Keith, Dustin, and I will be around to coach you through it, and I know a great variation for male subs. With them, you don't have to go around the boobs. Nothing is sexier than seeing your sub wearing your ropes."

David regarded Autumn regretfully. "I didn't bring ropes. Maybe next time."

"Here." Jordan appeared out of nowhere. He handed a coil to David. "You can use mine. Amy's not one for public play. Yet."

Autumn fingered the rope. The silk caressed her back. "I'm game if you are." David didn't respond, so she lifted her arms. "It's okay if this is your first time. Everybody's a virgin once."

"It's been a while." David untied the knot holding the coil together. "You're going to need to be patient."

She encouraged with a smile. "I've got all evening."

Jordan took a few steps back to give them privacy. David worked quietly and with methodical meticulousness.

Autumn mostly watched his face, but her gaze was repeatedly drawn to the way his shoulders and arms moved. Muscles bunched and elongated, and the deeper he concentrated, the more he sucked the corner of his upper lip. Autumn was tempted to offer to suck it for him. Instead she chose to say something innocuous. "You're cute when you're concentrating."

He glanced up, surprised, and his knot-weaving fingers stuttered.

She raised her eyebrows. "Let me guess—nobody's ever told you that you were cute before?"

"You're not at all what I expected."

"You wanted a leggy blonde with huge fake boobs?"

He exhaled a laugh. "No."

"Botox lips and cherry red lipstick?"

"Hell, no. I just didn't think you'd be so forward."

"Ahh." She sighed knowingly. "I'm not demure, and that's a turn off."

"Not at all. It's refreshing. I like that you're lighthearted and that you feel free to tease and flirt. I'm having fun, and I didn't think I would." He went back to looping rope.

Autumn knew she wasn't the most beautiful woman in the world. Her looks were passable, and most of the time she downplayed them to fly under the radar. She did the same thing with her personality, though she was letting it off the leash more often tonight than she usually did. She watched him untie the knot and try again. "Maybe you want to ask Jordan for help." She used her whispering skills so nobody but David would hear. "I don't know how to tie that one either."

He looked around, but Jordan was working with another couple, so he signaled the original presenter who was walking around with his sub and giving pointers. David offered his hand. "You're Malcolm, right? I'm David Eastridge."

Malcolm nodded. "Jordan told me you were here tonight. Glad you could make it. Frankie speaks highly of you." His sub, still wearing the corselet her Dom had tied during the presentation, waited patiently as Malcolm talked David through making a double coin knot.

"That's it. Then do the same thing in the back. It looks good, and it'll keep the corselet from slipping too much when she moves." Malcolm and David moved behind her to work. "I hear you're looking into CalderCo?"

"No work talk." Malcolm's sub broke her silence with that hissed reminder.

"Sweetheart, you just lost one stroke of the cane."

Though Autumn couldn't see the sub's face, she could feel the palpable disappointment. Only a Painslut would be upset about one less hit with a cane. However, that wasn't what made her flinch. How, exactly, was David "looking into" CalderCo? That was where she worked as an accountant. It was her one anchor to the normal world, the cover for her extracurricular activities, and it paid for the majority of her sister's care. Did he know she worked there?

Oh, the questions she had and couldn't ask. Wait—yes she could. "CalderCo? That's a shipping company. I thought you were in analytics?"

"I am." David came around to her side. Malcolm showed him how to tie off the corselet and adjust the placement of the final knot. When he looked at her, his expression was shuttered. "How does that feel?"

She ran her palms over the ropes. "Great. And it looks fantastic." Turning around, she found Malcolm assessing the attempt with a critical eye. His sub was still pouting over her punishment. Autumn felt sorry for her.

"Malcolm, meet Bree. Bree, this is Malcolm."

"Nice to meet you, Bree." He turned to his sub. "This is my wife, Darcy. She and a few friends arranged this whole party."

"It's a lovely party. I very much enjoyed the first game. It revealed so much about technique and finesse."

Darcy laughed. "It did, didn't it? Amy said I'd like you."

"Amy is your sister? There's definitely a family resemblance. You're both so beautiful."

Malcolm put his arm around his wife and pulled her against his side, pinching her ass hard as he did so. "It's almost time for the next game."

Bliss parted Darcy's lips, a reaction to the pinch. "Layla's announcing this one, but thank you anyway, Master." Her eyes opened, and she focused on Autumn. "If you liked the first game, you'll love the second one. And later, there's one where your Sir will have to guide you, blindfolded, through an obstacle course, using only a crop and his voice. Then there's the gauntlet, if you're brave enough to walk down an aisle lined with sadists armed with paddles."

Malcolm rolled his eyes at his wife's near-orgasmic listing of the festivities. "Which you won't be doing in your condition."

"Congratulations." David caught on a few seconds before Autumn did. "When are you due?"

"In seven months. This is baby number two for us. Our son is eight months old. Yep, barefoot and pregnant, that's me since the day we met." From the sarcasm in Darcy's reply, Autumn couldn't tell whether the woman was happy or upset.

Malcolm grinned as he kissed Darcy's temple. "What can I say? My boys are powerful swimmers. They laugh in the face of both condoms and birth control pills."

"Let's see how amused they are when you get a vasectomy."

Autumn couldn't help but laugh at Darcy's dry tone. She clamped a hand over her mouth and buried her face in David's shirt to hide her laughter. He hugged her to him, and his chest shook with silent amusement as well.

"I'm going to get her something to eat. Pregnancy has made Darcy start hallucinating when she's hungry." With that, he dragged her off toward the barn.

Autumn looked up at David. With her body pressed to his and the way he held her, it was an intimate pose. "I bet she's a handful."

A slow grin lightened his eyes. "I bet you are as well."

She shrugged. "It's been known to happen."

The light in his eyes dimmed, and his mood grew sober. "I have really big hands."

This wasn't supposed to get serious. She dropped her gaze, severing the spell he was weaving. When she lifted it, she attempted to make his eyes turn lighter again. She was beginning to really like that cinnamon brown color. "All men think they have big hands."

It worked. He laughed.

Chapter Three

Never before in an op had David felt less like conducting that operation. As Darcy tied his arm to Bree's, he couldn't seem to peel his gaze from the mysterious woman who might or might not be stealing from his father's company.

"How's that?" Darcy asked. "Tell me if it's too tight or too loose or needs adjusting. I'm not all that good with rope."

Bree grinned. "No need to be when your husband is so skilled. Is that what brought you together?"

Darcy laughed. "Not at all. When we met, I had an intense fear of being bound, and I hated cops. Malcolm, of course, loved bondage, and he was an undercover FBI agent investigating me for a bunch of crimes I didn't commit. We eventually resolved our differences."

David saw his opening. "Is that why he's no longer with the FBI?"

Her expression fell the smallest amount. "No. I'd never ask him to give up doing something he loved. Mal is very much his own man, and he doesn't always like to follow orders when they don't work with his objectives." She fixed David with a firm look that said she knew more about his situation than she would say out loud. "If you want details, you're going to have to ask him."

"The ropes are fine," Bree interrupted, and David was once again grateful for her presence. She seemed to have a way of charming people, setting them at ease, and defusing tense situations before they got out of control. "Is Layla going to go over the rules for the game?"

"Yes." Darcy looked past them. She raised her voice so Layla could hear over the din. "I think everybody's ready."

The object of the game was to get as many striped peppermint candies as possible from the plate near Bree to the fishbowl on his other side. He and Bree were positioned on the opposite side of a line, and her right wrist was bound to his left. The location of the peppermints was slightly out of reach for each of them.

"You lose a point every time you go over the line, and each peppermint is a point. Grab one at a time, pass it to your partner, and they have to get it in the fishbowl. Oh, and you can't use your hands except to touch your partner. You have two minutes. Go!"

David looked across Bree to where she needed to pick up a peppermint. "Lean over as far as you need. I'll hold you for balance." He held her hand. This was a trust game. "I won't drop you."

She flipped her braid behind her shoulder, revealing a shocking configuration of scars. They marred her shoulder a little, but most of the damage had occurred along her collarbone and neck. No details about this had been in her file. She distracted him with a confident half-smile. "Let's do this."

Bracing her foot against his—without crossing the line—she leaned over and picked up a mint with her teeth. Before he could pull her, she was back. He bent his knees to line up his mouth with hers. "This doesn't count as kissing."

With the peppermint effectively gagging her, she couldn't respond.

He used his tongue to take the candy, dipping into her mouth to snake it around the treat. His bowl was closer, and he was taller, so he didn't need her leverage to make the deposit.

She didn't dawdle. As soon as he was upright, she grabbed the next one. They worked quickly and efficiently, though each time his lips came into contact with hers, he had to force himself not to take his time and explore the sparks that kept igniting. Later he'd dazzle her with his tongue wrestling skills.

"Time!"

The verbal buzzer sounded as Bree was on her way to get another peppermint. David pulled her back to him, wrapped his free arm around her bare waist, and reined in the passion simmering in his veins. Her gaze fixated on his lips, and he wondered if she truly was a switch and, if so, was she in submissive headspace right now? Pushing aside the reasons his mission sanctioned his actions, he traced his thumb along her lower lip before cupping the side of her head with the hand still bound to hers. "This counts."

He closed his mouth over hers, taking what he wanted. She tasted of mint and a sweetness that had nothing to do with sugar. Her body softened against his, and she tilted her head a little more to give him better access. Chemical reactions burst through his senses in a series of tiny detonations that drove him to deepen his foray. She grasped his sleeve, her nails digging the slightest bit into his arm, and a soft, kittenish moan sounded in the back of her throat.

Though he wanted to cup her ass and thrust his thigh between hers, he ended the kiss. If he went against her limits now, it would sour her toward him, and he needed her close in order to conduct his investigation. Besides, he couldn't stomach Doms who didn't honor the agreements they made with their subs.

He released her slowly, making sure she had firm control of her faculties before letting go. When she smiled at him this time, it had a softer, subdued element that had been missing before now. "Yeah. That definitely counts."

"You won." Darcy's amused pronouncement cut through the mental mist binding them together and separating them from the crowd. "Do you want me to untie you, or maybe you want to stay this way?"

Bree laughed. "You can untie us. It'll be awkward in the bathroom."

"It's a portable potty. It's awkward even when you're alone." Darcy tugged at the knot and had it quickly unwound. "Congratulations on the win. You're in fourth place overall."

They'd missed a game that had gone on during the corselet demonstration, but David didn't care. "Thanks." He never took his gaze from Bree. She put her hair back in place, covering the worst of the scar. This wasn't the time to ask about it. "Hungry?"

"Yeah. A little."

On the way to the buffet, Bree held his arm the way he'd instructed, but now her grasp seemed more like a caress. He filled a plate with foods he thought she'd like. "I'm going to feed you."

He watched her struggle to not object. Feeding a submissive was an intimate experience for both of them. The rules she'd put in place were designed to keep distance between them, but he felt the kiss had shattered the miles. He led her to a table and guided her to a chair. Then he scooted his chair closer and repositioned her so that her legs draped over his. He hadn't touched her anywhere she'd prohibited, yet he'd managed to create sensual intimacy.

Try as he might, he couldn't think of a single thing to say while they ate. Each time he held a morsel of food to her mouth, he was mesmerized by the way her lips closed over the fork. Up close like this, he could see every light freckle dotting a path like stardust across her cheeks and nose. He wanted to tell her that she was beautiful, but the words stalled in his throat. He wanted to ask her about her shoulder and how she'd become involved in the lifestyle, but he knew she wouldn't answer. She'd deflect or tell him that she didn't talk about personal things with clients, and that would force a reality that would ruin the moment. And so they ate in silence, each watching the other and falling deeper into the precarious spell.

The rest of the night passed in a slow whirlwind of contests, demonstrations, and small talk. He made connections as well as he could with the agents at the party, and when he felt Bree rest her head against his arm, he knew the evening had come to a close. He walked her to her car.

"If you're too tired to drive, I can give you a ride."

She smiled, but there was nothing behind it. "I'll be fine. I'll stop at a drive-thru and grab some coffee."

"At least let me give you my number so you can text me to let me know you got home safely." He could find her number easily by looking through the CalderCo employee files or calling Dean, but she would be put off if he came on too strong.

Shaking her head, she managed a rueful smile. "I'll be fine. I had fun tonight, and I hope you got what you needed. You seemed to get along well with the agents and the other Doms."

He leaned against her door so she couldn't open it. "I had fun with you. Bree, I'd like to see you again."

She tucked a loose strand of hair behind her ear, a nervous gesture that had him wondering whether he should come on stronger or back off. "That's not possible. Look, you seem like a great guy. I'm sure you've made connections tonight, and eventually you'll meet someone you click with."

"We clicked." He went with his strength—dominance. Tracing the same path her fingers had taken, he caressed her hair. "And you know it."

"Dating a client is prohibited."

He decided to call her bluff. "You don't work for Beatrice, not officially. I know you're friends, and that you came here with me as a favor to her."

She nailed him with wariness in her green eyes. "I work for CalderCo, and you've been hired to start there next week. It's best that we have a professional relationship and nothing else. Besides, I don't date. I don't have the time or energy to pursue a relationship. It's not personal, David. Like I said, you seem like a great guy, but this isn't going to happen." Hand on the door, she stared expectantly, silently commanding him to move.

Going one step further, he opened the door. "I'm not conceding defeat, merely acknowledging that I'll see you Monday."

He watched her car as she drove away, frowning as he realized the thing was being held together by chewing gum and duct tape. Maybe his father didn't pay her enough at CalderCo, but working as a pro Domme, even occasionally, should have meant she could trade up for a car that could boast modest claims of reliability.

"How did it go?" Jordan Monaghan's voice floated over David's shoulder.

He turned to respond. "I don't know. She doesn't strike me as the kind of woman who would steal three million dollars."

Jordan nodded at the fading tail lights. "She sure didn't spend it on transportation."

"I'm meeting with my father tomorrow. I'll get it out of him why he suspects her."

"I ran her picture through our databases, but it could take a couple weeks to get a hit. And it's low priority, so it'll be bumped when someone needs the system for a case." Jordan jerked his head toward the barn. "Head back with me. We need more paddlers for the gauntlet. It's the final game. Too bad Bree is leaving. You guys are tied for second place. This could have clinched a victory."

David didn't get the feeling that Bree had wanted to win the games. He'd tasked her with having fun and making him look good, and she'd used the games to do exactly that. "I gave your rope to Amy. Thanks for the loan."

"No problem."

Malcolm took a position next to him as they lined up to man the gauntlet. "Darcy liked Bree a lot. She said to tell you that if you treat her like a suspect, you're going to ruin your chances with her."

"She may have stolen a lot of money from my father." David cared more that the missing money could cost hundreds of honest people their jobs. Any damage inflicted on his father was karma coming back to take a chunk from the old man's hide.

"My wife is a romantic. She's going with the theory that if Bree stole any money, then she had a good reason, like she's being blackmailed, or that she's being set up. And she thinks that you two make a cute couple."

David didn't want to discuss any of that. He created theories to fit evidence. Looking for evidence to fit a theory was shoddy investigative work. "Are we just supposed to paddle the subs as they run by?"

"Yep. Don't hold back, either. These aren't just subs. Some of the Doms are masochists as well. I'll owe you one if you go full out on Keith."

Thinking back to the information on the dossier, David was surprised at the request. "Isn't he your best friend?"

"And he's engaged to my sister. Fucker has it coming. I told him that she was off limits. This is one way I can get out my frustration. He's expecting it from me, but it'll be icing on my happy cake if he gets it from you too." Evil glee lit Malcolm's eyes, and David felt sorry for Keith.

But he still paddled full out. It proved a great way to channel the complicated emotions churning through his chest and stomach. The masochistic contestants ran by one at a time, and each race was timed. Most entrants ran quickly, but a few went slowly and savored the paddling. In the end, a couple David hadn't met won.

Thirteen years ago, he'd walked out on his father without a single regret. When his mother had passed away, everything that bound him to that life had gone with her. As he pulled into the driveway of the palatial estate, he noted how little had changed. Some of the landscaping was different. The magnificent sugar maple he'd loved to climb was gone, most likely a victim of age, but it had been replaced by another sugar maple. Mostly it suffered from a lack of color. His mother had loved to garden, and she'd spent more hours than he could count tending to roses or peonies.

The servant who answered the door was different. He'd grown up with Joseph, a man who always seemed to be ancient. Joseph's replacement was a woman, young and pretty. She welcomed him with a courteous smile. "Good evening, Mr. Calder. Your father is in the study."

"Eastridge." He'd taken his mother's name when he'd left. "My name isn't Calder." He didn't invite her to call him by his first name because he was sure the woman functioned as more than a maid, and it sickened him to see Bill Calder taking advantage of the innocent young thing.

"Sorry, sir. Can I show you to the study?"

"No. I remember where it is." He set off, noting as he walked the cavernous main hall that nothing had moved. All the portraits and paintings were exactly the same. It was as if time had stood still once he and his mother left. He found his father sitting in a leather wing chair. That was new.

"David, it's a pleasure to see you. I wasn't sure you'd come." He got to his feet, and David noticed other things that had changed. The thick mane of jet black hair on his father's head was shot through with grey, and it had begun to recede along the forehead, leaving a sort-of widow's peak.

"If I hadn't promised Mom, then I wouldn't have." He shook his father's hand. "This isn't a social call. We have business to discuss."

"I disagree." Bill said. He went to the wet bar and refilled his bourbon. "Can I get you a drink?"

"Scotch, neat." David frowned. "You disagree about what? I have questions, and I'll need answers before I start the investigation."

Bill handed him a short glass, and the two of them sat. "You've already begun the investigation. As much as it pains you to hear it, I know you. You're methodical and always prepared. You wouldn't be here if you hadn't done your research."

David sniffed his drink before taking a sip. It was firm and spicy, both dry and sweet. As expected, Bill Calder only stocked the best. "Research can only tell me so much. You still haven't said what you disagreed with."

"This is a social call. I'm having a civilized dinner with my son for the first time in over a decade. It's not just a social event, but a momentous one. Your mother would be so happy to see you here." Bill smirked as if he'd played an unexpected trump card.

It didn't work to tug at his heartstrings or stir latent guilt. His mother had known he would leave, and she'd given her blessing. She'd understood why he'd needed to go. David sipped again. "Let's get one thing clear: I'm not here for you. I have no interest in salvaging any kind of relationship with you. I'm here because I promised Mom that when you got in trouble and needed me to bail you out, I'd be here. This is a one-shot deal. I'll find your thief, get your money back, but then I'm Casper. There won't be holiday cards or birthday phone calls. After this, we're through."

Bill pretended not to hear, but that didn't surprise David. His father had always ignored him when he'd taken a stand. "She liked to tell me that my problem was that I didn't know how to handle a son who was exactly like me. I'll admit that I wasn't the best parent to you and that we had a contentious relationship when you were younger, but that doesn't mean we can't associate now that you're a man with a successful business venture of your own."

But it did. He hadn't forgiven or forgotten a thing. However, going down this road now wouldn't lead to anywhere productive. The maid came into the room. "Dinner is served." She retreated quickly, without waiting for further instructions.

David regarded his father through narrowed eyes. "Looks like you've moved on from Mom just fine."

Color drained from Bill's face. "Don't you dare. You have no right to cross that line. I loved your mother with every fiber of my being, and I lived to make her happy. She's been gone for thirteen years, and not a day goes by where she isn't my first thought upon waking and my last thought before going to sleep." His father breathed to get his temper under control. "However, it's my right to move on."

"With the maid." David knew he shouldn't have said it, but being around his father brought out his worst qualities. At the ripe age of thirty-one, being in his father's home made him feel like a powerless kid again—and he hated it.

The look of disgust on Bill's face spoke volumes. "Cammie? For God's sake, David! She's Joseph's granddaughter. I gave her a job because he asked me to. His health isn't what it used to be, so he only works two days a week. I tried to get him to retire, but he refuses. Cammie fills in another two days. I have a cleaning crew that comes out every Monday."

David followed his father to the elegant dining room, also untouched in the past thirteen years. He considered apologizing for jumping to conclusions, but he discarded the thought. He wasn't sorry. Cammie served dinner from the wrong side and in the wrong order. A decade ago, Bill would have shouted at the servant until she cried, or Joseph would have fired her and served dinner himself. As it was, Bill barely managed to hide his winces at the improper service.

When she left the room, David let loose his laughter. "Joseph didn't train her, I take it?"

"Oh, he did. She's not detail-oriented, as she likes to tell us. She's a free spirit who is exploring different art and creative writing classes at community college." Bill spread his napkin on his lap. "The chef is wonderful, so at least there's that."

David dug in. He was hungry, and he wasn't used to eating this late. The filet mignon was excellent, and he polished off half of it before firing questions at Bill. "Why do you suspect Autumn Sullivan?"

"She's in charge of the accounting department. Not officially, but almost all accounts make their way to her before they go to Carl Tucker, the actual head of accounting. I've noticed he has a knack for hiring talented people and rubber-stamping their work. Autumn is in a perfect position to skim money off the top."

David thought about the mischievous glint in Autumn's green eyes and the sad little clunker she drove. "I can't see her doing something like that."

"You've met her?" Bill frowned. "I should have known you'd be that thorough. Anyway, I told you that it didn't sit right with me. I've looked for alternate possibilities, but the trail only leads to her. And there's something else."

David waited for Bill to gather his thoughts. "I'm listening."

"Always the smart guy," Bill muttered. "It's hard to put into words. I know she's not above board, but my gut tells me I'm missing something."

"How do you know she's not above board?" David scowled. He didn't like to hear her character maligned. "What's your proof?"

"She, um...She maybe steals things. Not from me, but I had a PI follow her around for a few weeks. She takes jobs, usually with a partner, that require breaking and entering. She's good, though. The surveillance photos show her getting into the buildings, not what she does while she's there."

"Then you have no proof." David schooled his features to a neutral expression.

"None," Bill agreed. "Having her followed only led to more questions. That's why I called you. I want to know who is taking my money, and I want it back. I'm getting older, David. When I die, this all comes to you."

David finished his dinner. "Sell it off and give the money to charity. I don't want a dime from you."

"Tough shit." Bill's eyes narrowed. "Cammie, we're ready for dessert."

They didn't speak while Cammie cleared the table and brought out the final course—a fruit parfait, heavy on the fruit and short on the parfait. David lifted his eyebrows. "I expected something much more decadent."

"Cammie said Joseph and I were getting paunchy, and she put us on a diet."

David had noticed the smaller portion on his father's plate. "A free-spirited maid who isn't afraid to tell you that you're getting fat. I like her."

"Yes, yes. Now let's talk about your trust fund. My lawyer tells me that you haven't touched it. You know it matured when you were twenty-five? I had a registered letter sent to you."

He'd shredded the document. "I told you that I didn't need or want your money."

"The trust fund came from your mother. When we married, I told her that she wasn't allowed to spend her money, that I'd provide for everything she needed. So she set it aside in a trust fund when you were born. That's all from her, not me. Though, if you need money, son, just ask. I'm your father, and I'll never turn my back on my own flesh."

David saved the eye-roll for the drive home. Bill Calder talked a good game, but when it came down to it, he knew the old man wouldn't follow through with anything except what mattered to him.

Chapter Four

"Did you see the new guy?" Julianne perched on the corner of Autumn's desk.

Autumn blinked away the fog of concentration that had her living in a world inhabited solely by numbers. She peered at Julianne, puzzled. "Huh?"

"New guy—tall, blond, so hot that ice cubes have been put on the critically endangered list. Have you seen him?" Julianne fanned herself even though the object of her interest was nowhere around.

Autumn figured that Julianne was talking about David. Her expression soured, but it didn't relay the message to her pulse. "I don't have time to drool. I'm working, in case you haven't noticed." She looked around at the people seated at other desks in her department either on the phone or tapping at their keyboards. "This is why accounting always gets the productivity awards."

"You work too hard. It's important to take time to smell the roses. And let me tell you, this is one hothouse flower."

Autumn winced. "That was bad. I see your taste in reading hasn't changed."

"Romance novels make me happy." Julianne sighed. "I'm going to write one. I read the most horrid story the other day, and all I could think about was how I could do it better."

"Go for it. Use the hothouse flower as your hero. Maybe he'll take you to dinner and help you with your research." Autumn didn't like throwing David toward her friend, but she didn't have plans for him, and Julianne was the complete package. She was sweet and gorgeous, and loyal to a fault.

Julianne rolled her eyes. "If he asks me out, then he's probably a jerk. No thanks. I'll take fake lovers and a good vibrator any day. I'm finished with dating."

Autumn frowned sympathetically. Julianne had called Saturday to let Autumn know that her date was a dud. He'd attempted the goodnight kiss, but that had fizzled before it began. "At least the last one was forgettable. I advise you to forget him and focus on the future. You deserve to meet someone nice who will worship you for the goddess you are."

"You're so sweet. I'm going to get back to my office. Are you going tonight?"

"Yep." Autumn had a meeting for a potential job, so she'd have to leave Summer earlier than she normally did, but Summer would understand.

"I can't go. My mom is coming over. She texted something about curtains. I may be in for a trip to Bed Bath and Beyond." Julianne left, and Autumn buried her face in the spreadsheet on her monitor.

Except now she was thinking about David. If she hadn't been there as part of a job for Ms. B., then she might have put it on her list of top ten perfect dates. They'd both had fun, and that kiss—that kiss had almost made her forget who and where she was, which could be very dangerous for both Summer and her.

Autumn blamed her distracted state for the fact that she noticed the increased tittering of her co-workers a few minutes later. She looked up to see David entering Carl's office. Her boss wasn't a slave driver, which was one of the reasons she liked him. She kept one eye on the door as she worked. What would he say when he saw her? Anxiety pooled in her stomach, turning the jelly sandwich she'd inhaled at lunch back into jelly.

There was no way she was going to survive this. She went to the bathroom and splashed water on her face. *He's not joining the accounting department,* she reasoned. There would be little reason for them to have to interact. If she could just get through the first meeting, then the rest would go smoothly—as long as she didn't give herself away by staring at his lips. Then again, if she did that, she'd probably just blend in with the other women mooning over him.

Feeling much better, she dried her hands and face. One more deep breath, and she returned to her desk.

...To find Carl Tucker waiting there with Bill Calder—the owner of the company—and David. Carl smiled as she approached. "There she is."

Autumn pasted a friendly expression on her face. "I'm sorry, Carl, Mr. Calder. I didn't have a meeting on my calendar. How can I help you?"

"I wanted to introduce you to David Eastridge." Mr. Calder seemed to stumble over David's name. "He's going to be with us for the next few months conducting a quality review. I'm pulling you from accounting for now. Your job will be to get Mr. Eastridge anything he needs."

Her face froze. "With all due respect, I'm not a secretary, Mr. Calder."

Mr. Calder's face turned to granite, the dark kind with a smooth grain. "You're not an accountant, either. Your title is Assistant, and I'm telling you to assist Mr. Eastridge while he's here. I'm setting him up in office 2B."

Oh, but she'd rather quit. With three years at Calder Co on her resume, potential bosses wouldn't see the gaping black hole that existed in place of her past. If that failed, she could take on more of the type of work her father had taught her. Too bad Mr. Calder's face hadn't actually turned to stone. Where was Medusa when she needed backup?

"Ms. Sullivan, I know this is sudden, but please don't be upset. My usual assistant was unable to accompany me this time. I promise I'm not hard to work with." David interrupted her silent planning session with a winsome smile. "I can arrange for you to speak to her by phone if you need more assurances."

She stared at him as if he'd lost his mind.

"I won't ask you to bring me coffee, but I will need you to show me around the office and introduce me to key people."

"You look perfectly capable of meeting people without help."

Mr. Calder was quickly losing his temper, something Autumn had seen him do before. It wasn't a pretty sight, but she'd faced worse. "You can either do the job you're assigned to do, or you can look for employment elsewhere."

Carl put a hand on Mr. Calder's arm. "Sir, that's not necessary. I'm sure Autumn will be happy to assist Mr. Eastridge. She's working on a file right now, and she doesn't like to leave a job unfinished. Perhaps she can take the rest of the day to finish up here and hand off her assignments to others, and then she can start as Mr. Eastridge's assistant tomorrow?"

Leave it to Carl to find a compromise. While it might not be true, it gave both her and Mr. Calder an out that was more effective than David's assurance of being an affable boss.

"That's fine," Mr. Calder said, leaping on the solution.

Autumn didn't want to give in, but she forced herself to do it. *For Summer.* She was here in the first place for Summer. She channeled her inner twelve-year-old for the eye roll and accompanying sigh. "Fine. Tomorrow, then. I'll move my things to the desk outside office 2B. Carl, do you have ideas on who should take over which accounts?"

"Not really." He patted her shoulder. "Go with your gut."

Five o'clock came too soon. Autumn had planned to finish up with her most urgent spreadsheet tomorrow morning. Try as she might, there was no way she was going to get it done tonight. Her compatriots hadn't been thrilled about their increased workload, either, but they'd accepted the extra work gracefully. Stephanie Ceichelski had pointed out that anyone else would have been thrilled to work so closely with David. She even used his first name like she actually knew him. Autumn managed to hold back a derisive snort. If anybody at CalderCo knew him, it was her, and she was the only one who'd earned the right to call him by his first name.

She passed 2B on her way to the elevator. David stood in the doorway, casually lounging against the metal frame and nodding to people as they left for the day. When he saw her, he lifted his hand. "Ms. Sullivan, can I see you for a moment?"

Though tempted to keep going, she reasoned that he was now her boss, and it was never a great idea to piss off your boss before the first day. She felt her lips tighten as she tried to force them into a smile shape. "Of course." She went into his office, and he closed the door behind them. Though it had a window in the upper half, it still gave them plenty of privacy. "What can't wait until tomorrow morning?"

If this were one of Julianne's romance novels, he'd sweep her into his arms and kiss her senseless. But it wasn't. He gestured toward a chair, but she shook her head, refusing to get comfortable. "I wanted to apologize. I didn't know your boss was such a dickhead. I had no idea he'd threaten your job."

"He's not usually so...harsh. I think having you here rattles him, but I don't know why. After all, you're here because he hired you to conduct a quality assurance review. Right? You'll be analyzing resource allocation and employee productivity?"

"Among other things. For the record, I didn't ask for you. I asked for an efficient assistant who could get things done even if they seemed impossible. Calder chose you, and Tucker confirmed that you were the best suited for the job." He came closer, stopping just inside the perimeter of her personal space. "Autumn, I won't lie. I'm glad I'll be working with you."

She should really take a step back, but she wasn't willing to give up the ground. Instead she crossed her arms over her chest. "I still won't go out with you."

"Why not?"

"You mean, besides the ethical considerations?"

He shrugged. "I'm a contractor, not bound by an employee conduct code, which means I'm fair game. Or so I've been informed by at least three women today."

Did he honestly think his rating on the Office Desirability Scale meant anything to her? The number was obviously inflated by his status on the Fresh Meat Scale. "Then maybe you should take one of them up on their offer and leave me alone."

Leaning closer, he rested his palms on her arms. "We have chemistry. It would be a mistake not to see where it goes. Come to dinner with me tonight."

"I have plans already." She glanced at the clock on his desk. "I'd better get going if I'm going to have a chance of being on time."

He hauled her so close that her breasts grazed his jacket, and primal fierceness darkened his eyes. "A date? Or a *date*?"

"Neither. Or both." She didn't owe him an answer.

His mouth tightened, but he let her go.

"That could have gone better." Talking to Summer had always been her preferred way of venting. While she couldn't exactly vent to her about the thing that had been on her mind for the past three years, she could safely talk about David.

Summer, for her part, slept soundly.

Autumn dusted the dresser as she chattered, carefully wiping down every object and photograph there. Her father would have told her to get rid of the pictures because they posed a risk to their current identities, but Autumn didn't see the harm. Nobody here knew her and Summer as anything but Summer and Autumn Sullivan, devoted sisters who had the misfortune to be in the wrong place at the wrong time. The nurses liked Autumn because she brought them regular gifts, and housekeeping liked her because she kept the place clean. Not only could sitting there get boring, but Autumn's cleaning standards were a bit higher than the staff's.

"Friday night was perfect, though, as I already told you. Most Doms move too quickly. They want to get you tied to their bed or St. Andrew's cross before you've found out their middle name." Autumn touched Summer's face. She didn't know what it was like to be in a coma, but she figured that no human being could go without a loving touch for too long. The nurses sometimes gave Autumn strange looks, especially when she would lay down next to Summer, but she didn't care. This was her sister, and she treated her the way she would if she were awake.

"I know, I know. You're going to say that it's been a long time since I've gotten laid. I could say the same thing about you, Summer. I didn't tell you this, but I had a fling last summer with the UPS delivery guy. I'd meet him at his truck, and we'd duck inside while he took his break. Then his route changed, and I never heard from him again. It's not like we were soul mates or anything. He did the job I needed him to do." She finished with the dresser and took the wet sweeper from the closet. "I'm going to do behind the furniture today. It's that time of the month in more ways than one."

She scooted the dresser out and cleaned behind it. "Anyway, David is different. I think I could really like him, and that's dangerous. He's friends with all these FBI agents, and even though he says he's there to do a quality analysis, I kind of think that's a cover. I wish you could meet him because I think you'd draw the same conclusion."

The dresser creaked and groaned as she moved it back. It wasn't due to a struggle on her part; the thing was old and on its last legs. "I mean, I don't think he'll find anything wrong with my accounts. I'm very careful to keep them neat and tidy. I didn't swim much the first year you were here, so I had to get exercise from somewhere. Still, I was careful not to disturb the leaves or break any sticks. But when I realized you were going to be here a while, I took up swimming again. Had to. Bills to pay."

Though she spoke in code, if Summer was listening, she'd know that Autumn hadn't taken any B-and-E jobs the first year;

she'd supplemented her income by skimming a little from various accounts. It amounted to petty cash, and she'd taken less than ten thousand dollars. The totals were hidden in the books because she'd moved money around in a complicated shell game. After that, when she'd realized she was going to be with CalderCo for the time being, she stopped stealing from them and started taking jobs for hire. Her salary at CalderCo didn't quite cover the cost of Summer's care.

"I'm meeting someone tonight about a new practice schedule. I'll let you know how that goes." Finished with cleaning the small room, she slid onto the bed next to Summer and put her head on her sister's shoulder. "Are you in the mood to find out what Huck Finn is up to next?"

Summer's eyes opened, and Autumn's breath caught. She sat up and smoothed Summer's hair away from her face. "Summer? It's okay. I'm here. You're safe." Her sister wasn't on a vent, but she did have a feeding tube. "Don't freak out. You've been asleep for a while, and we had to put a feeding tube through your nose."

From the calm in Summer's hazel eyes, Autumn could tell that Summer knew where she was. Tears pricked at her eyes, and she struggled to keep from crying. The last thing Summer needed right now—and she might only be awake for a few minutes—was to have Autumn break down. She clasped Summer's hand.

"I know you have a lot of questions, but they'll have to keep for now. I sweep for listening devices all the time, but you know, the nurses kind of need them, so I can't get rid of those. For now, just know that I'm taking care of everything. You're safe. I swear it."

Summer squeezed her hand, showing that she understood. Then she squeezed it again, and the slightest bit of a frown creased between her eyebrows.

"What? You want me to read to you?"

The crease didn't go away.

Autumn sighed. "Is it David?"

The crease eased, and a sparkle came into Summer's eyes.

"I can't go for it. He's the kind of guy who'll dig into my past, and I'd hate to have to kill him."

The crease came back, this time more severe.

"I'm kidding. I'm not into wet work. Plus, he's not a bad guy. If you heard me earlier, I'm afraid he's in league with the government." She didn't want to tell Summer that she was sure David had followed her to Sunshine Acres. She didn't want her sister to worry.

Summer blinked, and Autumn knew she was fading.

"I love you, Summer."

Sometimes it was harder when Summer woke up. No matter how she prepared herself, Autumn always hoped it was permanent, and when Summer fell back into the coma, it was like losing her all over again. Heartache stabbing her chest, an hour later, she washed the evidence of tears from her face and dragged herself to the scheduled meet.

Without an umbrella, standing in the rain sucked. The temperature had dropped, both because it was night and because the cold front had moved in. David pressed closer to the building across the street from where Autumn was meeting with a man. The guy didn't look like anything special. He was middle-aged with a medium build and mediocre looks. Even his khaki slacks and polo shirt were nondescript. The pair drank coffee in the warmth and dryness of the shop, soft light pooling around them from the low-hanging bulb.

Autumn's expression had even become neutral. She spoke. He spoke. The man occasionally smiled or frowned as he asked a question, but Autumn seemed very subdued. Something wasn't right. After twenty minutes, the pair stood. Autumn left without once having made physical contact with the man, so if this was a pre-date meeting, it hadn't gone well.

She exited the shop and looked at the sky. He could almost hear her sigh as she noticed the rain. She ducked her head and trudged across the street toward her car, which wasn't far from where he was standing. Taking a chance, he hurried out of his spot and pretended he'd been walking down the street.

"Autumn?"

She didn't respond, and he frowned. He'd spoken loud enough.

Hurrying to the passenger side of her car, he tried again. "Autumn."

Now she looked up, but she didn't look surprised. "What are you doing here?"

"I'm staying down the street." He gestured toward the penthouse his father kept for nights he worked late. It was off-limits to him while David was staying there. "Nice night for a stroll, or so I thought until it started raining. Any chance you'll give me a ride home?"

She got in and reached across to unlock the passenger door. The car definitely wasn't one that someone who'd stolen three million dollars would be driving. It wasn't a Pinto, but it was nearly as ancient.

"You're a lifesaver. Thanks. Do you live nearby?"

"Close enough."

Noncommittal responses didn't sit well with him. He pushed a little harder, but he couched it as a joke. "I could look at your personnel files and search your address."

"Might as well, since you're already stalking me and all." Her tone was flat, but it didn't seem like she was angry. She turned the key, and the car roared to life for almost three seconds. A second try produced better results.

"Stalking you?"

She turned, nailing him with a glare devoid of heat or ice. "Are you going to pretend you haven't spent the last half hour standing over there, watching me while I met with a man who wasn't you and had coffee? I drank it extra slow just to see how long you'd stand out in the rain."

David paused to think through possible responses. Of utmost importance was the fact that she's spotted him, and she hadn't let on to the fact the whole time he'd been watching. Either she had experience being tailed, or this was one big, unlikely coincidence. He decided to play semi-innocent. "When did you first notice me?"

"When you followed me from the parking garage at CalderCo all the way to the nursing home." She put the car in gear and pulled into traffic. "You're good. Not great, but skilled. You're not in the FBI, but you're also not in analytics."

How much of his cover had been blown? And who the hell was Autumn Sullivan? He didn't think she'd pull into a deserted side street, kill him with an untraceable firearm, and go on about her life. She didn't give off a heartless killer vibe. "Actually, I am in analytics. I trained with Special Forces."

"What are you now? A mercenary?"

Surprised at how quickly this conversation was going where he didn't expect, he coughed. "Are you in WITSEC?"

"I'm asking the questions here, not you."

David found himself smiling at her Domina voice. She had great control, but it made him want to kiss her sweetly, and then tie her up and show her the ways in which life would be better with him in charge. It wasn't a sexist sentiment as much as it was a sexy one.

"If you're here to cause trouble for Mr. Calder, then you'd better think twice. I won't let you hurt him or the company."

Coming from her, the statement was shocking. "Why would you think I have bad intentions?"

"Stalkers generally think they have good intentions, but they don't."

"Mr. Calder threatened your job if you didn't work with me. He seems like a dick, and I'm sure he's an asshole boss." David stopped talking because he was going down a dark path and he didn't need to take her with him.

"Bill Calder gave me a job when I needed one. I didn't have the skills or experience, but he saw my potential. He hired me anyway and put me through training. I'll admit that he didn't show his best side today, which means something is stressing him out. I'm going to find out, David, and you'd better not have a hand in causing that man pain. Where do you live? I can only circle the neighborhood so many times."

David's brain short-circuited. He'd never heard anyone speak about his father this way. "He was going to fire you if you didn't do exactly what he wanted." She couldn't overlook facts forever.

She chopped the air with her hand to dismiss his concern. "He's all bluster. He might have fired me, but he'd have called me by dinner time to apologize. Either way, I'd be back at work in the morning."

No. His father was not full of bluster and he was not a generous man. She was clearly delusional. "What, exactly, could I possibly do to cause him pain?"

"If I knew that, I'd be accusing you instead of warning you. Where. Do. You. Live?" This time her glare had some heat to it. For some reason, that made David feel better. He liked the passionate side of her nature.

He pointed to the building she was passing, and she slammed on the brakes. He braced himself on the dashboard to avoid lurching forward. At least the hunk of junk had working brakes, so he didn't have to worry about her bashing into someone. "Why don't you come up? I'll make tea and try to justify following you tonight."

"Are you also prepared to explain why you arranged with Ms. B. to spend last Friday night with me when you knew we'd be working together come Monday?" She stared through the windshield, and her low tone was tight with suppressed emotion.

She had to be fishing. Nobody at CalderCo knew who he was or why he was really there. Jesse hadn't said a word about the mission to Beatrice DePau. He'd stumbled on the connection when doing a search of Autumn's tax returns. The connection had proved fortuitous. David opted to obfuscate. "Maybe when I saw your picture, I knew I had to meet you?"

"My picture doesn't appear on the Elite Solutions website, and though I'm listed under the Pro Domme page, it's only as Mistress Bree. Try again. Maybe the truth this time?"

At a loss, he could only stare.

"When you're ready to be honest with me, I'll come up to your apartment and listen to what you have to say. I'll have tea, or maybe you'll serve wine and I'll kiss you before I leave. Think about it."

He recognized when to retreat so he could live to fight another day. Pausing with one hand on the door handle, he leaned across the console to kiss her cheek. "Nothing I've said to you was a lie."

She didn't shy away from his overture. "And yet, it wasn't the truth."

He watched her drive away, her tail lights reflecting in the wet street. At least it had stopped raining. When she was out of sight, he headed back the way they'd come instead of going inside. His car was parked near the coffee shop. It was only four blocks, but it was late, and he had some calls to make. First, he tried Dean.

"What's wrong?" True to form, Dean wasted no time.

"I tailed her, and she made me."

Silence for a second. "It's not like you to be careless. How do you know she made you?"

"She told me. I followed her to a convalescent home—Sunshine Acres—where she spent about two hours. Then she went to a local coffee house to meet with a man." He related the details of his conversation with Autumn. "She's somebody, Dean. She managed to not answer a single question."

Dean cleared his throat. "She did give you a couple things, though. I'll have Jesse hack Sunshine Acre's medical and personnel records, but in the meantime, you need to talk to your dad. Why did he hire her if she had no experience or training? From what you've told me, that's outside his normal behavior pattern. Your dad knows more than he's letting on."

Though David had reported most of what his father had said to Dean, he'd left out the part where his father speculated about Autumn's extracurricular activities. Had Bree known she was being followed when his father had hired someone to tail her? He could see her leading the unsuspecting private investigator on a wild goose chase. That seemed like something she'd find fun. Still, if he knew anything about his father, he knew that Bill Calder only revealed the information he wanted David to know. "Probably. I'll ferret it out eventually."

"I just got the pictures you took of the man. Can you have your friends at the FBI do a search? We're pretty high-tech here, but facial recognition software is not helpful without access to state, federal, and international databases." Dean coughed.

David frowned. "Are you getting sick?"

"Maybe a little bit. Don't worry. I've stocked up on vitamin C, zinc, and cherry cough drops." He paused to hack up something disgusting. "I may send out for some chicken soup."

"Jordan fed a picture of Autumn into their system. He said it would take a week or more to get results. Send Jesse here as soon as he comes up with something. And make up a great resume. I can't pull strings to get him a job—I don't want anyone connecting us—and I'll have him tail her." He couldn't because she not only knew what he looked like, but now she'd be on high alert where he was concerned.

"Will do. I'll contact you as soon as I know more."

Go with your gut, kid. You have a fantastic sense of intuition. Her father liked to say that success was due to equal parts planning and luck. He'd maintained that Autumn had been born with a combination of great instincts and luck.

Autumn didn't put much stock in luck. Meticulous planning left little to chance, and if luck was supposed to have played a role in her life, then she was still awaiting its grand entrance. So she set to work. An Internet search of David Eastridge turned up some pretty interesting results that had her both relieved and anxious. Though he hadn't lied about who he was or what he was doing at CalderCo, as she'd suspected, he hadn't been truthful.

He'd evaded every question she'd asked, and she knew why. She also knew why Mr. Calder had been so rattled. It hadn't been David; it had been the reason Mr. Calder had been forced to hire him.

Just to be sure, Autumn called Beatrice DePau. Ms. B had been an associate of her father's. Autumn wouldn't call Ms. B a friend, exactly, because the two had a passive-aggressive relationship that had begun two years earlier when Autumn had been forced to go to Ms. B for financial help. Neither of them had quite walked away from that meeting with what they wanted, but both had established a grudging respect for the other. She trusted Ms. B to select good client prospects for her, but she wasn't willing to pay the price demanded for being allowed access to the best prospects.

The business woman picked up on the first ring. "Autumn, how are you, dear?"

"Great. Guess who is my new boss?"

"Did you get a new job?"

Autumn sighed. "Let's not play games. Why did you pair me up with David Eastridge last Friday—and as a submissive?"

"Darling, though you are an adequate Domina, you'd make a better submissive. I thought you might like David. He's very handsome." She covered the phone for a minute, issuing a muffled command to whomever was in the room. "I thought the two of you had chemistry."

Autumn couldn't tell whether the woman was smirking or if she thought she'd done something nice. "He asked for me. He knew who I was before he ever called you. I need to know what you know. Ms. B, this is serious. I know how he knew I work for CalderCo, but I don't know how he knew about my association with you."

"I don't either, dear. You're right. When his associate called to set up the date, he asked for you. I told him you were strictly a Domina, but he managed to convince me to arrange a meeting. I thought it went well. You said he was a gentleman, and that you had fun." The way she inhaled and exhaled, Autumn figured that Ms. B was now on her balcony, smoking.

"He blackmailed you? How?" The dirty side of Elite Modeling Solutions was something in which Autumn did not participate. Though the models were not, in fact, prostitutes, they served a more deceptive function. They were paid bonuses for obtaining sensitive information on the clients. Though Autumn didn't have proof—and she had no plans to go searching for it—her intuition told her that Ms. B was in the business of blackmailing clients.

"He did not blackmail me. Do you remember a few years ago when I had some issues with my grandson in Mexico?"

The details were vague, both because Ms. B never told the whole story and because it had happened not long after the accident. "Yeah."

"He's home, alive and well, thanks to Mr. Eastridge and his colleagues. I owed them, you see, and by providing an introduction to you, I have wiped out that debt." She threw the last part in there as a triumphant salvo. "I need to run, dear. I'll call you if I have a job, maybe next week, okay?"

"Sounds fabulous." Autumn injected enough dryness into her tone to evaporate Lake Michigan, but it went over Ms. B's head.

"Great. Ta-ta for now."

Chapter Five

Autumn went into work early. She didn't often do this because she had an on-again, off-again relationship with the snooze button. However, today she had a mission. A thrill of anticipation tingled in her belly. She was going to show David a thing or two about truth today. She'd dropped her things at her new workstation on her way out the evening before, so she quickly unpacked and got everything squared away.

By the time he waltzed in with the rest of the staff, she was elbows-deep in preparing the acquisition forms he would need in order to get the information he needed to do his job. She knew he was close by the way the pitch of women's voices rose and men's voices dropped. Both genders sought his attention. Though she knew it was just because he was handsome and new, she couldn't help the pangs of jealousy that pinged around and annoyed the heck out of her. In order to disguise her feelings, she dove back into her tasks.

"Good morning, Autumn." A stack of folders manifested on the other side of her desk.

She flashed her most winsome smile as she stood. "Good morning, Mr. Eastridge. I hope you didn't have a long walk back to your car."

He laughed, and it was the genuine article because his irises lightened. "Not too long. It gave me a chance to dry off a bit." He set a travel mug in front of her. Scrumptious aromas assaulted her senses. Too intent on getting to work, she'd skipped her usual morning cup. Next to the mug, he plopped a brown bag. "I don't know how you take your coffee, so I threw a bunch of cream and sugar in here. I made you a Turkish blend because it reminds me of you—exotic and spicy."

She looked from him to the mug and back. "This is for me?"

"Yes, and I brought you a refillable mug. It's much more environmentally conscious. If you rinse it out when you're done and give it back to me, I'll bring you more tomorrow."

Autumn couldn't remember the last time anyone besides Julianne had done something so thoughtful and unexpected. "Thank you." She gestured to the pile of file folders. "Are those for me as well?"

"Nope. These are mine. They'll stay in my office, and they'll never be logged electronically."

She tore her gaze from his face. Looking at him was like staring at one of those spinning disks with black and white swirls. It drew her in and threatened to hypnotize her into doing things she wouldn't normally do.

"Give me ten minutes, and then come into my office so we can discuss your responsibilities."

"Yes, Sir." She hadn't meant to say that. It slipped out, a response to his authoritative tone.

His grin grew. He scooped up the pile of folders and disappeared into his office. She watched for far too long.

"I heard a rumor that you moved to a new department." Julianne set a muffin next to the travel mug. She flung her enviable red tresses over her shoulder as she perched on the edge of Autumn's desk. "Congratulations. A lot of people are very jealous of you right now. There is talk of restructuring, and you're in a prime position to know who is getting the boot and who is getting the scoot. Also, you're in the perfect position to do a daily booty check."

"Thanks for the muffin." The thoughtful gesture touched a tender place in her heart. Julianne might be asking for the scoop, but she would have brought the gift even if there was nothing she wanted to know. Autumn understood the rumor mill that was the lifeline of too many workplaces. "They want details. Sorry, but I'm probably seven minutes away from being sworn to secrecy. If it makes you feel better, I'm pretty sure that nobody who is fulfilling their work responsibilities is in danger of losing their job."

"Why didn't you call me last night? I have questions."

"I was busy, and I don't know the answers to your questions."

Julianne rolled her eyes, blue this morning, thanks to the peacock-hued dress suit she wore. "I don't fear for my job. I heard you fought Mr. Calder on moving from accounting."

"David rubbed me the wrong way." Details would not be forthcoming. Julianne had no idea she moonlighted a few times a month as a professional dominatrix.

She arched one sculpted brow. "You looked cozy enough when I came up."

"We're working on our differences. He's not a bad person, I just...I really liked accounting." It sounded lame. There was no way to make accounting—or a love for it—not sound lame.

Autumn grabbed her tablet and got to her feet. "How about we have lunch? Right now, my new boss wants to tell me what I'm going to be doing with my days."

Julianne heaved a dramatic sigh that let Autumn know she expected some good gossip later because she wasn't getting it now. "Usual place and time?"

"Yes. I'll see you later." She took her mug of coffee into David's office. He was in his chair, bent over a file drawer behind his desk, sliding the files where he wanted them. "I can do that for you."

"Did you have a nice chat with your friend?"

"Did you plant a listening device in my desk?" Trick question—she'd already swept for bugs.

"Not yet. Put that on my to-do list, will you?" He tucked away the last file and faced her with a serious expression. "I love this answering-a-question-with-a-question bit we do, but at some point, I'm going to need actual answers."

She sat in the chair across from him. "Then I'm going to need actual questions. You don't want to know if I enjoyed talking to my friend. You want to know who she is and what we talked about."

He pushed a file toward her. "Julianne Terry, acquisitions, been with CalderCo for thirteen years, recommended you for hire."

Fine. If he wanted to know so badly, she'd throw him a catfish, which was like a bone, only it had sharp points, and it was given to hissing. "We talked about your ass. The office staff, in general, derives pleasure in admiring it, but they all wonder if you're going to fire theirs." She set the thumb drive on the folder. "I put this together for you. It'll be your first priority."

"What's on it?"

"If I tell you, it'll ruin the surprise, and where's the fun in that?"

He fought the urge to laugh, but not with resounding success. Shaking his head provided a little bit of recovery. "Autumn, I'm going to have to insist on straightforward responses."

"David, we're not at the point in our relationship where we've established enough trust for straightforward responses. You've got your brand of truthiness, and this is mine."

Wearing a look that said he'd like nothing better than to turn her over his knee, he put the thumb drive into the port on his laptop. His eyes moved as he looked over the file names, and then he tapped one. She knew which one it was because she'd labeled it "Open Me First."

He swore under his breath. "Fuck me. I told Frankie to take this down."

She'd taken a screenshot of the SAFE Security website. Autumn waited in silence, letting him look through everything.

"These are your files. Why are you giving them to me?"

"I figured that if you're going to do a quality assurance review, then you'd better start with me. As the person working closest with you, it's important to know what you're getting." She knew he heard the air quotes around "quality assurance review."

He sat back in his chair, rested his elbow on the arm, and studied her intently. "I'm ready to be honest with you, or as honest I can be at this point. But I'd like the same courtesy from you."

She had no problem telling him anything about CalderCo he wanted to know. "That sounds fair."

"Fine. My place, after work. You remember where I live, right? I'm in penthouse three."

"Yes, but I have errands to run first. How about seven-thirty?"

All the buildings where he lived looked alike, but Autumn had cased some of them before, so she could tell them apart. He lived in one she may have allegedly broken into six months ago. Digital security doors had so many flaws. If the right circumstances presented themselves, she didn't even have to override the system. For example, eventually someone with a lot of bags was going to need to get inside. As a passerby, she might hold the door for a parent struggling with a small child and a handful of bags from various stores. Slapping a piece of tape over the lock was simple, and nobody ever seemed to notice the move.

Though she could get in the building other ways, she chose to use the buzzer. He let her in, and she took the elevator to the top floor. His was one of four penthouse apartments, and when the elevator door opened, she found him waiting in the hall. He'd changed from his work clothes, and this was the first time she'd seen him clad in all casual attire. The jeans, she was sure, were the same pair from Friday night. He probably only had the one pair. On top, the jersey-style shirt advertised the Detroit Tigers. And his feet were naked. This was an unexpected development. She would not have thought he was the kind of guy who was ever barefoot.

An amused smile sparkled in his eyes. "Did you finish your errands?"

"You didn't follow me?"

"Trust has to start somewhere." He held out a hand, and because she didn't know what he wanted, she put hers in it. He tucked her arm under his and led her to his apartment.

It was huge. The entryway was as large as her entire apartment, not that she needed more space for what was essentially a crash pad. His place had an open floor plan. To her left, two walls contained floor-to-ceiling bookcases filled with books, pictures, and statuettes. Of course, the pool table dominated the space. The dining room was straight ahead, and the kitchen branched off from that. To her right, four steps down led to an opulent living room. Huge French doors off the dining room led to an outdoor patio. From her vantage point, she made out a table and chairs.

"This is the foyer, though it doubles as a library and pool hall." David swept his hand in an arc from left to right, pointing out what she could clearly see for herself, though now she noticed a hallway on the far side of the living room. "Dining room, kitchen, living room. Down the hall, you'll find an office, guest bathroom, and the master suite."

She looked around, seeing too much to make reasonable assumptions. "You're already finished unpacking. You must have had a busy weekend."

"The apartment came fully furnished. None of this is mine. I only brought what you saw in my car Friday night."

The SAFE Security website hadn't listed an address, and a search had turned up 123 Main Street, Anytown, USA, which is the address people used when they didn't want sensitive information getting out there. His lack of personal belongings indicated that he didn't plan to stay in the area for very long.

He released her arm and stepped away. "Take off your shoes. You can put them on the rug next to the door."

It wasn't a request, and he didn't bother pretending it was something it wasn't. A surprised laugh, short and dry, escaped. "You're already giving orders?"

"Yes."

It had been a long, long time since she'd allowed anyone to dominate her. Sure, she'd bottomed for him, but it wasn't the same thing, and she wasn't sure how much and what kind of control she was ceding. Still, trust had to start somewhere. "So, that's the way it's going to be with us, is it?"

"Unless you object."

She didn't want to object. No part of her was against this, and her intuition chimed in with full support. She slipped out of her heels, and now when she faced him, she had to tilt her face up even more. "I don't object."

A soft smile lifted the corners of his mouth. "Good. We're on the same page. Have you eaten?"

While she frequently grabbed something not memorable on her way to or from the nursing home, she hadn't today. "Not yet."

"Good. I made dinner." Taking her hand, he led her to the sliding door. "It's a nice night. We'll eat on the patio." He pulled out a chair and helped her sit. "Wine?"

Remembering the terms she'd unwittingly laid out the night before, a shiver of anticipation did cartwheels up her spine. "Are you hoping I kiss you before I leave?"

His eyelids fell to half-mast, and his light brown eyes became mesmerizing liquid pools. "I'm counting on it." She thought he might try for a kiss right then—she wouldn't have pushed him away—but he just repeated his question. "Would you like a glass of wine?"

This time she gave a straightforward response. "Yes."

He poured the wine and served dinner, a pilaf and some kind of white fish that was light and flaky with the right amount of lemon and dill. "Do you like it? You said you weren't picky, and I avoided shrimp. Though, it's amazing how many shrimp recipes go through your mind when that's the only dish you can't make."

She laughed. "Forbidden fruit. We always long for something the moment we're told we can't have it."

He regarded her with an intensity that made her feel like she was the only person in the world who mattered. It made the air hard to breathe. "What forbidden fruit are you after?"

"The truth." Her pulse was leaping out of control, and she had to take a moment to compose herself. It had been easier to banter with him when she had questioned his motivation. "Why don't you shower me with your truth?"

He sipped his wine, buying time, she knew, because he wasn't sure what he could and shouldn't reveal. "Truth comes in a lot of different flavors that are widely dependent upon a person's perspective."

Pretty words, but she was a master in manipulating a conversation, and she recognized that talent in David. "I said truth, not bullshit."

He laughed. "What do you want to know?"

"Why you're here. I figured out that Mr. Calder isn't nervous that you're here. It's the reason he had to bring you here and slip you in under a false cover that has him on edge." She nibbled on another bite of pilaf and watched him expectantly.

"Nothing I say to you tonight can leave this apartment."

"I know."

"Three million dollars is missing. It's enough to destroy the company. I've been hired to find the money, get it back, and figure out who is responsible."

She nodded. "I thought it was something like that. It makes sense now for you to have an assistant from accounting."

"Who very thoughtfully copied all her files for me. Thank you. I found some errors, but no irregularities."

A cold, slimy feeling slithered along her conscience. "Errors? What kind of errors?"

"Nothing out of the ordinary. Overall, they amounted to under four thousand, and they all happened in the first year you were with CalderCo learning the business of accounting. Your files have been nearly spotless since then." The encouraging smile he wore didn't feel right.

"You must think I'm a special kind of stupid."

"Actually, I think you're brilliant. Nobody's records are perfect."

Hers were. The "errors" concealed petty thefts she'd committed in order to pay for Summer's physical therapy, which wasn't covered by insurance. Therefore she didn't bother to argue. This was a great time to derail the topic. "I noticed the SAFE Security website is no longer available."

His only response was to press his lips together and barely lift a shoulder.

"And I talked to Ms. B. She told me what you did for her grandson."

"So you know I'm one of the good guys."

"Like truth, good and evil depend on perspective."

He laughed. "Now who's obfuscating?"

"Well, you're not exactly saying anything. You're letting me guess at the blanks."

Refilling her wine glass, he said, "I've told you the reason I'm here. You're wondering why I zeroed in on you, why I asked Beatrice for an introduction, and why I took you to the play party."

If he had the access she suspected, then she knew exactly why he'd selected her. "Yes."

"A lot of reasons, some of which I can't tell you due to client confidentiality. Suffice it to say that your history raised red flags, and when I found your connection to Beatrice, I arranged a meeting. I think that taking you to a play party helped me get to know you faster and more in depth than would have happened if you'd just been my assistant." He gathered their empty plates. "If you'll bring the wine, we can take this inside. It's getting a little chilly."

She hadn't noticed the temperature drop. Taking the bottle and their glasses, she followed him inside. The amount of light indoors made her realize how dark it had become outside. "Why don't you like Mr. Calder?"

In the midst of rinsing the plates, David froze. "I just didn't like the way he treated you."

She set the bottle on the counter near the living room. One wing of the U-shaped kitchen divided it from the living room. The counter functioned as a bar on the other side. "It's more than that. Your reaction was visceral, almost as if he'd attacked you personally."

He finished rinsing and dried his hands before picking up his wine glass. One more step forward, and he sandwiched her between his body and the edge of the counter. "Autumn, we said we'd be truthful with each other."

"We did."

"But we're not at the point where we're going to bare our souls and tell all, are we?"

The way he looked at her, the way he commanded her body and mind with his proximity and dominating gaze,

Autumn had never felt closer to anyone in her life. It scared the shit out of her. "No. We're not. This is temporary, I know."

His eyebrows drew together, two fierce slashes. "Temporary?"

"Yeah. You're leaving as soon as you save the company."

He put his glass down, and then he took hers and put it next to his. She knew by his expression that he was going to kiss her. He slid his fingertips along her neck and used his thumb to guide her head into the perfect position. "You're okay with temporary?"

It was all she'd ever had. Nothing in her life had been permanent—not her name or where she lived or who she was, not even the people she'd counted on to always be there. Her father hadn't planned to die, and Summer hadn't planned to spend three years in a coma, but it had happened, and she was alone. Perhaps that was the permanence she counted on most.

The way he held her meant she couldn't move, so she spoke. Her voice came out in a tiny squeak. "Yes."

He kissed her gently, tasting her lips with a teasing caress before abandoning them to explore other areas. His lips skimmed her eyelids and cheeks before wandering to her neck and shoulder. She felt drugged—safe, warm, and wanted—and it had been far too long since she'd let herself be so vulnerable.

"Who are you, Autumn Sullivan?" His low whisper took a moment to penetrate the fog he'd induced. "Who are you really?"

Once the question got through, the spell dispersed. She stiffened, and he stopped kissing her. "What's that supposed to mean?"

He exhaled hard, but he didn't move away. "You've only existed for six years."

Jerking from his hold, she whirled away and put distance between them. "Are your buddies listening in?"

"Are...What?"

"The other members of SAFE Security—are they listening?" Without waiting for him to answer, she began searching for listening devices. She felt under surfaces, looked inside vases, and took apart pens.

When she knelt to look under the dining table, he lifted her up. "Autumn, what the hell are you doing?"

She pushed him, hard. "What the hell does it look like I'm doing? You're the Special Forces mercenary spy guy. Figure it out."

He held his hands up, placating her by appearing to surrender. "I'm not a mercenary, I'm no longer in Special Forces, and nobody is listening to us. This isn't a sting. Though I apparently suck at it, I meant it to be a date."

"Then why did you ask me who I was?"

"Because I know that Autumn Sullivan isn't your real name."

"It is." Nobody could prove differently.

"It is now," he corrected. "But six years ago, you were someone else."

This was why she didn't let people get close. *This* was why she kept all relationships casual. Julianne was a sweetheart, but she was like most people. She'd never questioned Summer or Autumn's identities. She backed away slowly, heading for the door and wishing she had some kind of weapon to put between them. "Who do you work for?"

"Calder—that's all. I swear I mean you no harm, and your secret is safe with me. I'm here to find the missing money, not to put you in danger." He leaped for her, crossing the chasm between them with swiftness and grace. She didn't struggle against him because she knew he was stronger and better trained, so she held herself stiffly in his arms. "I swear to you that I don't mean to cause this kind of trouble. Please don't call the Marshalls because they'll move you. Not only will you have to start all over again, but I just found you. I don't know exactly where this thing between us will or won't lead, but I'd really like to find out, and I can't do that if you vanish. Plus, if you go, it'll definitely look like you took the money."

Autumn stared, fascinated and amazed. He truly thought she was in WITSEC, which was far better than the truth, and it afforded her easy outs if he asked things she didn't want to answer. Only it wasn't fitting in with the theme of the night. "I am *so* not ready to bare my soul."

"I understand."

Her heart was still racing, only the cause shifted back to something safe. She plucked at his Tigers jersey. "But I am ready to finish that glass of wine with you, and maybe I'll let you get to first base again."

He brushed his lips against hers. "I had my heart set on second."

"Not on the first date, David. I'm not that kind of girl this time around."

He closed his mouth over hers and sent her senses soaring.

Chapter Six

"You were right." Autumn fluffed Summer's pillow, lifted her sister's head, and placed it back underneath. "He's wonderful. Thoughtful—he brings me coffee in the morning. And those lips—he's a fantastic kisser. I wish you could see a picture of him. He kind of reminds me of a young Val Kilmer, circa 1987, only less cocky. He's confident and self-assured, but not in a way that shoves it in your face. It's subtle."

"That's new for you."

Autumn jumped and looked at the door. She put a hand over her heart. "Jeeze, Julianne. I didn't know you were coming. What's new for me?"

"Subtle." Julianne came to the bed and rubbed Summer's forearm. "I'm here, dear. It's Wednesday, so it's been four days since I've seen you. Lots to tell you, like the fact that your little sister landed the new office hottie. I told you about David, remember? I said he seemed like Autumn's type."

Autumn could admit that subtlety wasn't her strong suit, but it wasn't a new concept for her. "I can be subtle when I need to."

"I meant in your choice of dating companion. You tend toward men who are immature. They're nice and all, but they're not done cooking. I'm not throwing stones. How can I? I skip straight to the quintessential loser type. But I can admit to being a little jealous." Julianne looked at Summer. "Autumn wasn't kidding when she said Val Kilmer. He's tall, built, and blond. His hair is the thick kind that you just want to run your fingers through."

Autumn sat on the upholstered chair in the corner. "I'm sorry, Julianne. I was going to tell you, but it didn't seem real until I told Summer." She'd waited over a week to say anything to Summer. First she wanted to make sure that David didn't change his mind. They'd spent several evenings together over the past week, eating good food, drinking fine wine, walking hand-in-hand around the neighborhood, and kissing. Lots of kissing.

Julianne nailed her with a look that screamed, *You're a dumbass.* "I know how you operate. Summer may be your sister, but she's also the only real mother you ever had. She's my friend too. I often tell her things before I tell you. I'm not upset."

"Oh, good." Autumn exhaled in relief. "And I know you'll keep this between us. I don't want David to get in trouble."

Rolling her eyes, Julianne sat on the edge of Summer's bed. "Oh, please. I've seen him with Mr. Calder. The way the old man clears his schedule whenever David Eastridge calls for a meeting is almost pathetic. He made his assistant buy a thousand dollar espresso machine just to have the kind of coffee that David likes on hand. You'll get fired before your boyfriend would."

That didn't make Autumn feel better, but before she could say anything, Julianne screamed.

"Summer! Oh my God! You're awake!" She jumped up and down.

Summer had never woken up twice in one week. Autumn rushed across the room. She grabbed Summer's hand. "You're okay. Don't try to talk because you have a feeding tube down your throat. You're safe. I'm here, and you're safe. I love you so much."

Summer blinked several times, looking fearfully between Julianne and Autumn. A tear dropped from the corner of Summer's eye as it closed again. Autumn waited as long minutes passed, and then she felt Julianne's hand on her shoulder. She turned, and let Julianne hug her as she cried.

Julianne left a half hour later, dragging Autumn with her. "It's not healthy for you to just sit there all the time. If Summer could talk, she'd tell you that, and then she'd tell me to make you go home and get some sleep."

Autumn made sounds of agreement, but most of Julianne's well-meaning lecture didn't make it in the one ear to go out the other. Like a zombie, she went to her car, started it, and drove toward home. Then she shook herself out of the funk. She had things to do tonight.

The target was a gallery in Royal Oak, which wasn't all that close to her Ypsilanti home. She called David on the way, intending to leave a message, but he answered. "Hey. I thought you were hanging with the FBI guys tonight?"

The sounds of nightlife—probably a bar—provided background noise. "I am, but that doesn't mean I wouldn't answer when you called."

"Oh. Well, I just wanted to tell you that I'm not going to work tomorrow."

"Are you okay?" The background noise vanished. "Do you need me to come over?"

She sniffled, not because she was pretending to be sick, but because she'd started crying again, and she'd just noticed. "No. I'll be fine. I'm taking a personal day. I have some things I need to do."

"You don't sound okay. You sound like you're crying. Honey, I didn't look up your address. Text it to me." He used his Dom voice, and though she couldn't obey, it gave her the strength to stop the flow of tears.

"I'm not at home. I won't be home until late." She found an unused napkin on the floor of the passenger seat and wiped her face. One day she'd clean out her car. "I can come over tomorrow evening. How about six?"

"Autumn, let me help you. That's what I'm here for."

She laughed. Hearing his voice made everything seem not so bad. "You've already helped. I feel a lot better. Go back and have fun with your new friends. Maybe they'll offer you a job, and you won't have to freelance anymore."

His exhalation vented some of the frustration, but the rest came through the line with crystal clarity. "We're going to talk about this tomorrow, and I may very well spank your ass for this."

"Yes, Sir. The reports you need are in our shared folder. Have fun at all those meetings. Goodbye." She ended the call before he could say anything more. In reality, she could use a good solid spanking. It had been years since she'd been on the receiving end of one.

Ben—her partner for this heist—wanted to hit the target during the day, but having a day job made it impossible to case it for security, and so she needed to burn some daylight wandering around the vicinity. It drained her of personal days, but keeping up illusions was part and parcel of who she was.

Of course, she'd never before had a boss with a reason to question her for time off. Mr. Tucker had never taken an interest in her personal life. She found Ben sitting in his car on a residential side street. As she slid into the passenger side, she had to squelch the urge to laugh.

David had been jealous that she'd met this man for coffee. Not only was Ben about fifteen years older, but he completely lacked any air of authority. He had the kind of face that faded into the background, and he'd cultivated a demeanor to match. For a thief, it was a helpful cover. She'd worked with Ben several times before, so she was comfortable with his idea for hitting this target.

"Anything interesting happen?"

"I find it interesting that there's one guard on all day, and when the gallery is open, they have three. If they didn't want to get robbed, they really should reverse those numbers. I mean, who robs a gallery when it's open?"

Autumn shrugged. "Takes a ballsy thief with a catch-me complex. I prefer stealth and brains. Plus Royal Oak is all about the nightlife. That's too many witnesses. Did you get pictures of their system?"

Ben had spent the day as a plumber. Somehow the gallery's entire system had backed up, and Ben had saved the day, fixing it before toxic sludge could shut them down for costlier repairs. He handed over his phone.

Studying it, she mentally mapped the locks that would need picking—two doors stood in the way—and what it would take to get into the vault.

"The day guards change shifts at eight, and the overnight guard has a dentist appointment the day before. He should be nice and tired, perhaps even asleep, when we come in. I timed the entrance and exit with the guard's rounds. If you can do the vault in ten minutes, we can be in and out in sixteen."

She zoomed in on the security panel and the lock's dial. "Lockmaster 1559. It's about a year old. The fancy light displays look like they do a lot, but they don't. It has two-tier protection, but nothing I can't handle. If all goes well, ten minutes should be fine." Before handing the phone back, she was careful to make sure her prints weren't on it. This precaution was something her father had drilled into her from the time she was a toddler.

"Compensation will be as discussed. Half will be deposited into your account by midnight the night before, and the other half will be paid upon completion."

Nodding, Autumn said, "See you in one week."

"Bright and early," he agreed. "I'm thinking we're in by seven and out by seven-sixteen."

In the hustle and bustle of the early morning, they'd be in and out before anyone noticed them. Any store that didn't serve coffee wouldn't see its first employees for at least an hour. She exited the car. Her last job had been over a month ago, and Summer's PT bill was overdue. Unlike her rent, not paying meant Summer didn't get the care she needed. With rent, it took a couple months to evict, and even then it was cheaper to work with her than to kick her out. Her apartment sucked, as did the neighborhood, so there probably wasn't a line of renters waiting for it to become available.

Most of her income went to cover the co-pays and other expenses not eligible for insurance. Having a sister in a coma wasn't cheap, and her paycheck barely covered the basics. That said, Autumn would be lying if she said she didn't enjoy the intellectual and physical challenges presented by a well-planned theft. Though, because she lacked the ability to run and disappear, she opted to take a hugely discounted straight cut up front instead of a percentage of the sale once the item was fenced.

Ben drove off, and she strolled the streets alone. She needed to know the lay of the land. After the job was done, they'd separate and scatter. It was her job to devise an escape route.

David stared at the phone as the screen turned black. Something wasn't right. Autumn had been crying, and he wanted to know why.

But she'd rejected his offer of solace, and they'd only been together for a couple of days. Most of what he knew about her was due to research instead of conversation. Fighting his instinct to go after her, he returned to the table in the bar where Jesse sat with Malcolm and Keith. The night was young, and so many tables were empty.

"How's the wife?" Keith smirked as he sipped lemon water.

David didn't know Keith very well, but the man's reputation spoke for itself. He had a close rate above eighty percent. The air of danger and authority that shrouded the man was earned. He slid into the booth next to Jesse. "Wife?"

Keith's green eyes glinted with mischief, which reminded David a little of Autumn. "I've seen that look before."

He frowned at Jesse. "What look?"

Jesse grinned. "The one that says someone messed with your sub and you want to put them in traction.

"Malcolm wore that look when he was undercover investigating Darcy." Keith ignored the warning look Malcolm was giving. "I was his handler on that, and every time I met with him, he'd find some way to justify her behavior or why he wasn't going after her as aggressively as he could. Well, except to get her in bed. He knocked her up within a week of starting the investigation."

Malcolm glowered in Keith's direction. "She was innocent, and I kept telling you that. I got what I needed from her, and that investigation netted seventeen convictions."

"And one son."

"One awesome son." Malcolm took a swig from his bottle. "Maybe we'll have another boy, and then she'll want to try again for a girl."

Keith's laugh boomed, echoing across the bar. "Man up. It's not that bad. A couple days of soreness, and you'll be fine."

Jesse threw Malcolm a puzzled look.

Keith opted to fill him in. "Birth control and condoms have failed them, so Darcy told Malcolm he has to get a vasectomy."

Jesse snorted. "Who's the dominant in your house?"

"When you find your submissive soul mate, you'll realize how her wants and needs drive your every action." Malcolm's sage advice was wasted on Jesse. The man was thoroughly committed to casual play. He slapped Keith on the shoulder. "Do you agree?"

"Yep. There's nothing more powerful than when you're submissive kneels at your feet, looking at you with love and devotion." The naughtiness vanished from his expression as it softened. "But you have to earn it with yours. It's a two-way street. Be careful, David. Autumn isn't who you think she is."

David knew the parts of her she let him see, and he knew she kept so much more hidden. "Did you get a hit with the facial recognition software?"

"Not one."

It was disappointing, but not unexpected. "That's good. It means she doesn't have a criminal record."

Malcolm and Jesse exchanged a significant look.

And that irritated David. "What?"

Malcolm tapped his bottle cap on the table. "If she was in WITSEC, we'd get a hit. We wouldn't get much information—it'd mostly be a manufactured profile, and it would trigger a response from the U.S. Marshalls who'd be on our asses about why we were looking into one of their witnesses."

"She didn't say whether she was or wasn't in WITSEC, did she?" Jesse slid his question in smoothly. He was a man of few words, but when he spoke, he tended to make it count.

"No, she didn't. I took her evasion as wariness to talk about it with someone she didn't know all that well." And she'd let him think it was the truth. What had she said? He had his own brand of truthiness, and she had hers. Did that mean he couldn't trust a single word she said? "Maybe she had a traumatic past that she doesn't want to talk about. She has some serious scars on her left shoulder. Did you find out who she visits at the convalescent home?"

"Summer Sullivan. According to her birth certificate, she's 82, but the file photo shows a woman in her late twenties or early thirties. She's been in a coma for about three years. She looks enough like Autumn to be her sister, but Autumn Sullivan doesn't have a sister. According to what I've found, she has no family." Jesse paused, thinking. "I looked up Summer Sullivan, but beyond information pertaining to a deceased woman who would be an octogenarian if she were still alive, I found only one thing—a police report of the car accident. A car driven by Summer Sullivan hit the passenger side of another car, and then both cars were hit by a semi. Summer was severely injured—head trauma, contusions, broken bones—which led to the coma. Autumn suffered broken bones, and her left shoulder was impaled and pinned. They had to pry her out with the Jaws of Life. The driver and passenger in the other car were killed, and the semi driver escaped with minimal injuries."

David studied the label of his beer bottle as he tried to make sense of it all. "Maybe she's on the run from WITSEC. She freaked out when I asked her who she really was. She's terrified of being found by someone."

"Be careful," Keith said. "Don't make her a victim without proof. She could just as easily be the criminal in all of this. What if she and Summer tee-boned that car to kill whoever was inside? You have nothing on her more than six years old, and even that's sketchy. Most of your information is from after the accident."

It didn't add up, and he knew that getting answers from Autumn was going to take time he didn't have. He turned to Jesse. "Follow her. Be careful, though. She made me." Other details came back, and they didn't tilt the scales in her favor. "Fuck. She knows how to scout for bugs and spot a tail. Those aren't accounting skills."

"Don't worry," Jesse said. "I'm better at tailing than you are."

David glared. He was damn good at surveillance and tailing. "It helps that she's never seen you in person. She saw the picture of you that Frankie put up on the company website, but your hair was longer and you were smiling, so you looked like a completely different person."

Jesse scowled. "I smile plenty."

"Baring your teeth and smiling aren't the same thing."

"Then she'd better not see Jesse at CalderCo," Malcolm said, extinguishing Jesse's rising ire. "He can't be your inside guy. I'd offer to tail her, but she's met me. If she's that good, she'll notice me."

Dean had wanted David to utilize Malcolm. They were in the market for expanding SAFE Security, but new talent was difficult to find. David motioned toward Malcolm. "You're tech savvy. How about you go undercover in Jesse's place? We pay well."

Malcolm considered the proposal.

Keith snickered. "Darcy wants your ass out of the house so badly that she's inventing errands and chores. She told me that if I brought you home before ten, then I was dead to her."

"I'm in." Malcolm smiled. "I miss being in the field."

"And I hate being cooped up in an office. This is much more my speed." Jesse tapped commands into his phone. "I'm sending you the dossier on your cover identity. You start tomorrow morning at eight."

David arrived home to find his father waiting in the living room, enjoying a drink and the evening news. "Dad, what are you doing here?"

"Checking in. We can't discuss all the things we need to at work."

They certainly could. Autumn had scheduled a meeting for tomorrow, at which he intended to disclose his progress. "You can't just come in and make yourself at home."

Bill lifted one eyebrow. "It's my apartment."

"Not while I'm living here. Say the word, and I'll leave. I don't have a problem renting another place."

A familiar sigh issued from his father. He wasn't in the mood to argue, and he found David's attitude irritating. "What do you think of Autumn?"

He went with the change in subject. "She's a very capable assistant, and her accounting skills are above average. There are some discrepancies from her first year, but after that, she seems to have gotten the hang of her job."

Bill helped himself to a refill. "Have you ruled her out as the thief?"

He didn't want her to be the thief. "I've just started combing through the evidence. It would be a mistake to rule out anybody at this point."

"Office rumors say the two of you have become very cozy."

"You're going on rumors now?" David's personal life was none of his father's concern.

"I need to know that you're not going to let your dick get in the way of doing your job." Bill settled back in the chair and put his feet on the coffee table. "She's very attractive."

David thought about throwing one of those you-must-not-know-me-very-well-if statements at his father, but then he realized that Bill didn't know him very well. Though they were related by blood, they were effectively strangers. His temper evaporated. "It won't. You're right about her, though. The details of her life don't add up, and that makes her a prime suspect. I'm on it, Dad. I'll find out the truth, and when I'm done, you'll have your money back, and your company will be fine."

Bill got to his feet and offered his hand. "It's been good seeing you, David. Take care."

This reasonable man wasn't the one David remembered. He more closely resembled the man Autumn knew. It was a puzzling development. David shook his father's hand. "See you tomorrow."

Chapter Seven

The next morning, David worked his way through Autumn's flash drive like a madman. He had Malcolm hack her account and search for anything deleted or missing. "Look through her Internet history. See what she's been doing online."

It took less than an hour before David gave in and called Autumn. That's what a good boyfriend would do, right?

"Hi, David. Do you miss me already, or are you having trouble finding something?" She sounded both happy and amused.

"I was just wondering what you're up to."

She laughed. "I'm casing an art gallery that I plan to rob."

"Autumn." The warning came out a little sharper than he'd intended, especially when he remembered the tidbit his dad had thrown at him about her breaking-and-entering habit.

"Are you calling as my boss or as the guy who's making plans for second base?"

"Second base? Honey, I'm gearing up for a home run, only instead of a bat, I'll have a flogger, and the ball will be on the gag."

"Mmm." Her grin came through, loud and clear. "Ropes can be my uniform. I'm starting to see the appeal of baseball."

David loved the sport. "You don't find baseball appealing?"

"Don't know. I've never actually watched or played a game. I get the metaphors, though. Here's hoping you hit it out of the park." She laughed again. "I like you, David. You're going to be late for a meeting, though, so I'll let you go. See you at six?"

"Don't be late." Though she had a well-known habit of being late, he wasn't seeing that as a consistent thing. She'd been to his place early that first night, and she'd been to work early the next day. But then she'd been late the day after that. He didn't know what to make of it.

Jesse reported in at eleven. "She got up at the crack of dawn. I followed her to Royal Oak. It's about forty-five minutes away. It's a hip little town full of shops."

"I've been there." It had been years, but David remembered the city well. "They have a kick-ass fetish store."

"Yeah. It's definitely the heartbeat of the kink community. Anyway, she walked around a lot. About nine-fifty, she stopped for a chat on the phone that had her smiling and twirling her hair. Then she went into a bunch of stores, had an early lunch at a café, and then she left. I followed her to the county health department. She's in there now." Food crunched. Jesse had apparently picked up lunch while he waited.

David frowned. "Why would she need to go to the health department?"

"Don't know. Want me to check it out?"

"No. Just keep following her." He rang off with Jesse and immediately dialed Autumn. She didn't pick up, so he left a short message.

Perusing through her files led him to a cache of articles on aromatherapy and reflexology. Other than that, she'd already duplicated everything and given it to him on the thumb drive. It was a dead end, a maddening trip that netted no answers, and so he turned his attention elsewhere. Almost four hundred other employees needed to be investigated.

Autumn frowned as she listened to David's second voicemail. Three phone calls in one day—while he was at work—was excessive. He truly didn't like not knowing where she was and what she was doing. It had been so long since someone had cared at all about her whereabouts that she didn't know whether his actions were sweet or the sign of an unhealthy mind. She opted to err on the positive side. He hadn't demanded she tell him anything, and after her tearful call last night, he was probably worried.

Dominant men were driven to fix everything for their submissives, but this wasn't something he could fix. She took a deep breath and went into the nursing home. This wasn't her usual visiting time, but she planned to spend the evening with David, so this would have to do. Besides, did it matter what time she came as long as she was there each day?

Lorne greeted her at the door. He shuffled along slowly with Edith at his side. "You're early today, missy."

Edith frowned and patted him on the hand. "Don't yell at her, Lorne. She's not deaf. Turn up your hearing aid."

Ignoring Edith, or not hearing her, he shook his finger at Autumn. "You'd better have a good reason."

"He was going to have you watch the gentleman's choir. They're quite good." Giving up on the hearing aid, Edith explained why Lorne was upset.

"Oh, I'm sorry." Autumn smiled regretfully. "I have a date tonight, so I thought I would drop by early rather than skip a day."

Lorne turned to Edith. "That's why I'm leaving all my assets to this one. She might not be blood, but she's the best granddaughter I ever had."

Edith rolled her eyes. "She doesn't come here to see you."

"I come to see everybody," Autumn said. "I love you all." She hugged Lorne. "Leave your assets to your children. They love you, but they don't live nearby."

It took longer to disengage from the couple than Autumn would have liked. Lorne launched into updates on his children, grandchildren, and great-grandchildren, and Edith interjected her stories. While they were sweet, she just wanted to see Summer. For her part, Summer was resting quietly.

"Hey there, pretty lady. I brought you some flowers." Autumn took the wilting bunch out of the vase. She tossed them in the trash and refilled the vase with fresh water. "These have pink azaleas with little black flecks and some white lily of the valley for contrast. It's a sexy bouquet. Why sexy? Because life should sometimes be sexy."

Summer didn't stir. Autumn finished arranging the new flowers and went to the bedside. "How was PT today?" Without waiting for a response, she flipped back the covers on Summer's left leg. Laying for days on end destroyed muscles. She'd read from various sources that each day of inactivity took four days to a month to recover from. "Let's do a few more leg lifts. Your ass is not as tight as it used to be."

As she was taught, she lifted Summer's leg at the knee and ankle for the first series of stretches and moves. "When you wake up, I want you to be in good shape. I haven't seen David since I last saw you, so there's not much new to tell on that front. I went to the gynecologist today, got my plumbing checked. It's been a while, and I wanted to make sure everything was in working order. Apparently, BOB has done a great job of keeping away the cobwebs. I also got an IUD put in, and I stocked up on condoms. You can never be too careful, and David is too fucking hot to not have some mileage on him. I don't blame him. If I was in a position to come and go as I pleased, I'd have a few more notches on my bedpost."

She switched to Summer's other leg to repeat the exercises. "I took today off work, and he called three times. I didn't answer the last two because I'd turned my phone off at the doctor's office and forgot to turn it back on. Last night was hard for me, Summer. I want so badly for you to wake up and be okay. Even if you're not okay, I want you to be awake. I can deal with anything as long as I have you back. I miss you so much. I called him on my way home, crying. Just hearing his voice made me feel better. Is that pathetic or what? I've known him exactly one week. And he's only here for however long his investigation takes. Then he's going to leave. That's going to suck, but I'm determined to enjoy him while he's here."

She made it home with time to spare, so she mixed up a box of brownie batter and popped it in the oven before getting in the shower. Hopefully David would appreciate the gesture, if not the actual treat. She shaved her legs and landscaped just in case David felt like swinging for the fences. Chances were pretty good he'd score.

The light green skater dress with a diamond cutout in the back was the first piece of clothing she'd purchased in a long time. New clothes weren't really in the budget, but she felt the splurge was worthwhile. Summer wouldn't fault her. Looking in the mirror, she smoothed the short skirt over her hips and adjusted the way her boobs sat in her bra until someone knocked on her door.

People rarely knocked on her door. The neighborhood wasn't safe enough for solicitors to travel door-to-door, and most of the people who lived there couldn't afford whatever they were selling anyway. As Autumn generally kept to herself, those who lived in nearby apartments didn't feel free to drop by for an impromptu visit. She peered through the peephole to find David on the other side.

Delighted, she flung open the door. "You peeked into my personnel file to find my address." She opened her arms. "How romantic."

He frowned. "Is that sarcasm? Sometimes your delivery is so dry that I can't tell."

"No sarcasm yet, but if you give me a minute, I'll try to muster up some."

He came in, pushing her backward with his body as he kicked the door shut. He kept going until she hit the far wall, and then he devoured her lips with a demanding kiss. No teasing or nibbling this time—he claimed his territory with his tongue while his hands roamed her back, hips, and thighs. The man kissed with his whole body, awakening parts of her that she'd forgotten. Her breasts swelled against his chest, and she explored his arms, shoulders, and back.

When she raked her nails across the back of his neck, he moaned and released her lips. She gulped air, and he wandered south, biting her neck where it met her shoulder with precise viciousness. Red hot desire showered sparks through her body, and unfamiliar, incoherent noises squeaked from her throat. She dragged her fingers through his hair, looking for something to hold, and she dug her nails into his arm.

He lifted her thigh against his hip and thrust his leg between hers. The things he did to her neck left her mind and body reeling. When he fisted the hair near her nape and pulled, the pleasure pricking down her spine was nearly her undoing. He licked the column of her throat and captured her lips again.

The bulge in his pants came to life, and he ground his pelvis against her thigh. Tearing his kiss away, he pressed his forehead to hers. "You've been on my mind nonstop since last night." The rhythmic thrust of his pelvis and the way his fist tightened in her hair distracted her from processing the fierceness of his statement. She noted it, but that was all. Then the hand that held her leg high slid forward. He yanked her panties aside and stroked her wetness.

Autumn struggled to speak. "I picked up condoms today."

His eyes lit, turning an even lighter shade of pale brown. "Where are they?"

She pointed to a brown paper bag on the table next to the sofa, inches from where they stood. He released her, letting her hair and leg go at the same time. Though she was leaning against the wall, she stumbled, and he steadied her.

Her Dom steadied her. He looked out for her, and he cared about her. Suddenly she wanted to take care of him. She wanted to submit, and she wanted to be dominated. More than that, she wanted to taste him. Steady on her feet, she blinked up at him. "If you don't mind, I would like to suck your cock."

No hesitation on his part. "Get on your knees." He unbuckled and unzipped, and then he shoved his pants and shorts out of the way. "I'm not quite there. Finish making me hard, and then put the condom on."

It had been years since Autumn had found herself with a cock in her face. Her brain short-circuited for a second because she wasn't perfect, and she found herself staring at the thing.

With one finger hooked under her chin, he urged her to look up. "If you've changed your mind, tell me, honey. I won't be upset if you want to wait. I know this is fast."

She didn't want to wait. "It's not too fast. It's just...been a while for me."

He stroked her hair away from her face. "Open your mouth and pretend it's a popsicle. Licking and sucking works wonders. You can even use your hands to hold it steady. Really, there's no wrong way to do this, and I'll be sure to give you plenty of practice."

His dry humor worked to assure her that he wouldn't be judging her skill, or lack thereof. Who knew how rusty she was? She wrapped a hand around his base and stroked his soft, silky skin gently. He responded, and she licked the ridge around the head. In her hands and against her lips, he hardened, and then she took him into her mouth. She was just getting into it when he pushed her away.

"That's enough practice for now. Put the condom on."

Her hands shook with anticipation and nerves. It had been so long since she'd been intimate with anyone that she'd forgotten what it was like to do this with another person. She managed to get it on correctly, and he hauled her to her feet. The kiss wasn't unexpected, but the torrent of passion he unleashed on her was. She realized that he was barely keeping himself in check. Having this influence on him worked wonders for her confidence. It bounced right back.

He lifted her, yanked the crotch of her panties aside, and positioned his cock at her entrance. Slowly, she sank down his length. His cock stretched her walls, filling her pussy and marking her as his. She wrapped her legs around his waist and held onto his powerful shoulders as he fucked her with deep, slow strokes.

"Are you still okay?"

Her entire body trembled with emotions she refused to identify. Trapped between his body and the wall, she experienced true freedom. "More than."

He kissed her, taking her lips again and again as tension built in her core. She gasped and moaned, making desperate noises as the climax closed in. "Look at me," he commanded. "Open your eyes, Autumn. I want you to be looking at me when you come."

Not realizing they'd drifted to half-mast, she forced her eyelids to open. He caught her with the firmness and mastery of his dominant gaze. Something intangible passed between them, and she found herself surrendering to him. It scared her for so many reasons, and the liquid brown pull of his eyes remained a single anchor in the emotional storm. The moment she gave herself over, the orgasm slammed into her hard. Too stunned to scream, she let the endless waves wash over her limp body.

Mindless of her struggle, he increased his pace, fucking her faster and harder until he buried himself deep and cried out. The entire time, he kept his gaze glued to hers so neither of them could hide their souls. He held her as they came down. Silence surrounded them because there were no words to describe what had transpired.

Eventually he let her down. "I'm going to take care of the condom. Where's your bathroom?"

She pointed to her right. "Second door." The first door led to the bedroom. They were five steps from a mattress, but they hadn't made it.

While he went inside the bathroom, she straightened her dress and locked the front door. From as far back as she could remember, Autumn had been taught not to trust anyone who wasn't her father or sister. Over the past few years, she'd come to trust Julianne to a point. Did she trust David? Not completely, but probably more than she should. Definitely enough to actually surrender to him. Sure, she'd played at submission and surrender in the past, but she hadn't actually felt it in her soul. Not like this. Not the way she'd felt moments ago with David.

Kinky games appealed to her, and the idea of submission was an ideal she'd never fully embraced. Who, in their right mind, would turn over control of their life to someone else? She'd been in D/s relationships before, but they had always seemed more like playacting, and when she'd walked away from them, she hadn't given it a second thought. Relationships were a means to an end, and everybody was out to con you. Love, her father used to say, was the greatest con of all.

Except Autumn didn't have an end in mind. Wait—yeah, she did. She wanted to escape her life and all the burdens she had carried alone for the past three years. David offered slices of heaven. That's what she wanted from him. In surrendering like that, she'd successfully escaped for a little while.

"Autumn?" He came out of the bathroom, his clothes once again perfect, and frowned. "There was blood on the condom. Was I too rough, or is it that time of the month?"

Her brain took a moment to catch up. "Oh, sorry. I had a pap smear today. It's from that." And the doctor had said she might experience a little spotting for a few days with the IUD.

His frown deepened. "Pap smear? Is that why you took the day off?"

She couldn't help but smile at how badly it killed him not to know what she'd been up to. "My appointment was for late morning, so I did some shopping first. I bought a dress." She smoothed her hands over the skirt.

"You look very sexy in that dress."

"I was hoping you'd like it. I bought the panties and a matching bra as well."

His gaze traveled up and down, as if he had x-ray vision and could see through the fabric of her dress. "You'll have to show me later." The haze of desire cleared from his eyes. "Why wouldn't you tell me any of this last night?"

"Or today, when you called three times to check up on me?"

"I was worried. When you called last night, you were crying and you wouldn't tell me what was wrong." Crossing his arms, he leaned against the counter.

Thinking of Summer stabbed at her heart. "I can't talk about that, David. Please don't ask."

From the way his lip curled, she knew he hated the restriction. "Fine. Then tell me why you wouldn't tell me what you had planned for today."

How to explain to him that she valued her privacy and loved lording it over him? He was acquainted with her evil sense of humor, so it might not shock him. She opted for a non-answer. "It's hard to explain. Are you asking as the guy trying out for temporary boyfriend or as my boss?"

"Your Dom." He closed the distance and gripped her upper arms. "I'm asking as your Dominant. You didn't object a week ago when I made it clear who I am to you, and I'd be well within my rights to punish you for evasion and generally being a brat."

She dropped her gaze, not even thinking about why she was compelled to do it. "It's been a long time since I've had to answer to anybody. I'm not used to it. And, though I think it's been clear from the start because I've never tried to hide it, I am a brat, David. That's never going to change." The lessons her father instilled in her reasserted control, and she met his eyes once again. "I'm not going to suddenly turn into a weak, simpering submissive who does what you say or prostrates myself at your feet to beg for forgiveness. If you want to punish me, you can, but it's not going to get you anywhere."

For the longest time, he didn't move. He stared at her, and she couldn't fathom what he might be thinking. After forever, he said, "How long?"

"How long what?"

"How long has it been since you've had to answer to a Dom?"

A thousand responses flitted through her brain in single file, but he deserved a straight answer. "Truthfully, I never have. I've pretended to when it suited me, but I haven't really. You're the first man I've met who's strong enough to—" She broke off, wondering how much was too much. Information was power, and it was a mistake to give too much power to someone who was passing through her life.

"Autumn? Strong enough to what?" His grip on her arms had relaxed, and now he held her with tenderness. His tone conveyed reassurances she hadn't expected.

"To make me think I can let down my guard." She took a shaky breath. The emotional closeness he'd made her feel hadn't gone away, but she was far enough removed from the moment to question her temporary insanity. "I gave myself to you, David. I wasn't planning to do that."

He nodded. "You've always been the Domina. Have you given of yourself when you were the dominant?"

"No." She whispered. "I only played the Domina with clients that Ms. B. sent to me. That was mostly just tying them up, doing some impact play, and most of them wanted verbal humiliation. I'm quite good at that. This is different."

"Very. I won't be satisfied with fake submission, and I won't let you hold back." He folded her in his arms. "Why don't you pack an overnight bag? I'll take you to my place, we can order out, and we'll talk about us. And please bring the brownies. They smell almost as good as you."

"What? My apartment is too minimalist to stay in? We can get take out around here." As he released his hold, she glanced around her apartment. The walls were bright white, a color she'd painted them because she hated the dingy yellow-tan that passed for neutral but just gave everything an unhealthy pallor. She'd accented the white with bold reds and blues for the trim. The entire room, which was smaller than his foyer, contained a living area at one end and a miniscule kitchen at the other end. Rather than delineate room areas, the whole floor was covered in yellow linoleum. She'd covered that with huge rugs she'd rescued from a home improvement store's trash bin.

Though she lacked a dinette set, she had living room furniture. Her sofa, end tables, and coffee table were clean and in good repair. As he took in the details, he began to look more and more trapped. She almost felt sorry for him. Almost. "The bedroom is also fully equipped with a bed. If we want to try some bondage or flogging later, I have everything we need in my toy bag. And we can be as loud as we want. My neighbors don't care about noise."

He looked toward the door. "I'm kind of afraid to leave my car out there for too long."

"You think it'll get jacked?" She snapped her fingers. "You're right. Everybody in the poor neighborhoods get together whenever a Mercedes comes rolling up. We wait until they're busy, then we strip their car. We've got it down to sixty-seven seconds. We're going for the Guinness Book, though, so we're aiming for fifty-three." With that, she grabbed her bull whip from the front closet.

Eyes wide with shock, he followed her out the door. It opened to an outdoor walkway that led to stairs on either end. As she was on the second floor, she had a great view of the parking lot. She leaned over the railing to find a trio of teenage boys checking out David's precious car. They would, she knew, steal it if she didn't tell them to leave it alone.

She cracked the whip above their heads. They jumped as if it had been a gunshot. "Hands off the car. He's with me."

The oldest spread his palms, showing his innocence. "We're just looking, Ms. Sullivan."

The second oldest grinned. He had the kind of smile that would slice through butter. "You sure are looking good today, Ms. Sullivan."

The youngest tipped his cap at David. "Don't worry, mister. We'll keep an eye out for trouble."

David rolled his eyes and went back into the apartment. After another visual warning, Autumn followed, and she found him lounging on the sofa. "They're really a very charming bunch."

"I can see that. I'm starved. What's good around here?"

"Around here? Nothing. Give me a minute to throw some things in a bag, and we can get going."

Devilry sparkled behind his smile. "I'm fine with staying here. I've spent time in worse places. A foxhole in Afghanistan comes to mind. Besides, you've proven that you're more than capable of defending my car and my honor. Where did you learn to use a bull whip? That's a pretty serious instrument, and you let loose left-handed."

She went into the bedroom to pack, leaving the door open so he could hear her answer. "After the accident where I hurt my shoulder, I used it as PT. It has all the range of motion I needed to practice, and I didn't have insurance for real physical therapy, so that's what I did."

When she came out, she found him in at the counter, slicing the brownies into pieces. He pried them out and put them on a plate. "Where is your plastic wrap?"

She didn't buy things she didn't use. "I have plastic storage containers in the third cupboard." While he did that, she grabbed some things from the bathroom and threw in the bag of condoms.

He took her bag and handed over the brownies. "I've always wanted to learn to use a bull whip."

"I recommend wearing a long-sleeve leather shirt, thick denim jeans, and protective eyewear. And don't think you're getting that shit near me. I might like a good flogging every now and again, but I'm not into that kind of pain." She snagged her keys from the counter and followed him through the door. Halfway down the second flight of steps, she said, "Oh, wait. I really need to pee. Go ahead to the car. I'll be there in a minute."

While she did need to go, she also wanted to set her alarms. David didn't need to know she'd set up motion detectors in front of her windows and door. He'd just worry about her living all alone in an unsafe neighborhood, and she was more than capable of taking care of herself.

Chapter Eight

He bought the bathroom excuse. She hadn't gone after sex, and most women who weren't tied down found an excuse to freshen up afterward. He also bought that she'd been to see a gynecologist, but he didn't know why she'd use the county health clinic when her insurance would cover someone in private practice. Jesse had reported that after she'd left the clinic, she'd gone to the nursing home for an hour, and then she'd gone home.

When he'd arrived at Autumn's apartment, he'd given Jesse a break. Now that they were gone, Jesse would sneak into her apartment and go through her things. David didn't hold out hope he'd find much. Though she'd done some things to make it appear homey, the place lacked personalization. There were no photos or prints on the walls, and no personal items were laying out anywhere except the bathroom. Those things told him that she had recently shaved and she used discount shampoo. The rest of the apartment was clean—too clean to be a place where a person resided.

On the way to his place, he stopped at his favorite restaurant to pick up two of the daily special. Today was pasta and chicken in an alfredo sauce. As long as it wasn't shrimp, he wasn't worried. Autumn waited in the car. She picked at her skirt, smoothing it nervously as he drove.

"What's wrong?"

"Nothing."

"Autumn, if this thing between us is going to go anywhere, I'm going to insist on honesty. You might find it uncomfortable at first, but you'll get used to it."

She stared at him, her brow wrinkled in a half-confused, half-"fuck you" kind of expression. "I've never lied to you."

The veracity of that statement was up for grabs. On one hand, she hadn't told him any lies she wasn't passing off as truths to the world in general. On the other hand, she had let him believe falsehoods. "I know you're not in witness protection."

"I never said I was."

He struggled for patience, and he made sure his tone remained neutral. Attacking her wouldn't get him what he wanted. She'd proven more than capable of parrying his thrust. "You knew what I assumed, and you didn't bother to correct me. That's lying. But it's not what I meant. I was talking about being truthful about your feelings. I asked what was wrong. I'm not guessing that something's bothering you; I'm reading your body language. I know something is wrong."

"I think I pulled my shoulder throwing the whip. I didn't warm up first."

Patience only lasted so long. He hit the steering wheel with his palm. "Damn it, Autumn."

"Fine. I'm nervous, okay? Does it make you happy to know that?"

It kind of did. Getting the upper hand with her was challenging. "Why are you nervous?"

"I haven't..." She frowned and looked out the window. "I said earlier that it's been a while for me. I wasn't talking about D/s. I meant dating. I haven't been romantically involved with anyone in more than three years. I haven't even been casually involved, not like this."

This didn't surprise David. She had to be one of the most guarded, closed-off people he'd ever met. She'd perfected the art of keeping people out. He took her hand in his, giving gentle reassurance. "What made you decide to break your streak?"

"I like you. A lot. I'm wondering if I have the ability to open myself enough to let you in." She sighed, the sound of a weary soul. "And I'm wondering if I'm making a mistake by trying."

Manipulation or honesty? David didn't know how to take her confession. Even if she was attempting manipulation, he had to play along to see what her endgame was. "I think we all wonder similar sentiments when a relationship gets serious."

"Yeah?" She perked up a bit.

"Yeah. Look, I expected to come here and do a job. I didn't expect to come here, meet you, and start wanting more than a casual acquaintanceship. This is a shock to me as well, but I'm not running away."

"This might also come as a shock to you, but I wasn't raised the conventional way. I'm not sure how serious relationships are supposed to work. I know I'm going to mess up, and I'm terrified that you won't understand where I'm coming from."

They'd arrived at the parking garage below his building. He glanced over to see that she was struggling with anxiety. Actually, she looked close to having a full-on panic attack. "Breathe, honey. Slowly. Inhale for three seconds. Tap it out with your fingers on your leg. That's it. Exhale for three." He'd been trained in the military in basic responses to panic attacks.

Once she calmed down, he said, "The cure for your fears is to tell me about yourself. The better I know you, the better I will understand your perspective."

"Sorry. I'm not usually like this. I think having sex with you threw me off my game."

He couldn't stop the arrogant grin from taking over his features.

With an aggravated sigh, she got out of the car. He waited until after dinner—low blood sugar could account for some of her anxiety—to bring up things she kept hidden. He was playing with a handicap, though, because he knew more about her than he could reveal, and he was desperately trying to fill in huge blanks.

He relaxed on the sofa, and arranged for her to sit next to him and snuggle into his chest. This way he could hold her reassuringly and control the conversation. Or he could try to. She possessed excellent verbal skills designed, he now realized, to keep people at a distance.

"I thought you'd want to have sex again."

"Because I'm a dude and all I think about is getting some?"

She snorted. "If that's how it is, I might also be a dude."

He visually admired the rise of her breasts and the curve of her hip. "You're definitely not a dude."

"I could practice giving a blowjob some more."

Oh, and he'd thought he was going to control the conversation. He adjusted his junk to give it more room. "As you're aware, in a D/s relationship, it is imperative to talk about limits and preferences. I thought we'd start that discussion tonight."

She turned, sliding her chest along his, and said, "I've memorized your limits and preferences. I'm okay with everything you listed on the sheet you filled out for Elite Solutions. Just be careful of my shoulder. I can't keep my arm above my head for long periods. When I accidentally fling it up in my sleep, it kills for the next few days. And it can't take a lot of weight for very long."

He narrowed his eyes. "Have you experienced everything on my list?"

"No, but I figured we should start easy and work up to more complicated things. If I can't handle something, I'll safeword."

"Call me crazy, but I'm still going to insist on talking. I don't want to strap you to a spreader bar to find out the hard way that you don't know how to move around in one without whacking yourself in the face."

She pushed away, lifting her boobs off his chest. The way they moved in the low cut bodice of her dress drew his attention. She snapped her fingers. "I'm up here. What evidence do you have that I'm a klutz?"

"None yet. What if you panic when you're tied down, blindfolded, and unable to move? I'd rather know before we start whether you've ever done that before. This isn't negotiable, honey."

"Okay." In a fluid motion, she flipped around and ended up straddling him. "Fire away. What do you want to do with me first?"

That was easy. "Spank you."

She laughed. "I know, silly. You've already mentioned it. After that?"

An erotic image came to mind. His cock moved closer to her heat. "Bind your knees and wrists to a spreader bar. Lick your pussy. Turn you over and fuck you until you beg me to stop."

She traced a finger along his lower lip, and the raw emotion in her gaze arrested his breath. "What makes you think I'd ever want you to stop?"

"Because I won't let you come until you submit to me, until you acknowledge me by title and give me everything I want from you. Until then, I'll keep you on edge, torturing you because I get off on it."

The tiniest bit of fear clouded the submissive desire in her green eyes. "Besides submission, what do you want from me? Sir."

She added his title belatedly, but at least she was learning. Feeling benevolent, he smiled and gave her the sort of answer she would give him. "I'll know it when I see it."

A pouty frown marred her chin. "That could mean anything."

He flipped them so that his weight pinned her to the sofa. "Yeah, well, that's not all. I also want the truth. I want to know who you are and who you go to see at Sunshine Acres."

She shoved at him, anger giving her an unexpected amount of strength. She nearly heaved him away. "We've already discussed this. I am Autumn Sullivan, and it's none of your damn business what I do with my time when I'm not with you." She wiggled and bucked to no avail. Then she stilled. "There's a lot I don't know about you either, and I'm not being a dick about it."

"Of course not. You're the sweet submissive who'd never do anything to piss off her Master."

Her eyes flashed. "You're not my Master. I barely agreed to let you be my Sir. For the record, you failed your audition for boyfriend. That only leaves sex between us. There you go, David. That's who I am. I'm Autumn Sullivan, the woman who has meaningless sex with her boss. When would be the best time to ask for a raise?"

He shouldn't spank her when he was this angry. Really, he should let her up and go to another room until he cooled off enough to be rational. But damn it, he wasn't in the mood to want to be reasonable. He got up, hauling her with him, and dragged her into the bedroom. He hadn't brought more than the basic, portable equipment with him because you never knew when a hot brunette was going to light your fire.

That meant he had to improvise. He slapped neoprene cuffs on her wrists and ankles, and when she tried to peel them off, he quelled her with one hard look. "Take off your dress and lie face down on the bed."

"David, I—"

"Don't," he thundered. "The only words I want to hear out of your mouth are *Yes* and *Sir*. If I hurt your shoulder, call yellow. Otherwise, shut up and follow orders."

He knew that she could call red. That was an option. He'd respect her safeword, but she had no way of knowing that. She yanked her dress over her head, fuming wordlessly, and threw it on the floor.

"Pick it up and hang it neatly over the back of the office chair."

Her mouth might not have moved, but with eyes that expressive, it didn't have to. David read her fury without needing a translation. And he noted her brand-new pair of sexy panties and matching bra. She'd bought them with him in mind.

"Remove your panties and bra. Put them with the dress." He kept the hard edge to his tone, but he was having trouble holding on to actual anger, especially when she obeyed. "Bend over the bed, legs spread, ass in the air, and arms...behind your back." He wasn't sure about that last part. If she had trouble raising her arm for too long, holding it behind her back might be too much strain.

She bent over, rested her torso on the bed, and clasped her hands behind her neck. "I can hold this for longer."

Those words weren't on the approved list, but he let it go. He needed her to communicate with him, and this was a start. "This is going to hurt a lot."

"Put your money where your mouth is and let's see what you've got. Sir."

He'd never had a sub goad him before. For a few seconds, he debated gagging her, but then he rejected the idea. The amount of sass that poured out of her mouth would let him know where her mind was, and that was invaluable information. "You've earned extra for running off at the mouth."

"Whatever. So far all you've done is run off at the mouth." She wiggled her ass back and forth, taunting him.

He began the spanking with a steady tap designed to prepare her for the harder hits to come.

"Seriously? This is discipline? No wonder you're single."

This was going to require a glove. Good thing his bag was open and nearby. He snagged it without missing a beat. When she was warmed up, he ran his hand over her bottom. "You have a sweet ass. From now on, I'm going to call you Sugar." He delivered the next volley of harder hits without giving her time to respond. If she wasn't going to reveal her real name, then he was going to call her whatever he wanted.

When her pale bottom was bright red, he paused. His palm was covered, so he ran the inside of his wrist over her flesh. Waves of heat scorched his skin. "How are you doing, Sugar?"

"Still waiting for you to get started, dickhead." If possible, her tone was even more acerbic.

It was time to break out something with more bite. He selected a leather paddle. "I thought you said you'd never been on the receiving end before?"

"No, I said I'd never actually submitted. I've had my ass spanked by harder hands than yours. So far, your listening skills and your punishment are not proving impressive."

"Let's get to it, then. Batter up." With that, he spanked her so hard the outline of the paddle showed up on her ass.

She sucked in a breath. "Score one for dickhead."

It was a good thing he had masterful control over his temper, because if he let himself go, he'd dissolve in a puddle of laughter. Her sense of humor hit his funny bone in exactly the right way. Now that he knew what she could take, he set to work. He didn't count the blows. Instead he watched her body language and noted her breathing. After a time, fat tears began to seep from her eyes. He stopped when her torso began shaking. Taking her in his arms, he cradled her while she sobbed.

He smoothed her hair away from her face, kissed her temple and cheek, and murmured soothing noises as he rocked her back and forth. As she calmed, he let his hands wander over her skin.

"You needed this."

She clutched his shirt and sniffled. "Yes, Sir."

"You're a smartass most of the time. Why did I think it would disappear when you became my submissive?"

"I don't know, Sir."

"This is the kind of thing I would like you to tell me up front, Sugar."

"I didn't know, Sir. I've never been like this before. Doms usually stop when I keep shooting my mouth off."

Looking at the positive side, she was showing him a side of herself that she'd never felt comfortable enough to share with anybody else. He'd also figured out why she'd been unable to surrender. No Dom yet had proven himself worthy. A SAM—a smartass masochist—was a challenging submissive to dominate. "How's your ass?"

"Smarting."

"I love your sense of humor."

"Thank you, Sir. I'm fond of it as well."

He fisted her hair and pulled, forcing her to meet his gaze. Her eyes were red-rimmed from crying, but it only made the green of her irises stand out more. She was beautifully disheveled. "Let's get one thing clear, Sugar. I won't put up with you denouncing our relationship. This isn't meaningless sex, and I may not be your Master yet, but I will be one day when we're both ready to take that step."

"I'm sorry, Sir."

"And I am your boyfriend. You're mine, Sugar, and I'm yours. I may not know your name, but I know your heart, and I'll never let you hide that from me."

"Good luck, Sir. I sincerely wish you success."

He laughed, though it wasn't funny. She'd built some thick walls that he had to penetrate. He had every confidence he'd succeed. "To that end, I propose a compromise. Every Thursday night, you get to ask one question that I must answer with complete honesty, and I get to ask you one in return."

She blinked. "Tonight is Thursday."

"It sure is." If she agreed to this, then she was agreeing to tell him things she'd sworn not to reveal. He waited while she mulled it over.

"No. It's just going to piss you off when you ask me things you know I can't answer."

"Can't? Or won't?"

"Both." She winced as she sat up to rest her hands on his shoulders, but when she looked into his eyes, he recognized her silent plea. "David, in a month or six weeks, you'll be gone and we'll never see each other again. It's not worth the hassle. Can't we just enjoy our time together?"

"If I swore not to press you for your real name, would you agree?"

That stopped her. "I—Yes."

"Great. You can go first."

She hadn't expected that. "I probably should get dressed for this."

"No. You don't get to wear clothes until tomorrow morning when I say you can get dressed for work." Clothes were a type of armor, and he wasn't going to allow her to backslide when they'd made such progress.

"Okay. Um...Why do you hate Mr. Calder so much?"

Shocked, David's mind went blank, and he tried to stall for time. "What? Why would you think I hate him?"

Her mouth turned down. "This is honesty? I'm neither blind nor stupid. I've seen you with him, and I've heard you talk about him. You respect him, yes, but you also hate him. Not merely dislike, you outright hate him. If you don't answer honestly and truthfully, then I won't either."

He exhaled hard. She didn't pull her punches, even when she didn't know what a sore spot she'd hit. He ran a hand through his hair. "He's my father. Before last week, I hadn't seen or talked to him in thirteen years."

Her lips parted in shock, but otherwise she held it together well. "Go on."

"Growing up, he was a bastard. He was controlling and mean. Nothing I ever did was good enough. If I hit a home run in Little League, he screamed at me for not getting a grand slam. If I brought home a B on a report card, I hadn't tried hard enough. If I got perfect scores, then the class was too easy. As I got older, I started arguing back, and the things he said got worse. He criticized everything I did. I don't remember a single encouraging thing he said to me or an accomplishment that he told me he was proud of. My mom used to run interference. She'd calm him down and make me feel like I wasn't a worthless piece of shit. He was a different person with her. She made living there bearable. She got sick my senior year of high school, and she passed away when I was eighteen. I quit college and joined the military, cut all ties with Bill Calder. I even changed my name. Eastridge was my mother's maiden name."

She cupped his face, and fresh tears tracked down her cheeks. "But you came back when he needed you."

"Because I promised my mother on her deathbed that I'd be here when he got in trouble. He called, asking for my help, and I came to fulfill a promise. Nothing more. I've been very clear about that with him. Once I figure out where that money is, that's it. My debt is paid, and I'll never look back." He wiped away the tears she shed on his behalf. "I trust you to keep that information to yourself."

She nodded. "I was wrong. You don't hate him. You just don't know how to love him."

"He's not loveable." David grasped her wrists and held her hands while he kissed her palms. "Your turn, Sugar."

"You're really going to call me that, aren't you?"

"You bet your sweet ass."

"But not when other people are around."

"Especially when other people are around, and when they ask why I call you that, I'll tell them all about your very red, sweet ass."

"You're flirting with a sexual harassment lawsuit."

"Nah. You'd have to put your legal name on the complaint." He squeezed her sensitized flesh until she gasped. "I want to know who you go see at Sunshine Acres."

She sighed. "I knew you'd ask that. My sister, Summer. She was driving when we got into the accident that tore my shoulder up, but she was hurt worse. She's been in a coma for three years. I visit every day."

Some of that he already knew, and he suspected that Summer was her sister, not an elderly relative. Of course, he couldn't ask about the discrepancy. "Go on."

Her sad smile made his heart constrict. "She wakes up every few weeks, never for more than a minute or two. Whenever she does, she's terrified. When I'm there and she hears my voice, she calms down. Every time her eyes open, I hope it's permanent."

He threaded his fingers through hers, holding her hand to let her know he was there for her. "She woke up last night, didn't she? That's why you were crying when you called."

She sniffled but didn't cry. "Yeah. Julianne was there. She's Summer's friend. That's how I met her—she showed up at the hospital after the accident."

"And she helped you get a job at CalderCo. Does she know you're not who you say you are?" And, obviously, her sister's real name wasn't Summer Sullivan.

"I've never said it wasn't my name. That's your thing."

"You've existed for six years."

"So you say."

"When I run the name Summer Sullivan, what will I find?"

"A woman in a coma." She nibbled his lower lip. "If you're very nice to me, I'll take you to see her."

"I spanked you when you really needed it. That was nice."

She loosened his tie and unbuttoned his shirt. "You know what would be even nicer?"

"What?" He cupped her breasts, holding one in each hand.

"If you were as naked as I am." She tugged off his belt. "You might try using this for discipline next time. You might get faster results."

"Thanks for the critique."

She froze, staring at him with wide eyes. "David, I don't mean it as a critique. Those things I said when I was upset—I didn't mean them. The names I called you—Did I go too far?"

"No." He grasped the sides of her head and kissed her with all the tenderness in his heart. "I knew what you were doing, Sugar, even if you didn't. You were pushing me because you needed the punishment, and SAMing is your way of making sure you get it. Instead of asking for it harder, you called me a dickhead."

"You're okay with that?"

"Context, Sugar. We were in a scene. If you started spewing that shit now, I'd rethink the healthiness of this relationship." The fact that she was so concerned spoke volumes. He eased her so that she was lying on her back, and he covered her body with his. He touched her face and hair, and he reveled in the fragile trust and adoration in her gaze. They'd both shared something intimate, personal, and close to their hearts. David recognized the danger in what he was feeling for this woman who was not who she claimed to be.

Re/Leased
But he didn't think of that as he made love to her.

Chapter Nine

"Where you going?" David rolled over, but he didn't open his eyes.

Autumn didn't think he was quite awake, and it was a too early to make him get up for work. She didn't sleep well in strange places. Growing up, she'd moved around a lot, and it had always taken her at least a week to adjust. Her father used to rub her back and sing to her until she drifted off. Summer, on the other hand, could sleep anywhere, anytime, and in virtually any position.

"Bathroom." She whispered so that she didn't jolt him out of his semi-sleep state. He didn't respond, so she figured she was successful. The room in question was larger than her bedroom, and when she saw the luxurious shower, she didn't have the will to resist.

David came in after she'd finished shampooing her hair. "You said you were going to the bathroom." He sounded like a boy whose blankie had been stolen during the night for a clandestine meeting with the washing machine.

"I'm still here." She smiled into the spray. "The shower said, 'Psst. Autumn, check me out. I'm big and sexy, and I have more than one massaging head.' I was powerless to resist."

The door opened, bringing chilly air with it, and David joined her. His impressive erection already wore a condom. "And my dick said, 'Gimme more of that sweet Sugar.' He has a crush on your pussy, and he was very disappointed that she wasn't waiting for him when he got up." He wrapped one arm around her waist and hauled her against him for a kiss. The other hand spread her pussy lips and massaged her clit.

Autumn had already been thinking about David and his magic touch, so she was wet. "Well, it's a good thing my pussy has decided she gets off on hugging your dick. I say we get those crazy kids together and see what happens."

"Turn around. Brace yourself on the wall."

The moment she turned, she felt his hands on her hips, tilting her to the angle he wanted. He entered her with slow jabs, sliding deeper each time.

"Play with your clit. This is going to be quick and dirty, and I want to hear you come." His thighs pressed to hers, he pumped into her with graceless, frantic strokes. Fortunately, he'd found her sweet spot.

"Holy shit, Sir. Right there. Oh. My. God. Please don't stop." Her fingers kept time with his sloppy rhythm, and in minutes, a hard climax convulsed through her pussy, squeezing his cock and forcing his orgasm.

He fell forward, collapsing partially against her and the rest of the way against the marble tile. Marble—in a shower. He took a few moments to gather his wits, and then he sat on the bench along the far wall with his eyes closed. "Sub, you woke up too damn early. Wash me."

"You can go back to bed."

"That's the plan—after you wash me. Don't be bratty, Sugar. You'll just earn another punishment."

Autumn removed his condom, and then she took a detachable shower head to rinse his body before wetting his hair. After that, she took a break to put conditioner in hers. She liked to let it soak in for a while. As she shampooed his hair, his eyes opened, and he stared at her breasts.

"There's nothing like a spectacular pair of tits in your face first thing in the morning."

"I don't like that word."

"Morning? I'm not a huge fan either, but this kind of makes up for it."

"Tits. It's an ugly word. Boobs, breasts, knockers, rack—those are acceptable terms."

Confusion wrinkled his forehead and chin. "Let me get this straight: You're okay with knockers and rack, but not with tits? What's the difference?"

"It's too close to teats, and animals have those."

"Gotcha. Have I mentioned that you have a fantastic rack? I didn't get to play with them much last night. I'll make up for it tonight." He closed his eyes while she rinsed away the shampoo suds, and then he pulled her onto his lap.

She thought he might try to play with her boobs, but he just hugged her to him. She relaxed and let the warm water wash over her skin. He was truly a wonderful man. How had she managed to be so lucky?

After the shower, she tried to get dressed while he shaved, but he stopped her. "You stay naked until I tell you to get dressed. There's plenty of time before we have to leave for work."

"But I'm going to need you to take me home so I can get my car."

"We work at the same place. I'll drive."

"I go see Summer every day after work."

"I'll take you there. You said I could meet her."

That was going to be awkward. Her time with Summer was marked by unlimited topics of conversation. It had been that way before the coma, and Autumn hadn't changed a thing just because Summer couldn't respond. "Today might not be the best day. I haven't told her that you were coming."

The buzz of the electric shaver stopped. He checked his chin in the mirror, but he didn't appear troubled. "If you're not ready for us to meet, then I'll take you home after work so you can get your car. If it's still there and in one piece."

"You've seen it. If anything, the boys bring me spare parts I might find useful. One time, they surprised me by putting a new bumper on the rear."

He donned pants and a shirt, which made her feel extra naked, and he looked at her strangely. "You do realize the part was probably stolen."

It wouldn't be the first stolen item in her possession. "Who would come looking for it?"

Shaking his head, he led her to the kitchen, where he made cheese omelets and bacon. Nothing made a day better than starting off with bacon. He sipped coffee as he munched. "Are you busy tomorrow afternoon?"

"Probably. My boyfriend's dick has a crush on my pussy, so we'll probably help them get together at some point."

He laughed. "I like that idea. I have tickets to see the Tigers play. Would you like to go?"

"Sure. I've never seen a baseball game. I heard they were boring, but with you around, I'm sure it won't be."

"Boring?" He sputtered. "Whoever the hell said that doesn't know what they're talking about."

"My dad did. He wasn't much of a sports fan." To be fair, he had been an avid sports fan. He loved trolling outside venues for easy marks. Baseball and hockey games were where Autumn had perfected her pickpocket skills. She just hadn't ever been inside.

He perked up at the mention of her father. "Your dad? I don't think I've heard you mention him before."

Waves of sadness washed over her. "He died. Same accident that put Summer in a coma. We were very close, like you and your mom."

He reached under the table and closed his hand around hers. "I'm sorry, Sugar. I didn't mean to malign your father."

"You didn't." She attempted a smile to lighten the moment. "He was always chasing adventure, and so he found many things boring. Growing up, we never had a television for very long because, as Dad liked to say, life was for living, not watching."

"He sounds like a great guy."

Autumn gave him points for trying. "Mostly, yeah. But I'm not blind to his faults. During the winter, a TV somehow always found a way into our living room. I'm looking forward to the game. What time should I be here?"

The look on his face said she might never leave, and it made her feel warm inside. For the past three years, Autumn had led a cautious life. She made sure that her work and personal lives were separate. The only person at work who knew anything about her personal life was Julianne, and Julianne knew not to say anything. She was the kind of friend who didn't come around very often—the kind who respected confidences even when she didn't understand the reasons for keeping them.

Autumn had resisted making friends at work. She'd shut out friendly overtures, though she'd done it with maximum charm and professionalism so that people still liked to work with her. Some might call her manipulative, and they'd be right, but she didn't use her powers for evil. She used them to maintain privacy and a positive work environment. Things were going so well with David that she felt like she was ready to open herself to more people and new experiences. And remembering what her father had liked to say about living life also motivated her.

Of course, he was also the one who had taught her to be cautious about what she said and who she said it to. Until now, she'd taken that as a directive to keep people at arm's length. Reconsidering that strategy brought a smile to her face. Julianne was a friend who had no idea about the less honest aspects of her life. Why couldn't she have more than one female friend?

Today, she had lunch with Julianne as she frequently did. The round tables in the lunchroom fit at least six people, so they were rarely alone. This time, as their table filled up, Autumn smiled and greeted each person. It was amazing how that one gesture could jump start a conversation. Even Stephanie Ceichelski, who normally affected a holier-than-thou attitude that rankled Autumn's nerves, didn't bother her today. And as she chatted with the woman, the attitude disappeared.

After lunch, she walked with Julianne to the acquisitions department. "Are you going tonight?"

"Briefly." Julianne smiled shyly. "I have a date. It's a second date. I didn't want to say anything, but I'm excited. Autumn, do you know how long it's been since I've had a second date?"

"Eleven months. There was the guy who took you to a concert, so you felt obligated to agree to a follow-up dinner date even though he yelled obscenities through the whole concert." Remembering how appalled Julianne had been, Autumn laughed.

"It was a Kelly Clarkson concert. We were surrounded by kids, and he kept yelling, 'Fuck, yeah!' I was embarrassed." Even thinking about it brought color to Julianne's cheeks. "Anyway, it's been a while. This one isn't a pity date. We went ice skating, and we had a great time."

"Ice skating? It's summer."

"Indoor rink. They have those. The one we went to apparently has a bunch of Olympic ice dancers or pairs skaters that practice there. Who knew?"

Autumn knew. It was one of those trivia items that somehow lodged in her memory in the place where something important should go. "What is his name?"

"Jeff. He's thirty-three, single, never been married, and he's an engineer. He's nerdy, but in a cute way."

Autumn hugged Julianne. "I'm so happy for you. Let me know how it goes."

"I could say the same to you." She lifted her brows as a challenge, but Autumn didn't bite.

"We'll compare notes next time. I need to get back to work." She was already late, and she didn't want to put David in a bad spot.

It turned out not to matter. He'd left a note on her desk saying that he'd be out of contact all afternoon, but he'd be there at five to pick her up. This was why she'd wanted to get her car. Meetings, especially those held outside the building, lasted a lot longer than scheduled. She called Julianne to arrange a ride, and then she texted David to tell him to pick her up at Sunshine Acres at seven.

———

"Something wrong?" Jesse's question pulled David's attention from the text Autumn had sent.

He slid his phone back into his pocket. "Autumn got another ride home."

"This is a problem because why?" Jesse sat back, a wary, knowing look in his eye.

"Because she came clean about Summer Sullivan. As we thought, it's her sister in the nursing home. She's in a coma, the result of the car accident. Autumn was going to take me to meet her tonight." Part of David felt guilty for divulging a private matter his sub had trusted him enough to reveal. On the surface, it wasn't much. Why keep a sick family member secret? But he had the feeling she'd been trained from a young age to keep her mouth shut about a lot of things. He needed her father's name.

Jesse frowned. "You can't go another day? It's not like you're going to find out anything. She's unconscious."

Malcolm tapped his pen on the table. "It's important because she's letting him in. The more she does that, the more we know, and the better we can figure out who she really is. I see two problems with this part of the investigation. One: It has nothing to do with the missing capital, and it's draining time and attention that should be going to other things. Two: When she finds out what you're doing, and she will, she's going to be hurt in a way there may be no coming back from."

Jesse ran his hand over the scruff that passed for hair on his head. "I don't see how her feelings are relevant, but I agree with Malcolm on his first point. Following her is a waste of time. I spent last night going through her apartment and car. I found some puzzling things, but nothing to implicate her in this. She's poor. Her apartment is a shit hole in a shit hole of a neighborhood in the shittiest part of Ypsilanti. Drug deals happen out in the open in broad daylight on the streets, and the cops avoid that part of town."

"How is she poor?" Malcolm frowned. "I've seen her salary. She's not getting paid a ton, but it's enough to afford a small house in a decent neighborhood. If she budgets, she should be able to afford weekly entertainment and a yearly vacation."

"No way." Jesse shook his head. "Not the way she lives. There's barely food in the kitchen, and what's there is from the bargain basement dollar bin. Her furniture, though she takes care of it, is threadbare and secondhand. Most of her clothes are as well. She lives like she's making six bucks an hour."

"But she isn't." David frowned, thinking of how uncertain she'd been about the dress she'd bought with him in mind. Perhaps he'd misread her, and she'd felt guilty?

"I'm going to throw this all out in the open now, and then we're going to be done talking about David's girlfriend." He pulled up photos on his phone. "She has a drawer full of overdue bills, mostly for rent and utilities. It looks like she's had the heat and water turned off a few times. The vast majority of bills are for Summer Sullivan—physical therapy, blood tests, liver tests, endocrine tests, experimental medication, and other expenses not covered by insurance. She's in deep. Head-scratcher things: I found a 'Go' bag. It wasn't well hidden. Four hundred in cash and three fake IDs. The forgeries are a few years old, but the quality is good. And she monitors her door and windows with portable laser trip wires, probably hooked up to an app on her phone."

David swiped through the photos before handing the phone to Malcolm. What he saw made his stomach ill.

"A lot of the medical bills were paid in cash." Malcolm had noticed the same thing David had. "If she's been skimming a little off the top for three years..." He shook his head. "It wouldn't add up to three million dollars. That would take decades. Of course, she'd be able to take more and cover it up better with a lapping scam, but even that wouldn't net this much money. There's not enough capital flowing through CalderCo."

David thought about the discrepancies from her first year. He'd investigated them, but he hadn't thought to look at her books with an eye toward a scam. This meant he was going to have to go through her records again. He closed his eyes. "She works occasionally as a pro Domina. Last week, I hired her to go to the play party as my sub. It took some doing, and I had to pay double, but she agreed."

"She agreed because Beatrice DePau asked her to do it as a special favor." Jesse tapped his fingers to the rhythm of his thoughts. "I added up the receipts. If she stole all the cash money from CalderCo, then the total is a drop in the bucket compared to what we're looking for. She's not our guy. Can we agree and move on?"

"Yeah." David had thrown out several names where he'd noticed irregularities. Now that he thought about it, a lapping scam could explain some of the figures. But they needed to trace it, find out where the money was going.

"The FBI would pull warrants and look into personal finances," Malcolm said. "I'm not sure what kinds of resources you have."

Jesse's eyes sparkled. "We're not bound by the same restrictions. We just hack the accounts and take a look. They're all paid by direct deposit, so we already have the account numbers. That's half the battle."

As if it were a virus, that sparkle jumped to Malcolm's eyes. "Okay. Let's do this."

"Hey, do you and Darcy want to go with Autumn and me to see the Tigers? My dad has a box, and he's letting me use it." David hadn't planned to accept his father's offer, but he'd found himself asking Autumn to go, and now he was looking forward to the outing.

"Sure. Darcy would love to get out of the house." Malcolm scratched his chin. "Let me double check, though. She's going to need to see if my parents or her sister can watch Colin."

Jesse stared expectantly. "Are you going to invite me? I love sports of all kinds."

"No. I can't have Autumn making you. While she's not our prime suspect, she's not in the clear, and you'll need to keep watch over her. She's met Malcolm and Darcy already."

Jesse's expression soured. "Next mission, you get the shit part of the job."

David wasn't much help with hacking, but he was brilliant at analyzing accounts once they'd been opened. Malcolm and Jesse kept him busy for the rest of the afternoon. It was well past five by the time he stumbled out of that tiny, windowless room. He'd pored through so many account statements that his head felt like his brains had liquefied.

"Dean wants a report tonight," Jesse said on the way out. "He's expecting a call. I'll watch your girl overnight. It's best not to have her wake up and overhear anything."

Good thing Autumn hadn't been forced to wait on him. He called in an order for takeout on his way to Sunshine Acres. The entryway was deserted when he arrived. From the cacophony coming from the cafeteria, he figured the residents were eating dinner. He waited for several minutes at the front desk, but nobody showed up, so he set off down a likely hall in search of the coma ward. The place wasn't too large or convoluted, so he found it faster than he thought he would.

Pausing at the door, he watched Autumn peel back the covers from Summer's leg. He had no idea what she was doing, but it seemed like a bad time to interrupt. Stepping back, he listened as he waited.

"Let's do some leg lifts. You have sexy legs, sister of mine. Remember last time we went clubbing? That guy—you remember—he couldn't dance for anything, and he kept trying to pick you up. He was behind you, doing some kind of pelvic-thrust move, but it looked like he was having a seizure. You asked him if he needed an ambulance." Autumn laughed, and David found himself relaxing into surveillance mode. She had a musical laugh that made him smile whether he wanted to or not.

"Speaking of guys, David is supposed to come by soon. He's amazing, Summer. I really hope you like him. I told you he was very handsome, but I didn't get a chance to tell you about him."

She trailed off, and David almost poked his head into the room from listening so hard.

"He's amazing. I keep saying that, I know, but I don't know how else to describe him. He's funny, like he's got this cheesy sense of humor, and he thinks I'm funny, which is nice. And he understands when I run off at the mouth. Stop rolling your eyes. You're just as bad. Where do you think I learned it? Anyway, David gets me, mostly. Don't worry—I haven't told him anything I shouldn't." She lowered her voice, but the clear whisper carried to him. "He spanked me last night. Oh my God, it was incredible. It's like all this pent-up emotion and stress just melted away, and then he held me afterward."

He heard the rustle and creak of her moving around the room, probably to the other side of the bed.

"I think I'm falling in love with him. Don't laugh. I know how stupid that sounds. I've known him for a week, and already I can't imagine my life without him. Now, I'm not stupid enough to tell him that I'm falling for him. He's only here temporarily, which is one of the reasons I slept with him. It's out of character for me, I know, but he's different. He cares about me, and he likes me. He got jealous when I met with this guy for coffee. I mean, for starters, the guy was not attractive, so there was no competition there, but it was about a job."

More rustling and squeaking, and then he heard her sigh.

"Summer, I love puzzles. I can pick any lock, open any safe—well, I need practice with some of the newer models— but I've never been good at truly connecting with people. With David, for the first time, I feel like I'm starting to learn. I'm making mistakes, but they don't seem insurmountable."

Taking a deep breath, he breezed into the room, using a trajectory that made it seem like he'd been walking down the hall. Autumn was on the bed, lying next to her sister as if the two were just casually hanging out. She sat up, surprised. "I thought you'd call first."

He gestured behind him. "Want me to leave? I can go into the hall and call."

"No cell phones. There are a ton of Pacemakers around here." She climbed out of bed and slipped her arms around his waist. "Come and meet Summer." Turning back to the bed, she said, "Summer, this is David, my boyfriend. David, this is my sister, Summer. Say hello."

"Hi, Summer. It's nice to meet you." It was weird to be talking to someone in a coma, but he'd read anecdotal evidence that patients could hear everything. "I'm David Eastridge, one-quarter owner of SAFE Security, and I think your sister is an exceptional woman. She's had a long day, so I'm going to take her to dinner and make sure she gets to bed early. She might not get to sleep until later, but at least she'll be in bed."

Autumn's head snapped around, and she regarded him with wide eyes and parted lips. "I can't believe you said that to my sister."

He squeezed one of her ass cheeks. It felt perfect in his hand. "Sugar, I'm sure you've shared more details with her than that."

"Yes, but I'm her sister. You just met her."

He shrugged. "She's your sister. I'm sure she's a lot like you, only quieter."

Though she shook her head, a small giggle escaped, and that made him smile. She kissed Summer's cheek, and then she slid her hand into his. "Let's go. I'm starving." At the door, she turned back to look at Summer. "Bye, Summer. I'll see you tomorrow."

David opened doors for her and helped her into and out of his car. The entire time, he kept thinking about what he'd overheard. *I think I'm falling in love* floated around with *I can pick any lock, open any safe.* There was no way she was going to tell him everything, but he knew what question he was going to ask next Thursday. More than anything else, he wanted to know about this woman who called herself Autumn Sullivan.

He picked up dinner, more takeout, and drove toward her place. "I hope you like Chinese."

"As long as it's not shrimp, we're good."

"So, just to be clear, you don't have a shellfish allergy?"

"Why? Are you thinking of making me eat shrimp as a punishment? That's incredibly gross, Sir. It's right up there with golden showers." They'd arrived at her apartment building. People sat on lawn chairs in the parking lot and along the walkways. "Don't worry about the car. One warning is all it takes. They've seen me in my dominatrix outfits, so they know better than to piss me off."

He wasn't too worried about the SUV. It wouldn't be the first time his vehicle had been stolen or vandalized. That's why he registered it to SAFE Security. "You didn't answer the question, Sugar."

"No, I'm not allergic. I'll eat crab and other shellfish, but for some reason, shrimp grosses me out." She led him to the second floor and to her door. "You know, all these people think you're my boy toy."

He shrugged and held her screen door open as she unlocked the security door. The moment they stepped through, her phone buzzed. She tapped a pattern into the program, and the buzzing stopped. Rather than pretend ignorance, he asked point-blank. "Is that a laser alarm linked to your phone?"

"You can never be too careful."

"You just said my car was safe." He set the paper sack of food on the counter.

"Safe enough." She got out plates and flatware. "I'm more concerned about a surprise visit from my landlord."

If he hadn't researched her, he would have interpreted that as fear of an unscrupulous landlord. Since he had, he knew she wanted some warning before eviction happened.

This time, he played ignorant. "What concerns you about a surprise visit from your landlord, and do I need to kick his ass?"

Her movements slowed, and he knew she was formulating a true statement that didn't reveal things she didn't want him to know.

"Sugar, answer me right now."

"I, um, I don't always pay my rent. Landlords tend to object to that sometimes."

"Why not? This palace can't be all that expensive." He opened the containers and lined them up on the counter.

"The bills for Summer's care are sometimes a bit much. As long as I catch up within four months, they won't evict me." She looked at him, her eyes wide, beseeching him for understanding. "That's generally when I take a job with Ms. B. It's easy money."

"And you get to stretch your dominatrix muscles. It's hard for a switch in a relationship with someone who doesn't switch. I get it."

She paused, empty plate in hand, and studied the food choices. "I'm glad you get it."

"I'm going to want details after every session. And if you need to discuss planning, I'm willing to give you pointers." He took the other plate and began piling on the food.

Snorting, she followed suit. "Thanks, Sir, but it's not the same thing. The scenes are almost scripted by the client. They pick what they want, and as long as it's within my limits, that's what happens. There's rarely negotiation."

He looked around. The sofa was the only place to sit, so he crossed the tiny space and settled there. "Do you think there will come a time when you'll want a regular sub to scene with?" As he asked, he wanted to rewind time and take it back. If she did that, then she'd be establishing an intimate—even if it wasn't romantic—relationship with someone else. That was not acceptable.

"Never thought about it." She set her plate on the low table next to his and went back to the kitchen for napkins. The sofa bounced as she sat heavily next to him. "To be honest, before you came along, the idea of having a relationship of any kind was the farthest thing from my mind." She tied her hair back with a rubber band and dug into her food. "This is really good. Thank you."

"You're welcome. Tomorrow, we're going to have a home-cooked meal that we prepare together."

"I'm better at baking," she said. "I love to bake. It's both exciting and relaxing."

He thought about the brownies she'd made. They were tasty, but they were from a box. "I'll pick up some cake mix."

She nailed him with a glare that said she knew exactly what he'd been thinking. "I'll text you a shopping list. When I have the time, I prefer to bake from scratch."

"Then you'll bake from scratch. Hey, listen, I wanted to talk about protocol."

She swallowed the forkful of lo mien she'd been eating. "You want me to get naked?"

"Sometimes. I'll tell you when you can and can't wear clothes." When they were finished negotiating, he was going to make her strip down. Right now, they were outside of the dynamic. "You naturally fall into calling me by a title when we're alone together. I like that. You'll keep doing it. In mixed company, you can use my name, but if we're with friends who know about our lifestyle, then you'll continue to use my title."

"Yes, Sir." She put her hand on his knee. "I want to kneel when we start a scene."

Surprised that she'd take the lead on that, he nodded. "I prefer that as well. When we eat at home, I'll expect you to serve me, preferably on your knees. You know what I'm talking about?"

"Yes. And when we're hanging out, do you want me to kneel in a relaxed position at your feet?"

His pants were growing uncomfortably tight as images of that kind of domestic bliss flipped through his mind. "Yes, though a lot of the time, you won't stay there. I like to cuddle."

"Sir?"

"Yeah?"

"My bra is too tight."

He looked over, and her breasts strained against her shirt. They'd swollen as she became aroused. "You want to take it off?"

She was naked in about the same amount of time it took her to stand up. The skirt and her panties pooled at her feet. She kicked them away and knelt next to him. Her posture was perfect, and he had a prime view of her pink pussy. His dick jumped, trying to get out of his pants. Of course, he recognized her power play, so he didn't throw her over his shoulder, take her to the bedroom, and have his way with her.

"You're a temptress, Sugar, but I'm starving. Kneel up. You're going to feed me. No utensils."

She eyed the rice and noodles. "Yes, Sir, though if you want more than a few grains of rice or a single strand of noodle, that's going to be tough."

"You're a smart woman. I'm sure you'll figure it out."

She started with meat and vegetables, holding each morsel to his lips patiently. He scraped her fingers and sucked on them with each bite. As he did, she seemed to fall under his spell and settle into her submission. It didn't take long to notice that she wasn't feeding herself.

"Eat, Sugar. I insist. You're going to need the energy."

She fed herself from her plate, using her fingers to experiment with how to scoop up more rice or noodles. Then she smeared rice across her upper chest and climbed up to straddle him. "This'll work, Sir."

He sucked and licked, cleaning the food from her boobs. His forays widened, and he sucked her nipples to sharp points, which he rolled between his tongue and teeth. She cried out, throwing her head back and arching closer. He dragged a knuckle through her wetness, lightly petting her clit as he tortured her nipple.

"Arms behind your back, Sugar. Be mindful of your shoulder."

The scars, twisted and pink, showed evidence of a surgeon who tried to minimize the appearance of damage, but they were still angry and unfaded by time. She moved slowly, clasping her wrists and sliding until she had a good hold on her forearms.

"Does that hurt?"

"No, Sir. I just can't stretch it more than this."

Adequate physical therapy should have given her more mobility than that. He pushed aside the surge of anger at what she'd endured to focus on torturing her with pleasure. Dipping his head, he returned to his rough worship of her breasts. He plumped and kneaded the globe as he alternated long with hard pulls on her nipples. The kittenish moans and squeaks that poured from her throat made his dick throb.

Her hot little clit responded to his petting, swelling to hide the tip. With deft fingers, he pushed it back and forced her overly sensitive nub to endure this sweet torture. The noises she made turned desperate. "It's too much, Sir."

She hadn't called a color, so he ignored her protest.

Pinching the drenched flesh around her clit, he slowly pulled it, stretching it until she cried out. He held it in that painful position for three seconds, and then he let go. She panted as the pain subsided. Lifting her, he threw her over his shoulder as he got to his feet. He opened the bedroom door, took two steps, and set her on the bed. His good girl had kept her arms behind her back.

"Hands behind your neck. Lay on your back. Knees up and legs spread wide."

She scrambled to obey.

He spent some time looking at her body. She had an athletic shape, with muscles that testified to a life spent outdoors. She'd said that she hadn't played sports, and he wanted to know what physical pursuits she enjoyed. He'd love to take her hiking or rock climbing.

As he looked at the perfection before him, he removed his tie and shirt. And then he remembered something. "We left the condoms at my place, so I'm going to eat that luscious pussy, and then you're going to suck my dick."

She looked down, uncertain for a second. "I have an IUD, and I'm clean. Are you?"

"Yeah. Are you saying that you're okay with not using a condom? Think about it for a minute, Sugar. I don't want you to make a decision you'll regret later. I'm not pressuring you."

"I don't feel pressured. I want to feel you inside me, Sir. My pussy misses hugging Little Sir."

He settled on his stomach with his face above her pussy. "Never refer to my dick as little."

"Sorry, Sir. I meant it as cute."

"That's not better. Stop trying, Sugar. I'm going to eat your pussy, and you're going to like it."

"We'll see, Sir."

With her knees up and her legs spread, he had access to her thighs and cheeks. He smacked her hard on the inner thigh. "Don't be a smartass tonight." Without waiting for a response—she'd better not have one—he dove in. She tasted like heaven, and so he spent some time licking her from clit to hole, and then he took her clit into his mouth and sucked rhythmically. As he did, he increased the suction to pull at the nub harder and harder.

She screamed incoherent phrases. He caught key words like *yes* and *harder*, as well as shout-outs to a higher power. As she climaxed, her body bowed off the bed. It went higher than normal because she'd planted her feet on the mattress.

While she came down from that orgasm, he took off his pants. Mouth open to gulp air, she watched him with reverent anticipation, and he thought about what he'd overheard earlier. *I think I'm falling in love.* It was there, shining in her eyes. She might not be ready to utter the words, but she didn't bother to hide her feelings. *His sub.* She was his sub, and he was going to find out the truth so he could save her from herself.

As he entered her and her soft warmth enveloped him, he kissed her tenderly, and she kissed him back with equal affection. Without waiting for permission, she took her hands from behind her head and held him close as he once again made love to her.

Chapter Ten

Autumn woke feeling refreshed. She was alone and in her own bed, but that was okay. Sir hadn't stayed the night, citing an early meeting as an excuse. Autumn didn't know who he'd meet with on a Saturday, but she didn't question it. Perhaps his crew was in town, and he needed to catch them up on the investigation thus far. It freed her to head to Royal Oak and case the gallery on a weekend morning. By contrast with the weekdays, the streets were quiet, almost deserted. She liked the idea of having fewer people around, so she called Ben.

"It's dead here right now. Are you sure about Thursday?"

"The item I want will not be delivered until Wednesday, and I'm not taking a chance that it'll be sold before Saturday. Stick to the plan."

The plan was solid, though she was always looking for improvements. "Fine. See you later." She slid her phone back into her bag.

"Autumn?"

She froze for a moment, not recognizing the voice. She turned, and the morning sun temporarily blinded her. Shading her eyes, she recognized Stephanie Ceichelski coming toward her. "Hi, Stephanie."

"Isn't this a gorgeous morning? What are you doing out and about so early?"

"I thought I'd do some shopping."

Stephanie looked around. "Most of the stores don't open for another hour."

"Yeah. I probably should have checked times before I drove all the way out here. What are you doing here?"

Stephanie laughed and slapped Autumn's arm. "Silly. I live nearby. I'm picking up bagels and donuts. My future in-laws are coming for breakfast. We're spending the day on the lake."

"Which one?" Besides the Great ones, Michigan had a ton of smaller lakes.

"St. Clair. I packed extra sunscreen. I turn into a lobster if I'm not careful. You got plans for today?"

"Yeah. I'm going to see the Tigers."

Stephanie squinted. "Oh, yeah? I didn't know you were a baseball fan. I pegged you for more of a symphony and art gallery type of person."

Autumn had no idea why she'd think that. She'd never once mentioned an interest in either thing. In the three years she'd worked at CalderCo, she'd managed to turn every conversation about hobbies and interests around so that people talked about their experiences. Nobody noticed that she didn't share anything personal. People were too preoccupied with themselves.

Except Julianne. She was that rare person who made Autumn break some of her longstanding rules.

"Oh. I like those things too." Some habits were hard to break. "What about you? Are you a Tigers fan?"

"Nope. Hate baseball. If I want to see a bunch of men standing around scratching themselves, I'd visit an orangutan exhibit." Harsh, but Stephanie had always been a little hard to take. She patted Autumn on the arm again. "I've got to be going. I'll see you Monday at work. Have fun at the game. Are you going with anybody I know?"

Autumn shook her head. Technically, Stephanie didn't know David. She knew of him, but they hadn't formally met. "Have a great time bonding with the future in-laws." She didn't remember Stephanie mentioning that she was engaged, and she felt guilty for not paying attention. If she was going to make friends, she had to know these things.

Recon mission fulfilled, she headed west to the store she really wanted to visit, Noir Leather, but it was closed until noon. Briefly she considered picking the lock on the back door. It was off Main Street, and it backed up to nothing much. Then she rejected the idea. She'd left her lock picking set in the car. She had to be at David's apartment in Ann Arbor at one, so she left disappointed.

The soft breeze lifted away some of the late summer heat. Dean lounged on the patio wearing stylish shorts, designer sunglasses, and no shirt. The big guy had spent a lot of time outdoors this summer, and his bronze chest made David feel like he needed to take his shirt off more often. Dean needed to disappear soon, but he showed no sign he was outward bound. His eyes remained closed as he listened to Jesse's call. David sat at the table intently listening to his buddy.

"Royal Oak? Again? Where did she go?"

"Nowhere. The place was a ghost town. I think she's casing a place on Main Street, but I can't figure out which one."

David frowned. This was twice in one week, and he didn't think she had another appointment at the county health clinic.

Dean stirred enough to speak. "What makes you think that?"

"She walked around, stopping for a couple minutes at various places. Sometimes she looked into shop windows, and other times, she appeared to be watching people. At one point, she talked to a woman—brown hair, about 5'4, early- to mid-forties. Nothing about her stood out. They chatted for almost three minutes, and then they went their separate ways. Oh, her target isn't Noir Leather. She looked so disappointed when she saw it was closed that I felt bad for her. I think she wanted to surprise David with something to tickle his kinky bone."

Thinking about what he'd overheard in the nursing home, David hesitated before sighing. "I heard her tell her sister something about how she's good at picking locks and opening safes."

Dean's eyes flew open, and he frowned. "Those are my areas of expertise."

"I don't suck at it either," Jesse said. "It's only David who doesn't have the magic touch."

"Fuck off." David tapped his fingers on the table. None of this sat right with him, and pursuing it meant he was managing parallel investigations. Of course, Autumn wasn't in the clear with regard to CalderCo either. The image of her kneeling as she fed him dinner came to mind. The way she'd looked at him, the purity of her devotion—he didn't want her to be a criminal. "She can't be planning a robbery. Between work, taking care of her sister, and spending time with me, she doesn't have the time."

"Right," Dean said. "Because fitting it all into her schedule wouldn't be something she'd think about ahead of time."

"You could always order her not to do it." Jesse suggested.

That would work. Not. "Just keep watching her. I'll have her today and tonight, so you and Dean can take over looking at data. Where is she right now?" According to the time, she should be at Sunshine Acres.

"She went into the nursing home right before I called. She's there now. I'll let you know if she makes any detours on her way to your place. Oh, and Dean? I bought tickets to the game. Great seats—I used Eastridge's credit card." The call terminated before David could go off on his partner.

Dean chuckled. "He's pissed that you didn't ask him to go."

"She's good with faces. If she meets him, she'll make him."

"If she has experience spotting tails, she'll make him eventually."

David was rethinking that. "She only made me because she saw me follow her from the parking garage. What if she's not good at spotting tails, but she saw me because she was looking for me?"

Dean considered this. "We pay attention when people we're attracted to are around, and she does have a thing for you. I guess we'll see. I'll instruct Jesse to tell her that you hired him to follow her if she confronts him. Of course, we also like to rationalize undesirable behaviors in those we love."

Yes, David could admit he was struggling for objectivity when it came to Autumn. Though it would piss her off to know that he was having her tailed, it was safer than having her freak out and run Jesse down with her car. She wouldn't care about the dents. "Fine."

Jesse came by, and Malcolm and Darcy arrived early. "We dropped Colin at Amy's house, and we ended up sneaking out before he could notice and throw a fit." Darcy grimaced. "He's in the stage where he wants me all the time."

Malcolm rubbed her lower back. "That's why we need more kids. If the next one doesn't like me best, we'll have to try again."

The glare she hurled at him made David laugh. Malcolm might be the Dom, but that didn't guarantee him a win on this issue. David wondered how Autumn felt about the idea of children.

Dean and Jesse wandered in from the patio. Jesse sauntered across the foyer, smiling in welcome. He shook Malcolm's hand, but when he tried to do that with Darcy, she hugged him. "You kept my sister safe. That warrants a hug."

"I never say no to a hug from a beautiful woman." Jesse kissed her cheek as well.

Malcolm tugged her from Jesse's arms and tucked her against his side. He turned his attention to Dean. "You must be Dean Alloway." He offered his hand. "Malcolm Legato. This is my wife, Darcy."

The two shook hands heartily. "It's great to finally meet you face-to-face." Dean shook Darcy's hand. He hadn't been involved with guarding her sister, and so he didn't rate a hug. "Darcy, it's a pleasure. I'm looking forward to debriefing with both of you either tonight or tomorrow."

He wasn't asking, and as Malcolm's boss, he was within his rights to demand a meeting. However, Darcy wasn't an employee. Confused, she peered at Malcolm. "Is there something you want to tell me?"

"I'm working today. I'm supposed to give my impression about Autumn."

David knew what was going on. "And whether my judgment is impaired because she's my sub. Other perspectives, while not always comfortable to hear, are important to consider."

Darcy threw her shoulders back. "This is my day off. I intend to enjoy the game and the fact that I don't have to change a diaper for the next eight hours." Then she clasped David's hands in hers. "Lying ruins relationships. Ask Malcolm how he almost lost me. It wasn't pretty, David. Don't make the same mistakes, especially when you know she's innocent. Have you tried asking her? Putting all your evidence on the table, and saying, Autumn, I really like you, and I'd love to hear your side?"

"Knowledge is power," Dean cautioned. "Telling her what we know puts the ball in her court."

"I don't think that's necessarily a bad thing," Darcy said.

David gave a reassuring squeeze. "I've asked about a few things, and she won't give a straight answer. We're not quite to the point where I think she'll level with me."

Jesse and Dean gathered their electronics and paper files. Jesse slapped David's back as they headed out. "We'll be at the game pretending like we don't know you."

Autumn rang the bell a half hour after she was supposed to have arrived. She stepped off the elevator and stopped when she saw him waiting outside in the hall. He looked her up and down, noting how the neckline of her turquoise shirt revealed the tops of her breasts and showed off a tantalizing glimpse of cleavage. On the bottom, she wore white shorts that reached mid-thigh.

She lowered to her knees and bowed her head to the floor. Her positioning was perfect, and her face was inches from his bare feet. The powerful image searing into his soul, and he knew that no other woman would ever kneel before him. Darcy's warning haunted him, but he knew he couldn't rush her. Whatever the truth, Autumn was harboring some thick stone walls that he had to penetrate first. With her prostrate before him, he finally felt like they were making progress.

"Stand up, Sugar. I want a kiss."

She got up and melted against him, turning her face up so that he could ravage her mouth. Kissing her wasn't a controlled experience by any means. She was a drug that drove him to extremes, and the way she acquiesced to his dominance only fueled the fire. By the time he tore himself away, he was fighting for the control not to whisk her into the bedroom and show him how completely she belonged to him.

Her stunning green eyes took a moment to regain focus. Leaning against his chest, she smiled sheepishly. "Sorry I'm late. Summer's brain scan came back, and there were abnormalities."

The raging passion quelled in the face of her possible heartache. "Is everything okay? Do you need to be there today?"

"No. There's nothing I can do, and it was kind of good news to have increased activity. Maybe she's waking up." The hope in her voice smacked against his heart. He wanted her to keep hoping, but he'd read the research, and he'd talked to a longtime friend who was an expert in the field. The chances of Summer waking up were slim.

There was no way he would ever say that aloud. He hugged her closer and kissed her forehead. "Maybe. You know, I have a neurologist friend who owes me a favor. Would you mind if I asked her to look over Summer's charts? You'd have to sign a consent form."

Her brow furrowed as she considered the idea. "If she's not in the network, then insurance won't cover it."

"Don't worry about it. Like I said, she owes me."

Surprised gratitude mixed with a deeper and more infinite emotion, and she wiped the corner of her eye. "Yeah, sure. Thank you."

"Malcolm and Darcy are inside waiting for us. The game starts in a couple hours, so we'd better get going." He steered her toward the apartment.

"Oh. I didn't know they were coming."

"Is that a problem?"

"No, but now I feel bad for keeping three people waiting."

He chuckled as he opened the door. He'd taken her propensity for lateness into account, and she'd come with a damn good reason to boot. If she'd been early, he would have been scrambling to get Jesse and Dean out without her noticing. "It's okay. They were early."

The drive from Ann Arbor to Detroit was uneventful until Autumn asked Malcolm if he'd found a job. In the rearview mirror, he watched Malcolm lie smoothly. "I'm freelancing, doing some consulting work with IT."

David came to the rescue. "He's working for SAFE Security. There's a vast amount of data to analyze, and I've hired Malcolm to help."

Autumn brightened. "Oh, good. I was thinking that was too much work for one person. Really you should have your whole team here, though I guess the rest of them are probably out working on other cases."

More of his team was here than she knew. Frankie was the only one not in the state. She was working a delicate negotiation on a kidnapping where the client didn't want law enforcement involved. He tangled his fingers with hers and held her hand for the rest of the ride.

He parked, and they walked to the entrance. Autumn's pace slowed considerably as they approached the gates. He paused to let her take in the magnificence of the entrance. "It's impressive."

She panned the area, taking it all in. "That's a very large tiger statue."

Darcy tugged at Malcolm's arm. "Let's get our picture with it." She thrust her camera at Autumn. "Will you take it?"

"Sure." Autumn waited until they were positioned, and then she clicked several photos. Then she whirled, her hand shooting out to grab the wrist of a passerby. She twisted it, putting enough pressure near the base of the thumb to cause serious pain. The boy cried out, but she lacked mercy. She twisted harder. "You sincerely don't want to do that. My boyfriend is a mercenary, and he's not the forgiving type."

David wasn't sure what she was doing, but he knew he needed to intervene. Before he could say anything, the boy reached in his pocket and handed over a wallet—David's wallet. Too wrapped up in Autumn, he'd let down his guard. He checked to make sure nothing was gone. "Thanks."

Autumn eased the pressure on the boy's wrist. "This isn't the life you want. You should think about choosing another career." She let go, and the boy disappeared into the crowd.

Malcolm and Darcy returned, and Autumn gave Darcy her phone back.

"What happened?" Malcolm asked.

"A pickpocket tried for my wallet, and Sugar caught him."

A light blush stole up her cheeks, probably at his public use of the nickname. "Crowds make for easy targets. You have to watch out."

Darcy looked impressed. "It's a good thing you were watching. I'm not that observant." She gestured toward the tiger statue. "Your turn."

After handing his phone to Darcy, he slung his arm around Autumn's waist and steered her toward the statue. "I'd love it if you didn't call me a mercenary in public. It sends the wrong message."

"Yeah, but 'security specialist' just makes you sound like a mall cop. Nothing against mall cops, but they're not big, bad, and dangerous like you."

She made a good point, but it had holes. "That boy didn't think I looked dangerous."

"He was only paying attention to where you carry your wallet and whether you were distracted. Because you usually wear suits, you weren't used to paying attention to your ass. But I am. You have a nice ass, easy on the eyes." The posed for their picture. "If you want to put your wallet in my bag, you can. Notice that I carry it in front and above my hip. Also, it has a zipper under the floppy top."

Darcy showed the pictures to Autumn, before sharing them with him. "You two make an adorable couple. I like this one, where he's looking at you with the most awestruck expression. That's a keeper."

He showed Darcy and Malcolm how to get to the box, and then he walked Autumn around the park, showing her the history featured on the concourse. He talked a lot, opening up about his love of the sport and his childhood memories of Tiger Stadium, and she listened with rapt fascination.

"What about you?" He'd been selfish, and he finally turned the conversation to her.

"Me? I think you were closer to your dad growing up than you remember. He can't be that bad of a guy if he kept season tickets to a sport he didn't seem to love just because you did." She gestured toward their seats. "He got these tickets for you because he wants back in. He's trying, David. He's doing the best he can. You should meet him halfway."

David shrugged. He'd been friendly to his father so far. "I don't think we'll ever be close."

"Not if you don't try. My dad and I didn't see eye-to-eye on everything, but I loved him for who he was. Now that he's gone, I have many wonderful memories to comfort me when the hard days come around, like his birthday or the anniversary of his death. You'll always regret not trying." She slipped her arms around his neck. "One of the best decisions I ever made was to give you a chance. I like you, Sir. A lot."

"I like you too." He didn't care if they were standing in the middle of the concourse. He kissed his sub.

The game was enjoyable. By the seventh inning stretch, the Tigers were up by 3 over the Royals. Having a luxurious box meant they had a nice place to escape the heat. He and Malcolm went inside to order snacks, but Autumn and Darcy stayed outside. They'd chatted throughout the game, talking about anything and everything. He noticed that Autumn often steered the conversation so that Darcy shared the majority of the anecdotes. Now they stood on the other side of the glass, laughing and chatting.

"I wonder what they're talking about." He held a beer loosely between two fingers.

"It's best we don't know." Malcolm snagged two bottles of water from the refrigerator. "Darcy's doing a great job of drawing Autumn out, but she's still not saying much. It's almost like she doesn't have similar stories to share."

David turned away from the window. He moved to stand on the other side of the bar from Malcolm. "That's an interesting idea."

"Well, even if she went by a different name, she should have I-knew-someone-who or one-time-I stories. When Darcy talked about being a mom or having a mom, Autumn listened, but she didn't relate. When Darcy mentioned her experiences as a sub, the closest Autumn came was talking about being a pro Domme. Though she's aware of them, she doesn't have an opinion on political or social issues." Malcolm twisted the lid from one water bottle and took a long drink. The temperature outside was approaching the mid-eighties.

David looked out the window, noting that Autumn's smile was genuine. "It's like she's lived her whole life watching other people living theirs."

"Either she's looking to finally have those experiences for herself," Malcolm paused, weighing what to say next. It didn't take him long to arrive at a conclusion. "Or she's a sociopath who hasn't quite figured out how to blend in."

David shook his head. "She's not a sociopath. She feels things quite deeply."

Malcolm took the other water out to Darcy. She smiled brilliantly, her entire being lighting up just from being near her Master. They exchanged a few words, and then Malcolm came back inside.

"They're talking about floggers. Autumn said, quite regretfully, that you hadn't tried to flog her yet." Mal plopped onto the plush armchair. "Subspace has helped Darcy process a lot of the pain from her past."

David sat on the matching sofa. "We haven't had time. Her evenings are pretty full. She visits her sister every day after work. I was planning to scene with her tonight."

Just then, the women came inside. Autumn knelt at his feet, and Darcy knelt in front of Malcolm. He had the feeling they'd been colluding. He and Malcolm exchanged a puzzled glance.

David studied Autumn, looking for clues in her perfect posture and lowered gaze. Other than the impish gleam in her emerald eyes, he saw nothing. Of course, the gleam was enough to worry him. "What's up, Sugar?"

"Sir, I would like to give you a blowjob." She spoke so that her voice carried only to him.

His mind short-circuited for a second. He envisioned kicking Malcolm and Darcy out and letting her have her way. The window was tinted dark enough so that nobody would see them. His dick voted in favor of any scenario that would get him off. He exchanged another glance with Malcolm, and he realized that Darcy had made the same request.

He regarded Autumn suspiciously. "Is this a competition?"

"Yes. Darcy and I have made a friendly wager." She knelt up and crawled forward until she was between his knees. She ran her palms up his thighs. "If you're game?"

Across the box, Malcolm groaned. "I don't want to know what the bet is, and I don't care if you lose. I never turn down head."

David nodded. "I'm game, Sugar."

As if some silent starting gun had gone off, she tackled his fly with amazing dexterity. He lifted his butt to help her scoot his shorts out of the way. She wrapped her hand around his base and licked his growing length. Really, she only had to look at his cock and it felt the need to salute. She lifted his balls in her other hand, and he hissed when she sucked one into her mouth.

"Fuck, Sugar. That feels good."

She had a gentle touch, and the wondrous sensations she generated made him rock hard. She took her time, licking, sucking, and stroking in ways that made him moan and groan. This definitely wasn't a speed contest. She swirled her tongue around his sensitive crown, licking away the pearly drop at the tip before taking him in her mouth. She didn't deep-throat him, which was fine because her hands never stopped moving. He gathered her hair in one hand and held it out of the way so he could see her face.

She bobbed up and down, an expression of submissive bliss softening her features. The competition had dropped away, and she sought to please him with her service. For David, there was no more powerful aphrodisiac. He lost himself in the pleasure she offered, and he came with a gasp and moan that was a lot louder than he'd anticipated. She sucked as he climaxed, swallowing his seed. His eyes rolled to the back of his head, and he let his head flop back. She fixed his clothes as best she could and laid her head on his thigh.

When his muscles started obeying the signals from his brain again, he stroked her cheek. "Thank you, Sugar."

"My pleasure, Sir." She glowed at his praise. "I think we won."

"What was the contest?"

"Who could make their Sir shout the loudest. Malcolm was fairly quiet."

A glance over showed Malcolm in a near catatonic state, while Darcy waited with her head on his thigh. His hand was still tangled in her hair, but he wasn't moving. David chuckled. "If this is the mischief you two are going to cause, we're going to have to hang around them more often."

Autumn smiled softly. "I'm okay with that, Sir. As long as I get to be with you, everything else is just a bonus."

Chapter Eleven

Autumn floated on a cloud of happiness that David towed in his wake. Even the game was exciting—the anticipation of waiting to see who would strike out and who would get a hit proved to be much more engrossing than her father had predicted. They cheered for the home team, though David seemed equally upset when the Royals fell behind.

Darcy was wonderful. As great as it had been yesterday to take steps to befriend the people at work, this was even more so. In Darcy, Autumn felt like she'd made a true friend. They had so much in common, being sassy submissives who were devoted to their Doms, that the connection seemed instant. Of course, after spending the afternoon with Darcy, Autumn wasn't sure she had much more than an interest in the D/s lifestyle in common with her. But they liked one another, and she found Darcy both genuine and fun. They'd discussed the play party, and Autumn had complimented Darcy on how the games were fun icebreakers, and Darcy had shared the game ideas that hadn't made the cut.

That had led to the blowjob contest. David was not a quiet lover, so even though she'd never given him a complete blowjob, she was confident that she could get him to make some noise.

What she hadn't counted on was the way doing that had affected her. Giving him pleasure had made her soul sing. She'd never felt closer to another human being, not even Summer. Bowing for him when she'd emerged from the elevator and kneeling before him in the suite had touched her deeply. She'd given herself to him, and it was for real. Doing so gave her a sense of peace and purpose. If she was a black and white drawing, belonging to David had splashed color all over the place, transforming it into something wholly different.

They parted ways at the apartment, and Darcy gave her a tight hug that lasted for a long time. "When this is all over, you're going to have to come for a girls' night in."

Autumn had no idea what she meant, but she responded to the sentiment. "That sounds lovely."

As soon as the door closed, David lifted her up and spun her around. She laughed at his exuberance, and he kept going, not setting her down until they both fell on the sofa. They sat very close together. His arm draped around her shoulders, and her leg rested on top of his. He kissed her, a hard, brief press of the lips.

"Now that you've been to a game, what do you think?"

She snuggled into his hold. "It was a lot of fun. I liked Darcy and Malcolm. And you're in a very good mood. Did you have fun?"

"More than I thought I would." He situated her legs so they both draped across his lap. "So, was that your first sporting event?"

"Like I said, my dad wasn't into sports." He'd been into the events, though, because they usually made a good haul from picking pockets. Summer and Autumn, especially, were good at taking people unaware. Nobody expected two cute and innocent little girls to snag their wallet. Her enjoyment dimmed for a moment. Picking pockets hadn't been something Autumn had wanted to do, but it had made her dad happy, so she hadn't questioned it.

David stroked a thumb along her throat, jolting from the memory. "What about your mom?"

Autumn shrugged. "I never knew her. She died when I was little. Summer barely remembers her, and Dad always changed the subject if we asked about her, so we stopped asking. It sounds bad, but she was a stranger, an abstract idea, and so it didn't matter to us if we knew anything about her."

"Would you want to go to more games?"

Glancing at his crotch, she said, "You don't have to take me to a baseball game to get a blowjob. You're my Sir. Just tell me what you want. I love making you happy."

"That's not what I meant, but it's good to know you're comfortable submitting to me." His hands moved over her skin wherever her clothes didn't cover it. "I wondered if you had an interest in other sports, like maybe you played soccer in school, and you'd like to see a game?"

"Oh, we didn't go to school, and Summer and I didn't play sports."

His roaming hand stuttered. "You didn't go to school? Were you homeschooled?"

Hours of lounging around, reading anything and everything, had been punctuated with lessons in safecracking, pickpocketing, blending into a crowd, evading authorities, and whatever else her father had thought relevant. Their book collection had been a combination of garage sale finds and library castoffs. Summer had taught Autumn how to sneak into school buildings and steal textbooks. In that way, they'd learned math and science, and they'd been exposed to literature and social studies. Their curriculum consisted of whatever they could find to learn.

"Sugar?"

Blushing, she realized that her mind had wandered again. "Yeah. Homeschooled. Dad didn't trust anything the government had their hands on. He said that schools churned out robots, not people."

"Did you have friends?"

This conversation was taking a turn for the worse. She didn't want to think about the things she'd missed out on. Her family had been close-knit, and they'd loved one another unconditionally. "We moved around a lot. What about you? Did you play sports other than baseball?"

"Yes. I wrestled and ran cross country in middle school, and I did football and baseball in high school." He stroked her thighs and calves. "But you're changing the subject. We were talking about you."

"Really? Because I thought we were talking about blowjobs and how they do or don't relate to baseball. Baseball, you know, has some very useful terms." She placed his palm on her breasts. "Look how easily you made it to second base."

"You're mistaken." He slipped his hand under her shirt and folded the cup of her bra aside. "This is second base."

Just having his hand on her with nothing between them made her nipple pebble. She inhaled a shaky breath. "I like second base. But we did skip first base."

He closed his lips over hers, kissing her thoroughly and consuming her thoughts. She barely noticed how he slid her body down so that he was laying on top of her. She caressed his back and sides, ending with her fingers buried in his thick, blond hair. He teased her nipple and kneaded the globe. When he finally released her lips, she panted heavily. "I like first base, especially when you're stealing second at the same time."

He lifted her shirt and eased it over her head. The latch on her bra wouldn't cooperate as well, and so she waited patiently for him to ask for help. He didn't. After several more attempts, it finally came off. Autumn filed that away as another play party game idea: Unlatching a bra with one hand.

Plumping the breast he hadn't played with yet, he took her nipple in his mouth and spent more time at second base. His face became ruddy with arousal as he kneaded her flesh and plucked at her nipples. As she watched him play, power coursed through her veins. She was the one causing him to feel a rush of desire. She was the one whose breasts he wanted to touch.

His ministrations grew rougher, sending pleasant tingles straight to her pussy. It hurt, and it felt so good. The sensations were becoming impossible to distinguish, and she cried out. He grinded his pelvis between her legs, dry fucking her as his attention on her breasts crossed the line between rough play and torture. Her cries turned desperate.

With a hearty groan, he stopped and buried his face in her breasts. She held him, stroking the back of his neck as her heart beat against his cheek. "I'd like to scene with you," he said. "But we need to talk a little about your limits first."

"Okay." It came out breathy.

"Flogger."

"Yes."

"On your boobs."

She liked that he hadn't used 'tits' since she'd expressed a dislike for the term. "Yes. Not on the head or neck, stomach, or lower back. Be gentle with it on my pussy, and only do the thuddy stuff, not the stingy stuff."

"Okay. It's unlikely I'll flog your pussy. I'd hate to bruise something that my dick is so fond of. Vibrators?"

"Yes."

"Anal sex."

Rumors abounded that it could be very enjoyable. She chewed her lip as she considered his request. He wanted it, she knew, and she wanted nothing more than to serve him in the ways that would make him happiest. "Okay."

He lifted his head to study her face. "Have you ever had anal sex?"

She shook her head.

He smoothed her hair away from her face. "No anal sex, then."

"We can try it. I trust you, Sir." So much meaning was imbued in that simple title. She trusted him to take care of her, to see to her physical and emotional wellbeing.

"Thank you, Sugar, but let's table that for now. We'll talk about it in detail another time. Right now, I want you so badly that I just want to know what you're comfortable doing. This is our first real scene, and I want to limit it to things you're familiar with."

And that's why she trusted him. He could have used her however he wanted, but he refused to indulge his desires when she wasn't fully informed on what would or could happen.

"Questions?"

"Just one."

"I'm listening."

"What's third base? If first base is kissing, and second is hands on the boob, and a home run is fucking, what's left for third?"

He sat up, kneeling between her legs, and unknit the zipper on her shorts. Peeling them down slowly, he said, "I'll show you third base, and since you like challenges so much, I'm going to issue one. I'm going to make you come, and you can't make a sound."

Autumn was not quiet when David was doing things to her, but the gloating in his tone—as if he'd already won—got her goat. "What if I do?"

"You have to bake dessert wearing a butt plug and a remotely operated bullet. I'll be in control of the bullet, and I'll periodically spank you with the plug still inside."

That didn't sound so bad. "And if I don't?"

"I'll let you come as many times as you want to tonight, even if you forget to ask."

"When did you make it a rule that I had to ask to have an orgasm?"

"Just now."

It was a reasonable and commonplace rule. "All right. You're on."

He removed her panties and settled back on top of her, pinning her in place. "No noises, Sugar. No moans, groans, grunts, or those cute little purrs you make when you're getting going."

Rerunning the bases, he kissed her breathless before moving on to her breasts. They were already sensitive from his first at-bat. While he distracted her with his mouth, his right hand slid over her stomach, stealthily making its way south. His fingers tickled over her mons and parted her lips. He circled her clit, stroking it with varying degrees of pressure.

It felt good—so fucking good—and the fact that she had to concentrate on keeping from making noises meant all the tension went spiraling back into her pussy area, which made the pleasure that much more intense.

He slipped fingers into her channel. The fullness was almost her undoing. She groped for a throw pillow, which she smashed to her face. David immediately ripped it away. "No suffocating on my watch, Sugar." He tossed it to the floor and went back to playing with her breasts.

The fingers in her channel found her sweet spot. Her eyes rolled back, her body arched, and she stifled a sob. He massaged and jabbed, his pace increasing as she pumped her hips and thrashed her body in an effort to channel the excess energy. It was too much. Reason deserted her, and her body short-circuited. From a distance, she heard desperate cries, but the climax stole her ability to figure out what they were or where they were coming from.

Awareness returned, and she found herself gripping David's arms, her fingernails gouging deep grooves into his flesh. She let go suddenly. "Sorry, Sir. I didn't mean to hurt you."

He chuckled. "You totally lost the challenge, Sugar. Though, if it makes you feel better, I've never heard you make quite those sounds before."

She blinked, momentarily wondering what the hell he was talking about. Then she remembered. There was a butt plug in her future, which was kind of exciting because she'd never played with one before. "That was third base?"

"It was."

"It felt like a home run."

He stuck his fingers, wet with her juices, in his mouth and sucked them clean. "Tastes like a home run, but it isn't. A home run involves two climaxes."

"Then a blowjob would be third base as well."

"Nope. It doesn't get a baseball designation."

That tragedy couldn't continue. "Seventh-inning stretch."

"I'll take it. Listen, we're going to make dinner before our scene. I'm going to have you put your shirt on, but no shorts and no underclothes. I have an apron you can wear while we're cooking." He got up and held out a hand to help her off the sofa. "Go clean yourself up. I'm going to get the plug and the bullet. I'm going to love challenging you, Sugar. Whether you win or lose, it's going to be fun for me."

The bathroom had large mirrors all over the place. The woman who walked into the reflected bathroom shouldn't have been a stranger. Shocked, Autumn stared. The woman in the mirror greatly resembled her, but her lips and nipples were swollen. Her neck, chest, and stomach bloomed with evidence of a fading orgasm. Her eyes were wide with shock and soft with a gravity-inducing emotion. Even her hair had more body. She touched her face gingerly, wondering at the profound change being in love could make.

Just yesterday she had questioned how deep her feelings for David ran, and today she was sure. It was a fragile thing, new and tenuous, but it would strengthen over time. Her Sir would nurture it until it was an unbreakable cable that bound them together forever.

Or not. She splashed water on her face, washing away the girlish fantasies and false hopes. He was leaving in a few weeks, and for the time being, he merely leased a space in her life. She beat her wild emotions into submission with logic and reality. As she'd originally intended, she would enjoy this time with David and remember it fondly after he'd gone.

When she rejoined him in the kitchen, she found him taking things from the cupboard and setting them out on the huge prep surface in the center of the U-shaped kitchen. A pot of wild rice boiled on the stove. A grin spread across his face when he saw her approach. "Hey, Sugar. I missed you. Come here."

She closed the distance, and he wrapped her in his warm embrace. He buried his face in her neck and inhaled, and she did the same with him. The smell of him calmed her nerves and made her want to get that much closer. He must have felt the same pull. The shirt she was wearing didn't cover her ass, and his hand landed there.

He kneaded and squeezed, lifting it so that she had to get on her tiptoes. "Bend over the counter and show me this sweet ass, Sugar."

She bent where he patted, and the coolness of the granite penetrated the thin material of her shirt. He tapped her legs farther apart, and she cooperated. He traced a finger along her slit. She'd cleaned herself up, but her pussy kept weeping in anticipation of more of what David had in store. He added a little lube, and then he eased the bullet into her vagina.

"This might start to fall out as you move around. If it slips, let me know, and I'll put it back in place." As he spoke, he massaged gel into her sphincter.

She'd read about this and knew the procedure for safely inserting a plug. Of course, back then it had all been theoretical. This was somewhat more intimate and shocking than she'd imagined.

"Color, Sugar."

"Green, Sir."

"This shouldn't hurt. It's the smallest size. Relax and exhale hard."

She breathed out, letting it happen because it would get her one step closer to pleasing Sir. The plug slid in, stretching her temporarily before that sensation subsided.

"How does it feel?"

"Full, but good. It reminds me that I belong to you."

He smacked her ass, centering his hand on the plug. It surged forward slightly, giving her a taste of what it might be like if he fucked her there. "Good. I wouldn't want you to forget that you're mine, Sugar. Now stand up. We're having chicken parmesan, and I need you to slice the cheese."

She donned the apron and set to work with the mozzarella while he seared the chicken in olive oil. The bullet pulsed to life, distracting her from her task.

"When you're done with that, I put out all the ingredients from the list you texted me last night. You can start on dessert."

Finished with what? Oh, the cheese. She concentrated on breathing and cutting. "Are you sure I should have a knife in my hands while you torture me?" She hadn't meant it as a threat, but the dangerous way he arched one eyebrow in warning had her scrambling to explain. "Because I could get distracted and cut myself."

In response, he reached into his pocket. The speed of the pulses increased. "I'll finish with that. You start on dessert. It looked like ingredients for a cake."

"I was going to do cupcakes." With that thing buzzing in her pussy, her attempt at speaking was not smooth.

It ended up being slow going, and David finished prepping the chicken long before she was able to make any substantive progress. As she measured flour, she found herself freezing in the face of an imminent orgasm.

"Sugar, remember to ask first."

She prayed he was in the mood to watch her climax. "Can I come, Sir?"

"No, Sugar, and if you disobey, I'm going to spank you."

There was no way she could breathe through it. He'd trapped her in an impossible situation, and he'd given his evil side free reign. "Please, Sir!"

"Nope." He crossed his arms and leaned against the counter next to her. "One of my favorite things about this situation, Sugar, is that no matter what you do, you're going to fail. And that doesn't mean you're weak—it means I'm stronger."

Her knees buckled, and she slammed the bag of flour on the counter. He caught her, and he held her as the waves of climax washed through her system. As it subsided, the pulsing of the bullet ceased.

"I love watching your face when you come. You're so fucking beautiful, Sugar, and now that sweet ass is mine."

The game was rigged to indulge his dominant and sadistic sides. He carried her to the sofa and arranged her body across his lap. She did her best to get her knees under her and make sure her ass was in the air.

"You're mine. You will always bow to my will, and I will always take care of you." He spanked her with short, quick swats that stung. The sensation mixed with the residual languor of her orgasm in an interesting way. The spanking didn't last long—he stopped after five swats—but it grounded her and made her feel like she belonged—to David and in this world. She was no longer on the periphery looking in. Now she was part of something larger than herself and her duty to her family.

She slid from his lap and knelt at his feet. "Thank you, Sir."

He kissed the top of her head. "You're welcome, Sugar. Now get back in the kitchen. You're not finished baking."

She rose to obey, and the bullet started again. The occasional bursts came every ten or fifteen seconds. It was enough to distract her, and it felt good, but it wasn't going to get her anywhere. On the other side of the island prep space, bar stools provided a place for people to sit and converse with the cook. David perched on one and watched her work.

"It's not Thursday, but I have a question that needs answering."

She was wary of this because she didn't want him to ask too much about her father or her upbringing. What would he think of her if he knew anything about the unconventional way she was raised? She wasn't ashamed of her father, but she wasn't exactly proud of having the gift of light fingers. "I reserve the right not to answer, but you can ask."

His gentle smile made her feel less anxious. "What was your father's name?"

She folded the wet ingredients in with the dry. "Didn't that come up when you dug up the details of my past?"

"No. Nothing came up, Sugar. On paper, you have no past."

"Do I get to ask you something if I answer?"

"Of course. I'm not unfair when it matters."

"Brian Sullivan. My mother's name was Jenny Sullivan. I don't know the names of any grandparents, and I don't know enough about either of my parents to make a membership to Ancestry.com worthwhile."

He was quiet for a moment as he stared into the middle distance. She watched the wheels of thought churning through his mind. Distracting him right now would only remind him that he had an evil remote in his pocket and he wasn't afraid to use it. She spooned the batter into a cupcake pan where she'd already placed the paper wrappers. This kitchen was incredible because it had a double oven. She put the pan into the oven she'd preheated.

"You weren't lying. Your name really is Autumn Sullivan."

"That's what my dad told me." He'd changed her name frequently growing up, but that's the one he always returned to when they were holed up somewhere waiting for the heat to die down after a spate of robberies.

He shifted. "I'm still going to call you Sugar."

"I know." She'd come to like the term of endearment.

"Your turn. What's your question?"

He'd tossed her a softball question, and so she did the same. "How did you and your friends decide to form a security company?"

He gestured for her to come closer, so she did. Sitting down wasn't an option. Juices wet her inner thighs, and she still had a lubed-up butt plug in her ass. She stood between his legs and rested her hands on his thighs. He removed the apron, balled it up, and set it on the counter. Then he gave her his undivided attention.

"Dean and I met our first day of basic, and we hit it off immediately. He was like the brother I never had. He keeps cool under pressure, and he made sure I learned to do that too. We met Jesse and Frankie later, when we joined special services. The four of us were stunningly effective when we teamed up. We spent three years going on missions together. Then, when we got out, we decided that we liked helping people, so Frankie came up with the idea of SAFE Security."

"So Frankie is the brains of the operation? What's he like?"

"She is not the brains. We're all equal partners, and so we contribute equal amounts of brainpower."

Autumn frowned. "I didn't think women could belong to Special Forces?"

He shrugged. "They might now, but they couldn't then. She wasn't officially with us, yet there's no way we would have been half as effective without her. That's one of the reasons we weren't in a hurry to reenlist. One of our best friends and an awesome soldier was denied recognition of what she actually did."

"So you formed your own company. You're still doing a lot of the same things, but you're doing them at home, and you all get the recognition you deserve. What's she like?"

"Frankie? Sometimes she runs off at the mouth, but it's generally funny and not offensive, and she likes to stick her nose into everybody's business because she thinks she can do it better. She's strong, confident, smart, loyal, speaks three languages, and doesn't take shit from anybody. You'd like her."

She sounded fricking amazing. Autumn felt inadequate by comparison. "Did you like her?"

"She's one of my best friends. Of course I like her."

"No, I mean, were you ever involved with her?"

He peered at her through narrowed eyes. "You suspect her, but not Jesse or Dean? Dean's damned good looking. Jesse is a bit rougher, but he can be very charming when he wants."

That threw Autumn off. Her intent hadn't been sexist or to convey a lack of trust. She simply wanted to know if he'd ever been involved with Frankie. "I didn't know you were bisexual. That explains the manicure and manscaping. So, were you involved sexually or romantically with any or all of them?"

"None." He grasped her hips. "I was involved with none of them. I am, however, involved with you." With that, he extracted the vibrator from her pussy and undid his shorts. "Turn around and brace yourself. You're not to come, Sugar. Your goal is to not move while I get off in your pussy."

He entered her swiftly, his path easy because she was so flipping wet. She held onto the counter, and his powerful thrusts still lifted her to her toes. He pushed on her lower back, making her arch it, and he increased his pace. It felt good, but she kept her task in mind. This was about him. His pleasure was all that mattered. Before too long, she heard his cry and felt hot jets of semen bathing her insides. He collapsed against her, holding her firmly to his front as his cock softened and slipped out.

The oven chimed.

"Dinner is done. Go clean up and grab a towel for your chair. And lose the shirt. I want my sub naked."

"Yes, Sir."

Chapter Twelve

Excitement surged through David as he double-checked the tools and toys he'd selected for their scene. It had been far too long since he'd wanted to scene with someone. He'd never understood men who could sleep with any woman that came along. Sure, he'd found many women attractive since he'd first noticed their existence, but the act of sex without the emotional component left him cold.

Similarly, he didn't care to engage in a BDSM scene with a woman he barely knew. Casual sex wasn't his thing. The fact that things were moving so quickly with Autumn gave him pause, but not much. The connection he felt with her far surpassed anything he'd imagined possible. His heart had somehow become entangled in this mess, and he was no closer to getting answers about anything from her.

Asking *Are you planning a robbery?* was definitely a mood-killer. She would have been dressed and out the door before he could explain anything, and even then, the explanation wouldn't calm her temper. Perhaps having her father's name would turn up something so that he could avoid asking her altogether.

He sighed. This predicament sucked, though it was stunningly easy to push aside all the unanswered questions when she knelt before him and looked at him with trust and affection in those sexy green eyes.

"Are you all right, Sir?"

He turned toward the sound of her voice to find her kneeling on the floor at the foot of the bed. He'd been too lost in thought to hear her come in. She kept her posture perfect, but concern wrinkled her forehead. "Yes, Sugar. Thank you for your concern."

"If you're too tired, we can wait until the morning."

"I'm not tired." Especially not after seeing her naked body presented so prettily. She was a visual feast, and when he looked at her, he felt as if he'd never eaten in his life. "I'm going to tie you up and flog you first."

Since this place belonged to his father, it didn't have a St. Andrew's cross or anything suitable for tying a woman for flogging purposes. Modification had been needed, and David had no problem nailing four two-by-fours to the inside wall. On the other side, only a luxurious closet would be bothered by the noise. The two-by-fours were secured to the studs and positioned horizontally. Two were higher, shoulder-level and a foot higher, and two were lower, at ankle and knee levels. Each two-by-four had been sanded to silky softness, and he'd sunk heavy duty rings in key positions on each one.

He wanted to put things in her—a plug, dildo, vibrator, beads, or balls. Different materials would bring pleasure, but some would function strictly for torture. Glass—filled with water and chilled like champagne—would be hard and smooth, perfect for tormenting his sub. The bullet he'd used earlier had driven her to two orgasms before he'd stopped playing with the controls. He enjoyed both kinds of penetrating toys. With her in that position, showing him that her body belonged to him, it only made the urge that much harder to put on the back burner. He'd taken out the butt plug, and now he wanted to put a larger one in. But was it too soon? She'd never engaged in anal play, and he wanted her to enjoy it. That meant he had to go slowly. There would be plenty of time to push those boundaries.

"Come here, Sugar."

She rose and closed the distance.

"How does your ass feel now that the plug is out?"

"Weird, Sir. Empty. If you'd like to try something larger, I think I can handle it."

He kissed her forehead. "I may play a bit later, but not with something larger at this point. Go stand on the towel in front of the wall."

She positioned herself facing him. Her feet were shoulder-width apart, but he wanted them wider, so he altered her stance. He secured neoprene cuffs around her wrists, and he put a second pair just above her knees. Then he connected them to a spreader bar. He found that a sub could still close her thighs when a spreader bar was connected to her ankle cuffs. It was a matter of flexibility and how far she could turn her hip and knee joints inward. This way guaranteed she couldn't shield her pussy, not that Autumn was in the habit of physically misbehaving. Her mouth presented the most problems.

He attached her wrist cuff to the rings that were shoulder height. Her arms were bent at the elbow to relieve the stress on her shoulders—especially the left one. "How is that?"

"Perfect, Sir. I can't move, and my shoulder can stay in this position for a long time without getting sore."

"And how are you? Is your inner SAM planning to make an appearance?"

"Not tonight, Sir. I do not feel at all stressed out." She thought for a moment. "Of course, that could change. If you want me to be mouthy, I can. I'm very good at it. I can start with taunting you about ruining your manicure."

He shook his head as he chuckled. The manicure thing didn't bother him. He didn't get them nearly as often as Dean did. "Thanks, but I'll pass this time. Tonight is a chance for us to get to know each other's limits and boundaries. I'm going to warm you up with deerskin, and then I'll progress to more painful implements."

"Thank you, Sir."

The warm up didn't take long. He used a circular motion to get the blood flowing in her breasts and thighs, and then he switched to a rubber flogger with round falls that tended to band together. This would produce the thuddy sensation to which she'd consented. He lifted one breast in his palm so he could center the hit over her nipple. Large and rosy, they were so responsive.

She gasped and tried to breathe through the pain. He let the feeling dissipate before hitting it again. Subspace wasn't his goal; he wanted her to be aware of every single stroke. Over and over, he repeated the pattern, alternating breasts when he felt one needed a break. Through it all, she was a trooper. She cried out when the pain became too much to breathe through, and her chest heaved with the exertion.

By the time he stopped, beads of sweat dotted her upper lip and hairline. He blotted them away and looked into her eyes. "What's your color, Sugar?"

"Green, Sir."

"Good. You're doing very well. I'm going to give those luscious boobs a rest, but I'm not finished with them. Do you need ice?"

"No, Sir. I'm okay."

Her eyes widened at his sinister chuckle. He got the bucket of ice from the desk where he'd put the toys. Her flesh was hot, and the ice was going to be a shock. He held a cube against one nipple.

It took a second, but she gasped. He set the bucket on the table between the bed and the torture wall to free his other hand. Now he held cubes to each breast, pressing them mercilessly against her tender flesh. "Sir, please. It's too much."

Because she hadn't called a color, he ignored her protest. She tried to wiggle away, but she only succeeded in arching her back and pressing the cubes even harder. "Breathe through it," he counseled. "You can do this." She complied, and he held the cubes until they melted too much to be of use, and then he ate them.

He slid his cold fingers into her vagina, but her heat neutralized any affect he might have had. The ice cubes were long and thin, the kind made by the automatic ice machine on the refrigerator. He slid one into her pussy. She sucked in a breath.

"Does it hurt?"

"It's cold, Sir."

He pushed it deeper, and then he added two more. "Clench, Sugar. Hold these inside until they melt away."

Her struggle was beautiful to witness. Legs spread wide and standing up, she kept them for a lot longer than he thought she would. When they fell out and landed on the towel he'd spread under her, only small shards were left.

Relieved, she relaxed, leaning against the wall. Her face was mesmerizing to watch. She held nothing back, and she hid nothing. This woman could not have possibly done the things they suspected.

He kissed her, plundering her mouth with his tongue because he couldn't help himself. She melted, giving herself to him because it's what they both wanted. When it ended, he stepped back to survey the perfection before him. Her breasts were still red from the rough use they'd endured from him today, and her nipples made a tempting cherry on top.

Squeezing her areola, he said, "Get ready, Sugar. You're going to scream." The clover clamp was an item she'd okayed, but he was ready to remove it if she called yellow. These things had a terrific bite, and they were going to hurt. He eased it on slowly, letting her acclimate to the pressure as best he could, though acclimating was a relative term. She screamed before he let go, and he watched her face for any sign of the wrong kind of distress.

She tried to flail her arms and legs, but he'd secured her well enough. After a minute, she calmed. "Damn, that hurts."

"Yes, and I get off on your suffering. You do it so beautifully." He put the second one on with the same gentle care. She didn't scream, but she did take a little time to adjust to the pain. "Color?"

"Green, Sir." Her gaze drifted toward the ceiling. "My nipples hurt, but it's making my pussy really miss hugging your dick."

That wasn't in the plan yet. "Sorry, Sugar. Your pussy is going to have to wait." Her clit was another story. He plugged in the wand vibrator and held it to her clit. The power tool would bring some relief.

"Thank you, Sir." She moaned, and pretty soon those cute purring noises started deep in her throat. When she was close, he removed the clamps. She shouted as she came, and he kept the wand pressed to her clit. It would hurt, he knew, because she'd be oversensitive after the climax. She squirmed, struggling against it as he forced her to a second orgasm. Tears leaked from her eyes as she looked at him kneeling between her legs. She'd submitted so deeply that she didn't bother to beg him to stop.

He turned off the wand. "You're mine, Sugar, and I love playing with this body." He kissed her again. Yes, it was a reward, but she'd wrapped him so completely around her finger that he couldn't help but need to feel her lips moving against his.

When he released her, she searched his face, peering deeply into his eyes. "I love you, Sir."

Stunned, his mouth dropped open. His heart surged to hear the words, but his brain prevented him from replying in kind. Did he love her? Probably. But he didn't trust her, and that was a problem. He scrambled for a suitable response.

"Don't," she said softly, her tear-bright eyes soft with understanding. "Don't say anything. I didn't mean to interrupt. Let's just continue the scene."

"I'm going to turn you around," he said. "So I can flog your back." And so he could gather the wits she'd scattered.

She smiled, the excited kind a sub who was happy in a scene gave. He felt less bad about not replying. Eventually he'd have to address the issue, but that discussion was for a time they were both clothed and on equal footing. He untied her, turned her around, and retied her wrists and knees. Then he removed his shirt. He might not be able to give her the words, but he could get her to subspace. He could at least give her that.

Could she have a near-subspace-induced, drunken episode that was less embarrassing? Who the fuck mutters an *I love you* the first official weekend in a relationship? This is why she avoided alcohol—because she turned into an idiot when she wasn't in control of her emotions or tongue. And he'd looked so shocked and confused, like he was trying to figure out how he'd ended up going home from the bar with the crazy woman. *She looked so normal, officer. Not at all like a psycho.*

Facing the wall was better than facing him if she wanted to get her head back into the scene. He'd already checked her color, and now he started with the deerskin for the warm up. She leaned her forehead against the wall, and the plank of wood was the perfect height to rest her chin. As he changed floggers and began again, she tried to get her brain to stop berating her, but he wasn't using an implement with enough bite. This one had a pleasant thuddy-sting.

After a while, he paused. "Color, Sugar."

"Green, Sir. It feels very good, but if you don't mind, I'm okay with more sting."

"I can do that. Let's see what you can handle. I'm going to give you a ball to hold. If you drop it, I'll stop. It's a secondary safeword."

She was familiar with the concept, and she'd used the system before, especially when a gag was in play—only she'd been the Domina. He pressed it to her hand, and she closed her palm around the small, rubber bouncy ball. When he started in with the next flogger, her whole body relaxed into the rhythm. She barely noticed the change in technique, though the technical department in her brain noted that he was using a double Florentine method. Later she'd be impressed. Right now she was in heaven. Her mind floated a little, though it didn't take flight.

When he undid the snaps and took her down, she answered his questions absent-mindedly and followed his instructions without question. None of this registered as important enough to warrant much attention. The fog began to lift when she was lying on his bed. On her back with the spreader bar still attached to her knees, she stared at the ceiling.

"You have a skylight."

He chuckled, and she lifted her head to see that he was at a desk gathering items. "Yes."

"How did I not notice that before?"

"Because it was dark or I was busy blowing your mind." He dropped the items on the bed, and she noticed the towels and lube he'd already put there. "I'm going to bind your wrists to the spreader bar, but I need to know what your shoulder can handle. I can bind your wrists inside or outside of your knees. You will be putting weight on your shoulders eventually."

Due to having been stretched out for so long, her shoulder was starting to get a little twinge. She thought about it for a second. "Can you bind them to either side of my left knee? Or would that get in your way?" In that position, when she had to balance weight on her shoulders, her right would take the brunt of it.

"No, it's fine. Remember to call yellow if you need to, Sugar. I'd hate for a night of kinky sex to land you in the ER. It might end up being reenacted on a reality TV show." He attached the cuffs to the bar. Then he stood on the bed and threaded a heavy gauge rope through a ring in the ceiling. She watched while he tied one end to the spreader bar, hoisted the bar, and tied it off on the other end.

He'd looped it so that her legs kept it from slipping off. She lay on her back with her wrists and legs bound to a suspended spreader bar. Bared and spread wide, she was unable to move. Excitement zoomed through her veins, fueled by the unknown and a deep trust for this man who had become her Sir.

He sat cross-legged on the bed so that he had a prime view of her assets. She felt his fingers swirling patterns along her labia, teasing from clit to hole with a light pressure that made her crave more. "Your pussy is a lot like you. It has flaps and folds where secret plunder is stored. It's all here, waiting for me to discover every last bit and cherish it for the precious treasure it is." He leaned forward to nail her with a promise in his gaze that left her breathless. "It's *my* treasure, Sugar. I will defend my right to hoard it for myself."

"It's yours, Sir. I give it to you of my own free will."

He squeezed lube onto his fingers. "You're already sopping wet. This is for the first dildo. I'm going to see how much you can take. Feel free to scream, but remember to use your safeword if it's too much."

With that, he picked up the first dildo. It was neon pink silicone and had an average circumference. He slathered lubricant up and down it slowly, like he was masturbating and forcing her to watch. She couldn't see what other treats he had in store due to the position of her arms. It forced her to wait until he held it up to show her what he planned to put in her pussy.

It penetrated her easily. He moved it around, sliding it in and out leisurely, as if he was measuring how deeply he could push it before the hilt stopped forward progress. He rotated it, both spinning it like it was a screw and using her entrance as a fulcrum while he tested the give of her walls. By the time he finished, she was breathing hard. It had been pleasurable, yet he hadn't fucked her with it.

The next one was larger than she would have chosen for herself. It would fit with enough lube, but it didn't look like it would be comfortable. He treated this one to the same prep, and watching him pretend to jack off with a dildo turned out to be an incredibly erotic image. She relaxed to take this one. The head stretched her entrance, and he had to move it around, but it went in without causing pain.

It filled her. It stretched her tender tissues, forcing every bit of her sweet spot to slide along the textured surface. "Holy shit," she said. "That feels incredible."

He laughed, the low, melodic sound tickling over her wellbeing. "I'll keep that in mind for when you've earned a reward."

As with the first one, he didn't attempt to get her off. He slid it in and out, twisting and rotating to see how much give he could find in her vagina.

The third one was larger. When he held it up, she felt her eyes widen so much that she feared one might pop out. Though it wasn't as wide as his fist, it was nearly as wide as hers. "Oh, hell no. That will not fit, and if you break my pussy, you can't use it again for a really long time. Months. Maybe years."

With a sinister chuckle, he spread the lube on it. He also squirted some into her vagina and used his fingers to massage it into her aroused tissues. "It'll fit." He scissored his fingers at her entrance. "You have plenty of elasticity. Trust me."

This one took some time to breach the entrance. Several times, he used his finger to stretch and massage her delicate opening. She toyed with the idea of calling yellow, but she had no real reason, besides trepidation, to do so. Nothing he was doing hurt. Some of it was uncomfortable, but it didn't hurt.

"It's in. You're doing beautifully, Sugar. I'm so proud of you."

It didn't feel like anything, and she realized that her nerves had stretched so thin that she'd lost feeling. That couldn't be good. Then he eased it in a little more, and she breathed with relief. She definitely felt it. He was gentler with this one. Though he slid it in and out, he didn't rotate it or try to test whether her walls could take more.

And she realized one other thing: With a dildo this big, she was going to come. It didn't matter that it had skipped foreplay or that it kept a slow, gentle pace. Bondage turned her on, and the heat of her flogged skin against the coverlet took care of any additional foreplay she might require. An indescribable sensation stole over her, and without prelude, her pussy began convulsing. She cried out, lifting her ass off the bed as she came. He moved with her, making sure she didn't hurt herself.

As she came down, trembling from the force of that unexpected bonus, he slowly slid it out. Her pussy both celebrated and mourned the loss. She struggled to remember how to breathe normally. "Oh, Sir. That was incredible. I hope it hasn't ruined me for normal-sized dicks."

He slapped her inner thigh hard enough to leave a handprint. "No sass."

"It's a real concern." She tried to gesture with her hands, but they were bound. "What if my pussy can't hug your dick as tightly as it used to? Will your dick find another pussy to have a crush on?"

"I don't think that's a valid concern, but I'll assign you a hundred Kegels a day to keep your pussy strong. That will work out well for when I want to make you wear ben wa balls to the next baseball game. It's Wednesday night, by the way."

She'd planned to get to bed early Wednesday night. If they went to a game, even if she went home afterward, she'd get to sleep later than she wanted. Having a boyfriend was not convenient when planning a robbery. "It's a date." Actually, it would give her a wonderful excuse for calling in sick on Thursday. He'd believe that she was exhausted. Besides, if she went to the game, she'd have to skip seeing Summer, and it was logical that she'd want extra time with her sister the next day.

Next she felt him spreading lube in her ass. For a second, she panicked. What if he tried to stick one of those dildos in her ass? There was no way that wouldn't tear something that would prove painful on a regular basis until it healed. Then she remembered what he'd said about not wanting to push that limit yet, and she relaxed.

She felt a small bead slide past her back entrance. More followed, each larger than the last, but the final bead didn't feel larger than the plug had.

He rubbed a hand up and down her lower leg. "How are you doing, Sugar?"

"Fine, Sir. The anal beads are pleasurable."

"Good." He untied the knots holding the spreader bar in the air. Tossing the rope aside, he picked her up and turned her over. Now she was perched on her right shoulder and both knees with her ass in the air. He adjusted the placement of her knees. "I'm going to fuck you, and you're going to come."

"I'll try, Sir." Really, her pussy had been through a lot today. She wasn't going to be upset about not having another one. It mattered that he had one, though—a really big one.

"There is no *try*, only *do*. You will come, Sugar. That's not negotiable." He slid into her pussy, and she realized he was right—his cock felt as snug inside her as it always had. He set a quick pace, fucking her with hard jabs that felt so very good. He played with the beads as well, sliding them in and out in slow increments. It added another level to the riot of sensation in her pussy. Then she heard a motor whir to life. The wand vibrator pressed to her clit. Not climaxing ceased to be a fear. She came twice, screaming and sobbing the second time as the orgasm obliterated her senses.

She woke some time later in David's arms. The sweat and fluids had been washed from her body, and a thin sheet had been pulled to her waist. He stroked her hair and occasionally pressed a kiss to her forehead or temple. The next time he went in for a kiss, she tilted her face so that their lips met.

That kiss was soft and slow, an expression of feelings he hadn't been able to share verbally. It was enough for now.

Chapter Thirteen

Autumn woke up with a man's leg on top of hers. Luckily it belonged to David. She'd slept soundly, but it was still a strange bed and a strange room, so she'd awakened at the crack of dawn. It didn't matter how thoroughly he'd exhausted her the night before—she couldn't sleep there for more than a few hours.

She eased out from under him, but he snagged her around the waist and pulled her so that she spooned him. "Where you going?"

"Bathroom."

His eyes didn't open. "You said that last time, and you never came back to bed."

"Well, you probably shouldn't have such a tempting shower. I'm weak in the face of multiple heads."

He shifted so that his hand covered her breast and his face nuzzled her neck, but he didn't show actual signs of waking up. "I'll keep that in mind for our next scene."

She tried to move his hand, but he wasn't cooperative. "Sir, I really need to use the bathroom."

"Fine, but you'd better be back before my dick gets lonely."

She didn't relish lying in bed while he slept. It tended to make her tired. "Or I could make muffins for breakfast, and then when your dick wakes up, he can come out and get me."

It took a few seconds, but her proposal penetrated the haze of sleep. He loosened his grip. "Okay. I like blueberry and banana muffins. And walnuts. Those are good."

She slid from bed and let him get back to sleep. He'd decreed that she should remain naked, but he'd let her wear clothes while cooking last night, so she reasoned he wouldn't mind if she dressed in his bathrobe. The blue silk garment felt great against her bare skin, especially her breasts and back, which were still sensitive from the scene.

When she emerged from the bedroom and entered the living room, she was grateful the robe was extra long on her, falling to mid-calf. Sitting at the dining table, sipping coffee, was Mr. Calder. She froze. Never before had her boyfriend's father caught her coming from his room, particularly not while wearing a mere bathrobe.

"Autumn. I didn't expect to see you here."

"Well, I didn't expect to see you there. Would you like me to wake David?"

He stood, his face hardening as he walled off his feelings. It wasn't like she expected him to emote with her, but she didn't expect the complete shutdown. "No. I didn't mean to intrude. I merely had business to discuss."

"Business? On Sunday morning? With your son?"

Mr. Calder's brows rose. Though David didn't resemble his father—the elder man had darker coloring and hair, a shorter stature, and a thinner build—he'd definitely inherited his father's expressions and his air of authority. "He told you?"

"Yeah. I can see why you'd want to keep that relationship secret for now, but a ruse like that is difficult to maintain. He's your little boy, and you want to bond with him over more than company business." She smiled warmly. "Perhaps you should go with him to the baseball game on Wednesday. I hear there's nothing like attending a baseball game to facilitate father-son bonding."

He looked her up and down, and Autumn had the uncomfortable feeling that he found her not good enough for David. She hugged the robe tighter to her body. He picked up his coffee and headed to the door. "I'll be back in a few hours. Make sure David is still here."

The door closed, leaving her in an empty, silent room. Why had he stopped by so early? It was barely seven, and David liked to sleep. It was almost as if he'd been hoping to catch David unaware. A bit of sadness dimmed her sunny outlook. David hadn't been kidding about his father being difficult to get along with. But the fact that he had been there meant he was trying, didn't it? She pondered this as she threw together a muffin mix from scratch.

It had been years since she'd baked anything that didn't come from a box. When Summer had been around, they'd enjoyed experimenting with different recipes. They'd even fantasized about opening a bakery together. Summer had planned to paint tantalizing murals on the walls, and the menu would be hand-lettered—with scrumptious renderings of all the offerings next to the description. Autumn would have made the place robbery-proof. Now that she knew so much about accounting, she could handle that part and teach Summer how to keep the books.

David somehow made her want to spend more time in the kitchen. He'd enjoyed her cupcakes the night before, and she hoped that maybe when Summer woke up, they could set their dream in motion. If she could find someone as wonderful as David—even for a little while—then anything seemed possible.

She set the oven to automatically turn off when the muffins were done, and she headed back to the bedroom to wake up her sleepyhead Sir. She found him curled in the same position, so she tossed the robe over a chair and crawled beneath the covers. She sidled up to his warm body, and he shifted to let her get closer, but he didn't show signs of wanting to open his eyes.

No matter. She kissed a path down his chest and across his abdomen. He turned to lie fully on his back, and she took that as permission to continue. His cock proved more awake than the rest of him, and she spent some time teasing his sensitive crown. She ran the tip of her tongue along the ridge, and then she experimented with putting just the crown into her mouth and massaging it with her lips and tongue.

He groaned loudly. "Sugar, you're going to kill me if you keep that up."

She released him with a loud smacking sound. "Can't have that, Sir. I like you alive. It's easier to have conversations that way."

"Conversation? Are you talking to my dick or are you going to suck it?"

"I can do both. I can do this—" She put it in her mouth and bobbed her head a few times before stopping. "And then I can tell him how sexy he is with that purple crown and all those veins pumped and ready to have a good time."

He lifted her, repositioning her so that she straddled him. "He's not interested in conversation. He's more of an action hero, so get on, Sugar. You're going to ride me, and I'm going to spank that sweet ass while you do it."

That got her juices flowing even more than playing with him did. She positioned him at her entrance and slid down. Starting off slowly, she enjoyed the full feeling while she established a rhythm. He held her hips, and used his thumb to circle her clit.

"Faster," he ordered, smacking her ass in encouragement.

She obeyed. Heat and tension coiled in her pussy, and she found herself gasping and moaning. Yeah, she was vocal during sex, but so was he. Together, they made a loud couple. As he approached his climax, he smacked her ass more frequently, and each hit made her pleasure spiral even higher. She came, her body stiffening as she lost the rhythm. He held her hips and pistoned into her several more times until he climaxed.

He eased from her body and pulled her to his chest. "Have I told you how much I like waking up with you in my bed?"

"Not yet."

"A lot, though I'd like it more if you slept in."

"Sorry. I have trouble sleeping in strange places."

He stroked a caress down her spine. "Is it really so strange? I'm here. The bed is comfortable, and the sheets are soft."

"It's perfect," she agreed. "But it's still strange to me. It's not you. I've always been like this. It generally takes me about a month to acclimate to sleeping in a new place."

"A month of getting up early? I might be able to handle that." He tangled his hand in her hair and kissed the top of her head.

She laughed. "It's not like I'll be here every night. You can sleep in tomorrow."

"Where are you planning to be?"

"In my bed. Too many nights of sleeping like this makes me a bear, and I'd rather you didn't meet my grumpy side." Really, there was no need. She got up and took her clothes into the bathroom. "I made muffins and coffee. They should be done by now."

He joined her before too long, but he merely stared with a disapproving frown. "Why are you getting dressed?"

"Well, after breakfast, I'm going to go see Summer, and then I'm meeting Julianne for dinner." She'd shared her plans with him yesterday, so this was not news.

"I know, but I didn't give you permission to dress."

She brushed her hair and watched him in the mirror, trying desperately to keep her gaze at eye level. He had a very sexy body that made her want to undress and lure him back to bed. "I wore your robe when I went out earlier to make the muffins, which was a good thing because your dad was sitting at the dining room table drinking coffee. It was a tad on the awkward side. He said he'd be back in a few hours. I'd rather your dad not see me naked."

The frown morphed into irritation. "I told him not to do come in without being invited, but it looks like he chose not to listen."

Autumn didn't want to sow dissention between them. There was already too much. "He's your dad, Sir. He just wants to be part of your life. He's trying. You could meet him halfway. I invited him to go to the game with you on Wednesday."

"You what? Why? That's time I wanted to spend with you."

"Well, I can come too. I thought the two of you could do some father-son bonding, maybe start building bridges over your differences. As different as we were, I loved my dad, and I'd do anything to have him back. While your dad is still alive, it's not too late."

He got into the shower, still frowning, but now he glowered. "I should spank you for this."

"If it'll make you feel better, my ass is always up for that kind of fun."

"It wouldn't be fun. It would be a punishment."

She perched on the counter next to the sink, watching him lather up. "For what? Caring about your relationship with your father? You're reaching, Sir."

"He's an asshole." He slid the door open and pointed at her before grabbing a towel. "You don't understand because he hasn't shown you exactly what kind of a bastard he is, but trust me, I know." He rubbed the towel roughly on his skin.

"Maybe he is, but back to my earlier point—he's trying. Meet him halfway. It won't cost you anything to try." She set her palms on his chest and stared deep into his dark brown eyes. "I took a chance with you even though you started off as a stalker. It turned out to be one of the best decisions I've ever made."

"It wasn't stalking. I was investigating you." His negative mood fell away, and he wrapped his arms around her. "All right. My dad can come to the game, but you're coming too. I need a buffer."

"You should invite Malcolm and Darcy too. The more buffers, the merrier." And she didn't necessarily welcome four hours of having to navigate tense conversations between grown men who should know better. There wouldn't be a blowjob contest, but that's the price David had to pay for not mending fences before now.

Autumn was in the middle of dishing intimate details about her weekend to Summer when the perpetrator of those bedroom crimes called. Smug smile firmly in place, she answered. "Miss me already?"

He laughed. "Yes, but that's not why I'm calling. Remember the friend I was telling you about? The neurologist who owed me a favor? She'll be at Sunshine Acres around two o'clock. I gave her Summer's room number, but she can't check her out or look at her records without a release from you, so she's bringing it by."

Stunned, Autumn didn't quite know how to respond. Not only had he remembered his offer, he'd followed up on it immediately. After several false starts, she finally managed something. "Thank you. I can't believe you remembered."

"Sugar, this is important to you, so it's important to me."

Hot tears pricked at the backs of her eyes. She hadn't expected this level of thoughtfulness. It was one thing to offer, but she'd found it rare for people to actually follow through. "You're so very sweet, Sir."

He cleared his throat, and she imagined a tinge of red staining his cheeks. "Her name is Tess Wycoff. She's blonde, around 5'5, about fifty years old, and kind of scrawny. Don't tell her I said that. She's touchy about words used to describe her build. Oh—she just texted me to have you get any records you can together so she can take them home and go through them."

Those records were at her apartment. A check of the clock showed that she had a half hour before Dr. Wycoff showed up. "I will. Thank you so much, Sir. I'll call you tonight."

Just in case she didn't make it back in time, she jotted a note to the doctor and taped it to the whiteboard that detailed who was in charge of Summer each day. A half hour was enough time. She could make it if she hurried, there was no traffic, and a miracle happened. This was not the time to be in denial about the challenges she had with time schedules.

She arrived at her car to see someone standing next to it, peering into her back seat. It took a moment for her to recognize Stephanie from work.

The woman looked up as Autumn approached. She straightened, and surprise turned to an almost wooden smile. "Autumn, I thought this was your car, but I wasn't sure. This is so strange—bumping into you twice on the weekend in two different cities. It's like fate is trying to tell me something."

Autumn had no idea what in the world Stephanie was rambling about. She wanted to get going. "I didn't know you had a relative here."

"I don't. I'm looking for places that might take my great-aunt. She's not doing well and needs round-the-clock care. Is this where your sister is?" She tilted her head as she waited for Autumn's reply.

Having a sister in a coma wasn't common knowledge, and Autumn knew that Julianne would never spread gossip. Had she mentioned it in passing and Stephanie overheard? Abruptly, Autumn brushed aside the concern. Keeping Summer a secret was stupid anyway. "Yeah. The staff here is pretty nice."

Stephanie nodded as if she'd come to a decision. "This is what God is trying to tell me. Running into you yesterday and today—this is the place where Aunt Rachel belongs."

"Oh, then I guess I'll see you around. I have a time-sensitive errand to run. I don't mean to be rude, but I have to get going." With that, she unlocked her door and got in. She lived fifteen minutes away. Her files on Summer were organized, but hidden. It would take ten or fifteen minutes to get them out. Shit. There was no way this would work. She dialed Julianne.

"Hey, hon. Are we still on for dinner?"

She pressed the accelerator to beat a yellow light, but she had to brake hard for the next one. "Yes. Listen, David has a doctor friend who is coming to take a look at Summer, and I have to run home to get her records. Only she's going to be there before I can get back. Is there any way you can drop everything and go to Sunshine Acres right now?"

"I can be there by two. Is that okay?"

"It's perfect. I appreciate this so much." She punched the gas as soon as the light turned green, but she found herself having to slam the brakes on again when someone pulled out in front of her. Only she wasn't fast enough, and her car slammed into the back half of the vehicle.

"Autumn? What happened?"

"A car pulled in front of me, and I couldn't stop in time."

"Are you okay?"

"Yes."

Julianne snorted. "Why am I asking you? No, you're not. If you were bleeding and had a broken bone, you'd still tell me you were fine."

"I'm going to let you go now. Get to Summer, okay? I'll be there as soon as I can." Her sister was not going to lose out on a chance to be seen by a specialist. Autumn got out of the car, but she swayed before taking a step and had to lean against the door.

"Miss? Are you okay?" A stranger was in her personal space.

She tried to move away, but her legs wouldn't cooperate. "Fine. Is the other person okay?"

The stranger peered into her eyes. "They have airbags. You don't. Did you hit your head?"

The time between hitting the car and getting out of hers was a blur. "I don't think so." The stranger was coming into focus. He was about her height, and his hair was in neat cornrows. She stared at him, concentrating on his rich, brown eyes and the friendly concern she recognized there. "They pulled out in front of me."

"I know. I saw it happen. You were both on your cell phones, and they didn't stop for the light." The way he looked into her eyes made her feel like a patient.

The man swam in an out of focus, and things didn't quite make sense. She focused on the stranger who seemed concerned. "Are you a doctor?"

"I am, and you need to go to the ER. You did hit your head. It's bleeding. I've called an ambulance."

"I don't have time, and I'm okay."

He guided her to the curb and helped her sit down. She didn't know why she went with him. Time was ticking, and she needed to get Summer's records for Doctor Wycoff. "Well, you have to wait for the police to make a report and give you a ticket anyway, so why don't you just let the EMT's check you out?"

An hour later, she found herself sitting on a bed in a hospital while a nurse took her vital signs and enough blood to feed a vampire. "What in the world are you going to do with that?"

She smiled. "Run tests. It's our job to make sure you're okay before we send you back into the big, bad world."

"I'm not staying here." She got out of bed and searched for her bag. The doctor who'd helped her to the curb had been nice enough to get her things from the car. "My sister needs me."

The nurse's face got a don't-fuck-with-me look. "Call your sister and tell her that you need her."

Autumn blinked. "She's in a coma."

"Well, then she won't miss you for a while. You have plenty of time for the CT scan the doctor ordered." She put her hands out. "Get back in bed, sweetie. You're not thinking straight right now."

"Listen to the nurse, Sugar. That's an order."

Hearing David's voice made harsh realities intrude. Big tears started forming in her eyes, and she looked up to see him standing in the gap between the curtains that partitioned her from the rest of the people in the ER. "But Summer—"

He shook his head, a firm warning not to argue. "Tess understands. She'll drop by tomorrow." He turned sideways to pass the nurse, and he helped her back into bed. "Right now, you're going to rest and wait for the test results. You may have a concussion."

"The orderly should be here in about ten minutes to transport you to radiology." The nurse made her pronouncement and left.

"I don't remember hitting my head. It was a fender-bender. That's all." She rested her face against his chest, and he held her loosely, though he was tense.

"What were you doing in your car? You were supposed to stay at Sunshine Acres and wait for Tess."

"Summer's records are at my apartment. I asked Julianne to wait for the doctor, and I went to get the files."

Some of the stiffness left him, and when he spoke again, most of the irritation was gone as well. "We'll grab them when I take you home to pack a bag. You'll be staying with me tonight."

She wanted to sleep in her own bed. "Sir, that's not necessary. I'm sure all this is a waste of time and money."

"We'll see about that." He eased her back on the bed, and then he sat in the visitor's chair. His presence filled the tiny space, and she found having him close to be so very comforting.

"How did you know I was here?"

"Julianne called me." He rubbed his palm down the thigh of his pants. "I tried to call you, but your phone goes directly to voicemail, so I called a friend to find out where the ambulance took you."

He certainly had convenient friends. Might as well see how convenient they were. "Do you know where my car is? I kind of need it."

"It's been towed. I had it delivered to a body shop I trust. They'll call when it's ready."

Visions of bills to come floated before her. "That's okay. It's just a couple of dents, nothing that needs to be fixed right now."

The way he pressed his lips let her know that he wasn't in the mood to negotiate. "You're not getting it back until my mechanic clears it. I'll loan you one of mine until then."

She blinked. "*One* of your cars? How many cars do you have?"

"As many as I need. Stop arguing, Sugar. Thank me and shut up about it. When it comes to your safety, I'm not cutting corners."

Corners needed to be cut. Going around them was always too expensive. But he regarded her with a menacing scowl, and she knew when not to poke her bear. She'd just have to make sure her extra job this Thursday really paid out. They hadn't planned to go after the safe, but maybe while Ben was occupied with the paintings he wanted to steal, she could see if there was any cash on hand. She hated to do it, but it looked like she had no choice.

By nightfall, she found herself in David's car, riding shotgun. He didn't say a word as he drove to her apartment. Julianne had come by to let her know that Summer was fine. Autumn had been forced to stay in the ER until the doctors gave her a clean bill of health. She'd merely been shaken up, not seriously hurt. Well, car accidents tended to shake her up. The last one had cost her a father and almost a sister.

"Are you angry with me?" She broke the silence. "I'm sorry, Sir. I didn't mean to interrupt your plans. Really, I'm okay staying by myself."

He dragged a hand through his hair. "I'm just tired, Sugar, and worried about you. And I'm feeling guilty. This wouldn't have happened if I had given you more than a half hour's notice."

Reaching over, she twined her fingers with his. "It's not your fault. I know it's hard to accept that you aren't in control of every factor in the world, but you aren't. You were doing something incredibly thoughtful for me, and then you dropped everything to come to the ER to be there for me when I needed you. Those are the only things you get to take the blame for." They'd arrived at her apartment building, so she unclicked her seatbelt. "And I'm okay. I know I'll probably be a little sore tomorrow, but at least nobody was hurt."

He came around to assist her out of the SUV, but she was too quick. The whole way up the stairs, he hovered behind her with his hands out to catch her if she stumbled or fell.

At the heavy security door to her apartment, she held a hand against his chest. "I love that you care, but please stop. I will tell you if I'm feeling faint or dizzy or any of the other symptoms on the warning list. I promise."

A half-step back was all he was willing to cede, but she'd take it. As they went inside, the alarm on her phone went off. She fumbled for it to enter the deactivation code while David turned on the light. A quick scan set off a warning bell in her head.

She grabbed David's arm to keep him from touching anything. "Someone has been here."

"Your alarm went off?"

"No." The alarm would alert her about intruders who didn't know how to avoid detection. That left a whole class of savvy criminals who could bypass her security. She looked closer at everything, noting minute details.

"Then what makes you think someone was here?"

She opened a drawer in the tiny kitchen where she kept Summer's unpaid bills. "Someone has been in this drawer. These aren't exactly how I left them." She put them back and went to the sofa. The left cushion didn't fit quite right, and so it had to be forced into position by tucking the cover a certain way to level it out. "This has been moved as well."

David grasped her arms and forced her to face him. "Sugar, maybe the accident shook you up more than you thought. What you're saying doesn't make sense."

Careful not to hit the bruise at her hairline, she pushed her hair back. "I know it might sound a little crazy, but I set little traps in case someone breaks in and tries to go through my things. My dad was always paranoid about the government intruding in our lives, so I grew up with this habit. I turn every third, seventh, and twelfth letter, and I have a certain way of putting the cushion that won't automatically reset if you lift it up and put it down, even if you try to tuck the cover in."

He frowned. "I'm not going to lie. It does sound crazy. But everything you've told me sounds like you grew up living on the run. It makes sense that you would still use those precautions even though there's no need."

Yeah, her father had possessed some odd quirks, but everybody did, so that was unremarkable. It was one thing for Summer to make comments about their dad's oddities, but it was entirely different when someone outside the family did it. "I'm going to reset everything, and then I'll get some clothes."

"I'm a seasoned traveler with a lot of packing experience." He went into the bedroom. "I'll pack your clothes."

She didn't want him going through her drawers, but after sounding like she was half-baked and paranoid already, she didn't care to rock that boat. Nothing in there was a secret anyway. She quickly reordered her unpaid bills and refolded the sofa cover so that it was exactly the way she wanted. In the past week, she hadn't spent much time at home, so this could have happened anytime in the last several days. Her level of vigilance was flagging, and that led to danger. *Dad taught you better than this.*

Chapter Fourteen

Having been in her bedroom once before, David scanned it to see if he could spot anything out of place. He hadn't exactly been focused on memorizing the placement of her belongings last time. When Autumn was around, he had trouble doing his job. She commanded his full attention, and he liked giving it to her.

If he had been raised by a paranoid father and trained in keeping himself off the radar, where would he set traps? Few pieces of furniture meant easy answers—the closet and drawers. He hadn't looked in either place last time, so he set to work going through her closet and drawers. While Jesse was always careful, he hadn't been looking for small traps that would only make sense to the person who'd set them. This way, he could take the blame for anything out of place.

In a box on top of the dresser, he found a cache of photos. Riffling through, he found the oldest in the bunch and took pictures of them with his phone. The backs lacked any kind of identification like names, locations, or years.

Autumn came in, her troubled green eyes scanning the room for anything out of place. She frowned when she saw that he hadn't been looking in the right drawers. "What are you doing?"

He flipped through several of the old photographs. "You were a cute kid. Is this your dad?"

She peered at the one on which he'd paused. It showed her and Summer on a beach with plastic shovels and buckets. A man with red hair and a slight build helped them shape a sandcastle. All three sported joyful smiles. "Yes. I think I was about four and Summer was six."

"A day at the beach. Where was this?"

"I don't know." She took the photo and her forehead wrinkled as she thought. "Maybe Texas. We spent some time there. Summer might remember. I was too young." Then her face softened and her eyes grew distant. "Dad had his quirks, but most of my memories are things like this. He structured his whole life around us. I don't remember a time he wasn't there when I needed him."

David looked through a few more photographs. Most of them were of Autumn and Summer. Brian Sullivan was in very few pictures, which made sense if he was the one with the camera. "Who took that picture?"

"I don't know. Maybe a friend of my dad's was there. Or a stranger. People at beaches tend to be friendly and helpful to one another." She stood next to him as he went through more, and he took that as permission to keep looking.

He stopped at one with Autumn sitting on the floor with her hand on the dial of a complex safe. She couldn't have been more than fifteen. That type of safe had a combination that consisted of six numbers that reset any time a mistake was made, and it had two-tier protection. "What are you doing here?"

She fingered the edge of the photo. "Dad used to put my birthday presents in a safe, and I had to guess the combination. It was a game we played."

It was a game a thief would play to pass along his skills to his offspring. "What if you couldn't guess right?"

"Then I tried again." She laughed and patted his arm. "Like I said, it was a game. He never put anything in there that couldn't keep for a long period of time. But the gift rarely mattered. I thrived on the challenge."

While he continued to look through photos and surreptitiously snap pictures of his own, she gathered her things from the closet and other drawers. He tensed when she went to the closet, as he hadn't been there yet, but she didn't indicate that anything was amiss. "Why don't you have some of these in frames?" He held up one of Summer and her in formal dresses. They appeared to be in their mid-teens. "This is a special occasion?"

Sadness clouded her irises, and she turned away quickly. "No. Sometimes Summer and I dressed up because we wanted to." She slid the lone nightstand several feet, covering her upset with physical work. "I just need Summer's records, and then we can go."

She knelt down, a metal nail file in hand. He watched as she used it to pry up a linoleum tile, and then she lifted a section of the subfloor. "Did you stash a safe in the floor?"

"Where else would you put one? Closets and behind paintings or panels are too obvious. Nobody looks in the floor." She lifted out several small lockboxes before reaching into the void.

He went closer to watch, but she spun the dial too quickly for him to see the combination. Once open, she extracted a thick accordion folder. There was nothing else in the safe. She closed it, replaced everything, and stood up. He caught her as she swayed. She dropped the folder to hold onto him.

"Thanks."

"For the time being, no kneeling, and be sure to get up slowly."

"Yes, Sir. Can you move the table back for me?"

He made sure she had her balance back before doing the strong man work. "Let's head out, Sugar. We're both ready for an early bedtime."

David maintained a subdued tone for the remainder of the evening, coddling Autumn as much as she would allow until they both went to sleep. He liked sharing a bed with her. Since she was within arm's reach, she couldn't possibly get into trouble.

The next morning, she woke early, and they argued as they ate breakfast.

"Take the day off, Sugar. You were in a car accident. People will understand."

The scraping of a knife across toast communicated intense irritation, and the heat in her eyes threatened to blacken the toast. "It was a fender-bender. I'm fine, and I'm going to work. I don't give a rip what people do or don't care about."

"You didn't sleep well," he pointed out. It was a rather reasonable point.

"I slept fine. I got up at two, took some more ibuprofen, and went back to sleep." She washed two more pills down with coffee. "I'm not even all that sore."

If reasonable wasn't going to work, then he'd appeal to the submissive side that should delight in her Dom taking care of her. "I will give Summer's files and your consent form to Tess. You don't have to worry about it."

She gestured across the table with a butter knife. "If you don't want to loan me a car, just say so. I can ride in with you, and Julianne can take me to see Summer and then home."

"You're staying with me tonight."

"Negative. Sir, I like you, but we just started going out. I don't want to be one of those couples who are glued to each other and get a blended name like Davumn or Auvid. See? It doesn't even work with our names. I need personal space, and so do you. It's healthy to want some time apart. I'm going home tonight, and we'll go to the game together Wednesday." She polished off her food with gusto, and he was glad to see that she felt well enough to eat.

"What about Tuesday?"

"Julianne's mom invited me to a purse party. Or maybe it was a kitchen party? I committed to it weeks ago. As much as I'd like to, I can't cancel." She helped herself to more bacon. "She'll track me down with the catalog and order forms, and she knows where I live."

He snagged the last slice of bacon before she polished it off. "But she's probably afraid of your neighborhood, so you've got that working in your favor."

She laughed, which effectively ended the disagreement without David getting his way. This was not how D/s relationships were supposed to work. He gave the orders, and she obeyed whether or not she agreed. Of course, if she let him have that much control over her at this early stage, their relationship was doomed to fail. He needed a woman who knew her own mind and who would advocate for what she wanted.

And she had a point: They'd been together for just over a week, and it was unreasonable to expect her to spend every moment with him. Jesse would be busy for the next couple days.

He called Jesse at lunch to bust his chops. "Hey, buddy. I wanted to warn you that Autumn is aware that someone has been in her apartment. That's sloppy work to not put the envelopes and the sofa cushion back the way she had it."

"What the fuck? I put everything back."

"Well, she noticed things out of place. I tried to convince her that she was seeing things, but—man—she has the place set up as well as any paranoid nutjob we've ever run into." He scanned lines of account data while talking.

"Wait until your girlfriend hears you called her a nutjob." Jesse grunted. "She's skipping lunch today. Did you not pack her anything?"

"No. Where is she?"

"The little diner around the corner. She's with a bunch of ladies from CalderCo."

"And she's not eating?"

"That's what I said. Listen, I put the mail and the cushions back exactly. She had some letters turned different ways, and I made sure to put them back exactly the way she had them. And the sofa—she had some weird fold thing she does with the cover to keep the cushions level. I put it back, David."

It didn't make sense. While it was unlike Jesse to mess up a search, there was no denying that her place had been disturbed. He sighed. "Why would someone else break into her place and look around?"

"Don't know. I'll put Dean on it."

David agreed that they needed reinforcements. "Oh— before you go—I found a box of photographs on her dresser. How did you miss those?"

"There were no pictures anywhere. I looked in every box, drawer, and cupboard. Nada."

She must have hidden those things in the floor as well. "Where did you find her 'Go' bag?"

"Upper right shelf in the closet. It was behind a bunch of stuff that looks like it belongs to Summer."

"Okay. You're going to have to do another search. She hides things under the floorboards. There's one under her nightstand. I'm taking her to a baseball game Wednesday night, so do it then."

Jesse sighed. "You're not keeping her with you tonight?"

"She won't stay. She came up with a thoughtful argument that contained evidence about how our names don't sound right blended together." David paused on a line of text. "I gotta go, bro. Call Dean."

He hustled down the stairs to the IT cave where Malcolm was hiding. When people who knew anything about computers were readily available to a workforce, tons of problems spontaneously cropped up. Yet when people had to file work orders, so many things took care of themselves. Keeping Malcolm out of sight meant he could work on his assignment uninterrupted.

As expected, he found Malcolm holed up in the tiny, windowless room that had more than its fair share of air conditioning pumping into it. Of course, with all the computers and monitors, it needed great ventilation. He wasn't alone, though. Keith Rossetti reclined in an adjacent chair, his feet propped on the table below a monitor.

With a grateful grin, Mal stood up and stretched. "What time is it? I keep forgetting to take breaks."

"It's lunchtime for most of the staff." He held out his hand to Keith. "Hi, Keith. Nice to see you again."

Keith dropped his feet to the floor and leaned forward to shake hands. "Likewise. Mal was filling me in on your adventure this weekend. I'm a little jealous."

David perched on the edge of a table. "I have the box again Wednesday. I was about to invite Malcolm and Darcy, but you and Kat are more than welcome to join us. It seats twelve, so there's plenty of room."

Malcolm frowned. "If he comes, then nothing fun is going to happen with the subs. They'll just giggle and gossip—and we will not benefit from any fun bets."

"Yeah," Keith said dryly. "*I'm* the mood-killer. You're the one who would flip out if you saw your sister give me a blowjob. I can't even discipline her when you're around without you getting a bug up your ass for a week."

"See? This is why I told you not to date her." Malcolm rolled his eyes. A monitor down the line came up with a notice, and he tapped a few keys.

"You told me not to date her because I was an asshole. She cured me of that, so you have no excuses left. Admit it— you think nobody will ever be good enough for Kat." Keith turned to David. "We'll be delighted to join you. I'll let Kat know so she can be sure to get out of court in time, and I call dibs on Mama L for babysitting."

David and Dean had a relationship like this, where they knew one another so well that they rehashed the same arguments and pushed each other's buttons. "Great. Malcolm?"

He flashed a regretful frown. "I have to pass. Darcy has a client in town, and we're doing the business dinner thing."

Keith rubbed his hands together. "I wonder what interesting challenge Kat and Autumn will come up with?"

"None." David regretfully imparted the grim news. "Autumn invited my father. She's under the impression that spending time together will help us mend fences, build bridges, or some other architectural feat."

Keith greeted that news with a thoughtful frown. "I have a shit relationship with my parents too. One thing that rocks about being with someone so positive is that she can push you to do things, like give someone a chance, when you don't want to. What's the worst thing that can happen?"

Honestly, David didn't think anything bad would happen. His father always behaved in mixed company. "I guess we'll see." He turned to Malcolm. "I actually came down because I found something, and I want your opinion." He took over one of the keyboards, tapping out commands to bring up the data he wanted to share.

Malcolm's eyes moved over the lines of data. Keith moved to get a better view, and David stepped aside to let him see. Both men had more experience with these types of crimes than David did.

David shared his findings thus far, more for Keith's benefit. "Someone is going into the accounts after the fact and changing numbers. It looks like money is being moved around until it's 'lost' in the system, and then the thief can transfer it to a private, untraceable account. It's almost genius."

"Yeah." Malcolm scratched his chin as he read. "All of the transactions happen before or after hours, or during the lunch hour."

Keith pointed out several codes. "Either every person on staff is involved in a conspiracy to commit embezzlement, or someone has other people's logins and passwords. These are all from different accounts."

David was more inclined to believe theory two. "Can you trace where the logins are occurring?"

"I can do better than that," Malcolm said, his fingers flying over the keyboard. "I can cross-reference it with arrival times, departure times, and sick days. I can also sync attendance lists for scheduled meetings. That way we'll find the transactions that happen during business hours."

David and Keith leaned forward expectantly.

Malcolm paused and shot a dirty look over his shoulder. "It's going to take a few days. That's a shitload of data."

He and Keith leaned back in unison.

"You made it sound like the information was forthcoming." Keith smacked Malcolm's shoulder hard. "I got all excited about getting to arrest someone."

David had looked forward to clearing Autumn of all suspicion so he could concentrate on finding out her secrets. "I have something that you might be able to do." He showed Keith the pictures of the photos he'd taken at Autumn's apartment. "I think her dad was a shady character. Maybe you can run him through the database?"

Keith swiped through the selection. "Do you suspect him of something?"

"He's deceased. Autumn said his name is Brian Sullivan. Maybe you can turn up something that will shed some light on why she's only existed for six years. I don't think it has bearing on this case, but I want to know." So many questions remained unanswered, and there was a lot Autumn didn't know about her own life. Things she said and habits she'd developed didn't sit right with him. Something more was going on. At the heart of the issue lay the fact that David wanted to fix it for her. "It's personal."

Keith forwarded several of the images to his work email. "I'll run them, and I'll call you if I get a hit."

"Thanks."

On the way back upstairs, he stopped by the cafeteria and snagged a couple of lunches. Autumn most likely thought she was staring at more financial problems with her forthcoming hospital bills and the cost to fix her car, but that was no excuse to skip meals. His phone rang, the call from his mechanic friend, as soon as he got back to his office.

"Eastridge."

"David, this is Larry. I've taken a look at the car, and you're not going to like this."

"It's a piece of shit?" That wasn't news.

Larry chuckled. "I've seen worse. Anyway, I banged out the dent. That's as good as it's gonna get, but then when I put it up to do a general systems check, I found that the brake lines had been cut."

The urge to kill something presented first, but he channeled that violent rage into the need to do something productive. "How long would the brakes work after the lines are cut?"

"It would take a couple stops before the fluid ran out. She was dry when the accident occurred. There was no way she was stopping."

Red and violent hues clouded his vision. The accident hadn't been her fault. Who the fuck would want to hurt Autumn? For the most part, she was quiet and kept to herself. Nobody could have a reason to hate her enough to want to cause her serious harm—or even death. "Document everything. Send pictures, and save the parts. I'll get them when I pick up the car. When will you have it fixed?"

The sounds of tapping on a keyboard came through the line. "I have to notify the authorities, but once they sign off, I can have it fixed in about three hours."

David didn't want this going out on a general alert. "I'm going to give you the name and number of a couple FBI agents I'm working with on this. Call Keith Rossetti, and if he's not available, try Jordan Monaghan." He rattled off the numbers before thanking Larry and ending the call.

"Are you all right?"

He looked up to see Autumn standing on the threshold, her hand on the frame and concern marring her forehead. "Come in and close the door." He gestured to the seat across the table. "I thought we were having lunch together today?"

The concern deepened, but she also harbored a bit of mischief in those green eyes. "We never had a conversation about that. You're my boss. I think it would look a little weird if we spent our lunch hours huddled around your desk. People might think we're sleeping together."

With a chuckle, he motioned to the salad and sandwiches he'd picked up. "I haven't eaten. Have you?"

"No, but I'm not hungry. Did you not notice how much I ate this morning?"

He had, but he knew better than to comment. A healthy appetite in a woman was sexy, but women tended to see such things differently. Until he knew how she'd take it, he kept such observations to himself. "That was six hours ago. I insist you eat something."

Reluctantly, she took a ham sandwich and unwrapped it. "You never answered my question."

Since he wasn't in the habit of giving out information, he probably hadn't. "Which was?"

"Are you all right? You looked troubled when I came in."

How much should he tell her? If he were in her position, he'd want to know that his brake lines had been tampered with. "My mechanic called. He said your brake lines had been cut, so there was no way you were stopping when that car pulled in front of you. The accident wasn't your fault."

"Cut? Who would cut my brake lines? And why?" She put down the sandwich. "It doesn't make sense."

"Where did you go after you left my apartment?" The parking garage under his place was guarded, not that it mattered. Given the timeline, the tampering had happened sometime after she'd left his place.

"I went directly to Sunshine Acres. The car was fine. I was there for about twenty minutes before you called, and then I left. I'm guessing it happened there. It doesn't make sense. Who would go to a convalescent center—really it's full of geriatric patients—and do that?" She leaped to her feet and paced in front of the desk, taking small nibbles of the sandwich as she thought. At least she was eating. "Maybe it's the same person who broke into my apartment."

David didn't want to go down that road because it would lead to revealing some uncomfortable truths he wasn't ready to share. He knew Jesse wouldn't do anything. Jesse—he was the key. "Sugar, my mechanic is notifying Keith or Jordan, and I'll follow up with this additional information. We'll get to the bottom of it. In the meantime, you can stay with me."

She stopped pacing and regarded him warily. "David, I can't do that. I like you. I really like you, but there are times when I need my personal space or I'll go crazy. I promise I'll be careful. I'll call you and text you and report in, but I won't go into hiding, and I won't use you as a shield."

If Jesse hadn't been assigned to follow her, he would have fought harder to get his way. He'd have played the Dom card and ordered her to do what he wanted, but he knew when to stop pressing. Autumn was a strong, capable woman who refused to be intimidated. He respected the hell out of that, but he was going to protect her whether she wanted to be protected or not.

"Fine. Sit and eat. Tell me about your morning."

"My morning?" She sat. "I got the files you requested and put them in the shared folder. Then I went to acquisitions and chatted with Julianne. She demanded proof that I'm feeling okay. She's almost as bad as you with that stuff." She paused to chew and swallow. "I played a lot of solitaire and read an article about something called Resting Bitch Face. It explains several people I've met. Mostly I was bored. You really don't give me much to do. I could still be doing my accounting work and be your assistant."

"No." Not only did he enjoy having her where he had unlimited access, but he didn't want her touching accounts until this matter was resolved. "I need you."

She rolled her eyes. "Sir, that was cheesy, but sweet."

"It was neither." He hadn't meant to sound maudlin, but she'd read correctly into his tone. "I need an assistant, and you're excellent at the job."

Finishing the sandwich, she wiped her hands on the miniscule napkin and put the wrappings in the trash. "You're pretty self-sufficient. Most of the stuff you need, you get without involving me. I feel like I'm spinning my wheels and wasting the company's time. I wish you'd give me more to do."

"Would you be offended if I sent you to my apartment to make dinner? That way, when I get home, we could eat, and you'd already be naked." He meant it as a joke, but her face darkened.

"Don't be an ass. I'm in accounting, David. I like my job, and I take pride in my work. I like to be productive. I may be your girlfriend, but that doesn't mean I will let you devalue me by suggesting that I belong naked and in the kitchen."

Oh, he'd stepped into it big time. He hadn't meant to walk that minefield. "Sugar, I didn't mean—"

"And that's another thing." She stood and stared down at him, irritation and hurt mixing behind her eyes. "At work, you need to call me by my name. You mean 'Sugar' as a term of endearment, I know, but when you use it here, it's demeaning. And it's not quite a term of endearment, either, if you recall your reasons for choosing the name in the first place."

He hesitated. He'd chosen it because she had a sweet ass, but he didn't know if now was the time to acknowledge that. He got to his feet and spoke from the heart. "Autumn, I don't do lines very well, and I think I may have crossed a few too many too quickly. You're mine—my sub, my girlfriend, my lover—and you're my assistant. I can't look at you and not see the total package. I never meant to make you feel devalued or demeaned. I'm sorry." Perhaps he was more like his father than he was comfortable admitting. He'd grown up feeling that way, and he'd never meant to make anyone—especially someone he cared for so deeply—suffer like that.

Her frown didn't ease. "There's a lot more to my package than that." She held up a hand when he tried to speak. "Don't. You can be very suave and persuasive, but not generally with words. That's not your strong suit. You're a man of action. I get that, so I'm going to let you prove with your actions that you know there's more to me. That's the truth I want you to prove. Don't let me down."

Chapter Fifteen

David kept his promise to make sure she was given productive tasks for the next two days, and he had plenty of meetings to keep him busy. Autumn didn't know when he had the time to do the job for which he'd been hired, and after each meeting, he seemed increasingly contemplative. She wished he felt comfortable enough to use her as a sounding board, but she understood why he didn't.

When she breezed into his apartment building on time for once, she hoped to find him pleasantly surprised. But when he opened the door, his first reaction was bafflement. He greeted her with a hug and a brief kiss. "You're early."

"I thought you said six?" With a frown, she glanced at the clock on the bookshelf. "It's six o'clock now."

"Yeah, but for you, that usually means six-fifteen at the earliest."

She gave him a sour look. "I can leave and come back if you want."

He herded her through the threshold. "Not necessary. How was your meeting with Tess?"

When Autumn had left work early to meet with the neurologist, she hadn't harbored high hopes. It turned out to be a good thing. "She looked through the files and did some basic tests. She didn't say anything I haven't already heard. Summer has a closed-head injury, and they don't know enough about how the brain works to know why she's in the coma or how to wake her up. She said she wanted to look into a few options, but she didn't want to make promises. Thanks for trying, though."

His face fell, which surprised Autumn.

She put her hand on his cheek. "Sir, it was a long shot, really. Every few months, they do a fresh workup on Summer—brain scans, blood tests, everything—but they never find anything new. I used to get my hopes up, but I've learned not to. It's just too disappointing."

"But you were excited when I told you she was coming." He kissed her palm and held her hand.

True. She had let her hopes elevate a little, but sometime in the next day, she'd reasoned with herself. "I was mostly excited that you cared enough to ask a friend for a huge favor like this—for me. I—It's—Nobody had ever done something like this for me. Which brings me to something I wanted to talk to you about before we go." She glanced around the apartment. "Where is your dad? I thought he was going to the game?"

"He is. He'll be meeting us there. Malcolm and Darcy weren't able to make it, but Keith and Katrina will meet us there as well. I'll get my keys." Dropping her hand, he turned away and went to the kitchen counter. "That's what you wanted to talk to me about? You thought I told my dad not to come?"

The thought had crossed her mind more than once, but she didn't think he'd go through with it. "No, actually, I wanted to apologize." She followed him and dropped her purse on the dining room table. "I was out of line Monday. I flew off the handle when I really shouldn't have. I overreacted."

He tapped a key on the granite surface as he thought. "You were upset, and you had reason to be. Someone cut your brakes lines. That's serious shit. I've been sneaking out of the office every day to make sure they're okay, but that doesn't cover when you're at Sunshine Acres."

All her office friends had been shocked to hear about the car accident, and they'd been so supportive since then. She hadn't shared more details. Nobody needed to know that the accident hadn't been an accident. "I meant the other stuff. You don't demean me or make me feel devalued. I know you want to take care of me. That's part of who you are, and I like that about you, but I grew up learning to take care of myself. It's going to take me some time to get used to letting you protect me."

He came closer and took her hands in his. "Still, you made some good points. I shouldn't call you pet names at work. It's unprofessional, and it can create problems in the way people perceive your skills."

Okay, it was nice that he recognized and acknowledged the line between their professional and personal relationships. But she had to be more honest. Isn't that what he'd asked her to do? It wasn't an easy path to navigate, and she took a careful step. "I also am a little afraid, Sir. I don't want to come to rely on you too much. You're not from around here, and you'll be leaving. I'm okay with the built-in expiration date—I went into this without blinders on—but I think if I let myself depend on you the way you want, I'm just going to get my heart broken. This is supposed to be fun, not serious. Some of the things you're asking from me—those are serious things." Not to mention that she'd already slipped up and fallen for him. And then she'd stupidly uttered those three dumb words during a scene. At least he seemed to have forgotten them.

Though he didn't release her hands, he stared out the fabulous floor-to-ceiling windows that let him look out upon the cityscape. His mind was probably back home, imagining what it would be like to return to his normal daily routine. Then he pressed his lips together, firmly resolute, and met her gaze. "Maybe this started off that way, but it's not like that anymore. Not for me. When this case is done, I don't want to leave you here. I've hated not being able to spend time with you for the past two days. I can't imagine not seeing you or hearing your voice. This doesn't have to end when the case is over, not unless you want it to, because I don't, Autumn. I don't want to walk away from you and what we have."

She launched herself at him, and he held her tightly. Once again, she felt the enormity of what he hadn't said. One day soon, he would find the courage to take that step, just as she would find the courage to come clean about the side of her life she was keeping from him.

They met up with Keith and Katrina at the huge tiger statue where Darcy had made them all take pictures. This time, Keith was the sentimental one, insisting they get pictures in all sorts of combinations—both women, both men, all four, and individual. David cooperated enthusiastically, though Autumn thought it was overkill.

She pulled David aside on the way in. "Is he doing surveillance or something, and the person he wanted pictures of was in the background?"

He laughed. "I think he's one of those record-the-moment people. It's okay. I like having more pictures of you on my phone. This way I can rotate which shot of your gorgeous self is my wallpaper. I should get a picture of your ass." He stopped, and when she stopped with him, he motioned for her to continue. "Keep walking, Sugar. That skirt hugs your curves in a very dangerous way."

She couldn't believe she was doing it, but she resumed walking along the concourse. As outlandish as the idea sounded, she put a little extra wiggle in her walk. Moments later, he caught up. "Did you get what you want?"

"Yep."

"Can I see?"

"Maybe later."

"Why not now?"

The impishness of his expression glassed over. "Hi, Dad."

"David." Mr. Calder shook his son's hand before greeting Autumn. "Autumn, it's a pleasure."

David introduced Keith and Katrina, and more cordial handshaking happened before they entered the suite. Tonight, it was set up differently. Last time, David had ordered food delivered halfway through the game, but this time, a caterer had already visited. Drinks and platters of hors d'oeuvres were set along a buffet counter on the side. Like Katrina and Keith, Autumn slowly scanned the room, taking it all in.

"Dad, you didn't have to do this. Thanks. It was thoughtful." Some of David's neutral demeanor vanished, and it made Autumn's heart sing.

"Yes, Bill, thank you so much. It's very generous." Keith smiled, which meant he looked a lot less dangerous. Luckily he seemed happy most of the time.

Autumn and Katrina echoed the sentiment.

Mr. Calder flashed a benevolent smile, and Autumn wondered if he'd done this to be manipulative. It fit with the way David talked about him. Then she shook the thought away. She was letting his negative attitude taint her impression of the situation, and she needed the opposite to happen—she needed David to recognize and appreciate the good in his father.

"Go ahead and dig in. Opening pitch is in ten minutes." Mr. Calder took the first plate, and began filling it.

Autumn looked to David, who took two plates and held one out, but when she went to take it, he didn't release his grip. "Unless you're okay with me choosing for you?"

Lowering her gaze, she let go of the plate. Joy vibrated through her body. "I'd like that, Sir. Would you like me to get you a drink?"

"I'll have a beer. Get yourself something, Sugar, but no alcohol. The doctor said to avoid it for a few weeks." He kissed her cheek and turned away to fill the plates.

Outside the suite, in the box seats, they sat in a line, with Autumn between David and Katrina. Mr. Calder sat on David's other side, and Keith guarded the aisle.

Katrina set her plate on her lap, threw her head back, and sighed with pleasure. "I love my kids, but it's so nice to not have little fingers grabbing food off my plate." Keith tried snagging a chicken wing, but Katrina slapped his hand—hard. "Get your own."

With a smartass smirk curving his lips, he took the wing anyway. "I love it when you think you're in charge. It's cute."

"For every wing you take, I'm pushing the wedding back one month."

Keith shrugged. "I'll tell Mama L everything, and you'll get one of those lectures that start with 'Katrina Marie.' See how well that plan works for you."

Katrina sighed and turned to Autumn. "I swear my parents like him better than me sometimes. My mom will spontaneously bring over one of her famous Italian dishes or homemade ice cream, and it turns out that Keith had called earlier to rave about her cooking."

They seemed like a happy couple. Autumn smiled. "It's great that your parents like him. Are you close with his as well?"

Keith laughed, the highly amused kind that indicated trouble.

"No," Katrina said. "They like me, though, especially his mom. She helped save my life one time, and ever since then, she likes to keep in touch to make sure we're all doing well."

"She's happy that we've adopted Angie and Corey, my sister's biological kids." Keith and Katrina exchanged a significant look, and Autumn concentrated on eating her dinner of finger foods.

David put his hand on her leg, but he continued discussing baseball with his father. The in-depth analysis was beyond her, and that was okay. David was reconnecting with his father over a shared love.

"The adoption was finalized yesterday," Katrina continued. "It was the first time I ever cried in court. When the judge pronounced us a family, I couldn't help it. Angie is almost five, and Corey is sixteen months. Anyway, she hugged me so tightly and petted my hair—and she called me 'Mom' for the first time."

"And she called me 'Daddy.'" Keith beamed. "If she didn't already have me wrapped around her cute little finger, that would have done it. Katrina's family was there, and we took a ton of pictures. God—even my parents showed up. I was shocked."

Katrina turned to Autumn. "It was one of the best moments of my life. I know Corey won't remember, but I hope Angie will. My first memory is from when I was about that age—four-and-a-half. I was wearing a dress with a long tulle skirt, and so were my older brothers. They had agreed to be backup dancers for me, and I remember being so ecstatic. They couldn't dance for shit, but they tried so hard." She chuckled, most likely picturing it in her head. Then she smiled at Autumn. "What is your earliest memory?"

Always content to let people talk about themselves, Autumn had to scramble to answer that unexpected question. She had planned to congratulate them, not share her own experience. She tried that route first. "Congratulations. I'm sure she'll remember it. I mean, it's a huge deal. Does she remember her mother?" Okay, maybe that interested her more. Autumn not only lacked memories of her mother, she didn't have pictures to look at and wonder what her mother was like.

"My sister is in prison for the next decade or so. We take the kids to visit every month," Keith said. "But my sister wasn't a great mom, so Angie doesn't really want anything to do with her. I don't blame her. My earliest memories are of Savannah, and they aren't pleasant. Corey doesn't remember her at all. He'll usually interact with her freely."

Katrina put a hand on Autumn's arm. "David tells me that you're close with your sister like I was with my brothers before they decided little sisters were passé. I bet your first memory involves her."

Now that she had some time to consider, Autumn remembered. "I was in a room that my dad had rented, and I couldn't sleep. My sister, Summer, and I were sharing a bed, and I snuggled into her because I was always afraid in a new place. I remember her hugging me close and telling me that everything was going to be all right. And it was."

David squeezed her hand, and when she looked at him, sympathy and understanding blazed from his eyes. Like Summer's hug, it made her feel better, like she'd be safe as long as he was around. She liked that feeling.

The rest of the night was filled with friendly and fun conversation. Autumn left feeling as if she'd made a new friend in Katrina. On the way home, she held David's hand.

"Stay the night," he said.

"I can't." She wanted very badly to stay with him. "I'm exhausted, and I didn't bring my things. How about tomorrow? I can come over after work, and we can spend the whole evening together. Alone."

"What about Summer? Don't you want to stop off and see her?"

Autumn had planned to call in sick, but she couldn't tell him that now. He'd never leave her side. He'd probably drag her back to the ER for more scans. She shrugged. "I'll take a long lunch and eat it with her—if that's okay with my boss?"

He kissed her passionately. "It's okay with your boss."

Autumn dragged herself from bed well before dawn. Though she didn't hold out hope for money being in the gallery's safe—all transactions were likely done electronically—she needed there to be. Ben might be able to fence the goods they'd steal, but Autumn couldn't afford to be part of that. Plus she didn't trust Ben enough to part company without her payment for services rendered. There was no honor among thieves.

This was going to have to go toward rent. Her landlord had served the final warning with a date for eviction proceedings, so that meant she needed to catch up. If she didn't get enough from this job, she would need to take another, and it would have to be one with a larger payout.

After that, she'd start thinking about paying David back for the repairs on her car.

The drive to Royal Oak didn't take as long because rush hour was still two hours away. By that time, she planned to be on her way home. She'd call off work, pay her rent, and go see Summer. Later, she'd contact Ms. B. to see if she had any Domina jobs available. To be honest, Autumn was finding that she really loved being in the submissive role with David as her Dom. She didn't relish having to pick up a flogger and be the boss again. It had always been a role for her, an act that she hadn't minded until now.

She parked at a meter, but she didn't feed it quarters. It wouldn't be enforced until six, and she'd be gone by then. Several other cars were there, workers from the coffee shops and bakeries in the area. Ben met her at the back door of the gallery. It was around the corner from the main strip, and access to the secured rear door was off the small alley and next to an industrial-sized trash bin.

"Good to see you. Any problems?" He greeted her with a brief smile, and his gaze never stopped scanning the area.

"Nope. Let's do this." She extracted a torsion wrench and a hook pick. Inserting the torsion wrench a little, she tested the give to see whether the lock opened clockwise or counterclockwise. It had a firmer stop when she wiggled it clockwise, so that meant she needed to work it in the opposite direction. She applied a constant, slight force, and carefully inserted the hook pick.

Slowly, she counted the pins and tested their give, adjusting her torque a little so that she could push them up and have them spring back down. Next, she pushed the last pin—the most stubborn one—until the faint *click* told her that it had set. Then she tested it to make sure it had set correctly. The lock had six pins, so she repeated the process five more times. With all the pins set, her torsion wrench turned easily, and the door opened.

The guard, as expected, was sound asleep in the break room. Next to the door, a keypad counted down the seconds until the alarm would sound. Ben punched in a code, and the small red warning light turned green. They crept down a short hall and into the storage room.

Autumn quietly closed the door to dampen any sound they might make. Ben's target was in the safe, so she got out her stethoscope and set her pad and pencil on the floor. The pad showed two line graphs, which she'd need a little later. This safe was made of an alloy that didn't conduct sounds as well as a safe made of metal, but that really only mattered to beginners. Though she estimated, based on the make and model of the safe, that it had five numbers in the combination, she needed to test it to make sure. She placed her stethoscope near the dial surface and twirled the dial. As she did so, she moved the bell end around to find the best amplification.

Turning the dial counterclockwise, she listened for two clicks close together. Once she found the spot, she repeated this twice more to verify it. Then she parked the wheels, positioning the dial 180 degrees opposite so that she could pick them up to find out if there were actually five numbers in the combination. Ben hovered nearby, giving her the signal to get moving. She ignored him. Breaking into a safe like this was a precision operation. She needed silence and no distractions. His part had been easy—reconnaissance. Plus, he was the one who wanted the item. Beyond the fact it was a painting by an up-and-coming Phoenix artist, Autumn didn't know anything about it. Not only did she not need to know, but she didn't care.

After she confirmed there were five numbers in the combination, she prepared to figure out what they were. Setting the dial to zero, she listened for clicks and recorded them on the graph. When watching people crack safes on the big screen, Autumn was always amazed that they never showed the math part of safecracking. She'd always excelled at math.

She found the first two numbers and was heading for the third, when the sound of the back door opening ruined her concentration. Ben wasn't the type who could handle a physical threat, and neither was she. Nonetheless, her father had taught her to react quickly. The front door wasn't where she wanted to exit, but she would do it to avoid arrest. She grabbed her pad and pencil, and she tucked her stethoscope away. Ben froze, his gaze darting between the back and front as he tried to figure out an exit plan. The store room where they hid had one door and a window. Autumn was at the window in seconds. It was a slim one, clearly not up to code or meant to be used as a fire exit. Ben was going to need to squeeze his larger-than-average frame out. She could get him out of this, but not without some serious scrapes and bruises. If they ran DNA tests, he'd better hope that the government didn't have a match hiding in their database.

A box cutter sat on top of a pile of cardboard boxes that had been flattened. Intending to use it to slice the screen open, she snatched it up, but a big hand closed around her wrist. "Drop it."

She followed the hand up a long arm to a face that did not belong to a police officer. He looked familiar, and Autumn realized that she'd seen him before, but she hadn't realized he'd been following her. He was damn good at his job. She knew without a doubt that this was Jesse Foraker, one of David's SAFE Security partners. Muscular and toned, he had a military bearing and an alpha-male attitude. His pale blue eyes brooked no refusal, and so she relaxed her grip. "What are you doing?"

"Stopping you from making an even bigger mistake." Like her, he spoke quietly, and she realized that he didn't want to wake the guard either.

Glancing back at Ben, she recognized Dean Alloway, another of David's partners according to the SAFE Security website, with a gun pointed at her partner. Ben held his hands in the air, and he looked like he was ten seconds from pissing his pants.

"Someone spotted you already. They called in a suspicious activity report to the police. We need to go now." Dean used the gun to indicate that Ben should leave through the back door.

Autumn didn't want to follow—Jesse didn't have a gun pointed at her—but since the operation was blown, she didn't see another alternative. She followed Dean, and Jesse brought up the rear. Once they got outside, Dean motioned down the alley and nailed Ben with a hard stare. "Scram."

Ben ran off, keeping a pace faster than Autumn would have thought possible. Sheer terror could do that for a person. She turned to Jesse. "Thanks for the warning. I don't suppose you could fail to mention this to David?"

He held out a hand. "Give me your keys. Dean will take care of your car, and you're coming with me."

She didn't want to go with him, but she didn't see where she had options. He had saved her from being found by the authorities in the midst of a robbery, but he could still turn her in. His company had a good relationship with law enforcement. If she wasn't mistaken, it was Jesse who had introduced David to Jordan, Keith, and the other members of the FBI that David now called friends. Not only that, they were bigger, stronger, and trained in physical combat techniques. This wasn't a battle she could win, and that rankled almost as much as the fact that David had set his watchdogs on her in the first place.

They already had the upper hand, so she resolved not to give them anything else. Schooling her features to remain relaxed, she handed her keys to Dean. "Be kind to Poco. He sometimes takes a little sweet talking to get going, and be sure to check it out first. Someone cut my brake lines a few days ago."

"I'm aware." Dean took the keys. "Autumn, David already knows everything. There's no point in trying to hide it."

She looked from Dean to Jesse. "How long have you been following me?"

Dean left without responding, and Jesse put his arm around her shoulders to steer her in the opposite direction. "My car is this way."

Five minutes later, she found herself sitting with her right hand cuffed to the hardware that allowed the car seat to slide back and forth. Restrained like this, she couldn't ditch him at an intersection and run for the hills. Of course, he knew where she lived and worked, so there was no point in running anyway. With Summer stuck here, she couldn't disappear and start over elsewhere. "I'm cooperating," she pointed out.

Jesse started the big, black SUV that was a twin to David's. His stone-faced expression didn't crack. "I appreciate that."

She was quiet for the first twenty minutes as she thought about David's reaction. He was going to be pissed, no doubt about it, and it was unlikely that he'd turn her in, but what did this mean for their relationship? This proof of his lack of trust spoke volumes. Did this mean he thought she had stolen the three million dollars from his father's company, even after she'd turned over all her files?

Before her worries could spike out of control, she turned to Jesse. He was a handsome man, somehow harder than David, and his hair was shaved so close to his head that she couldn't tell whether it was light brown or blond. "He's had you following me since I spotted him and called him a stalker, hasn't he?"

"Yes." Jesse's monosyllabic response didn't make her feel better.

This whole time, he hadn't trusted her. Had he only slept with her to keep her close? Was everything he'd said and done part of an act designed to get her to reveal where she'd hidden the three million? It was a pointless ruse—she hadn't taken it. If she had three million dollars, she wouldn't need to hire out her skills as a thief or a Domina.

It didn't matter whether David's opinion of her had changed because she no longer knew what had been real between them. How he must have hated having to scene with her and sleep with her—and now the gloves were off. He didn't have to pretend. Her heart broke, and she realized he must have been laughing at her the whole time. Those three words, uttered in the heat of the moment, came back to haunt her. She'd been nothing more than an amusement to him. Well, she wasn't going to explain a thing. She hadn't taken the three million, so there was no proof that could point to her, and she didn't think Jesse and Dean had proof of her intent to rob the gallery.

Heading to David's probably meant an apartment full of mercenaries bent on finding out what had happened to David's father's money. Her father hadn't prepared her for an interrogation. He'd only taught her how to avoid capture. Of course, he couldn't have foreseen mercenaries with the cunning of criminals and the morals of law enforcement. No matter—she could do this. Her heartbreak wouldn't matter to him, so she couldn't let it impair her. The thing she really wanted to know was: How low had David sunk to knock her off guard in order to find money she didn't have?

————

David ran his fingers through his hair again, not caring that it struck straight up. He paced from the huge windows overlooking Ann Arbor's cityscape to the sofa, and back again.

"That's not going to make them get here any faster." Malcolm sat at the dining room table, papers spread out around the laptop he tapped on.

"I'm not ready for this. What the hell was she thinking?"

"You overheard her talking about being good with picking locks and cracking safes. Jesse said he thought she was casing the place, though he wasn't sure which one it was." Malcolm gathered the papers and arranged them neatly in one pile.

This wasn't happening. "But she—she's not like this! She's not the kind of person who breaks into places and takes things that don't belong to her. She's kind and sensitive, shy and—"

"Secretive. Desperate. Don't forget that last one. Desperation will drive people to do things they wouldn't normally consider. And then there's what Keith found out. David, the man who raised her messed her up. You saw the file the FBI has on him." Malcolm closed the laptop and went deeper into the kitchen to pour coffee.

The photo of Autumn's father had returned a hit almost immediately. His name wasn't Brian Sullivan, though that was one of his aliases. And facial recognition had found a match for the photos of Autumn and Summer as children. He dreaded telling her what he'd found as much as he dreaded confronting her about the robbery. He was furious about that, and Autumn didn't react well to his temper.

David followed Mal into the kitchen for coffee. He needed something to help him calm down. Malcolm poured a second mug and handed it over. "Have you thought about the approach you want to use?"

"It's Thursday." He sipped the strong brew. "I'll just ask her." The buzzer sounded. "That'll be them."

A few minutes later, Jesse escorted Autumn through the door. He'd handcuffed her wrist to his. As soon as David locked the door, Jesse unlocked the cuffs. "She behaved. Well, after she misbehaved, I mean."

From the moment she walked in, Autumn watched him. She didn't even look away when Jesse removed the cuffs. David was struck by the sadness and resignation that turned her eyes dull green. He hated seeing her this way, but she'd created this situation, and he couldn't have sympathy for her now. If she had any chance of reforming, he needed to be strong—for her.

"Have you eaten?"

Jesse rubbed his hands together. "Nope. I'm starved."

He'd meant the question for Autumn, but now that he thought about it, he was hungry as well. "Great. Why don't you run out and get breakfast for all of us?"

The sour look on Jesse's face said enough, but he followed up with a verbal response. "I'm not your errand boy."

"I can whip up something." Malcolm disappeared into the kitchen, and the sounds of pots and pans banging hopefully meant a good meal was on the horizon.

"Autumn, have a seat." He indicated the seat at the dining table where he wanted her to sit.

She frowned. "You know, I'd love to stay, but I don't have time. I'm going to be late for work."

"You're working from home today. Now sit." His tone was sharpened steel, and she obeyed, though she didn't bother to lower her gaze to show her submission.

She folded her hands neatly on her lap and stared at them.

He took the next seat, turning it to face hers. "Autumn?"

She met his gaze, and he recognized defensive defiance.

"Would you like some coffee?"

"No. I don't want anything from you."

She was pissed at him? What the fuck? He leaned over her, propping a hand on the back of her chair and crowding her personal space. "You don't get to be pissed at me, Sugar. You're the one who almost got caught robbing an art gallery. Tell me why you did it."

Facing him without fear or acknowledgement of his dominance, she scowled. "No."

He shook his head. "It's Thursday. That means you owe me one direct and fully honest answer."

"You cashed this one in on Sunday. Perhaps you should learn to ask better questions." Now she crossed her arms over her chest and regarded him with a mulish slant to her lips.

He had the urge to blister her ass—for so many reasons, and her backtalk nearly put him over the edge. He shot to his feet and jerked her out of her chair. Holding her by the arms, he gave her one shake. "Don't fuck with me, Sugar. You've earned one hell of a punishment already, and I'm not in the mood to deal with your mouth."

She stared at him, no hint of fear or acquiescence in her eyes. He threw her back into the chair so that she sat down hard, and she only pressed her lips together, a sign that he was in for a long day.

The apartment had fallen silent. Malcolm stared at him, assessing the situation. Jesse had joined him in the kitchen, and he watched as well, though without speculation in his eyes. Jesse knew he'd never hurt her, but Mal didn't know him so well.

The buzzer rang, and Jesse let Dean in. His buddy's clothes were impeccably neat, as always, though he'd been pulled from bed unexpectedly early just as the rest of them had.

He studied Autumn, looking for any chink in her armor and finding nothing. This was going to be difficult, and the direct approach only made her dig her heels in more. He circled back for something less confrontational. "When did you start planning the heist?"

She rubbed her arm where he'd grabbed her. He had no doubt it hurt, but she wouldn't have bruises. He'd held her tighter than that during a scene. Finally she spoke, her voice so soft he knew it carried only to him. "Three weeks ago."

Before they'd met. He heard the subtext. *This has nothing to do with you.* "Who was your accomplice?"

"The man you saw me having coffee with the night you stalked me and I gave you a ride home."

And she'd agreed to go out with him. That had been the beginning of their relationship. "What's his name?"

"Ben. It probably wasn't his real name. I didn't give him mine."

"How did you meet him?"

She shook her head, indicating a refusal to answer. It was likely she had contacts across many criminal sets, and there was no way she was giving them up. They'd probably come after her if she did, so he let it go—for now. "What was your target?"

This time, she shrugged. "He was after a painting."

He frowned. If she didn't know him that well, why would she agree to break into a place that had nothing she wanted? "What were you after?"

"Nothing."

David blinked. He believed her. "Nothing? Then why do it?"

She looked away, gazing at the dawn breaking through the window. It wasn't an evasion, more of an indication that the conversation was over.

"Sugar, I need an answer."

Her head snapped, and he saw that she'd channeled her sadness into vehemence. "You need an answer?" She set a hand on the back of his chair and leaned forward, getting in his personal space. "*You* need an answer? I think not. It's my turn, David. How about you tell me all about who ruined the brakes on my car?"

Taken aback, and not just by the quick change to her Domina persona, David's mouth gaped, and he stared. Jesse would never do that to her.

She rose to her feet, her slow ascent highlighting her dominant position. "Nothing to say? You had me tailed. This whole time, you had someone following me and reporting on what I did and where I went. So, tell me—who was in a better position to cut my brake lines than your man?"

"Jesse didn't tamper with your brakes."

She continued as if he hadn't spoken, her voice sliding down to a silky hiss. "And why would he do that unless it was on your order? It was convenient, having a doctor friend who could take a look at Summer. And the time crunch—that was brilliant. You knew I wouldn't have the records, that I'd need to go back to my apartment for them—that I'd do anything for Summer. It was the perfect leverage, wasn't it? Getting me to confide in you so you could find out and prey upon my weakness. If you wanted me dead, I just don't understand why you didn't kill me outright. You're a mercenary. You have to have experience with assassinations and hiding the body. Did you get off on using me? Was this fun for you?"

Though she tried to hide it, he glimpsed the raw pain that ripped her apart. He also recognized that she'd derailed his interrogation. He rose slowly, mimicking her move and forcing her to step back. Then he gripped her upper arms and hauled her against him. "Jesse didn't tamper with your brakes, and the rest was coincidence."

She snorted. "I suppose he didn't break into my apartment and search it, either."

"I did break in," Jesse said, but he wasn't successful in putting a dent in Autumn's growing rage. "You have a very clean and neat place. And some interesting security measures."

Her body relaxed, and she slid her palms up his chest. "I shouldn't have trusted you in the first place. I knew better, but you fake sincerity very well. And I'm one hell of a target—alone and isolated. You're good at your job, but I'm not stupid, David, and I know what you want from me."

Her tone and the way she melted into his hold were in direct contrast to the substance of her message. David frowned. "What do you think I want from you?"

She broke away abruptly, and he let her go. She turned toward the window, and then she went to stand next to it. "I didn't take the money, and I don't know who did. I break into places and rob safes. Computer hacking isn't my thing. I'd never even used a computer before I started at CalderCo. I gave you everything I had, and I told you that you were barking up the wrong tree. Now I know why you didn't want my help looking through the data. Did you even bother to look at anybody else?"

"Yes." Malcolm set three plates on the table. "We looked at everybody else. Now eat, Autumn, because both of you need to have clear heads, and neither of you do."

Jesse and Dean joined them, each carrying their own plates.

Autumn glanced at the omelet waiting at her seat. Her stomach growled so loudly that he heard it. Shades of indecision flickered over her face, but she opted to join them. Three bites in, she narrowed her eyes at Malcolm. "When did you become a mercenary for SAFE Security?"

"I'm just a tech geek." He smiled cheerfully. "I sit in a dark room in the basement and hack into everybody's files in search of that elusive three million. Unlike you, I'm actually very good with computers. Why hadn't you encountered them before? They're awfully hard to avoid."

She took another bite. "Apparently not."

So many things made sense now. Darcy's comment about being friends "once all this was cleared up" now had context. She'd known they were investigating Autumn, and she'd hoped to see Autumn vindicated. At least she hadn't been faking it. Her father had warned her repeatedly about people who pretend to care. Just when she'd thought it was safe to open her heart and make friends—or fall in love—his advice was proving too valuable. She never should have let down her guard.

Her heart ached. Part of her wanted to get up and leave, but a perverse majority wouldn't let her walk out without David's telling her to go. As long as she was here, there was hope that she might be wrong about him. Perhaps he would take her in his arms and show her how he felt?

Food disappeared from her plate, and she stared at the empty disk.

"Do you want more?" Malcolm's question broke through her increasing melancholy. "I can make another one."

She looked up, staring at him openly. He didn't have a horse in this race, and she didn't get the sense he hated her. But how reliable was her intuition? She didn't get the sense that any of them disliked her, though David's actions certainly indicated hatred. It took a moment, but she reminded herself to answer him. "No, thank you."

Just to get away from David for a minute, she stood and gathered her plate and glass.

"I'll get that." Dean took it from her. "You and David have a conversation to continue."

"We're done talking."

"Sugar—" David tried to take her hand, but she jerked it away.

"Don't touch me."

"Let's go into the living room."

"No." She parked her ass back on the chair and folded her hands on the table. "I can't think of anything more we have to discuss."

"I have questions, and you're going to provide answers. Did your father teach you to pick locks and break into safes?"

She was not answering questions about her father. She'd been a fool to even mention him to David, and now she reverted to tried and true methods of avoidance. "Did your father teach you to be controlling and overbearing?"

His nostrils flared, but she didn't know if she'd scored a direct hit or pissed him off—maybe both. "Autumn, I warned you. Answer me, or I will spank you."

She turned to face him, her chin high, and she challenged his threat. "No, you won't. I won't let you. Perhaps Jesse didn't tamper with my brakes, but he knows who did it, which means you do too."

"Autumn, I swear I didn't see anybody around your car except that woman you talked to." Jesse met her gaze, his pale blue eyes nothing but sincere.

She countered with incredulity. "You were watching my car, but you didn't see who did this? What the hell kind of tail are you?"

"I wasn't watching your car. I was watching you. There's a tree I can stand behind where I have a clear view of you in your sister's room, and unless you're looking for me, you're not going to see me."

With a jolt, she realized that she *had* seen him, but she hadn't thought anything of it. Many people hid out over there to take an emotional break from visiting a loved one. Sunshine Acres had a hospice section, and lots of emotional trauma went on there. She turned away, again staring out the window at the spectacular sunrise. The beauty out there seemed incongruent with what was going on in here.

David grasped her chin, forcing her to face him. "Did you father teach you how to break into places and rob them?"

Was he really going to try this tactic again? Autumn sighed. "My father was a good man. He was kind and caring, always there for me, always supporting and encouraging me. I'm not the one with Daddy issues, David—you are."

He stood swiftly, lifted her up, and threw her over his shoulder. The air rushed from Autumn's lungs, and she was momentarily stunned.

"Are you sure you want to do that?" Dean asked.

"I don't need an audience." In seconds, David had carried her to his room. He tossed her on the bed, where she landed hard.

She put her hand to her stomach. "You took a real chance doing that right after I ate. You almost got to see an encore of my breakfast."

"Get up." The Dom was in the house, and Autumn found herself obeying even when she didn't want to.

She was nervous as all hell. Had he read her mind? Did he know her deepest desires? Did he have Clue One that she needed him to prove that he cared about her?

His grim expression and the hands perched on his hips didn't bode well. "I can't be in a relationship with a woman who keeps secrets—big secrets—from me. Autumn, you either tell me everything right now, or I will release you."

Release her? He'd never given her a collar. She wasn't sure if he'd been a real Sir to her, or if he'd been pretending. It hurt, and she hated herself for being weak. This man had never loved her. He hadn't even bothered to lie to her about it. He'd never given himself to her the way she'd given herself to him. They'd both kept secrets, and many were still hidden. "Then it's official. We're through."

She turned away to hide the way she swiped at the tears spilling down her cheeks. *Don't fall apart in front of him.* She breathed through the pain, but it didn't help. She felt his hands loosely grip her shoulders, and even that light touch sent searing pain directly to her heart. "Autumn, I never used you."

That lie cut deep, and she couldn't take more. She shook him away and faced him, tear-streaked face be damned. "But you did, and I was desperate enough to let you."

She marched into the kitchen, grabbed her stethoscope and lock picking kit, and faced Dean. "Where is my car?"

He studied her face, and she scowled to hide her feelings. Finally he spread his palms. "I dropped it at your apartment and took a cab here."

Great. Now she was walking home. It was only seventeen miles away. No sweat. Malcolm came out as she waited for the elevator. "I'll give you a ride home."

"Thank you, but that's not necessary."

He got on the elevator with her. "Oh, but it is. Darcy would kill me if she found out I didn't."

Chapter Sixteen

"You fucked that up." Dean strolled into the bedroom through the door Autumn had left open. She'd been too upset to want to slam it on her way out. He felt like shit about the way he'd handled the whole affair.

Jesse dragged the chair from the vanity closer to where David sat on the edge of the bed. He swung a leg over to sit backward, and he rested his arms on the seatback. "This is why we let Frankie and Dean handle interrogations. I lack patience, and you not only lack patience, but you have no finesse."

Dean perched on the corner of the bed, creating an intimate triangle. "What did you hope to accomplish by breaking her heart?"

He hadn't meant to break her heart. He'd envisioned the questioning going a completely different way. In his mind, she'd opened up and told him everything, and then he'd held her hand as the others presented the information Keith had dug up on her father. It was going to hurt to hear how deeply he'd betrayed her and her sister, but her Sir would be there to help her weather the emotional storm.

Instead of a hero, he was the villain. This wasn't supposed to happen. He swallowed. "I told her that if she couldn't be honest with me, I would release her. She said it was over, and she left."

Dean winced, and Jesse shook his head. "You asshole. Even I knew she was crying out for understanding." Jesse was known for not caring about a woman's emotional state. He was all about having a good time and moving on. "I tried to help you out, but you blew up every lifeline I threw your way."

Is that what he'd been doing? It had sailed clear over David's head. "I thought you were buying into the way she was trying to control the conversation."

"Usually we're on the same page," Jesse said. "But with her, I'm not sure what book you're reading. I don't think you know, either."

Dean chuckled. "He's in love. Be patient. This is new for David. He's spent the last three years dabbling in emotional entanglements so that he knew exactly when to cut and run."

Nothing they were saying was untrue. However, this time, David hadn't bothered to devise an exit plan. He didn't want out. "Is she out there with Malcolm?"

"No. Malcolm took her home." Dean rubbed his palm on his pants. "We had to assure him that you had no intention of spanking her."

"Maybe she needed me to." David pinched the bridge of his nose and thought about the first time he'd spanked her. She'd displayed attributes of a smart-ass masochist, a submissive who verbally eggs on her dominant. "She's a sometimes-SAM, so maybe the sass was her way of telling me that she needed it."

Jesse snorted. "You were not in a headspace that would allow you to be objective or reasonable. Dealing with a SAM is tricky because she walks a fine line between submission and topping from the bottom. You can't be pissed off when you're in a scene with one. And today is not the right day for a scene."

"Jesse is right—she needed your understanding and acceptance." Dean got up, nervous energy driving him to pace. "It's hard to give when you don't quite trust someone. Has she ever lied to you?"

This was the source of many disagreements. "Besides using a false name the first time we met, no, she hasn't lied. But she hasn't told the whole truth either."

Dean waved away his concerns. "The name thing doesn't count, and you don't always tell someone the whole truth when you're getting to know them."

That's what she had claimed. David didn't like it coming from Dean as much as he'd hated hearing from Autumn. "I needed to know the whole truth about her father."

"She's not ready to give you that." Dean paused by the window. "She doesn't even know the whole truth about him, or about herself. But she told you what you wanted to know about the robbery. That's something, David. She's emotionally skittish—you knew that even before you knew the reasons why. Pushing her like this was wrong. It was too much for her to handle without you giving her the emotional support she needed."

He rubbed his eyes. Lack of sleep hadn't helped him have a clear head. "What now?"

"Now?" Dean tapped the window frame. "Now you and Jesse will pay a visit to the bank in the Cayman Islands where Malcolm traced two hasty transactions. You need to find out whose name is on it."

"It won't be Autumn's." Though he was vehement, he spoke quietly.

"I don't think it will be." Dean turned, crossed his arms, and leaned against the window. "She may be good at some things, but the long con isn't one of them. This is a crazy long con, and whoever did this has an exit strategy, which Autumn does not. She's tied here because of her sister. However, right now, all the evidence we have points directly to her."

"With big, neon signs," Jesse added. "Any court would convict."

Every user account that had been tampered with led them to one computer—Autumn's. The hacks had happened before and after hours, or on days when the account owner was out of the office. Malcolm had traced each transaction to Autumn's desktop. In some cases, she'd signed out of her account, and someone had signed in again minutes later.

David nodded. "What will you be doing while Jesse and I are gone?"

"Following Autumn. Whether she is involved with this or not, someone tampered with her brakes, and someone called in a suspicious activity report that nearly led to Autumn being caught. In all respects, she covered her bases. This robbery should have gone off without a hitch. It was a good plan." Dean wiped a hand across his eyes, the first sign that he wasn't operating at full strength. "And she's being set up at CalderCo. It's too much to be coincidence."

Dean was right. David frowned. "Then you go to the Caymans. I'll stay and watch Autumn."

"Negative." Dean frowned, and his entire demeanor transformed. Nobody would mess with this menacing man. Though David wasn't afraid, he knew he wasn't going to win this argument. Dean was the de facto head of SAFE Security for a reason. "You're too close to this. You'll focus on her and not what's around her. She's seen our faces, so I won't worry about hiding."

This was going to piss her off even more. David closed his eyes. "I'm going over there to talk to her. I can't leave it like this."

Jesse got to his feet. "I'll book a flight with an open-ended return date. Getting information from banks there is extraordinarily difficult."

Autumn spent the rest of the morning crying. By noon, she'd fallen into a deep sleep, and when she woke up, David was sitting on the floor under the window. The back of his head rested against the wall, and he'd closed his eyes.

"What are you doing here?" She wasn't going to ask how he'd been able to come in without a key. He'd probably made a duplicate of hers.

He lifted his head and opened his eyes, but he didn't otherwise move. Profound emotion stained his eyes dark brown. "Making sure you're okay."

"I don't see why you care."

He shook his head. "You're right. It makes no sense."

Disgusted, she sat up and threw off her covers. "You can leave now."

"No."

Her jaw dropped. "No?"

He didn't move. "No. You like to refuse to do what I want, so I'm refusing to do what you want. I want to stay here. I want to know things, Autumn. I need to know why you wanted to rob that gallery. Give me this one thing. Help me understand how the vulnerable, fragile, sassy, resilient woman who wrapped me around her finger is also an accomplished thief."

This part of her life wasn't one she wanted to share with him—not because she didn't trust him, but because she knew he could make her feel ashamed of some of her greatest accomplishments. This was at the core of who she was, and his rejection—even his disapproval—would irrevocably wound her. But maybe that's what it would take to make him leave her alone so that she could rebuild the walls around her heart. She picked at a thread on the hem of her shirt. "If I tell you, will you leave?"

He considered this. His cheeks puffed out, and he exhaled loudly. "No, but after you tell me, I have some things I need to tell you."

This was intriguing. He wanted to open up to her? This was going to be an even exchange? Maybe she'd been wrong about him. Maybe he hadn't been faking it with her. They'd both acknowledged his lack of skill with verbal communication. She dared to let herself hope, but she also knew better than to make a full confession. "Everything I tell you is just a story. Allegedly, it's how I was raised."

"To steal?"

She loved her dad more than anything, but she also knew the way he'd raised her hadn't been completely honest. "Yes. I'm good with puzzles, and I have a light touch. I grew up learning to count cards, pick pockets, and trick people with street scams. As I got older, Dad taught me new skills."

"You mean he taught you and Summer, don't you? Allegedly?"

She looked away. "Yeah, but Summer wasn't great with puzzles. She can't pick a lock or open a safe without a drill or explosives, and she loathes explosives. Also she didn't have a light touch. She was great with art and sculpture, good enough to allegedly do a few forgeries." Thank goodness she'd prefaced this by telling him it was made up. "As much as we loved the challenge, we also hated it. When we were kids, and we didn't know quite what we were doing, it was fun. Once we grew up and got tired of sneaking and lying, we started resisting. Dad never forced us to do a job, but he could be very persuasive, and I had a hard time refusing him anything. Summer is the one who finally convinced Dad to let us stop. We didn't want to live on the run anymore. We wanted to have jobs and maybe enroll in college—normal stuff."

"That was six years ago?" The worry lines between his eyebrows and on his chin were back.

"He left us alone for three years, and then one day, he showed up on our doorstep. God, I was so happy to see him. Summer was too. We were close. Growing up, we only had each other, and we'd missed him terribly." Thinking about what happened made the tears start up again. Grief over loss never quite went away, and sometimes, like now, it washed over her as if it had just happened. She let the waves crash and begin to settle down.

"He wanted you to pull another job." David waited until she had her emotions under control to continue. She was grateful he hadn't tried to hug her. She wasn't sure she could handle it quite yet.

She lifted a hand and let it drop. "We said no. Summer helped me stick to my guns. It was hard, but I refused to help him. He did it anyway. Summer and I were trying to stop him when the accident happened. She crashed into his car on purpose, but then an eighteen wheeler came along and crashed into both cars. Dad's friend—I don't know who was in the car with him—ran away. He died, and Summer...She was just trying to stop him."

"And now you pull jobs to help pay for her care, don't you? That's why you work as a pro Domina as well?" He came to sit on the bed next to her, but he didn't try to touch her.

"Ms. B. was a friend of my dad's. She doesn't like to give me work, but if I call her up and beg enough, she'll throw me something every now and again. Safe clients. You know, most of the models have sex with the clients. I don't." She understood Ms. B.'s reticence, and she shared it herself.

"Why didn't you ask me for money? I would have given it to you." He tried to touch the back of her hand, but she pulled it into her lap and tucked it under her other hand.

"I don't want your money, and if I had started pumping you for it, then you would have thought I was some kind of gold digger. That's not who I am."

He ran a hand through his hair, which already stuck up in a thousand directions. "I'd rather pay for your sister's medical bills than have you end up in prison. You're not a criminal, Sugar."

She didn't want to be, but she couldn't deny the sense of accomplishment she derived from breaking into a place, moving around undetected, and leaving without anyone the wiser. "No, but I do like puzzles. The best gifts my dad ever got me were those safes. Beating them was such a thrill. I loved it." And this morning, she had been in her element opening that safe. Even now, she had an urge to go back just to see if she could crack it. Really, she just needed a few more minutes. "Where does this leave us? Do I still have a job?"

Now he touched her lightly, the trace of a caress on her jaw to turn her to face him. "You definitely have a job, though I'm thinking you should take tomorrow off as well. Come back Monday. Don't take a sick day. I'll tell my dad that I have you working from home. I have to go out of town tomorrow to take care of some things, but I should be back Tuesday or Wednesday. For now, I'll put you back in accounting. And us? I just know I don't want to lose you."

She didn't want to lose him either. Their talk had the opposite effect she thought it might—he believed her, and he didn't want to be finished with her. Opening up to him hadn't driven him away, and it had made her feel closer to him. Though his declaration wasn't much of a clarification, it was enough for now. "We should talk when you get back."

"Yeah." He squeezed his eyes shut and pinched the bridge of his nose.

"Headache?"

"Dread. I have to tell you something, and I know you're not going to like it."

What could he have to say that could possibly be worse? She already knew about his mother and his negative relationship with his father. She rubbed his shoulder. "Is it worse than when you released me?"

He looked up, and the pain in his eyes apologized more eloquently than his words. "I'm sorry about that, Sugar. It was wrong of me, and I won't do it again. I generally learn from my mistakes."

"That's promising." She leaned in to kiss his cheek, but he caught her lips with a tentative brush of his. It felt so good, like coming home, and though he'd kissed her last night, so much had happened since then that it seemed like forever ago. Then he deepened it, and passion exploded. All the pent-up feelings that had built up inside streamlined in the direction of that pressure valve. She ran her fingers through his unkempt hair, and he eased her back until her head hit the pillow.

He touched her—soft caresses over her clothes that teased and had her fumbling for the buttons on his shirt. He wrapped his hands around her wrists, halting her actions, and he ripped his lips from hers. "Wait. Autumn, I have to talk to you first."

She relaxed, and he released his hold on her wrists. "Okay. What's this thing I won't like?"

"There are two things. First, Dean is going to be tailing you while I'm gone. It's for your safety, Sugar, and you don't have a say in this."

For a second, she wondered why he felt she needed someone to watch out for her, but then she remembered the brake lines. And Jesse had said that someone had called the police on her that morning. It could be a coincidence—one perpetrated by a random dickhead and the other by a concerned citizen, but she wasn't a huge believer in coincidence. "Why not Jesse?"

"Jesse is going with me. Dean is trying to get Frankie here so they can switch off. She's wrapping up another case right now, but it may take a few days."

While she wasn't crazy about the idea of being followed, she also appreciated having someone look out for her. "I'm okay with it. Do they want to come in and hang out with me? It can't be fun sitting in a parked car all day. I have a bathroom."

"But if someone is targeting you, I'd rather they not see that you have protection. We want to catch the person doing this."

"Makes sense. This is what gave you a headache?"

"No." He eased his weight from her and sat up. "Let's go in the living room."

She followed him, worried because his tone had gone flat. "Is something else wrong?"

He sat down and patted the cushion. Once she joined him, he opened a manila envelope and poured out the contents. He spread out several pictures. Most were familiar because she recognized the people, but not the pictures.

She picked up the one familiar pair. One depicted her as a four-year-old, and the other was of Summer as a six-year-old. They were grainy because they'd been blown up. "This is from my shoebox. You took my pictures?"

"I took pictures of your pictures."

"You're right—I don't like hearing this. You had no right to do that without my permission." She set them back down and snatched up the one familiar photo of her father. "Why would you do this?"

"For all the reasons you already know and some I can't tell you yet. I wanted to know who you were, why you've only legally existed for six years. It's impossible to be completely off the grid. Autumn, your father wasn't who you thought he was." He dug a photo from the bottom of the pile and handed over a picture of her father that she had never seen.

He was younger, but she recognized his handsome face, sparse freckles sprinkling his cheeks—just like the ones on her face—and the magnetic charm that oozed from his pores. "This is my dad."

"This man's name is Eugene Bowen. He served six years for a string of robberies, though he was suspected of a lot more."

Autumn held her breath. She'd always known that her father's name was an alias. He'd never hidden his true nature, and growing up, they'd frequently changed their names. "So what? I knew he'd spent time in prison. That's why he took such extreme precautions to keep the government away from us."

"You knew his real name?"

She shook her head. "I only knew the names he told me. We used aliases a lot, but we always reverted to the Sullivan name when we were alone."

"That's why you and Summer chose to use it when you came out of hiding?"

"Yes. They're our real names, David. I never lied to you about that."

He smoothed her hair away from her face. "No, you didn't. I'm sorry I doubted you, Sugar. You had no way of knowing it's not your real name."

She bristled at his claim. "Look, just because my dad didn't start out with that name doesn't mean it's not mine. Summer and I grew up with it. It's our name more than Bowen ever could be."

Next he picked up a paper that had FBI letterhead. "Eugene Bowen had a family when he was arrested. He had a wife and two daughters. Summer and Autumn were two and four when he was convicted. His wife, Jennifer Bowen, had information on several important criminals. She cut a deal with the Feds, divorced him, testified, and then disappeared with the kids into WITSEC. He tried to find them when he got out, but he was unsuccessful. So he found two more little girls playing in a yard, and he—"

"No." Autumn shot to her feet. She wasn't going to listen to this tripe. He had no right to denigrate her father's memory. All the previous hurts of the day fed her anger, sharpening it to a dangerous point. Fists clenched, she stomped her foot. "Don't. Get out of my apartment."

He stood, but he made no move to leave. "Sugar, I know this is hard to hear, but I'd rather you heard it from me than from the FBI. The man you knew as Brian Sullivan kidnapped you and your sister. He renamed you, and raised you as his own."

"No." This wasn't real. Why would David say things like this to her? Had his apology been a ruse so he could hurt her even more? She was stupid and sentimental. Her father had warned her about these weak spots that someone would eventually exploit. Damn her for wanting so badly to trust David. Her heart and head felt like they were going to explode. "Get out."

"Sugar—"

"Don't. Don't call me that. I hate you, David. I think you get off on being cruel to me, and it stops now. I never want to see you again. We're through. Now get out before I call the police."

He tried to grasp her shoulders gently, but she circled her arms to sever the contact. Then she lost control. She swung her fists wildly. She'd never been a violent person, and she had no idea how to fight, but some primal force deep inside drove her to hurt him the way he'd hurt her.

Only it didn't quite work that way. David was a skilled fighter. He deflected her fists. Through a thick sea of fog, she heard him tell her to stop, but it didn't seem real. None of it seemed real. She kept fighting, hitting and kicking at him with everything she had until she couldn't move or breathe.

When her brain snapped into gear, she found herself wrapped in a blanket—swaddled, like an infant—and sobbing against David's chest. He'd somehow subdued and bound her, and now he lay next to her, his arms around her, and one hand caressing a soothing rhythm up and down her spine.

"It's going to be all right," he said. "I promise we'll get through this."

"I hate you." Her voice came out hoarse and raw, and it hurt her throat. Even swaddled in that blanket, she shook from a chill deep that had seeped into her bones.

"No, you don't." He kissed her forehead. "You're upset."

"I want you to leave. I never want to see you again, David. I may be upset, but I wasn't kidding. This is over. Let go of me and get the fuck out of my apartment." Tired of crying, she embraced her anger. She rolled away from him, and the blanket loosened, freeing her.

He came around the bed and knelt in front of her. "If that's what you really want, then I'll go. I'll give you space for now. But I'm a phone call away, Sugar. Always."

She watched him go. The front door opened and closed, and she heard the deadbolt engage. The anger remained far longer. She showered, fuming the whole time. Who the hell did he think he was? Just because he wished he wasn't related to his father didn't give him the right to try to tear her away from hers. Brian Sullivan had been a great father—the best she could ever hope to have. He'd been devoted to Summer and her. Though her upbringing was unconventional, they'd been happy. David was jealous—that's why he'd fabricated this elaborate story. He wanted to corrupt her memories and shatter her family ties.

Baking always helped her cope, but she didn't have ingredients. Or money to buy them, thanks to Jesse and Dean interfering in her little venture. The days she had left in her apartment were numbered, and so was the amount of time Summer had left at Sunshine Acres. A state-run hospital was in her sister's future, and thinking about that made Autumn's heart ache with grief and helplessness. She hated feeling helpless, and she knew Dean wouldn't let her supplement her income the only way she really knew how. And so she threw on shoes and grabbed her bag, but instead of getting in her car, she stomped over to where Dean was parked.

He rolled down the window, baffled. "Can I help you?"

"I need money."

"How much?"

She started high. "A hundred."

Dean fished a couple of Benjamins from his wallet, which the pickpocket in her noted was kept in his inside jacket pocket where it was most difficult to lift, and handed them over. "You're not supposed to know me."

"Fine. Pretend I'm a working girl, and you're paying for services rendered."

He frowned. "David fucked up again, didn't he?"

"If by 'fucked up,' you mean that I'll kill him if I see him again, then yes, he fucked up." She tucked the bill into her bag and set off in the direction of the grocery store. The two block walk would help get her mind off David's assholery, and it meant she didn't have to get on the ground to check her brakes.

Dean followed from a safe distance. Her phone rang several times, but she didn't answer. The only person she would speak to right now was Julianne, and none of those had been her ring tone. On her way home, she saw Dean talking on his phone, probably reporting to David.

Julianne called while she was mixing batter for a cake. "Please tell me that you took the day off to sleep in and have sex, and that you're not sick."

Autumn laughed, and though it was genuine, it sounded foreign. "I slept most of the day, but I'm feeling better now." It wasn't quite an answer to what she'd asked, but it would do. "How are you?"

"Great. My mom is dropping off the stuff you ordered tonight. I'll bring it when I come to see Summer. Will you be there?"

She glanced at the clock, mentally rearranging her baking schedule. "Yes, but probably not until seven."

Julianne giggled. "I'll see you at eight. And guess what? I went out with the same guy again. That's twice in one week, which is a new record for me. I'll tell you all about it when I see you."

"I'm looking forward to it." Hanging out with Julianne was exactly what the doctor ordered. After the hell David had put her through today, she needed to retreat somewhere safe to lick her wounds.

Chapter Seventeen

Autumn awoke the next day, relaxed and refreshed. She hadn't cried herself to sleep. After visiting Summer, she and Julianne had spent two hours at a café just talking. The topics shifted with their thoughts, and by the time Autumn arrived home, she'd managed to push David out of her head. He didn't deserve to occupy valuable brain space.

She didn't know if David had, in fact, arranged for her to work from home, so she went to work. Since he wasn't expected to be there, she felt relatively safe with that decision. Because she had no accounts, she started with David's emails—the internal ones that he mostly had her deflect. Within an hour, a shadow loomed over her.

"Good morning. I didn't think you'd be here today." Malcolm flashed a sympathetic smile.

She didn't know how much he knew—or thought he knew—about her, so she didn't comment. "Hi, Malcolm. I meant to thank you for giving me a ride home." By the time she'd arrived, she'd been barely holding herself together. She didn't recall saying a word to him.

"You're welcome."

"David isn't in today. He's expected back early next week."

Confusion wrinkled strategic places on his face. "I know. When I saw that you were here, I came to see how you're doing."

"Fine." Channeling the good feelings from last night, she summoned a brilliant smile. "I'm over it. Two weeks is a short time for a relationship, but it seemed a lot longer than that. It was time to move on." Her smile faded. "Wait—how did you know I was here?"

"I check the sign-on codes every morning and confirm them with the closed circuit security feed." He pointed to something that Autumn had thought broadcast the wireless network signal.

"Those are cameras? Good to know. I'll refrain from picking my teeth when I think nobody's looking."

He chuckled, a mercy laugh. "Look, I know you're newer to the scene. If you want, Darcy's available to talk to you about D/s relationships. She'll keep whatever you share with her between the two of you." He handed over Darcy's business card. "That's her cell number, and I wrote her email address on the back. It's a lot easier to navigate this world when you have someone you can trust to talk to."

Trust? No fucking thank you. Julianne was the only person left who she trusted, and even that friendship had limits. She'd been right not to share details of her life with anybody. David had provided a necessary lesson. But she didn't say any of that to Malcolm. She took the card. "Thank you. That's sweet and thoughtful."

"You're welcome. Now for official business—David wants to know if you're planning on answering the phone when he calls."

"I think we've said everything that needs saying, so I don't see the point."

Malcolm opened his mouth to reply, but Mr. Calder interrupted. "Autumn, where is David? He was supposed to send a status report this morning, but he hasn't." Clearly irritated, Mr. Calder scowled, and Autumn recognized a resemblance to David.

"He's out of town, Mr. Calder. He plans to return early next week. Can I take a message?" This was her real boss, and she treated him with respect. He didn't have control over how evil and heartless his son had turned out to be.

"No. I called, but it went to voicemail." He pointed at her. "If you call, he'll pick up. You wouldn't mind calling him on your cell phone for me?"

Cheerfully, she rummaged through her bag. "Sure." She dialed, and David picked up on the first ring.

"Autumn. I'm so glad you called."

"Hang on a sec." She handed the phone to Mr. Calder, who took the phone into David's office and closed the door.

"That wasn't nice," Malcolm said. "He's worried about you, and there's a reason he's avoiding his dad. He's trying to protect you, and you're making it very difficult for him to do that."

"I'm fine." The first twinges of guilt seeped into her bones. She'd never been vindictive a day in her life, and even though David had it coming, this didn't sit well with her. "And I don't want anything from him." That wasn't exactly true, but if she kept saying it, then eventually it would become her new truth. That's how brainwashing worked.

"You're a pretty good liar, but I'm better at detecting them." He leaned down and lowered his voice. "Autumn, Keith wants to talk to you about this. He'll do a DNA test first to make sure you're a match."

She did not want to discuss this, not with anybody. Her father wouldn't—couldn't—do the horrible things these men so casually accused him of doing. "No. I won't get a test, and I won't consent for Summer to have one. These are lies David made up because he wants to hurt me. Don't get sucked in, Malcolm. I thought you were better than that."

Frowning, he rubbed his jaw. "David didn't make up anything. Keith fed photos into facial recognition software that ran it through every government database to find a match. He left the evidence with you so that you could look through it. Maybe tonight you'll do that. If you have questions and you're still too angry with David, call me." He took Darcy's card and scribbled his number on it. "I'm on your side, Autumn."

The door to David's office opened. Mr. Calder emerged, red-faced, and handed her phone back. "Thank you."

"You're welcome." She spoke to his back because he hadn't stayed for pleasantries.

"I'm heading back downstairs. I'll stop by this afternoon to see how you are."

Before he could disappear, she said, "Are you my tail for when I'm at work?"

"No. But I won't lie and pretend that I'm not looking out for you." He threw her a two-fingered salute and headed toward the elevators.

She stared at the phone on her desk, wondering how David inspired such loyalty in his friends, when it rang. She hadn't given David a special tone. Julianne only had one because she'd fiddled with Autumn's phone one afternoon and changed it herself. But his name popped up, all the confirmation she needed. She answered. "Nothing has changed."

"Fine, but don't pull that shit again. The next time you call me, it had better be because you want to talk to me." Hardness edged his tone.

She heaved a dramatic sigh. "Then I probably should delete your number."

"Be good, Sugar. We're going to have a long talk when I get back."

Rather than respond—he sucked at listening to things he didn't want to hear—she ended the call. Half expecting him to call back, she watched her phone until the screen went black. It did not ring. After a few minutes, she realized how pathetic it was to wait for his call, and she shoved it back into her purse. The rest of the morning passed uneventfully. At lunchtime, she slung her bag over her shoulder. She'd brought a half-dozen brownie chunk cupcakes to share. Nothing improved a dessert dish like adding brownies.

She stopped when she saw Keith striding toward her. Mr. Calder was with him, as was another man who was unfamiliar. Mr. Calder knew that David was out of the office, so why had he brought people to see him? She put on a friendly smile worthy of any professional assistant. "Gentlemen, how can I help you?"

Keith's granite face betrayed nothing, but the other man looked guilty. Mr. Calder regarded her with smugness and glee. "I think you've helped yourself to enough, Ms. Sullivan." He motioned Keith and his partner forward. "Agent Rossetti, Agent Adair, arrest her."

They stepped forward. Agent Adair said, "Autumn Sullivan, you're under arrest for fraud and embezzlement. You have the right to remain silent."

Keith took handcuffs from his pocket and locked one around her wrist. He leaned down and growled. "Ask for a lawyer, and then shut up." While Agent Adair finished

Mirandizing her, Keith snapped the other cuff on. He'd handcuffed her in front. He took the sweater from the back of her chair and draped it over the cuffs. At least he preserved some of her dignity while escorting her out of the building.

Mr. Calder followed, beaming the whole way. "I knew David would find out who did this, and now he's off finding where you've hidden the money. It's over, Ms. Sullivan. You're going to prison for a long, long time."

"Thank you, Mr. Calder." Agent Adair dropped back, putting distance between Mr. Calder and Autumn.

Mr. Calder laughed, almost maniacally. "You have tons of evidence. It's all in the box of papers I gave you. David had it at his apartment, hidden in a closet so the little hussy wouldn't find it. She thought she could use her feminine charms to sway him, but he was too smart for that trash."

Keith helped her into the back seat of his car. "Don't pay attention to him."

Don't pay attention? The car door closed with the same finality she'd soon hear on a jail cell. How could she ignore the fact that David had fabricated evidence to send her to prison for stealing three million dollars? No wonder he'd saved her from being arrested yesterday. It made sense now. He'd wanted the arrest to be for this. The car pulled away from the building, and all the employees on their lunch break gathered on the sidewalk to gape and gawk.

A normal person would cry, but she'd done enough of that yesterday. David had obviously found her guilty before he'd stepped foot inside the front door. When he hadn't found anything incriminating, he'd made it up—and he'd enlisted Malcolm's tech genius to help. She supposed she deserved it for trying to have a different kind of life from the one her father had raised her to have.

"Keith?"

"Don't say anything, Autumn. I have to report every word."

She had to know. "How bad is it?"

"It's bad. Did I hear you ask for a lawyer?"

Agent Adair chimed in. "I did. I heard it. She wants a lawyer. Isn't your fiancée a lawyer?"

"She's a prosecutor. Autumn needs a defense attorney."

"Autumn needs a public defender," she corrected. "Because Autumn is unemployed."

They took her to the Detroit field office for processing, and very soon she found herself alone in a jail cell awaiting arraignment, trial, or sentencing. Autumn sat on her bunk, stared at the floor, and thought about the kind of hate that would drive a man to do the things David had done to her.

————

"He did what?" David closed his eyes and counted to ten. The day had not gone well, but he and Jesse had expected this to happen. Bankers in the Cayman Islands prided themselves on discretion. It would take several days and much bribe money to chip away at that confidentiality.

"Your dad went into your place, found the evidence you'd gathered condemning Autumn, and had her arrested. Keith Rossetti walked her out. He put a shirt or something over the cuffs so people wouldn't see them." The static came to a crescendo before the line cleared. Dean added, "I know you want to come back, but don't. As soon as the judge sets bail, I'll post it. I called a friend of mine who agreed to represent her, so she has a fantastic lawyer. You'll do more good if you stay there and find evidence to exonerate her."

Dean was right—David wanted to rush back so he could be by her side. She no doubt blamed him. In addition to being afraid, she would feel betrayed—or this would reinforce her decision to cut him from her life. He had no choice but to stay. The only way to prove his love and loyalty would be to make this problem go away.

"Dean? Make sure she knows, okay? Tell her why I'm here." The call dropped, so David didn't know if Dean heard his request, but he trusted his buddy to take care of Autumn.

He punched the wall, putting a hole through the thin wallboard in their hotel room. Jesse peered at him curiously. "What's Autumn done now?"

"My fucking father had her arrested. 'Give him a chance,' she said. 'He's not that bad,' she said. I shouldn't have listened to her. Asshole hasn't changed at all. He tricked her into calling me, and I told him that I was closing in on the money." He jerked his hand from the hole in the wall and examined the cuts on his knuckles.

Jesse looked at his fist. "Flex it, dumbass."

He did, making sure nothing was broken. "I've hit harder things."

"How did your dad get the evidence?"

"The apartment where I'm staying belongs to him. I've warned him to stay out, but he doesn't. He comes in whenever he wants, and apparently, he'd taken to going through my things." He flexed his fist again, but the fading pain wasn't strong enough to distract him from the rage boiling in his veins. "He's dead to me. Promises to my mother be damned. This is unforgivable. I told him that I'd cleared her."

Jesse wrapped ice in a towel and handed it to David. "But you'll finish out the case so you can clear Autumn. Let's switch tactics. We tried being nice, but maybe we need to take a leaf from Autumn's book."

Breaking in was a last resort move, a *pis aller*, because it would burn a bridge they might need for other cases. Just by suggesting it, Jesse was proving once again that friendship came first, not that David had ever doubted it. There would be time later to cultivate other contacts. "Are you sure?"

"I have the blueprints already. I stashed them in the lining of my suitcase." Jesse's eyes gleamed. "I love this part."

"So does Autumn. I kind of wish she was here." On this beautiful Caribbean island—they'd rent a house and spend most of the time naked.

Jesse extracted the blueprints and spread them on the table of the hotel room's patio. "I know, Romeo. Get your head out of the clouds. We need to figure out entry and exit points, and then we need to case it to check out the security."

David put distracting thoughts on the back burner and studied the plans. The next morning found him sitting at a table outside a café, sipping iced tea as he digested breakfast. Though he wore sunglasses, he still squinted against the bright tropical sun. Jesse emerged from a shop down the street, a plastic bag with whatever tourist item he'd bought to fit in dangling from one finger. He took the seat opposite David.

The brim of Jesse's baseball cap shaded his buddy's eyes, though he also wore sunglasses. When staking out a location with the intent to break in, it was best not to seem like they were watching the place. "Too many." Jesse muttered, referring to the guards patrolling the place. "The shops on either side have incredible security. The bank definitely thought ahead with that."

"They probably own the storefronts so they could install whatever kind of security they want." David drummed his fingers against his knee. "It's clever. Keep that in mind for next time we consult on bank security for a bank that's not in a stand-alone building."

"I think our best bet is going in when they're open for normal hours. You cause a distraction, and I'll sneak into an empty office and hack their system." Jesse fell silent, assessing all the problems with the plan. "It's a long shot that I'll be able to hack it fast enough."

"Charm offensive," David suggested. "Marlene, the account rep we met with last night, kept playing with her hair and looking at you."

"You want me to get into her place, see if I can find her logon information?"

David eyeballed his buddy critically. What he proposed wasn't out of the ordinary, but it could cross some lines that Jesse might not want to cross. "She wasn't unattractive."

"She had a nice shape. I'm not opposed to loving and leaving."

"You never are." David snorted.

"I believe in love at first sight," Jesse said. "When I see the woman I'm meant to spend my life with, I'll know immediately—like you did with Autumn."

David removed his sunglasses so that Jesse couldn't mistake his reaction. "I didn't fall in love with her the first time we met."

"No—you fell for her when you saw her picture. Meeting her just confirmed it."

He'd been struck by her beauty, and the melancholy hiding deep in her eyes had tugged at his heartstrings. He hadn't fallen in love. Even now, he cared for her deeply, but that wasn't the same four-letter word. "I liked her. It's different."

"You loved her." Jesse set his sunglasses on the table, the gesture communicating that the gloves were off. "It's in your voice when you talk about her, and it's guided your entire investigation. Frankie thinks you took the case because you wanted to get closer to Autumn, and the promise to your mother was a convenient excuse. This isn't the first time your old man has contacted you, asking for help. You fell in love with her the moment you saw her picture. You're just too chicken-shit to admit it."

"She's kept things from me."

"More excuses, Dave. You've known her for a little over two weeks, and she came with a fairly blank background. That means you had to get to know her the old-fashioned way— through spending time together and actually talking." Jesse hooked an arm over the back of his chair, slouching like an alley cat. He appeared relaxed, but he was ready to shred someone at a moment's notice. "Throw away all the stuff related to this case and look at what's left."

What was left when his questions were gone? Simple—a woman who'd freely given her submission and her heart. Hard truths smacked David like a lead-lined bat. "She told me that she loves me."

"And so naturally you ignored it, strong-armed her into justifying her actions Thursday even though you knew what motivated her, and then you released her."

Though sarcasm dripped from Jesse's words and left a palpable slime trail, David didn't try to avoid it. "And then I apologized and told her that her father was a kidnapper. It's all she has, and I tried to take it from her. She's right. I hate my father, and I didn't even try to figure out how she could blindly love the man who raised her." He'd devastated her, and a few hours later, he'd been on a plane.

"Now that I've sufficiently torn you down, are you going to admit you believe in love at first sight?" Jesse smirked because sometimes he was a jerk, and sometimes David needed his head jerked out of his ass.

He'd uttered the words before to a few long-term girlfriends, but what he'd felt for them paled by comparison to his feelings for Autumn. This was love. "Yeah. I do."

"Great." Not one to gloat for long, Jesse switched topics. "Marlene gave me her number. I'm going to see if she wants to meet for lunch. I'll pass her cell phone to you. Malcolm can talk you through the hack. Just be sure to get it back to me as soon as possible. If we get what we need, then I'll end it there and we can grab a flight back. If not, then I'll extend the date so you can search her house."

They'd run these kinds of protocols on investigations before. It was fairly straightforward, but it would go even faster if they had a full crew present. He waited while Jesse made the call. The conversation started slowly, with banter and flirting, so he took a walk.

Dean picked up immediately. "I've been trying to call you."

Immediately on high alert, David paused in front of a window full of jewelry. "My phone doesn't show a single call or voicemail. What's going on?"

"International coverage can be tricky. I'll have Frankie look into the problem. Anyway, I couldn't get a judge to do a bail hearing for Autumn until Monday morning."

That meant she would spend three nights in jail. The coffee he'd just enjoyed settled like poison in his stomach. "She doesn't sleep well in strange places."

"I have a lawyer for her. We're trying everything, but they've had massive budget cuts, and night court is only a TV rerun. You know what the problem is? We've turned down every job in Michigan until last month when Brandy Lockmeyer called in a favor that Jesse and Frankie owed. I have no contacts here in the DOJ."

Another thing that was David's fault. He'd avoided the state where his father resided, and that was crippling their ability to be effective when Autumn needed him the most. He'd let her down spectacularly. This would definitely get him a Boyfriend of the Year award. He squeezed his forehead as if a solution would ooze out, but nothing happened. "Keep trying. Did you tell her I had nothing to do with this?"

Jesse, finished with his flirty call, leaned against the jewelry store's window and waited for David to finish his call.

"Tomorrow is visiting day. Keith, Jordan, and Agent Liam Adair have been 'questioning' her just to get her out of there, and they're making sure she's eating well. Oh—Keith took a DNA swab during processing. He's running it against the samples provided by Sylvia and Warren Zinn years ago when the FBI started keeping that kind of data on file for missing kids."

The line crackled awfully, and David had to piece together most of what Dean was trying to say. "Keep me posted, and get her out of there as quickly as you can." Once again, the line was dead, and David didn't know if Dean had heard the last part.

Jesse adjusted his cap. "They didn't set bail?"

"No. She's still in that shit hole."

"Dean will take care of her. He knows what she means to you. We all do." Jesse tugged David's sleeve, and the pair sauntered down the street to the next recon point. "Plus she's useful. I've never seen anyone with such a natural gift for picking a lock. She didn't leave a scratch."

"Please tell me you have a lunch date."

"Nope. She's visiting her sick auntie, but she's free for dinner. I'm picking her up at seven. That'll give us time to check out places to take her that are more conductive to our plan."

Nothing was proceeding as quickly as David wanted, but he had to be patient. He knew this operation would take time. It wouldn't be so bad if his father hadn't interfered. Autumn didn't deserve to be put through this hell. She'd been through enough.

Chapter Eighteen

Sleeping in jail wasn't as bad as Autumn thought it would be, though she didn't delude herself into thinking this was how she wanted to spend the next five years. As far as sleeping in new places went, she actually got a decent night's sleep because it reminded her of falling asleep on a subway or a train with her head on her father's lap and Summer on his other side.

Julianne visited on Sunday. She cried most of the time, and Autumn found herself in the exhausting role of having to comfort a friend when she was the one in dire straits. Before Julianne left, Autumn extracted a promise that she'd keep visiting Summer at least three times a week.

She saw a judge first thing Monday morning, and the bail was set at ten thousand dollars, which apparently was reasonable considering the crime. However, it was so far out of the realm of possibility that Autumn didn't bother getting her hopes up. Julianne might have helped out if it was five hundred or a thousand, but nobody she knew could come up with that kind of cash. And so she resigned herself to her new quarters.

To her surprise, Dean came forward as soon as the amount was entered into record, and he paid the bail. Autumn had assumed that bail paying would be a long, drawn-out process by which someone would need to fill out a lot of paperwork, and then they'd take an hour to get her out. But she was wrong. Dean had already filled out the paperwork. He simply handed the cash over to the appropriate person, and the officer who had escorted her in took her directly to a room where she could change back into her clothes.

Twenty minutes later, she stood face-to-face with Dean and tried to figure him out.

He pressed his lips together. "I'm so sorry you had to stay in there all weekend. I tried to get the judge to set your bail on Friday, but he wouldn't."

"Why did you pay my bail?"

He took her hands in his. "This wasn't supposed to happen, Autumn. I swear it's a mistake. David was furious when he found out what his father had done."

Autumn didn't want to hear about David. She extracted her hands from between his. "Dean, thank you for this, but I don't want to hear you justify David's actions."

He nodded. "I understand. David is flying home tonight. He can explain everything to you then. Can I take you home?"

"Sure."

He'd parked in a garage down the street. "Are you hungry? We can go out to lunch."

She wasn't hungry. Keith, Liam Adair, and Jordan had taken turns using their badges to pull her from the jail for home-cooked or fast food meals. This morning, Keith had brought bacon, scrambled eggs, and toast, courtesy of Katrina. "I really want a shower, and I want to sleep in my own bed." Digging through her bag, she came up with the plastic container full of cupcakes. When she opened it, the concentrated aroma wafted out.

Dean glanced over. "That smells incredible. Did you make them?"

"Yeah. I had planned to share them Friday at lunch, but I was arrested before I could eat." She taste-tested one to find the plastic had done its job. "Still moist. Want one?"

"Yes, please."

They finished off all six.

"The FBI searched your apartment. Keith supervised. He tried to make sure they were respectful of your things." Dean glanced over several times as he waited for her to respond. "I thought you should know."

She'd expected as much, so she wasn't surprised. "Did David tell them about my hiding places?"

"No. We found that information unnecessary to share with law enforcement."

"Even Malcolm? Did he know too?" She was a little miffed that David had shared her secret. She'd hoped Dean would be puzzled by her question.

"Yes, but he works for us."

"His best friends are FBI agents."

Dean shrugged. "Malcolm understands the importance of strategic sharing. David tells me that you're an expert when it comes to not sharing more than you need to. That's actually a very useful skill in our line of work."

"It looks like my dad taught me useful skills after all."

"Many," he agreed. "David, for example, sucks at picking locks, and I've never seen him successfully crack a safe without a drill and a little C4."

Autumn laughed, thinking of all the times Summer had failed to get into a safe. She'd stomped around, pouted, and thrown more than fits. "Patience isn't his strong suit."

"It's really not." Dean touched her arm lightly. "Remember that, Autumn. You're the patient one, and he will test your patience often. Love the man, love his flaws."

David needed practice learning to love her flaws, not the other way around. Well, maybe that wasn't fair. She'd taunted him and pushed his buttons something awful. No wonder he'd released her. But then he'd come back, and then he'd given his father manufactured evidence to arrest her. Lastly, he'd sent Dean to bail her out of jail. Where did that leave them?

When they arrived at her place, Dean followed her into the apartment. He went through the three small rooms, checking everything. At last, he stuck his hand in his pocket. "Anything out of place?"

Autumn shook her head. She'd looked as well. The couch cover wasn't how she'd left it, and she was sure her mail drawer was messed up as well.

"I brought your car back here, so you have that." He handed over her car keys.

"Thanks."

"Do you want me to stay?"

That was unexpected. "I'm fine. I plan to charge my phone, take a shower, call Julianne, and go see Summer. Who knows how many visits with her I have left?"

"All of them." His eyes glittered hard. "We'll make this right, Autumn. We will catch the bastard who set you up."

His vehemence put a huge dent in the hard line she'd taken against David. In the past two weeks, he'd wreaked havoc with her emotions, and she knew he wasn't the only one to blame for everything that had gone wrong between them. The playing field had been full of potholes from the beginning, and they were not navigating them all that well.

"Dean?"

"Yeah?"

"Thank you—for everything."

He nodded. "I'll be around. If you need me, just call. I'll send you a text with my number so that you have it once your phone is charged." He hugged her, and though she expected it to be awkward, it wasn't. If she had a brother, this is what a hug from him would have felt like.

With her phone moderately charged, she called Julianne at work. "Guess who is out of jail?"

Julianne sobbed. "I'm so relieved. They dropped the charges?"

"No. Dean, who is a friend of David's, paid the bail."

On Sunday, she'd related an abbreviated version of her problems with David to Julianne, strategically omitting mention of any crimes she may or may not have intended to commit. Julianne sucked in a breath, but at least she stopped crying. "When is David coming home? I heard from a friend who knows Mr. Calder's personal assistant that David won't return Mr. Calder's calls."

Autumn didn't know how to process that. She was too confused when it came to David. "I'm going to see Summer this afternoon. I wanted to let you know. You can still go tonight, but I won't be there. Which isn't news to you because we'd thought I'd still be in jail."

Julianne laughed. "Actually, I'm happy you're out because I can't make it to Sunshine Acres. My mom broke her hip, and I'm staying with her to take care of her for the next few weeks. Surgery is scheduled for Thursday."

"When did this happen?"

"Friday. I didn't want to tell you because you had enough to worry about."

She sure did, but that didn't mean she didn't care about Julianne or her mother. "I'll stop by to see her tomorrow. It's not like I have a job anymore."

The sigh came through loud and clear. "I'm sorry about that, hon. I'll tell Mom she'll see you tomorrow. That'll brighten her spirits. She loves seeing you."

Dean followed her to Sunshine Acres. She parked where he could keep an eye on her car and still see her in Summer's room. It wasn't an ideal spot, but she wasn't going to complain. It was kind of nice to have a guardian angel.

Not sure how much to share with her sister, she sat quietly with Summer. Mostly she wanted Summer to wake up, hug her, and tell her that everything was going to be all right. She'd listen and help Autumn sort out her complicated emotions for David. Summer always had great insight into what motivated people to do the things they did. Autumn desperately wanted to believe that David's intentions were pure, but at the same time, she couldn't come to terms with why he'd make up with her just to tear her apart with vicious lies about her father.

"Summer, I really need you to wake up. I miss you so much."

Her sister's eyes opened, and Summer stared. The fear was gone, and questions simmered in her eyes. The feeding tube prevented her from saying anything. Autumn perched on the edge of the bed, and sandwiched Summer's hand in hers.

"I love you so much, Summer, and I wish I knew the magic cure to make you stay awake."

Summer blinked twice, and a twinge of hope made Autumn's heart race. When they'd been children, they'd devised ways to communicate through facial gestures and blinking. It had been helpful when working a crowd to see how much money they could pickpocket.

"Blink twice if you can understand me."

Summer blinked twice in rapid succession.

Autumn struggled to keep the tears at bay. "We'll use twice for yes and once for no, okay?"

She blinked twice again.

"Do you remember the accident?"

Summer blinked once.

"Do you remember Dad coming to visit?"

Two blinks.

"Do you remember trying to stop him?"

Two blinks.

Okay, then it was just the accident she didn't recall. "Do you know that you've been in a coma?"

One blink, but so many questions waited. She'd never stayed awake this long, and they'd never been able to communicate. Autumn sniffled to keep from crying. "I've been here every day talking to you. Did you hear me?"

Two blinks.

"Do you remember anything I said?"

One blink. Autumn pressed the call button for the nurse.

"Are you in pain?"

One blink. Then Summer glanced at the feeding tube. Two blinks.

"I can't imagine that's not bothersome, but it's your feeding tube, so it's necessary. Can you move?"

Summer's fingers twitched, and she gripped Autumn's hand. It was a weak hold, but it was something. Tears rolled down her cheeks.

"Autumn, did you need something?" Today's nurse, Janet, hovered in the door. Autumn wasn't one for bothering the nursing staff. She'd cultivated goodwill by making their workload easier.

"Summer is awake. She opened her eyes about two minutes ago, and she's been answering yes-no questions with blinks."

Janet came to Summer's bedside, and smiled brightly. "Good afternoon, Summer. It's good to see you responding to the new medication so soon." As the nurse spoke, she peered into Summer's eyes and took her vital signs. "I'll call the doctor."

Janet left, and Autumn continued talking to Summer. "I didn't know about the new medication. My boyfriend has a doctor friend who agreed to come see you. I knew she was going to try some things, but she didn't tell me what."

Summer's eyebrows twitched, and Autumn took that to mean she was trying to raise them. Face muscles were not easy to exercise.

"You want to know more about the doctor?"

One blink.

Heat crept up Autumn's neck. "My boyfriend?"

Two blinks.

"His name is David. We've only been together for a couple of weeks, but he came by once to meet you."

Her eyebrows twitched as soon as Autumn stopped speaking.

"He's a Dominant. He's mostly nice, and we get into fights because we're both strong-willed. He has kind eyes and a great sense of humor." She wiped a tear from her cheek. "He's a great kisser. Remember what you always said about great kissers?"

Two blinks. Summer was fond of saying they gave great oral.

"Well, it's true."

Summer's eyes closed, and Autumn waited for them to open, but they didn't. "Summer? Please wake up."

Nothing happened.

"Please? I'll do anything." The tears came faster.

"Dr. Wycoff will be here in ten minutes." Janet put a hand on Autumn's shoulder. "I'm sorry, Autumn. But the fact that she was awake for so long and responsive is a positive sign. Don't give up hope."

Janet stayed with her, providing hugs and tissue, until Dr. Wycoff showed up. Tess Wycoff was a tiny woman in her mid-forties with super frizzy black hair, rectangular glasses, and a calm demeanor that loosely contained a hellish bundle of energy.

She strode in as if nothing unusual had happened. Beaming a smile at Autumn, she said, "I hear that Summer woke up for a little while?"

Janet handed over the medical chart. "For about seven minutes. She responded to verbal communication, and her vitals were normal. Heart rate was a little high, but that's to be expected."

"I talked to her." Autumn blew her nose. "I asked her questions, and she responded by blinking once for no and twice for yes. She said she hears me when I talk to her, but she doesn't remember anything I'm saying."

"Okay. Anything else?"

"She isn't in pain, but the feeding tube bothers her."

Tess nodded, her gaze pinned to Autumn as she listened. Once Autumn finished, the doctor looked over the chart. After several seconds, she examined Summer. She opened her eyelid and shone a light in. "I've been giving her a new medication.

Its target use isn't for coma patients, but it stimulates a section of the brain that is dormant in Summer. I was hoping to kind of jump start it."

"So...This was a one-time thing? It jump started it, but only for a few minutes?"

Tess finished her examination. "I don't know. Like I said, it's highly experimental. My hope is that it keeps jump starting it until her brain remembers what it's supposed to be doing and keeps doing it. However, it could be that it was a one-trick pony."

More tears came, hot ones that burned the rims of her eyes. "Is there anything I can do?"

"You're doing everything you can do. She said she hears you, so keep coming here and talking to her." Tess reached up and put her hands on Autumn's shoulders. "Honey, I'm not giving up, and neither should you. If this doesn't work, I have other ideas based on her test results. Right now, I'm going to order some tests, which means Summer is going to spend some time in my hospital. Why don't you go home? Call David and have him take you to an expensive restaurant and treat you like a princess. I won't have results today, but I promise to call tomorrow."

Numb, Autumn nodded. Tess didn't need to know that David was out of town or that their relationship status was a huge question mark juxtaposed with a cornucopia of emoticons. Autumn didn't feel like company right now. She wanted to curl up on the sofa, wrapped in her old comforter, and look through old pictures.

On the way out, she avoided letting Dean see her blotchy face. It was a good thing he was keeping his distance and pretending not to follow her. When she arrived home, she found flowers waiting on the walkway in front of her door. The tag indicated that the accounting department had taken up a collection. Flowers were a weird choice, though. Did they think she'd been sick, or were they rallying around her to show support? Nevertheless it was a nice gesture. She brought them inside.

She'd left her phone home to charge, and it rang as soon as she walked through the door. The number wasn't familiar, so she let it go to voicemail. She changed into comfy clothes, got the rest of the brownies from the refrigerator, and curled up on the sofa with the photos. Her phone blinked, and checking it revealed sixteen messages—not a single one from David, but she hadn't expected to hear from him. People from CalderCo—many of whom she'd made recent overtures of friendship—wanted to know how she was. Some, she knew, were looking for gossip, but a few were sincere with their wishes.

It felt really good to know so many people cared.

She called Julianne to let her know the latest news about Summer. Laughing and crying happened, mostly at the same time, but the call was cut short when Mrs. Terry called Julianne to help her in the bathroom.

This day had been nothing short of miraculous. When she'd awakened in that jail cell, she'd assumed it was where she would end the day as well. But then Dean had paid her bail, and he'd confirmed that David cared about her. Then Summer had come out of the coma for far longer than she ever had before. Autumn began to believe that maybe her life was going to turn out okay. Wallowing in hope beat drowning in sorrow any day.

The manila envelope David had brought lay on the coffee table next to the shoebox. She looked from one container to the next, wondering if she had the courage to look as closely at the contents of the envelope as she had at the pictures in the shoebox. She reached for the envelope, but her hand landed back on the box, and she pulled out another handful of photos from her childhood.

A knock at the door pulled her from a nostalgic walk down memory lane. Dean had said that David wasn't due until late, but maybe that had changed as well. Maybe David was coming early—with news that he'd found the information he needed to clear her name and make his father drop the charges.

But opening it turned out to be disappointing. Stephanie Ceichelski stood on the other side wearing a track suit and a bright smile. She thrust a basket at Autumn. "Care package."

Autumn took it. "Thanks. Do you want to come in?"

Stephanie breezed past. "Can I be the first to say that this could not have happened to a better person?"

Frowning, Autumn set the basket on the kitchen counter. Had she misunderstood Stephanie—or maybe her friend had phrased the sentiment badly? "Um, thanks."

"Ooh—that's quite a glare." Stephanie pulled the curtain to the single window in the living room. The late evening sun hadn't provided enough light for the room, so it didn't cast the room into darkness because Autumn had turned on the lights.

Autumn hadn't noticed a glare. "Can I get you anything to drink? Or are you hungry? I have brownies. They're a few days old, but if I put them in the microwave for a few seconds, they're soft and chewy again."

"I love your brownies."

It took a few minutes, but she set a plate of brownies and a glass of water on the coffee table for Stephanie. The woman was looking through Autumn's shoebox of photos. Autumn wasn't sure how she felt about that.

"This one is my favorite." Stephanie held up a shot of Autumn standing alone, staring into the distance. The desert stretched behind her, and the whole thing looked desolate. Except Autumn knew that it had been taken at a rest stop in Utah. Her father and sister were behind the camera, only six feet away. She hadn't been alone.

Another odd statement. Autumn sat on the other end of the sofa from Stephanie. "Your favorite?"

"Yes." Stephanie dug in her purse, frowning as she riffled her way to the bottom. "There it is." She pulled out a gun and pointed it at Autumn. "You're making my life quite difficult, Autumn Sullivan."

Alarmed, Autumn jumped up. "What the hell? Put that away."

"Sit down and don't move. I don't want to shoot you. It's not in my master plan, but you've already forced me to change a lot of my plan, so I guess I can live with it." The whole time, she smiled as if discussing how rain had canceled a trip to the beach.

"Stephanie, what are you doing? And why?" Fear beat a staccato rhythm in Autumn's chest, but she controlled it.

"What and why—great questions. For months, I followed you. You had no life. No real friends, no family, no love interest. You were perfect. Then you had to go and get a boyfriend, and you're making friends. People at work actually like you. They think you're sweet and shy." Keeping the gun aimed squarely at Autumn's chest, she snagged a brownie and stood.

Autumn tried again. "You don't have to do this."

"Yes, I do. It's what I do, Autumn. It's what I live for. This is who I am."

"You eat brownies and point guns at people? I think you have it in you to put the gun down and talk to me."

Stephanie laughed, the slightly hysterical cackle of a person losing their last shred of sanity. "I stole three million dollars from CalderCo, and I left a digital trail that leads to you. It's a great story I've built over the past thirty months, and you even have that sister in a coma and a drawer full of medical bills. You pay your bills late, and you've had your heat shut off twice. You're perfect, Autumn. I've done this for years, to so many people who lived on the fringes of society. Really, I'm doing you a favor."

"By setting me up to take the fall for embezzling?"

With a dramatic roll of the eyes, Stephanie huffed. "You're not going to prison, silly. You're so distraught over what you've done that you're going to kill yourself." She extracted a pair of latex gloves from her pocket and put them on. Then she lifted a plastic bag from her purse.

Through the clear, thin container, Autumn recognized a prescription bottle.

Stephanie opened the bag, took out the bottle, and set it on the table next to the brownies. "Take them."

Autumn waved toward the gun. "Or you'll shoot me? Go for it. I'm not going to kill myself." And Dean was outside. He'd be here in a heartbeat, and Stephanie wasn't going to win against a trained mercenary.

"Yes, you will. I wanted to wait a bit, draw this out. I do so love watching the downward spiral of an innocent woman in a hopeless position. The trial would have been spectacularly boring, but I would have gone just to see you beaten down. Then, when you were at your lowest point, I'd step in, and you'd gladly take the out I'm offering. Sometimes I don't even have to suggest it. Some of my victims beg for a way to end their suffering." Stephanie warmed to her topic.

"You've done this before—set up people to take the blame for money you stole?"

"It's who I am." Stephanie's smile turned dreamy, and then it abruptly vanished. "It was not in the deal for you to get a life. Nobody was supposed to care if you lived or died. So you have to die now."

"No." Autumn had no problem refusing to do this. She set her jaw and crossed her arms over her chest.

Stephanie sighed. "I was afraid of this, so I'll give you a choice. You'll take the pills, and I'll let you write a quick will to ensure your sister is taken care of. Otherwise, I'm going to kill her. I have a partner, you see, and he's waiting outside Summer's room at Sunshine Acres with a syringe full of wonderful stuff. It'll stop her heart. One word from me, and she's only a memory. Your choice."

Autumn had been raised by a man who taught her the tricks of a good bluff. "I don't believe you."

Stephanie slid her cell phone from her pocket and activated voice commands. "Call Dearest." Several seconds passed, and Stephanie said, "Hello, Dearest. Autumn requires proof." She tossed the phone to Autumn.

"Who is this?"

He chuckled. "Summer Sullivan is a pretty girl. It says on her chart that she woke up today for seven minutes. Such a pity. Do you think she'll wake up if I check to see if her pussy still works?"

Disgusted and afraid, Autumn handed the phone back to Stephanie.

The evil woman said, "Thanks, Dearest. I'll call soon with an update."

If she didn't take the pills, then Summer would die, and who knew what else that horrible man might do to her first?

Her sister couldn't fight back, but Autumn could buy some time. "Two letters."

"Two letters?" Stephanie sneered. "Like *F* and *U*?"

Autumn wouldn't give this woman the satisfaction of thinking she'd broken her. "Those, I'm sure, work for you. I was talking about letters, as in messages you write on paper addressed to a particular person. It's not rocket science."

Stephanie went to the kitchen and grabbed two envelopes from the unpaid bills drawer. She threw those and a pen to Autumn. "You don't have paper. Write on the back of those."

Taking out the papers inside, she looked for one with a blank backside. "I see you've been through my things."

"I have. You're quite pathetic. You have nothing of value, and the only keepsakes you have are in that shoebox."

It wasn't true, but she did keep everything hidden. The shoebox of pictures spent most of the time hidden. She'd only brought them out recently, a fact that Stephanie seemed to have overlooked.

The first letter went to Julianne.

> *Dear Julianne, I'm sorry to leave you like this. You're a wonderful friend. Thank you for being there for me for the past two-and-a-half years. Take care of Summer. Love, Autumn*

The second went to David,

> *Dearest David, Our time together has been the best of my life. I could not imagine a smoother relationship—not one single disagreement on anything, not even when I threw up on your shoes. That bout of food poisoning sucked charcoal.*

"Put a confession in there, or Dearest is going to get another call."

I cannot imagine your shock when you find out that I stole three million dollars from CalderCo— and after you came all this way to make it more efficient. I cannot live with myself for committing this horrible crime against your beloved employer. The weight of my guilty conscience is too much to bear. I wish you well in your future endeavors. Please remember me fondly. Love, Autumn

Stephanie snatched the letters away and read them over.

"Anything else?" She hoped to hell that David understood the small clues she'd tried to leave.

"Remember me fondly?" Stephanie snorted.

"I've known him for two weeks. It's not like we were engaged." Autumn injected maximum derision into her tone. "Would you like me to get all gushy and declare my undying love? Because he won't buy that load of crap."

"Fine." Stephanie motioned to the pills. "Take them."

Autumn poured the small pills into her palm. "What are they?"

"Prescription sleeping pills. You'll go to sleep and never wake up."

Drawing on the depths of her reserves, she put the entire pile into her mouth and chased them with the glass of water she'd meant for Stephanie to have. The reality of her actions hit her, and she didn't have the strength to speak.

"Lay down on the sofa. Cover yourself up. It was nice of you to get the blanket. You'll look so peaceful."

Autumn wrapped herself in the comforting cocoon.

"It won't take long." Stephanie's voice had taken on an awestruck quality. "Thank you for this. It's been so fun, and this part is always the most fulfilling."

She fought it for as long as she could, but eventually her consciousness faded. *Save me, Sir.*

Chapter Nineteen

"This day is never going to end." David yawned again, and the yellow barrage of headlights in the opposite lanes blurred.

Jesse drove east along I-94 to where David's apartment waited. "Maybe you should call Autumn and tell her that you'll see her in the morning? I bet she's already asleep."

"Probably, but I'll wake her up."

Their trip had been moderately successful. Through Jesse's skillful handling of Marlene, they'd hacked into the bank's secure network remotely. The accounts they needed were easy enough to find, but no names were attached. That's how a shady bank did business—with numbers instead of names. The fucking bank didn't even know who their clients were.

Still, they'd come away with IP addresses for where the deposits and withdrawals had originated and an account history going back almost twenty years. This wasn't the first time this person—or persons—had run this scheme. As far as long cons went, this one had served this criminal pretty well for a surprising length of time.

They'd found enough to cast serious doubt on Autumn's guilt, but not enough to exonerate her. It was progress.

They covered most of the distance in silence. Jesse stopped by Dean's car, which was parked in the lot of a building adjacent to her apartment complex. Dean got out of the car and stretched his long legs.

"How was the trip?"

"Productive. Jesse will fill you in. How's Autumn?"

Dean yawned. "She's fine. I followed her to Sunshine Acres. She parked so I could watch her car and her, which was thoughtful. Then she came home. There were flowers at her door. I sent a text asking who they were from, and she said the accounting department sent them. I thought perhaps you might have, but far be it for you to think of sending flowers to your girlfriend who just got out of jail."

David glared. The thought had occurred to him. "I couldn't get a cell signal until we landed. It was annoying as hell."

Jesse coughed into his fist, but it sounded like, "Excuses."

Dean chuckled. "She talked on the phone, then a friend came over, and she pulled the shade, so I don't know what happened next. Girl talk, I guess. Her friend stayed for about a half hour, and it's been quiet since then. I told her that you'd be in late tonight."

That's the part he really wanted to know. "Does she blame me?"

"I don't know. I told her that it was a mistake, that your father jumped the gun and you were furious, but she told me not to justify your actions. I said that you'd explain everything when you got back." Dean stretched again. He handed his keys to David. "I'm going with Jesse. It's your turn to watch your woman."

"Thanks, man. I appreciate you watching out for her." They exchanged a very manly hug, and then he slapped Jesse's shoulder. "See you tomorrow."

Fatigue dropped away, and he almost ran to her door. He knocked and waited, but she didn't answer, so he knocked again. Nothing. Though it was very late, he pounded on the metal door. He'd left his key at home, and she wasn't answering. Punching the speed dial code for Dean into his phone, David growled. "She's not answering. I need the key."

Dean chuckled. "Pick the lock."

"That'll take too long. I could kick it in faster."

Jesse took the phone. "Get a huge radio and stand under her window blasting *In Your Eyes*. Serenade her with some Burt Bacharach—*Can't Take My Eyes Off You*." Laughter came through the phone as he warmed to his taunts. "Pound on the door even more and tell her that you can't quit her. Ask her to rescue you right back."

"You've seen too many romantic comedies." David snorted. "First you go on and on about love at first sight, and now you're flinging ideas for romantic gestures from movies at me. What the hell is wrong with you? Just turn around and give me the fucking key."

"Here it is."

David spun around to find Dean standing there, smirking hard as he tried not to lose it.

"You're an ass."

Dean held up the key. "I'm an ass with a key to the door separating you from Autumn."

David snatched it and unlocked the door, but when he went for the deadbolt, he found it already open. Shooting Dean a frown was all it took for his buddy to lose the mirth. David pushed the door open. A lone bulb from the kitchen lent enough light for him to see Autumn on the sofa. In three strides, he closed the distance. "Autumn?"

She didn't move.

He shook her shoulder. "Sugar? I know you're tired. You probably haven't had a good night's sleep all weekend, but wake up."

She didn't stir.

He pulled back the covers, and the hand tangled in them fell limply to her stomach. He shook her harder. "Autumn? Wake up."

Now he started to panic. He put his ear to her chest. Her heart beat was faint, so he felt for a pulse. The light came on, and he felt Dean behind him. "Suicide notes. David—she wrote one for you."

"Her pulse is thready, but she's breathing and her heart is beating." He slapped her cheeks to rouse her. "Sugar, what did you take?"

"David, the note is weird. She says you guys never fought, and she mentions throwing up on your shoe and charcoal. Did she throw up on you?"

"No." He slapped her harder and shouted. "Sugar, come on—wake up."

Jesse rushed in. "What's going on?"

"Autumn took something," Dean said. "Can you make her throw up?"

He lifted her. Jesse helped, and together they sat her up. David shoved his fingers down her throat, all the time feeling like his heart was lodged in his. She gagged, but nothing came up.

Jesse picked something off her cheek. "I think she tried to spit them out."

David swept his finger around her mouth and came up with fifteen or twenty unswallowed pills. They were tiny, and he recognized a popular anti-anxiety medication. "She tongued them. Who was here, Dean? Someone did this to her."

"Charcoal." Dean repeated the word several times. "She needs her stomach pumped. I'll call an ambulance."

Lifting her in his arms, David headed for the door. "We can get there faster. Let's go."

Jesse drove like a madman, and Dean helped navigate from the passenger seat. David sat in the back with Autumn draped across his lap. He kept slapping her cheeks and calling her name. As they screeched to a halt at the hospital's emergency entrance, her eyes fluttered open, but her glassy-eyed stare saw nothing. Dean ripped the door open, took Autumn, and ran through the automated doors. David followed, shouting orders to the nurses. People responded to his authoritative tone and rushed to help.

"Pump her stomach. She took sleeping pills or anti-anxiety meds." He fished the leftovers from his pocket and thrust them at the nurse. "I don't know how many, but this is what she didn't swallow."

He tried to follow the gurney as they wheeled it back, but a burly orderly put a hand to his chest. "Sir, you have to stay out here. Let them work. The nurse has some questions, and there's always paperwork."

Before David could take a swing at a man who dared suggest he calm down and fill out forms while the life of the woman he loved hung by a thread, Dean stepped between them. "Where is the waiting room?"

Jesse came through the sliding doors next. "I called Jordan. A team from the FBI is on the way." He turned to the orderly. "They need to keep everything—it's evidence. Bag it. Go. Tell them."

Mentioning the FBI impressed the orderly. He pointed toward the sign indicating the location of the waiting room, and he took off down the hall.

"Her apartment is a crime scene. I closed the door, but I didn't lock it. A team will be there soon to process it."

Lights. Bright lights blinding her, hurting her head. "Come on, Autumn. Open your eyes. That's it. Keep them open. We need you to stay awake."

She blinked, trying to clear the cobwebs. Her throat felt like it was on fire. "David." It was the only word that made sense, but it came out slurred and unrecognizable.

"That's it, Autumn. Good girl. We pumped your stomach, but whatever got into your bloodstream will need to work its way through." The person speaking came into focus. He wore a white lab coat and colorful scrubs, and he supported her back, forcing her to lean forward. A woman who seemed to be a nurse stood nearby.

"David." She tried again, calling for the one person she needed. His voice came from a distance, raised with ire and authority. She perked up and tried reaching toward the sound, but her arm only twitched.

"That's it. You're doing well." The man rubbed her back, and she sincerely wished he'd stop.

She wiggled, trying to get away, but she was too weak. It felt like struggling through quicksand.

"That's it, Autumn. Fight it." The nurse dabbed a tissue around Autumn's mouth.

David appeared in the open doorway, and she lunged for him. The man in the white coat stopped her from moving.

"Sir, you can't be here. It's family only."

Summoning all her strength, Autumn lifted one arm and uttered a plea. "David."

"Sugar, you scared the shit out of me." He came to her, and he took her in his arms. She melted into him, sagging with relief. He'd saved her. He'd been there when she needed him most. He cradled her head in his palm, leaning her back to kiss her forehead. "I'm going to find who did this, and they're going to pay."

The man in the white coat regarded David warily. "You're her husband?"

David didn't look up. "Two FBI agents are waiting for you to give a statement, Doctor Perditis. They're in the hall."

"Summer." She ignored the pain in her throat. She needed to know if Summer was okay.

He searched her eyes. "They threatened Summer?"

Tears made his face blur. She nodded.

"That explains why you'd do this. I'll have Jesse and Dean check on her."

As he said their names, Jesse and Dean came into the room. Jesse waved, but Dean looked like someone had run over a puppy and forced him to watch. "I'm so sorry, Autumn. I let you down."

She shook her head, and the tears that had been welling in her eyes spilled over. There was nothing he could have done.

The doctor gave up trying to evict her three badass mercenary visitors. He wouldn't know they were security specialists, but one look at David, Dean, and Jesse, and most people didn't argue. Except Autumn—she'd argue with anybody. "MarySue, start a saline IV. Mr. Sullivan, your 'brothers' can stay for a few more minutes, but that's all. I'll be back with the test results to talk about next steps." After flashing a polite smile, he left the room. The nurse followed, but she returned in seconds with materials for an IV. Someone must have been waiting in the hall with them.

David rubbed her back, and it didn't annoy her like when the doctor had done the same thing. "You can make up for it by making sure Summer is safe. She needs a bodyguard."

Dean nodded. He took her from David and crushed her with a hug. "I'll call first to warn them." He turned to leave, but Autumn snagged his shirt. She was weak as hell, and it took a supreme effort, but Summer was worth it. He stopped. "What do you need, Sugar?"

"Hey—only I get to call her that."

Dean ignored David's menacing growl. He waited for Autumn to speak.

"Here." She pointed to the name of the hospital. "Doctor took her for tests. She...She woke up."

David hugged her harder. "She came out of the coma? That's wonderful news."

Autumn squirmed until he eased up, and she shook her head. "Few minutes."

"I'll find her. For the record, if anyone asks, she's my sister-in-law." Dean threw her a two-finger salute and left, closing the door behind him.

"MarySue, can Autumn have some water?" Jesse pulled up a rolling stool and sat down.

MarySue pushed him back, stool and all. "After I get this IV going." She eased Autumn from David's grasp. "Sir, I'm going to need you to step back so I can work." The nurse had courage where the doctor did not.

Reluctantly, David moved to stand next to Jesse until the nurse finished poking around Autumn's arm for the vein that would prove the most painful target for her evil needle.

Autumn had always disliked needles. This experience sealed the deal, and now she officially hated them. Another nurse brought a Styrofoam cup filled with water. Apparently nobody had informed the hospital how bad it was for the environment.

When she was gone, Jesse rolled closer. "Let's have it, Sugar. What happened?"

"Son of a bitch." David pushed Jesse, sending his stool careening into a machine that beeped in protest. "No. The next one of you who calls her that is going to get his ass pounded."

Jesse lifted a brow. "That sounds like sexy fun. Autumn may not want to share you that way, though."

Autumn tried to laugh, but it hurt too much. She sipped water, and the cool liquid soothed her throat.

"There we go," Jesse said. "There's that smile. Now let's hear it. Any details, however small, are crucial in helping us catch the person who did this."

Agent Rossetti came in then, accompanied by Agent Adair. Autumn's heart plummeted because the last time they'd appeared together, she'd spent three nights in jail. She didn't want to go back.

Keith wore a very serious expression that wasn't quite a scowl. "We have some questions, Autumn. I know you're tired and your throat hurts, but as Jesse said, any detail can be crucial. Start at the beginning."

"Stephanie." She looked meaningfully at Jesse. He'd seen the woman talking to her while he'd been tailing her. "Brakes."

Jesse searched the photos on his cell, and then he gave it to her. "Stephanie Ceichelski?"

Autumn nodded. "Had gun. Partner with Summer." She sipped more water, but her throat was as soothed as it was going to get. "She called him Dearest. Let me talk to him. He described Summer, read in her chart that she woke up." Remembering the threat to her sister's life hurt worse than her throat. "I hid most of the pills in my cheek, but I had to swallow some. She stayed until I passed out."

David held her hand, lending silent support as she answered questions that both Keith and Liam posed. He grunted when she mentioned that Stephanie had confessed to setting her up, and he held her water cup nearby so she could sip frequently.

When she finished, Liam put away his notepad and rubbed his hands together. "Gentlemen, I know you'd like nothing better than to get out there and go after this couple, but I have to warn you against interfering in our investigation."

Keith nailed David with a firm glare. "Stay with Autumn. We'll call if we have news."

All four men shook hands, communicating warnings and counterwarnings with manly grips and two-handed clasping.

When they were gone, Autumn turned to David. "Did you find out anything on your trip?"

He shrugged. "We have account numbers and passwords, but no way to link them to a specific person."

Jesse paced. "Ceichelski is long gone. She's done this before, so she knows how to have an exit plan. I need to search her place. I'll get Malcolm to focus on analyzing the evidence with an eye toward nailing this bitch."

David's phone rang. "It's Dean." Ignoring the No Cell Phone sign, he picked up. "How's Summer?" Pause. "That's great to hear. I'll tell Autumn. I'm sending Jesse to you. He has news." Ending the call, he faced Autumn with a brilliant grin. "Summer is no longer in a coma. She woke up about an hour ago. Dean spoke with her for a little while, but now she's sleeping. He'll call the moment she wakes up, and I'll take you to see her."

Stunned, Autumn shook her head. "I don't believe it."

"You think I'm lying?" David scowled. "Damn it, Sugar. I thought we were past that."

"No, I—" Words wouldn't come. Her brain stopped working, and she cried. She had nothing for herself, but plenty when it came to Summer. The sound of a single clap snapped her out of it. She glanced up to see Jesse standing next to David, and the pair glared at one another.

David rubbed the back of his head. "What was that for, asshole?"

"She's in shock, and you're trying to make it about you. This is why you two keep fighting. You don't listen to each other, and you're too defensive." Jesse took her hand between his. "Autumn, it takes a special woman to put up with David for any length of time. It's a good thing you're special." He kissed her cheek. "I'm going to debrief Dean. Don't break his heart while I'm gone."

She stared at the door for several seconds after it closed behind Jesse. "I like him. He's a little gruff, but when you get to know him, he's really sweet."

He sat next to her hip and took her hands in his. "I'm sorry, Sugar. I need to learn to read you better. I don't usually suck at that, but when it comes to you, my common sense short-circuits. We got off to a rocky start, and that was mostly my fault. Apparently I fell in love with you the moment I saw your picture, only I failed to realize it."

It felt like she'd waited a lifetime to hear those words. She lifted a trembling hand and cupped his cheek. "I love you too, Sir."

He covered her hand with his, cementing their bond. "I was confused. The holes in your history made me look for lies where there were none, and then the clues Stephanie left that made it look like you were the thief—I interpreted everything wrong. You asked for time, and I didn't give it. You gave yourself to me, and I didn't treasure your gift the way I should have. Can you forgive me, Sugar?"

She already had. "Love the man, love his flaws. We're going to argue, Sir. We're going to fight. I'll always be a smart ass, and maybe you'll learn to be patient. Can you live with that?"

"Yes, but I'll never release you again. That was a mistake, and I don't make the same mistake twice."

Happiness filled her, but now that she felt safe and secure, exhaustion overwhelmed everything else. With a smile on her lips, she closed her eyes for a second.

The hospital sent her home in the morning with a warning that she'd be tired for a couple of days. David rubbed a crick from his neck—the result of having slept in the single, uncomfortable chair—and helped her into the wheelchair.

"I can walk," she protested.

David pushed her from the room. "Indulge me, Sugar. Let me take care of you."

She relaxed and let him take control. "We're not leaving yet, you know."

"That's why we're going to the elevators. Dean said Summer woke up a half hour ago, but a team of medical people have been in there the whole time." He leaned down and kissed her cheek. "They might not let you in right now."

"I'll wait."

"Or I can take you home, give you a shower, make lunch, eat it naked."

She laughed at the image he presented. "I'm very tired, David. You might be destined for disappointment if you want to scene."

"Take a naked nap," he continued. "We could see where that leads. Is your throat still sore?"

"Yes, but it's getting better."

"I'll make you some hot tea with honey. It's imperative that you heal completely."

"Oh, definitely. I'll invite Darcy and Malcolm over. We can have another contest."

He pressed a brief kiss to her lips. "I love you."

She laughed. "I love you too."

As soon as they emerged from the elevator, Jesse greeted them. "You're looking better." He looked David up and down. "You look like you slept in a chair." Jesse, of course, appeared well-rested.

Autumn reached for his hand. "Jesse, have Keith or Liam called with an update?" Nerves squeezed her windpipe. Had they arrested the woman who'd set her up and tried to kill her?

His grin faded. "No. She fled. There's nothing at her house, and her car was found abandoned in a parking lot near the airport. They're checking the security feeds to see what flight they got on."

"Cayman Islands." David spat the location. "It's where their money is. Judging by their account history, they'll spend some time there before they start traveling and spending like crazy."

"Let's find out for sure, and then we'll set up a mission." Jesse scratched his chest. "Dean went to the hotel to crash. He stayed up all night. I guess Summer woke up a few times."

"Did she ask for me?"

"Dean told her that you weren't feeling well, and that you'd sent him to watch over her. He might have told her stories about his many adventures, and some of those might have been graphic or sexual in nature." Jesse shook his head. "Hopefully she wasn't too traumatized."

Autumn couldn't imagine what Dean might say that Summer would find shocking, though she could think of a few things Summer might say that Dean would find shocking.

They ran into a gaggle of doctors emerging from Summer's room. When they tried to sidle past, David and Jesse spread out and used their presence to keep them from escaping. The doctors appeared momentarily flummoxed.

"Oh, for Pete's sake, David." Dr. Wycoff pushed past the larger men in front of her. "They're doctors, not assassins."

David and Jesse let the doctors leave, and then David greeted Dr. Wycoff with a hug. "Hi, Tess. Thanks again for taking Summer under your wing."

Dr. Wycoff held her hand out to Autumn. "What happened to you?"

Autumn waved away the concern. "Some serial killer decided it was my turn. Good thing my boyfriend is a mercenary." There was no way David wasn't going after Stephanie and her accomplice.

Dr. Wycoff pushed a tangle of black frizz out of her eye. "That explains the big guy who spent the night with Summer. I'm glad you're okay." She looked to David and Jesse. "Did you catch him?"

"Her," Jesse corrected. "Not yet. That's next on the agenda."

"Okay. Cool. Well, your sister is going to be fine. After the test results came back last night, I modified the meds, and she came out of the coma. We'll keep her on the meds for a little while, due to the nature of the beast, but in a few weeks, we'll wean her off them."

Autumn clasped her hands to her heart. She'd waited so long for this news. "You're sure?"

"Yeah. Absolutely. Of course, it'll take time to figure out what else happened. It's not uncommon for coma patients to suffer small strokes, and we won't know what physical or mental capabilities are left intact for some time. She'll need intensive PT before she'll walk again, but preliminary testing turned up no atrophy."

Her nefarious activities were now fully vindicated. Those small thefts had paid for extra physical therapy, which had been necessary. Autumn grinned, and David shook his head.

"What's next?" David asked. "She's not staying here for long, is she?"

"She'll need to be in a residence-based rehab facility for at least six months." Dr. Wycoff looked directly at Autumn. "I'm not going to lie—it's expensive, and insurance will only cover a portion of what I recommend."

David put a hand on Autumn's shoulder, but he addressed Dr. Wycoff. "Do whatever she needs. Send the bills to SAFE Security."

"David, I can't let you do that." Autumn tried to rise from the chair, but he held her there with one hand.

"Sugar, I don't recall giving you a choice." He used his Dom voice, and the glint in his eye promised that he wasn't playing around.

She settled back into the wheelchair. "Can I see my sister now?"

As soon as David stopped the chair, Autumn sprang up and tackled Summer with the kind of hug only a little sister can give. Summer managed to move one arm to weakly hug her back. They'd removed the feeding tube, but lines led from under the hospital gown to various pieces of blinking and beeping equipment, and she had an IV in the arm she wasn't using to hug Autumn.

"I love you," Summer whispered. "Thanks for not abandoning me."

Autumn eased back. "I'd never leave you." David pulled a chair close for her to sit on, and then he guided her into it with a firm-but-gentle pressure that let her know she had no choice. "Summer, this is David, and that's Jesse. David is my boyfriend, and Jesse is a friend of his. You met Dean already."

A light blush bloomed on Summer's neck and ears. "Dean. Yes. He's a smooth talker, that one."

Later, when David and Jesse weren't listening, she'd ask for details. David squeezed Summer's hand. "It's nice to see you awake."

The corner of Summer's mouth quivered with an attempted smile. "It's nice to be awake."

Jesse leaned against a wall, crossed his arms, and nodded a silent greeting.

"He's the strong, silent type until you get to know him." Autumn winked at Jesse. "Then you find out he has a marshmallow heart."

"Is it your shift as my bodyguard?" Summer tried to joke, but Autumn could tell the effort it cost to utter each word. "And what's this I heard about a serial killer?"

Autumn's eyes widened. "Dean told you about that? What the hell is wrong with him?"

"You said it. In the hall. The door was open." Summer closed her eyes for a long second, and the effort it took to open them was obvious. "I hate being so tired. I slept for three years. Jesus—three years. I can't wrap my head around that. Serial killer?"

Autumn wasn't going to make her sister say more, but she wasn't quite feeling up to sharing the whole story. She glanced at David, sending a silent plea, which he understood. "A woman has been setting your sister up. She made it look like Autumn embezzled a bunch of money, and then this woman planned to kill her, make it look like suicide, and get away with the cash. Only your sister was too smart."

Losing the fight, Summer closed her eyes again. "You're okay?"

"Yes. I'm fine—a little tired, like you—but fine."

"Autumn?"

"Yeah?"

"Where's Dad? He wouldn't leave if I was in the hospital."

She hadn't been prepared for this. Her hopes had centered around fantasies that involved Summer waking from a coma, not on what would happen afterward. She swallowed the lump in her throat. "Dad didn't make it."

Summer opened her eyes slowly, and it cost her much energy. "That's what I thought. He didn't suffer?"

She shook her head. "It was immediate."

"Good. I'd hate for him to suffer." Her eyelids drooped. "Tired. Sorry."

"Don't be sorry. I'm going to go home and get some rest, and I'll come back later, okay?" But Summer was already asleep. If David hadn't been there, she might have cried, but his presence gave her the strength to trust that the doctor was right—Summer was going to take a nap, not slip back into a coma.

"I'll stay," Jesse said. "Go on home. I'll call you when she wakes up."

"Thank you." She hugged Jesse and got back in the wheelchair so David could take care of her.

Chapter Twenty

David drove to her apartment. "Do you want to get your things, or do you want to stay there?"

Sitting in his passenger seat, she stared up at the door to her apartment and appreciated that he was being so thoughtful. What she wanted now was very different from one week ago when she'd warned him about needing space. "I want to be where you are." It was more than not wanting to be alone. She needed proximity to her Sir.

"I can stay here with you. I didn't get a ton of sleep last night, so we can take a nap. I can see how tired you are, Sugar." He regarded her with a gentle smile.

She nodded. "I don't want to go to your apartment because I don't want to see your dad. I'm very upset with him."

His laugh roared through the vehicle. "That's priceless. Dean moved all my things while I was gone. We're renting a suite at a hotel."

That sounded nice. "Let's get my things, then. I don't particularly want to be in my apartment after what happened."

He held her hand the whole way, and when they arrived at her door, he held his hand out for the key.

She stared at his empty palm "I thought you had it." She tried the door and found it unlocked. "My car is still in the lot. That's a good sign."

"We might have been too focused on getting you to the hospital to remember to lock up. I'll go first anyway. You stay here." He entered carefully, and when he returned a few moments later, he shrugged. "It looks the same to me."

Autumn found nothing changed—except the picture with the image of her staring into the desert was missing. "She took a photo of me."

"A trophy." David put an arm around her. "It's common for serial killers to keep something from their victim. We'll get her, Sugar. We'll get it back."

She threw a bunch of clothes into her lone suitcase that she'd salvaged from a discard pile at a yard sale. It had needed some repair, and she was handy with a needle and thread. As an added safety measure, she extracted her irreplaceable treasures from their hidey-holes in the floor. David took the suitcase, which freed her up to get the shoebox of photos and the manila envelope she hadn't yet touched.

David nodded toward it. "Do you still hate me for that?"

She shook her head. It wasn't his fault. She'd blamed the messenger and misconstrued his intentions. "I haven't looked at it."

"That's okay. It'll keep for when you're ready." He stowed her things in the back of his SUV. "I should probably tell you that Keith took the DNA evidence he collected during processing to test against what's on file."

She froze. "He had no right."

"He has a duty and a responsibility. Two people lost their daughters a long time ago, and they never found out what happened to them. At the very least, it'll let him rule you out."

She was silent all the way to the hotel. When they arrived, David unloaded her things and dropped her at the front door. She waited in the lobby, quietly thinking about a nameless, faceless couple who'd spent the last twenty-six years wondering if their little girls were dead or alive. When David rejoined her, she said, "I don't have to meet them if I don't want to."

"You don't. But Summer might want to, and that's her decision to make."

Her protective instincts and her hackles both rose. "I agree, but we can't lay this on her right now. She's spent the last three years in a coma, and she just found out our dad died. She's been through enough for now."

He waited for the elevator doors to close before responding. "Take it one day at a time, Sugar. Today, you're going to take a nap, eat something decadent, and have at least one orgasm."

She could handle that.

Dean was still asleep when they arrived, so they crept quietly to David's room. "Shower." She stripped out of her sleep pants and the old shirt she'd been wearing when Stephanie had decided to visit. "I smell like a hospital."

David followed her, peeling his wrinkled clothes away and dropping them on the floor. He washed her hair, massaging her scalp and the back of her neck, and then he cleaned every inch of her skin. His possessive touch lacked heat, yet it brimmed with reverence. Afterward, he dried her the same way. She waited for the tenor of his caress to change, subtly alter as it became demanding, but it didn't. He tucked her into bed, and then he curled his body around hers.

"Sir?"

"Yeah?"

"I miss you."

He tightened his hold. "I'm right here."

She turned, rubbing her body against his, and slid her hands up his chest. "My pussy wants to give Little Sir one hell of a hug right now." She brushed her lips across his, ending with a teasing nibble.

"Sugar, yesterday you almost died."

Wrapping her hand around his dick, she coaxed it to life. "Today I want proof that I'm alive. Show me, Sir. Please love me."

He kissed her, the slow slide of his lips taking easy possession, and his hands roamed her body. She'd longed for his touch for far too long. Though it had been days, it seemed like months. He hadn't restricted her movement, so she indulged in a leisurely exploration of his body. Soon his kisses deepened, and urgency dictated their actions.

He rolled onto his back and drew her on top. "You're going to ride me, Sugar. Keep your eyes on me. I want to watch you come."

"Yes, Sir." She slid down his length, the fullness marking her as irrevocably his. She rotated her hips to establish a rhythm. His thumb found her clit, and his other hand cupped her breast. He caressed her gently, circling her clit slowly while his other hand wandered over her skin. Tension took its time curling in her abdomen, but she didn't care if she ever came. The feel of him inside her, the connection they shared—that's what fed her soul.

Then he pinched her nipple, twisting it viciously. She cried out, and heat flooded between her legs.

"Don't stop, Sugar."

"Yes, Sir." Her rhythm had stuttered, and she worked to reestablish it.

He sat up, knocking her off balance, but he caught her as she fell back. Tangling his fist in her hair, he brought her face to his and possessed her with his kiss. He licked her throat and dipped his head to tongue the nipple he'd abused. "You're mine."

Completely.

"Say it."

"I'm yours, Sir, body and soul."

He flipped her, spread her legs even wider, and pounded his body into hers. She came hard, her pussy convulsing with pleasure as it sucked a climax from him. He collapsed, and she wrapped her arms around him to keep him where she could feel his heart pounding against hers.

When they emerged much later, after a well-deserved nap, they found Malcolm, Dean, and Jesse sitting on the twin sofas watching television. Dean glanced up. "Keith will be here in ten minutes."

Autumn clutched David's hand. "He found them?"

"Don't know. He just said he'd be here in ten minutes."

Jesse stretched, scratching his belly where his shirt rode up to reveal his toned abdomen. Autumn let herself enjoy the view for a second, until David snagged her around the waist and drew her to him.

"Seriously?"

"If some woman flashes you, I'll understand if you don't immediately look away, Sir."

He chuckled as he bit her lower lip. "We'll see about that."

"Apologies," Malcolm said. "From the noise level, we thought you two finished earlier. Unfortunately, we have a meeting to start." He set file folders on the coffee table. Dean and Jesse each took one. David let her go, and he grabbed one as well. "This is a summary of everything I've been able to pull together about Stephanie Ceichelski. I was able to tie her to many of the recent transfers thanks to David's decision to install software on each employee's computer that snaps a picture every time someone attempts to login."

Autumn read over David's shoulder. "Wow. Talk about invasion of privacy. Did you get pictures of people picking their noses?"

"Yep." Malcolm grimaced. "It no longer amazes me what people do when they think nobody's looking. Anyway, I got what we need. In addition to that evidence—it's more recent—I've found building security footage that shows her using Autumn's computer on many occasions. The time stamps match the transaction times. I didn't have time to run them all, but I got enough to convince a judge to drop the charges against Autumn."

Relieved to have an end to her legal nightmare in sight, Autumn steepled her fingers over her lips. "Thank you."

Dean sucked in his cheeks. "I'll have you meet with her attorney first thing in the morning."

"Having a list of transactions definitely sped up my process. Give me another day or two, and I'll have everything you need to get a conviction." Malcolm handed out another folder. "This is a list of other probable victims, based on the times and locations in the transaction history. I'll turn this over to the FBI today so they can start the investigation. If we had facial recognition software, I would have run a search for Stephanie's other aliases, but I'm sure Liam will get around to doing that soon, if he hasn't already."

David studied Malcolm. "Are you missing the FBI?"

Malcolm ruffled his hair. "Little bit. I miss their resources, but I don't miss being pulled from one case and assigned to another because of politics or the budget. Same result, though. We protect the innocent and put away the guilty."

A knock at the door interrupted any deeper thinking Malcolm might have been compelled to do on the issue. Jesse let Keith in. Greetings happened.

Keith took a seat on the sofa next to Malcolm. "The woman known as Stephanie Ceichelski left the US through Detroit Metro last night at nine-forty. We believe she was accompanied by a man in his mid-forties." He set two photos, both enlargements from airport security cameras. "About five-ten, weight about one-sixty, receding hairline, full beard and mustache. We've sent a warning to authorities in Mexico, which is their eventual destination."

Jesse looked up from the photo. "Mexico? Were there any layovers?"

"Atlanta."

"Look through security there. They probably changed their flight plans. I'm betting they went to Grand Cayman to get their money, and from there, they can disappear anywhere, especially if they have a boat." Jesse wiped his palm on his head, thinking.

"That would explain why the Mexican police couldn't find them." Keith tapped out a quick text. "They're traveling under the aliases Jennifer and Jeff Johnson, though if they've done this as often as she bragged, they probably will ditch those and use fresh ones in a new location."

"And change up their disguises," Autumn added. She wasn't sure if that had occurred to these men yet. "Dad always had Summer and me change our style of clothes and the way we fixed our hair when we changed names. Often we got a different haircut altogether."

Keith stared at her for a second, coolly assessing her for who knew what. Autumn briefly wondered if perhaps Malcolm had slipped up and told his best friend that she had tried to rob an art gallery. Then she rejected the thought. Agent Rossetti would be duty-bound to arrest her if he found out what she'd attempted to do.

"That's all I have about that topic." He set a sealed envelope on the table. "This is for Autumn."

Now it was her turn to stare.

"Test results. You don't have to open them now, but I'd do it sooner rather than later. There's a court order pending that would compel testing Summer's DNA." He came to her and parked a hand on each shoulder. "The right path isn't usually the easy one, but you have one hell of a support system."

"Summer is awake," Autumn said. "It should be her decision. Just like this should have been mine."

"I haven't had kids for very long, but I can't imagine the hell my life would be if they were suddenly taken away." Keith released her, spreading his hands wide. "I'd rather be sorry for something I did than something I didn't do."

She didn't get the sense that he was sorry at all, but she also couldn't muster up any anger. "I'll remember that and use it at a convenient time in the future."

"Thanks." David sucked all the moisture out of the room with that statement. "Like she needs more ammunition to fuel her smart-assery."

Malcolm and Jesse saw Keith out, and David hugged Autumn.

"Are you okay, Sugar?"

"Yeah. But the FBI isn't going to get Stephanie, are they?"

"It doesn't look that way." Dean picked up the photos that Keith had brought.

The door closed. Though the suite was sizeable, the entryway wasn't separated from the living room. Malcolm and Jesse returned wearing grim expressions.

"It's going to take another day for them to go through airport security footage," Malcolm said. "Then they'll need a warrant, and then they'll have to navigate international red tape. It would be so much easier if we could just go to the Cayman Islands, catch them, and sit on them for a day while we wait for the paperwork to catch up."

Dean nodded. "Sounds like a plan. Jesse, book the flights."

Autumn frowned. "Who is with Summer right now?"

"Jesse sweet-talked his FBI buddy Brandy Lockmeyer into providing a pair of agents to babysit. She's fine. I talked to her an hour ago, told her you'd be back after dinner." Dean gestured to David. "Are you okay with Autumn coming along?"

David sighed. "Last time I went without her, she got arrested and someone tried to kill her. I'd rather keep her with me."

"She can't leave the country," Malcolm said. "She's out on bail. They'll arrest her as soon as she gets back. I'll meet with the lawyer tomorrow, but the judge is going to want Autumn there when the charges are dropped."

"Don't meet with the lawyer until we get back," Autumn said. "Nobody needs to know where I went, and I think Dean means for you to come on the mission."

Dean and Malcolm had a silent conversation. Autumn thought it consisted of Dean telling Malcolm that he hadn't meant for him to come, but he was fine with him tagging along.

However, Malcolm took something else away from it. "I'm going to pass. You hired me to consult on the tech end of the investigation, and I've done that. This mission is going to be dangerous, and right now, I'm not in a position to take that chance just for the sake of adventure. If you need anything, call me. I can be tech support, but that's all. Besides, I think you've got it handled."

Dean nodded. "I can respect that. Frankie is on standby in case we need her. Autumn, do you have a passport?"

"If you're willing to call me Alisha Applebaum, I do."

Jesse frowned. "I looked through all your fake licenses, but I didn't see passports or that name. Where were you hiding it?"

"Not telling." She softened the blow with a wink. "But if you'd like to hire me to consult on unexpected places to hide things in virtually any setting, I'm available. I have no job, and my Sir won't let me work as a thief or a pro Domina anymore."

"I never said you couldn't work as a pro Domina." David thought for a second. "Though I wouldn't want that to be your main source of income. I'd never get to see you."

Malcolm packed up his things. "I'm going to take off. Autumn, Darcy would like to have you over for a girls' night soon. Give her a call when you get back." Dean walked him out, the duo conversing in low tones that Autumn couldn't overhear.

"Fuck it all." Jesse pounded on the table next to his laptop. "I can book two tickets in the morning and two for tomorrow night. I can't find four together until the day after tomorrow."

David went to peer over Jesse's shoulder. "Book two for the red eye and two for the evening. You and I can go out first, and Dean can bring Autumn later."

"No." There was no way Autumn would let them relegate her to backup. "I'm going on the first flight. She tried to kill me, David. I want to be the one to catch her."

"Sugar, Jesse has skills that you don't. I need him. Dean will make sure you're safe." Concern softened his eyes to light brown.

"Seriously?" She snorted. "I was sneaking around and breaking into places when all you had to worry about was whether the popular girl in eighth grade knew you were alive or not. We're talking about tracking down Stephanie and her accomplice, capturing them, and babysitting them until the warrants come through and the authorities arrive."

Jesse grinned, but said nothing even though David looked to him for help. Finally, David said, "You might be able to track them and break in, but you won't be help in subduing them. Stephanie has a gun, and I'm pretty sure you've never held one before."

She scoffed at that. Her father hadn't liked guns or violence, but he'd understood the necessity in knowing how to use a weapon. "I know my way around a gun, which, by the way, you're going to have trouble getting. The Caymans are part of the British Commonwealth, so the only guns available are illegal—and I know my way around the contraband community. Do you?"

David breathed, and his lips moved as he counted ten. "You make some good points," he conceded. "But if I have Jesse, I won't need a gun. We can take them down using force."

"I'll distract them by being unexpectedly alive, and you can sneak in and bash them over their head with a big stick." She wiped her hands together as if they'd agreed on a plan. "Simple. Quick. I like it."

He'd done well with keeping his temper in check while he listened to her ideas, and now he was finished. She could almost see his temperature rising. "I don't want you to be a target."

Autumn agreed with that sentiment, but she had different ideas about what it meant. "Fine, then let me do this. She made me a target, and I want to give back the bull's-eye, preferably in a way that bruises."

Jesse chuckled and poked David's rib. "I don't think you're winning this one."

Dean twisted the cap from a bottle of water and leaned against the counter dividing the living area from the kitchenette. "I concur. Book David and Alisha Applebaum on the first flight. You and I will go on the second one. David and Autumn can spend the day tracking down our targets and doing recon on their hideout. By the time we get there, they'll be ready to go." He mimicked the wiping of hands. "Hashtag problem solved. Hashtag Dean rules."

Autumn considered adding a "big ego" hashtag, but she liked that his solution supported what she wanted, so she refrained. Instead, she turned the full force of her begging face on David. He gave in gracelessly. "Fine. Go grab your bag. I'll take you to see Summer now."

Chapter Twenty-One

Autumn had never been on a plane before, and though she had several passports with different aliases, she had never been out of the country. Well, they'd visited Canada when she was little, but that didn't count. Canada looked so similar that, if it hadn't been for the stop at the booth on the border, she wouldn't have known they'd arrived anywhere different from the US.

David let her sit by the window, and she spent a lot of time staring at the clouds and looking at the patches that made up the civilization on the ground. He held her hand, patiently answered a million questions, and watched her with soft eyes and an amused lift to his very kissable lips.

Once they landed, he retrieved their bags and hailed a cab to take them to the hotel Jesse had booked. He'd been quiet for most of the flight, but now that they were ready to begin the investigation, worry lines creased his forehead.

Autumn went to where he sat on the edge of the bed, lost in thought, and knelt before him. Nothing happened for the longest time, and then she felt his fingers in her hair.

"I don't want you to leave this room." He gripped the sides of her head and tilted her face to his. "I've never loved anybody before, not like this. I don't want to put you in danger, Sugar. When I found you the other night, and you wouldn't wake up—" He closed his eyes and pressed his forehead to hers. "I can't go through that again."

She slid her fingers along his smooth cheeks, a light reassurance. "I knew you would save me."

He chuckled bitterly. "What if I had gone home instead? Or what if my flight had been delayed, and I got there too late?"

"But you didn't." She traced a finger along his bottom lip. "My faith in you has never been misplaced, even when I thought it was. Now I'm asking you to trust me the way I trust you. Sir, I can do this. This—way more than accounting—is my skill set. I've pulled off small jobs for the past three years because I didn't want to chance getting caught, but don't let that fool you into thinking I'm small time."

"Tell me," he said. "What's the most dangerous job you've ever done?"

"Sir, I'd rather not discuss that right now."

He sat up, putting inches between them, and she put her hands back on her knees in the proper position. "I insist, Sugar. That's an order."

She debated. The job had involved sweet-talking her way into a smuggler's bed. She'd distracted him while setting the stage for Summer and her to return and rob him. Their father had been livid when he'd found out about it, even though Autumn had left out the part about seducing a target. It was likely that David had done similar things. In his line of work, sometimes a honeypot angle was the best one. He'd been upset all the times she'd abbreviated the truth, so that wasn't an option right now. Finally, she asked, "What's the punishment if I don't?"

"I'd love to confine you to this room, but I know you too well to think you'd stay." He went to stand in front of the window. "No punishment. I want you to trust me enough to tell me everything, so I'll wait until you're ready."

Oh—he didn't play fair, but he had a point. She was afraid he'd judge her harshly. "Miami. Summer and I robbed a drug smuggler's safe. I seduced him to get inside and set it up so that we could break in the next day when he had a deal scheduled. It was a cash business, and it ended up being a huge score. We got away with almost a half million."

He'd turned away from the window, and he watched her with an impassive expression. At least he was listening.

"He had a crew, armed with automatic weapons, and a compound that was reputed to be impossible to penetrate. It was a challenge, a dangerous one, but we did it. We got in and out without being detected." And it hadn't been easy. Timing guard routes, dealing with unexpected smoking breaks—they all seemed to be smokers—and overcoming various electronic security measures had taken planning, precision, cunning, and a quick reaction to wrenches that were inevitably thrown into every plan.

"That's a significant haul. What happened to the money?"

She pressed her lips together. "We gave it to Dad in exchange for letting us settle down and have normal lives. We'd hoped it would be enough. He was always chasing that one big job that would set him up for life."

"And you were the good daughter who wanted to take care of him." He exhaled hard. "Sugar, did he tell you that was a dumbass move?"

"Yeah, but he was proud of us, so we ignored the rest. But, Sir, the point is that I can do this. You can count on me. I don't panic, and I don't crack under pressure."

He hauled her up by the arms and devoured her with a ravenous kiss. She hadn't known a man could move that fast. Melting against him, she submitted to his strength and the assault of passion. He needed this from her, and she gladly gave everything.

Suddenly he ripped himself away and held her at arm's length. "Sugar, if you get in trouble, there's no safeword. These people won't play around. I don't like the idea of you being in danger."

"Sir, I'm not crazy about the idea of you being in danger, either. But I understand and accept who you are. You need to do the same with me." He'd struggled with that the whole time, but mostly because she had kept pieces of herself from him. She waited, giving him the time he needed to come to terms with the fact that she wasn't a delicate flower who needed to be sheltered from the big, bad world.

After forever, he nodded. "Okay. I can do this." He repeated it twice, and she knew he was trying to convince himself. "You can do this. We can do this together. For fuck's sake, let's get started before I change my mind, handcuff you to the bedpost, and wait for Dean and Jesse to get here." His phone rang before he could say more. For once, he didn't turn away to take a call, and that demonstrated the extent to which he'd accepted Autumn's place in this mission. He put the phone on speaker.

The reception unclear, Jesse's voice crackled on the other end. "They disappeared in Atlanta. Neither of them caught a connecting flight. We searched the boarding footage for every flight."

David frowned. "How could they disappear?"

"They left the airport." Autumn thought about how she might vanish if she'd scored a huge haul. "They probably took a shuttle to a car rental place."

"They'd need ID to rent a car." The tap of the keyboard, ironically, came through clearer than Jesse's voice.

"They didn't rent a car," Autumn said. "They went somewhere nearby, probably a hotel or restaurant, and used the bathroom to change their looks. Stephanie's hair was pretty long, so I bet she cut it and changed the color. Her partner either shaved his head or dyed his hair. Or they have wigs. If they're smart, they significantly changed their style of dress, though it wouldn't stand out in their surroundings. They don't want to be memorable."

David stared at her. "Jesse probably thought of that already."

"Some of it, yeah," Jesse agreed. "They could have taken a cab or bus, or they could have stolen a car. I can hack surveillance for the area surrounding the airport, but those aren't networked systems. I'll have to hack each individual server. Even with Malcolm's help, it'll take days."

"Then we'll have to draw them out." Autumn unzipped her suitcase while David scratched his head.

"How, exactly, do you think you're going to accomplish that? We have no idea where they are or where they're going." Thoughts flashed behind David's eyes, darkening them to almost black. She knew he was trying to think of a plan that didn't involve her too much or put her in imminent danger.

"We know where their bank is, and we know they haven't claimed the accounts yet. They set them up remotely, so there's no picture or anything on file. Start at the bank. Follow the money." She slipped her hand into his. "You have the account numbers, right?"

David gripped her hand. "Yes, but I don't see what checking the balance will do. The bank works with numbers only—no names or addresses, and the phone number we found led to a burner cell."

"I see where you're going." Jesse's connection cut in and out, making it difficult to follow him. "I can hack their system to change the personal information and security questions. You can claim the money and run. It'll clear Autumn, and you can return the money to your father."

"Not quite." Autumn didn't actually care about returning the money to Mr. Calder. She wanted Stephanie's head on a platter, and she wouldn't mind a side dish made from her boyfriend. "I want to spend it to draw them out. For whatever reason, they're waiting to claim the money and start their new lives. I want to find out the names they're using and post my picture on the account. I want them to know I'm spending their money."

David sputtered. "We are not using you as bait."

Jesse coughed discreetly. "That's pretty much why she went with you, man."

He sprang to his feet and loomed over the phone, which might have been intimidating if Jesse had been able to see him. Then again, probably not. Jesse knew David too well to find him intimidating. "She was supposed to deliver the element of surprise while I physically subdued them."

"This'll be more fun." Autumn grabbed his arm. "Let's go shopping, David. Let's spend your dad's money. Not only will we draw out the bad guys, but you'll be able to passive-aggressively get back at your dad. They will be surprised, and you'll still get to whack them over the head with a big stick." Given the tension running through his body, that method might not be enough to exorcise all his pent-up energy. "Or you can kick their asses, and I can hit them over the head with a big stick. We should probably pick up a big stick while we're out."

Her strategy worked. Some of the tension eased, and he laughed. "Jess? Use my standard answers to the security questions."

"Sure thing. Only one problem."

From the way he scrunched his face, David had expected smooth sailing. "What's that?"

"We can only hack the bank from inside."

It had to be easier than that. "You can't access it remotely or send them a virus that will let you in?"

Jesse chuckled. "In the real world, viruses have to be tailor made for a specific purpose, and they can take months or years to write. And the systems for the bank we need are on a local network. I'd need physical access to their server. The fastest and easiest way in is to use a terminal in the bank like we did last time. It looks like Marlene needs a date."

David wilted a little. Autumn eyed him suspiciously. "Who is Marlene?"

"A woman who works at the bank." He gestured to the phone. "She likes Jesse."

Static sounded louder and then it leveled off. "I can keep her out of the way while you sneak into the bank and change the information. But that leads to another problem."

This one, Autumn had realized as well. "Someone at the bank—probably Marlene—may recognize David if we go in together to claim the money. With the amount we're getting, someone in charge will want to meet with us. I'll have to claim the money with Dean."

David pursed his lips. "I don't love this idea."

She slid her hand up his arm. He wasn't going to love any idea that included her or put her in the line of fire. "But it's a good plan."

He couldn't argue with that. "Fill Dean in, and we'll see you guys when you get here."

The call ended, and Autumn looked up at David. "You have standard answers to security questions? That's not exactly a wise strategy."

"I don't use them for my personal accounts. We all have basic protocols and code words we use that come in handy in situations like this." He offered his arm. "Let's do some recon. I've been here before, and I want to show you escape routes."

"Most men would just want to take a stroll through the neighborhood with their girlfriend. This is so much more romantic." She put her arm through his. "Lead the way, Sir."

"I can't tell if you're being sarcastic, or if you really mean it."

She laughed. "Probably a little of both. I never go anywhere without planning an escape route. I kind of like that your mind operates the same way. It makes me feel less freakish."

He scowled. "You're not a freak."

"Or I'm merely your kind of freak. I'll take it." They reached the street. Afternoon sunshine blinded Autumn. She put her hand up to shield her eyes. Scanning the street turned up a few options for dealing with that problem.

He turned her in the opposite direction. "You're going to need a new outfit for your debut tomorrow." Wearing dress pants and a blue striped shirt, his only concession to the heat was to choose short sleeves, and he'd left his tie off. Dashing and handsome, he cut a fine figure. Her clothing, however, didn't quite scream "I heart designer labels." With a sly grin, he steered her toward a boutique. "I'm going to love dressing you up."

They went into an upscale boutique. The young woman working the sales floor ignored Autumn, but she took note of David. "Good afternoon, sir. I'm Bella. Can I help you find anything in particular?"

David scanned the racks. In seconds, he'd chosen a stylish, scoop-necked dress with green accents. He held it up to her. "It'll bring out your eyes, Sugar." He nodded to Bella. "She'll need to try this on."

Autumn followed the salesgirl into the fitting room. She generally avoided stores like this unless she was going to use a five-finger discount. Of course, David frowned on stealing and they couldn't chance being arrested before they could commit fraud and identity theft, so she didn't entertain the thought for long. Bella flashed one of those smiles that revealed more contempt than anything else. Autumn made sure her response matched. The uppity hussy hightailed it out of there.

"I like it," David said as she modeled for him, desire and approval turning his irises caramel. He adjusted the bodice, though it didn't need it, and he ran his fingertip along the edge of the dress where it exposed the swell of her breast. His delicate caress sparked a longing that traveled straight to her pussy. She gasped, and the small noise captured his attention.

He slid his hand up, fanning out his fingers and skimming them along the back of her neck to tilt her head back. Then his lips claimed hers, devouring them as he pressed her back to the mirror. Autumn was ready to throw caution to the wind when a loud throat-clearing interrupted them. David released her slowly.

Three shades of red stained Bella's face. "Would you like me to ring that up for you?"

David looked Autumn up and down. "She'll need shoes and a hat, one with a floppy brim to keep the sun out of her eyes."

She appreciated that David had noticed her need, but she'd hoped for sunglasses. It was easier to case a place if people couldn't see her eyes. "How about sunglasses instead?"

"You'll have both. And matching underthings." He gave Bella the correct sizes for her bra and panties.

"That's not necessary, Sir."

He lifted a brow. "I'm all for you going commando, but not tomorrow. If something should happen, I'll want your modesty preserved."

What did he think was going to happen in a bank? She laughed. "Right. Because if my dress flies up while they're checking my ID, we'll want everyone to know that I color coordinated my panties with the rest of my outfit."

"I could get you a red dress," he suggested. "And then I can spank your ass to match."

The idea of a spanking made her need new panties anyway. A half step put her against his chest. "We have plenty of time before your buddies get here, Sir. If you need some stress relief, I'd be happy to donate my bottom to the cause."

He kissed her hard, a furious press that promised she'd be donating more than just her bottom tonight. "I want to spoil you." He wound his hand in her hair and closed his fist, pulling her hair in just the right way. "Don't make the mistake of thinking you get a say in the matter."

This was the fun-loving man with whom she'd played games at the play party that first night. She loved when he was like this, so she let the matter lie. A lock of hair had fallen over his forehead. He was overdue for a haircut. She coaxed it back into place, loving the fact that she alone had the right to touch him like this.

Bella returned with a pale green silk bra and matching panties. David held them up, looking from the clothing to Autumn and back again. "I'm going to have to see these on you." He followed her and Bella back to the changing room, and when Bella tried to take the items to hang them inside, David held them out of reach. "I'll handle this. Why don't you go lay out a selection of hats on the sales counter?"

Inside the cubicle, Autumn lifted a brow at the speed with which David dispatched the sales girl. "You're going to watch me change?"

He latched the door. "I'm going to help, Sugar." With a devilish grin, he motioned for her to turn around. "I'll get your zipper."

"There is no zipper." The dress had short sleeves and a sweetheart neckline. Still, she turned around and lifted her arms. If he wanted to undress her, she wasn't going to argue.

He didn't disappoint. She felt his hands glide over her waist and hips, stroking down her legs until he reached the hem that fell to just above her knees. Then he lifted the soft fabric up and over her head, baring her to him. Due to the thin straps, she'd ditched her bra, and so she stood there in her panties while he returned the dress to the hanger. "Take off your panties."

She thought he might make a move, but he merely exchanged her panties for the pale green pair and matching bra. He helped her with the bra, latching it into place and reaching into the cups to adjust her girls. She stood in front of the mirror now, and he remained behind her. He teased her with his nearness and the almost-touch of his chest against her back. Her nipples pebbled, and gooseflesh traveled down her arms and across her abdomen.

"Are you cold?" He traced his fingertips down her arms and hips.

"No, but I could use some warming anyway."

He turned her to face him, and his fingers continued their gentle trek over her flesh. Desire turned his eyes to that lusty caramel hue, and his eyelids had fallen to half-mast. She wanted so badly to kiss him, but she'd surrendered herself to his mastery, and so she waited for his permission.

Silently, he touched her, his palms gliding over her exposed skin, eliciting soft gasps as he woke up every nerve ending in her body. He even knelt down to touch her legs until they trembled. Only then did he remove her panties. He stood, opening the fly of his pants as he did so. She wanted to touch the full erection that sprang free, but he lifted her so swiftly that she could only grab his shoulders for balance and wrap her legs around his waist. And then he was inside her, and his tongue plunged into her mouth to gag them both.

The mirror was cold against her back, a counterbalance to the heat coiling in her core. David pumped his hips, his cock sliding in and out with slow inches. He'd fucked her harder and faster, but this slow inferno threatened to take her to a peak she hadn't yet visited. He fisted her hair at the nape and pulled as he silenced her with his mouth on hers.

That didn't entirely stop noises from escaping, and David wasn't exactly quiet either. She came first, the climax exploding over her. Seconds later, his orgasm detonated, and he buried his face in her neck as he cried out.

They both trembled as he withdrew his cock and set her back on her feet. He held her for a few precious moments as their wits returned.

"So," she said. "I guess you like the bra, but not the panties?"

He chuckled. "They'll do."

They emerged from the fitting room holding hands. Bella blushed as she rang up their purchases, and none of the other salespersons would meet their eyes.

The store didn't sell sunglasses or shoes, so they spent another hour strolling up and down the streets in search of the items they needed. By the end of the excursion, he'd spent more on her than she's spent on three months' rent—when she paid it. Casing a bank with David turned out to be fun. Unlike in the shop, he behaved in a low-key manner. The last thing they wanted to do was draw attention. It proved a little challenging to keep her hands to herself. She felt like a woman on vacation with her lover, and it was difficult not to act like it.

By the time they returned to the hotel, exhaustion from the early flight had caught up with them. They took a nap, and Autumn slept wrapped in the familiar home of David's embrace. Of course, she woke up first. By the time David roused himself, the room service she'd ordered had been delivered. Wearing only light robes, the lounged on the balcony to enjoy the tropical breeze as they munched gourmet seafood dishes.

"Are you nervous about tomorrow?" A warm wind rippled through his hair.

"Excited. I haven't done a bank before." She sipped some wine. "I wish I was partnering with you, but working with Dean might be easier."

He regarded her thoughtfully as he chewed and swallowed. "How so?"

"I won't be distracted by his sexy eyes, his luscious ass, or the way he looks at me."

Scrunching his nose, he said, "It's wonderful to hear how attractive you find my best friend."

Autumn laughed. "Don't get me wrong. He's cute enough, but I was talking about you. It isn't easy to keep my mind on my job when I would rather spend my time staring into your eyes or checking out your backside."

The scrunching disappeared, and he snagged another bite. "I didn't sate you enough in the dressing room?"

Heat traveled up her neck. Never in her life had she been so daring. "The thing about you is that I can't get enough. Having some just makes me want some more. Like right now, I keep thinking that you're only wearing boxers under that robe."

He licked sauce from his fingers. "And I keep thinking that I never finished stretching your ass enough to fuck it."

She swallowed, though she hadn't been chewing. "If you have enough lube, and you go slow enough, I'm sure it'll be okay."

"I don't want your first time to hurt."

Autumn shrugged. "I'm not afraid of a little pain, especially not if it brings you pleasure."

He squeezed his eyes closed. "Sugar, I want to spank that pretty ass, put a dildo in your pussy, and then I want to fuck your ass. I don't want to be gentle, and I don't want to go slow. I want to hear you shout incoherently. I want to feel you submit to me. And I want to make you come until you collapse."

"I'm okay with that, Sir."

"Autumn—"

"Sir, we only have a few hours before Dean and Jesse will be here. I say we take advantage of our privacy before it's gone. Also, I know the safewords. You have to trust me to stop you if you're hurting or harming me." She reached across the table and touched the back of his hand. "I trust you to stop if I call red."

His gaze searched her face before dropping to her shoulder.

This time, she frowned. "Are you afraid to scene with me?"

He looked away, taking in the ocean view without really seeing it. "I'm afraid of losing you. This whole operation could go pear shaped, and you could get hurt. I hate having you here because it goes against my need to protect you."

Autumn tried to turn the situation around to look at it from his perspective. "David, after this is all over, what is going to happen with us?"

His attention snapped back to her. "What do you mean?"

"I mean, when you picture us having a life together, what does it look like?"

"I don't—I haven't really thought about it. I guess I assumed that you'd move to Kansas City with me. I have a great apartment downtown. You'd like the area—great restaurants and tons to do. We'd find the best rehab facility for Summer so that you could have her nearby."

She hadn't known that he lived in Kansas City. That explained why he had rooted for the Royals. "Did you think I'd stay home while you went out on all these dangerous mercenary missions?"

"Well, yeah. I mean, of course you'd want to spend as much time as you could with Summer. But you mentioned wanting to go back to college. You could do that."

He knew nothing of her hopes and dreams. College hadn't been a serious thought. She'd never been to a traditional school a day in her life. Pressing her lips together, she struggled not to say the unkind words that came to her tongue first. That was a defensive response, and he didn't deserve it.

He must have sensed her rising ire. "Or you can take classes. Maybe you can get a job in accounting. I know some people who'd hire you."

She nailed him with a fierce glare. "How about you give me a job? I can plan and carry out heists and cons. That's essentially what you do."

He gaped. "I know you and Summer broke into that drug dealer's compound, but that was once, and it's a miracle you're both alive."

"It's not a miracle. It was good planning. Apparently you've forgotten that we're here to carry out a mission that I pretty much planned. Jesse came on board with tech support, and you're the muscle." She stood up and wrapped her robe tighter. Dean was the eye candy, but she wasn't going to say that right now. "My brains would be an asset to your company, which you'd see if you'd bother to take an objective look."

He followed her inside, but before she could go far, he wrapped his hand around her upper arm and jerked her against his chest. "When it comes to you, Sugar, I'll never be objective. I love you. I want to give you the things you need— roots, love, affection, and eventually a family. There's nothing rational or objective about what I feel for you." His grip tightened, and now he had both her arms in his grasp.

"Fine." Her temper thinned in the face of his vehement declaration. "I'll ask Dean and Jesse when they get here. They'll be both rational and objective. We can look at this mission as an audition for me." She wanted to belong to him and with him, but not as an afterthought. Besides, she'd go crazy with jealousy if he was always out there having adventures while she was at home making brownies and vacuuming the floors.

Though she loved to bake, she could do it between missions as a way to blow off stress.

He gave her a little shake, enough to let her know that she was skating on thin ice. "SAFE Security is owned by four people, Sugar. We all get a vote, and mine is a resounding 'no.' Do you honestly think that my three best friends will go against me?"

"Perhaps." She met his gaze with a challenge. "David, it's not in my nature to be a housewife."

He grasped for anything. "You once said that you and Summer were thinking of opening a bakery. You could do that. I'd front you the startup costs."

She shook her head. "I am who I am, David. That's never going to change. Just do this for me—don't say no. Don't say anything. Give me a chance to prove myself."

Rational thinking must have broken through his emotional response. "Fine. But don't hold your breath." His grip on her arms eased.

Planting a kiss on his jaw, she wiggled closer. "You won't regret it, Sir."

He sighed. "You always try to deflect a serious conversation with sex."

It was true. She'd done this several times to get his mind away from topics she'd rather not discuss. "I never claimed to not be manipulative, Sir. It's one of the things you like about me."

"It's exasperating."

She kissed a path along his neck. "Would you like to spank me now, Sir?"

"Yes. I'd like to tie you up and not let you leave until the op is over."

That would cause difficulties because she was the bait. She nibbled her way back up to his lips. "You sound frustrated. Let me help."

Gripping her hair, he forced her to her knees. "Not a word, Sugar."

He needed her submission. This scene wasn't about easing her heart or mind; it was about giving herself over to him. Her ulterior motives melted away, and she relaxed against his hold. The tension of his fist eased, and he caressed her face with his other hand. "Is this relationship contingent on you getting your way? If I refuse to employ you, does that mean the end of us?"

Though his tone whispered across her with a soothing cadence, there was no mistaking the gravity of his questions. Autumn licked her lips. "No. I love you, Sir. Nothing will tear me from you, but that doesn't mean I'll let it drop. You showed me what it was like to live, and I'm not going back into a fringe existence."

The color of his eyes lightened as he accepted her reasoning. He released her hair and settled onto a wicker occasional chair. "I'm going to spank you now. Lose the robe and take off your clothes."

Autumn did as he ordered, draping the robe, shirt, and panties over the back of the matching occasional chair. Then she draped her body across his lap, lifting her bottom to await his pleasure. He caressed her flesh with deft hands, his palms sliding roughly over her skin.

"Why are you getting this spanking, Sugar?"

The only time Autumn had ever asked a bottom to explain a spanking was when her client had wanted humiliation or to be told they were bad. But she hadn't misbehaved, not really. It took a second for her to formulate a response. "Because you want to spank me."

"Precisely. This is for me. I'm going to spank you until I've had enough, and then I'm going to fuck that pretty pussy. If I want, I'll spank you again and fuck you again."

That sounded ambitious, but she was up for it. "Thank you, Sir."

"You'll think of me every time you try to sit down." With that, he began spanking her. He started out with short swats that stung, but soon he progressed to thumping wallops that had to be leaving handprints on her behind. Autumn gasped, and her breathing became uneven, but she didn't permit herself the luxury of crying out, not even when tears burned a path from her eyes to her hairline. This was for David, her Sir, and her pain or pleasure was an irrelevant byproduct.

It didn't hurt in the conventional way. Her skin was on fire, and her ass throbbed with pain, but her pussy received a different message, and that pleasure overrode everything else. Soon her brain short-circuited, and she relaxed against the onslaught. He kept going. She didn't bother to try to count or to keep track of how long it lasted. It didn't matter. That lightheaded floaty feeling settled over her consciousness, and when it began to clear, she realized that his fingers were probing her vagina. They explored slowly, not to give pleasure but to stake out their territory.

"What a wonderfully wet pussy you have, Sugar. Your juices are dripping down your thighs." He scissored his fingers open, stretching her weeping tissues.

She gasped at the way he made her feel so full.

"You've taken four fingers. It wouldn't take much more to get my whole fist inside."

Only if he wanted her to call red. They had not discussed crossing that boundary.

He withdrew his fingers. "One day. I'm not in a hurry." Then she felt his fingers probing her anus. "This, though, I think I'll take today. Relax, Sugar. Let me prepare you."

He massaged and caressed the delicate muscles guarding her entrance. Like the plug he'd made her wear, it felt both foreign and good. After a time, he withdrew from playing there as well.

"Get up. Crawl to the bedroom and get on the bed with your face down and ass in the air."

She slithered to the floor, but when she tried to crawl, she felt his feet nudging her knees.

"Wider. Don't close your legs at all."

It made for awkward crawling, but she managed to get to the bed in a timely manner. David went into the bathroom and washed his hands. When he joined her in the bedroom, he stood behind her and checked out her ass. Then he slid her body back so that she knelt on the edge of the bed. He massaged her from clit to hole, carving quick circles through her juices.

"I'm going to use a condom for this, Sugar."

"Thank you, Sir."

"While I'm fucking you, I want you to masturbate. Put your hand down and play with your clit. You're going to come too."

She altered her position to put her weight on her right shoulder while she touched herself. "I'm close, Sir. That was a wonderful spanking."

"My pleasure."

"Yes. Your pleasure," she echoed. "I want nothing more than your pleasure, Sir."

She felt his tip at her sphincter and his hand on her lower back.

"Relax, Sugar. If it hurts, call yellow."

"I will, Sir."

He pressed forward, easing past that muscle. It didn't hurt, though it wasn't pleasant for a few seconds. He stroked her hot ass, sending waves of pleasure through her system. "The tip is in. What's your color?"

"Green."

"Keep playing with your clit."

She hadn't realized she'd stopped. She started again, and he penetrated until his thighs pressed against hers. Having him deeper felt much better. He slid back and forth, acclimating her to the sensation. She gasped and moaned as her ministrations to her clit bore fruit. Her movements sped up, and so did his. The orgasm coiled in her pussy and somewhere near the base of her spine. She cried out as it exploded, and her hand dropped away. He didn't tell her to keep going.

He grasped her hips as he fucked her with a primal ferocity. Her body moved, roughly pulled back to meet his frantic thrusts only to be met with that opposing force. Grunting and growling, he made her into a vessel for his pleasure. Autumn relaxed, submitting to his passion and the role he needed her to assume. She was his, and she was giving him what he needed.

Finally, he surged forward one last time as he cried out her name. Then he collapsed, knocking her knees out from under her as he crushed her between his body and the mattress. His heartbeat thudded erratically against her back. When it slowed, he withdrew his cock, rolled to his back, and pulled her to snuggle against his chest. Neither of them spoke as he hugged her to him and stroked her hair.

When her body cooled, she looked up to see if he was asleep. Though his eyes were closed, she knew he was awake. "That was pretty intense."

"Yep." He scratched at his brow and moved a lock of hair away from his forehead.

"I bet it would be even better if you put a vibrator in my pussy. You'd feel that, right?"

"Yep. If I had brought toys, I'd do things like that to you."

She smiled. "I think I'm looking forward to going home."

Chapter Twenty-Two

The *snick-click* of someone using a keycard on the door to his suite woke David. Autumn was sound asleep, so he eased his arm from under her. By the time he tugged on a pair of boxers, light shone from under the door. Intruders didn't typically turn on lights, and so he headed to the common area. As he'd suspected, Jesse and Dean had arrived.

"Hey," he whispered as they set their bags near the entryway. "How was the flight?"

Dean visually swept the suite. "Uneventful."

"You know, when it was just us, you rented a room with two queen beds. You bring the little woman along, and suddenly we need a suite?" Jesse shook his head. "She already likes you."

"It'll go on the expense report," he assured Jesse. "CalderCo will be billed the full amount."

Dean inclined his head toward an open door. "Is that my room?"

"You and Jesse are sharing. It has two beds, but one is a fold-out."

"You fucking suck," Jesse said. "You could have just got two rooms with double occupancy."

David blinked at the unexpected vehemence. On many missions, hotel accommodations weren't available. They'd slept in cars and camped on the ground.

"He's tired," Dean explained. "He spent all day trying to develop an algorithm to hack into the bank. And then when he tried to call Marlene to soften her up before our arrival, she wasn't exactly welcoming."

"Apparently she thought it was a one-time deal. She's married." Jesse scowled. The pretty banker had been all over him on their last trip. "I'll convince her to meet with me tomorrow, and that'll be your chance to sneak in to plant the security information we need."

David had every confidence in Jesse's ability to charm his way into another dalliance with Marlene. "I'll let you get settled. We'll review the plan over breakfast. I should warn you that Autumn gets up early."

Jesse smirked. "Looks like you're losing your touch. You used to be able to exhaust a woman in to a semi-comatose state."

David chose not to rise to the bait. "She doesn't sleep well in strange places."

Dean leaned close and dropped his volume. "The DNA tests on Autumn and Summer came back with a positive match. Apparently their younger brother is an FBI agent out of Kansas City. He had it set up to automatically notify him if anyone accessed the files, and he called in favors to get the results expedited."

This was not news he wanted to discuss with Autumn right now. She had been through so much recently, and to say she hadn't reacted well last time was an understatement. He couldn't begin to imagine the depth of her anger or sense of betrayal at finding out that her entire life had been a lie.

"That's so close to home." He passed a hand over his eyes. "Don't say anything until after the op is over. I think she should be with Summer when they hear the news."

"Rossetti already talked to Summer."

Autumn wasn't going to like hearing that. "How did she take it?"

"She didn't try to kick his ass or accuse him of lying. Apparently she has vague memories, but she thought they were nothing more than dreams. She wants to see Autumn as soon as she gets back." Dean clapped a hand on David's shoulder. "Go back to bed. Tomorrow is going to be one hell of a day."

When David slid back under the covers, Autumn turned to him and snuggled closer. "Was that Jesse and Dean?"

"Yeah." He kissed her forehead. "Go back to sleep, Sugar."

————

Autumn woke to a darkened room. The heavy curtains blocked out all light, but she estimated that it wasn't far past dawn. David's arms surrounded her, and his chest pressed against her back. She lifted his top arm gently, but he stirred anyway.

"Get dressed before you go out there. Dean is an early riser too." He mumbled most of the words, but she understood him anyway.

Turning, she kissed his cheek. "What do you want for breakfast?"

His hands slid down her back and cupped her sore ass cheeks. "Pancakes. But before you go, my dick wants a hug."

His cock stirred against her belly, but he didn't make a move. She giggled. "You're not even close to being awake."

"Nope," he agreed as he rolled onto his back. "You're going to have to do all the work."

She coaxed his dick fully awake with her hands before she straddled him. Not once did his eyes open, though he now wore a pleased grin. Since he wasn't participating, she decided to play first. She ran the tip of his cock through her slit, stimulating her pink parts. She rolled and pinched her nipples as she rubbed his crown against her clit.

She hadn't realized that her eyes were closed until a sharp crack rent the air, and fire seared the aching muscles of her left butt cheek. She looked down at David, a question in her gaze.

"I said a hug, not a floorshow."

Not at all recalcitrant, she shrugged. "You're the one who wants to sleep through sex."

Wordlessly, he managed to flip her over and thrust his cock into her pussy in one smooth motion. He hooked her left leg behind the knee and hiked it as high as it would go. She gripped his shoulders as he set a frantic pace. Thanks to the foreplay in which she'd indulged, she climaxed less than a minute later, which was good because he came as well.

He collapsed and rolled away. "Pancakes."

Autumn jumped in the shower before she headed to the common room. Wearing cargo shorts and a white button-down shirt that wasn't buttoned, Dean lounged on the balcony. He smiled as she joined him. "Coffee?"

"Yeah, thanks." Remembering David's reaction to when she'd checked out Jesse, she refrained from taking a closer look at Dean.

He rose and went to the coffeemaker. "Cream or sugar?"

"Black is fine. I was going to order room service. Do you want anything?"

He chuckled. "I ordered for everyone when I heard that you and David were up."

It took Autumn a second to realize that he'd heard them having sex. Heat traveled up her neck to stain her cheeks. "Um, thanks."

He set down a steaming mug in front of her. "No problem. We should talk about our part of the operation."

She thought so as well. Working with a new partner was always challenging. It helped that she trusted him, but if they were going to play a couple claiming their money, they had to appear natural together. Any mistakes would put the operation in jeopardy. The charges against her hadn't been dropped yet. Though the case leading to her was circumstantial, it could still lead to a conviction. They needed hard evidence that Stephanie had set her up because right now, they only had Autumn's word against Stephanie's.

"We're a wealthy couple." She sipped a little bit of heaven to find it not all that good. "This is horrible coffee." He'd already set cream and sugar on the table, so she helped herself.

"I've had worse." He smacked his lips together. "Not much worse, though. Wealthy—that's a given. When we go to the bank, let me do all the talking."

Autumn shook her head. "I don't think so. The account is mine. You're the arm candy in this scenario."

Dean's brows drew sharply together, making him look almost dangerous. "You've never done anything like this before. We can't take the chance that you'd panic and fuck it up."

She scoffed at his assumption. "I kept my head just fine when you surprised me at the art gallery."

His brows relaxed, but his posture remained tense. "Why don't you give me a brief overview of your resume?"

This time, she snorted. "Not a chance. Let's just say that I can remain calm in a variety of situations, and I'm great at thinking on my feet. One thing I know is that we can't go in there with you and me vying for dominance."

"Agreed. I'm the dominant."

"No. We're equals. We should flirt and appear to be in love. You're wrapped around my finger, and you can't deny me anything."

He chuckled. "Or how about this: You worship the ground I walk on."

She shook her head. "That's clingy and pathetic. A handsome man in love can charm an entire room. That'll take attention away from David sneaking into Marlene's office."

The balcony door slid open, and David joined them. He pressed a kiss to her lips before pouring a mug of coffee for himself. "Are we arguing over the op?"

"We're negotiating," she said. "Dean will eventually realize I'm right."

Dean stared out over the horizon. "She thinks I should act like I'm you—pussy whipped."

David sat down. His hair was wet from his shower. Drops glistened in the early morning light. "It'll keep attention away from me. Women like seeing a man in love."

"That's what I said." She was a little miffed that he didn't dispute being pussy whipped. His dominant personality precluded anything that would reduce him to such a pathetic state. "And he's not pussy whipped." Okay, she wasn't going to keep her mouth shut.

David chuckled. "That's Dean's way of saying I'm in love with you."

"Oh." It didn't sound that way. She suspected that Dean had suffered his share of heartbreak. "So Jesse diverts the attention of Marlene, the banker whose login information you stole. David will sneak in to change the security questions on the account. Dean and I will stroll in, get a bankcard issued, and then we'll go on a shopping spree to draw out Stephanie and her accomplice."

"That's the plan." Dean said. "If anything goes sideways, follow my lead."

She nodded. At least Dean had agreed to her plan. It helped that David was on board. The door to the suite slid open again, and Jesse joined them. He showed off his magnificent chest by wearing only loose cargo shorts. She smiled. "Good morning, Jesse. Did you sleep well?"

He shot David a dirty look as he poured coffee. "Sleep better when I don't have to share a bed with a fucking cover hog."

Autumn looked to Dean, who shrugged. Then she fixed Jesse with her most sympathetic look. "Maybe you should try snuggling? You could share body heat."

David laughed. "I can picture it now, Dean spooning you from the back. That would be a very cozy picture."

Jesse glared, but Dean shook his head. "It'd never happen. Jesse farts in his sleep."

Before the conversation could degenerate further, Autumn cleared her throat. "What's the plan for when we lure Stephanie here? How are we going to catch her?"

Jesse sat down across from Autumn. "I have a few ideas."

A knock at the door interrupted their conversation. David rose. "I hope that's breakfast. I like to plan on a full stomach."

Not one to give up, Autumn turned back to Dean. "You should practice staring at me like a love-struck fool."

————

The bank was sandwiched between a bakery and a travel agency. Dean held the door for her, and she walked in like she owned the place. Out of habit, she noted the locations of the guards, counted the tellers, and scanned for the location of security cameras. Jesse had convinced Marlene to take an early lunch while Dean had quizzed Autumn on the answers to the security questions that would let her access the account.

A woman greeted them. She wore a conservative dress suit, and the white lapels of her blouse were neatly folded over the black lapels of her jacket. She smiled brightly. "Welcome to First National Cayman. Is this your first visit?"

Autumn looked around, taking in the opulent fixtures and filigree all over the place. If they'd done this right, David had sneaked in behind them and evaded the greeter. "It's our first visit to this island paradise. It seems that we've left our debit cards at home, though."

"Oh." Her smile dimmed with sympathy. "My name is Meaghan. Are you customers with First National?"

Dean parked his hand on her lower back. She'd worn the pale green dress with darker green accents that David said brought out her eyes. Dean's outfit, the same one he'd been wearing that morning, matched the vacation vibe that hers had. He flashed a charming grin at Meaghan. "We have several accounts here."

They did? Jesse hadn't shown her numbers for multiple accounts. Autumn didn't want to let Dean take them on a fishing expedition. "Honey, we only need cards for one account."

"I want to check the balances in the other accounts." Dean gritted his teeth like a long-suffering husband should, but he followed up by kissing her cheek. "My lovely bride doesn't exactly keep track of her receipts."

Autumn rolled her eyes. "I didn't buy the yacht. That was you, dearest."

"But you outfitted it like a palace. And then you surprised me by wearing that sexy little number with the Italian heels." He pulled her close and nipped at her earlobe. She squealed, more out of surprise than anything else. They kept up the ruse for a few more minutes, buying David time to change the information that would let them claim the account. Finally David sneaked behind Meaghan, throwing a nasty look at Dean—whose arms were still around Autumn—before exiting the building.

"Right this way." Meaghan motioned them to follow. "I'll set you up with Olaf. He'll help with anything you need." Meaghan and Olaf exchanged a smile, and then Olaf gave his attention to the clients.

"Welcome, friends. How can I help you today?"

"We left our bank cards at home." Autumn took a piece of scrap paper, wrote the account number, and slid it under the elegant bulletproof glass. "We'll need temporary replacements."

Olaf tapped in the numbers. "I'll need to ask you several security questions."

"That's fine." Dean leaned against the counter next to her, putting his back to the teller so that he could survey the bank.

"What was the first street you lived on?"

Autumn smiled as if remembering it fondly. "Mulberry."

Olaf flashed a short smile. "Your mother's maiden name?"

"Eastridge." The information was David's. These were his security questions.

"And the name of your first pet?"

"Ringo. He was an Irish setter."

"Thank you. Now I just need to see your identification."

Autumn exchanged a glance with Dean. This bank operated using account numbers, not names. He nodded slightly, and she handed over her passport.

Olaf studied it, and she smiled at him when he glanced up to compare the picture to her face. "Thank you, Ms. Applebaum. We do have to put your name on your debit card. Would you like one for Mr. Applebaum as well?"

"That would be lovely," she said. Dean's identification didn't include an alias. "But he left his passport in the hotel safe. Just issue one for me, and we'll come by tomorrow to pick up my husband's card."

Olaf smiled. "If you like, we can scan his fingerprint as a form of identification. It's on file."

This information wasn't something Jesse had uncovered. "That's okay." She leaned closer, and so did Olaf. "I'm not with my husband." She gave an exaggerated wink and pressed her finger to her lips. "Don't tell." Hopefully Olaf and Meaghan didn't compare stories.

His lips thinned as he struggled not to react. "Very good, Ms. Applebaum. I'll have your replacement card in a few minutes."

Dean leaned down. "You're good at this. And you're glowing. I think you like it."

"I love it." She slid her arms around his neck. "Think of this as a job interview." She followed up with the same wink she'd thrown at Olaf.

Dean chuckled and looked toward the sky as if an angel might swoop down and save him. "My dear Alisha, that is a committee decision."

She pretended to pout. "That's what David said."

At least it wasn't an outright rejection.

Thirty minutes later, David seated her at a sidewalk café across town. "They have excellent desserts here, Sugar. Are you in the mood for something sweet?"

"Absolutely, Sir."

"I'll be right back."

She waited while he went inside to get their food. Most people liked to choose their food, but she liked when David did it for her. It made her feel protected and cherished. She felt a little sorry for Dean and Jesse, cooped up in the hotel staring at the wireless feeds from the airport security cameras that Jesse had managed to hack.

David returned with an ice cream sundae floating on a thick brownie. One dish and two spoons. He scooted his chair close enough to touch hers, and handed over a spoon. "I want to be in our hotel room, feeding this to you naked."

She let the first decadent bite sink into her palate and slide down her throat. The hand-whipped ice cream was a frozen taste of heaven. "With you naked, me naked, or us both naked?"

"Both. If you're going to make those faces when you eat, I may have to watch you feast on something else."

"Little Sir?" She giggled.

"Damn it, Sugar. I told you not to call my dick little."

She laughed harder. "I might need another spanking."

He lifted her onto his lap. "I might be just the man to give it to you."

Cupping his cheek, she lifted her eyebrows. "Might be?"

"Am." He gave her ass a little whack under the table. "I was doing the flirting thing." Before she could say more, he stuck a spoonful of ice cream into her mouth. "Careful, Sugar. I'm adding everything up, and I will tie you up and cash in later."

She pressed kisses from his ear to his collarbone. "Now you're just saying things to turn me on."

"Are you wet?" He used that gravelly Dom voice that she couldn't resist, and he slid the hand that had been on her knee up her inner thigh.

"I might be."

"Might be?" He slid his hand closer to her pussy.

She clamped her thighs together. This was a public place, not a fetish club where nobody would mind. "Am."

"Relax. There aren't many people around right now, and nobody can see where my hand is. I've been discreet." A bit of silk joined the gravel, and he used the tone that could not be denied.

She relaxed and let him slide his hand up her thigh.

"You're going to come, and you're going to do it silently."

"Sir, I suck at this game."

He chuckled, the evil kind that proclaimed his power. "Look at this as a chance to redeem yourself." He eased the crotch of her panties out of the way and drew a finger through her wetness. "Very wet. Feed me some ice cream, Sugar."

She fed him, bite after bite, as he stimulated her clit and slid his fingers into her dripping vagina. Soon her hand shook, and she dropped the spoon. It clattered to the ground with a noise that could be heard above the roar of a monsoon. She leaned down to pick it up, his fingers still deep inside. He circled her clit with his thumb, and when she righted herself again, he pumped his fingers slowly. It was too much. She buried her face in his neck, bit his shoulder hard, and came on his fingers.

While she slumped against him and recovered, he scooped ice cream with fingers that were still wet with her juices and slurped the mixture with loud and obvious satisfaction. "Perfect," he said. "I've never had better cream. Just the right amount of sweetness and sass."

"I love you, Sir."

"I love you too, Sugar." He took her spoon—the one that hadn't dropped—and fed her a bite.

They spent the afternoon wandering around the island. David insisted Autumn try on expensive clothes, and he made her purchase the ones he liked. They shopped excessively, buying clothes and gadgets for Dean and Jesse. Autumn wanted to bring souvenirs back to her friends and family, but David reminded her that everything they bought would need to appear on the expense account. The next day, she bought a pair of jet skis, and they spent some time on the water. She would have bought two pair, but Dean and Jesse were once again stuck in the room watching surveillance feeds. By the time evening of the third day rolled around and they returned to the hotel, she hadn't spent as much money as she'd expected.

Standing alone on the balcony, she frowned into the middle distance.

"Penny for your thoughts?"

She looked to find Jesse leaning on the railing next to her, watching the sun set on the ocean. "It's beautiful."

"I agree, but that's not what you were thinking." He opened a bottle of beer and handed it to her. Then he opened one for himself.

She took a sip. "I guess I was hoping that Stephanie was already here, and spending her money would draw her out faster. We had everything delivered to the hotel. That should be easy to track. And then linking Alisha Applebaum to me should be a piece of cake for an identity-thief-slash-embezzler like her."

"Three days is plenty of time." He gazed thoughtfully over the horizon as he sipped. "The hotel is too public."

"And having three mercenary bodyguards is probably a deterrent as well." She watched the sun dip lower. "David and I should rent a cabin somewhere remote."

He chuckled. "I like the way you think. Have you said anything to David?"

"Not yet. He won't be in favor of making the bait so easy to snag. I was trying to figure out all the counterarguments first." She sipped, staring at the sunset in the silent moments as they both contemplated this conundrum.

"Dean and I should bring it up," Jesse said at last. "We scoped out a location already that affords the tactical aspects we require. All that's left is to set up security and move you two lovebirds out there."

She turned to him. "So you and Dean have already come up with the plan, and it was your job to get me on board?"

"Looks that way."

"Because you know our best bet in getting David to agree is for all three of us to gang up on him?"

Jesse didn't bother to look guilty. If anything, he was proud. "Are you mad?"

"That you manipulated me? No." She sipped the cold beverage. "I'm kind of pissed at myself for not using this as leverage to get you guys to hire me as a consultant."

Jesse's brows lifted. "Hire you? And risk David planting grenades in my boots?"

"The greater the risk, the greater the reward. I'm a valuable asset. I have contacts all over the country, I speak fluent Spanish, and I can open any lock." Okay, that last boast was a little out of date. There were plenty of locks she'd never encountered and security systems she'd only ogled over the Internet.

He shook his head. "Autumn, I think you'd better consider other career options."

She admired his loyalty. Summer was the only person in the world who was that loyal to her. Suddenly she was homesick for her sister.

Jesse misread her reaction. He hugged her. "Please don't cry. Maybe you can help out with some of the smaller stuff. I'd love if we had someone to schedule flights and accommodations. Maybe order supplies and make sure bills got paid. We could use an office manager."

The patio door slid open. "Why are you hugging my sub?"

Jesse transferred her to David. "She looked like she was going to cry."

Autumn smiled up at David. "Jesse said I could be the firm's office manager."

He stroked her hair away from her face. Remnants of the sunset reflected from the water and made his eyes shimmer. "Were you being manipulative, Sugar?"

She'd been pretty straightforward with Jesse. "Not on purpose, Sir. Jesse said I couldn't be a mercenary, and I was struck by how loyal he is to you. Then I started thinking of Summer and missing her. That's when he hugged me and offered me a job."

David glared, but he aimed it over her head, and it nailed Jesse. "You hired an office manager without consulting the rest of us?"

"Nope. I said we could use one, and I may have implied that Autumn would be a good candidate for the position, but I most certainly did not hire anybody." Jesse lifted his half empty bottle in a silent toast. "You're welcome." With that, he went back into the suite.

David studied her thoughtfully. "You're not going to let this go, are you?"

"Let me consult my Magic 8 Ball." She mimed shaking the toy and turning it over to read her fortune. "My sources say no."

Dean stuck his head outside. "David, Autumn, team meeting now."

The fact that he'd included her as part of the team made Autumn feel pretty darn good. Perhaps he and Jesse were secretly in favor of having her work at SAFE Security. She followed David inside and took a seat next to him on the sofa.

"Our plan isn't working," Dean said. "Rossetti called. The FBI thinks Stephanie and her accomplice might be traveling as Bruce and Madison Olivetto. Jesse and I found them by hacking into the docking logs in the marina. They've been here for two days, and they most likely have some kind of plan for snatching Autumn and getting the money back. However, the marina is too well protected. We need to lure them out."

David sat back, his arms crossed and his lips pursed. "Do they have eyes on us?"

"Probably." Jesse drummed his fingers against the table. "If I was in their position, I'd stay on a boat, keep an eye on you from a distance, and move the second I thought she was alone."

"We're not leaving her alone." David didn't bother to consider that idea. "This bitch has already tried to kill Autumn once. I won't leave her vulnerable again."

Dean and Jesse exchanged a glance. "We have another plan."

"I'm listening."

Autumn listened as well while Dean and Jesse outlined their idea for David and Autumn to rent a cabin and wait for Stephanie to come to them. She thought it was a great plan— except for one thing.

"What if they just go to the bank while we're on our secluded beach and take out all the money? That's what I would do. Heck, I wouldn't bother with revenge or killing anyone. I say we drain the account first, and then take the money to the cabin with us. They'll be online, watching the balance drop. That's guaranteed to draw them out." Autumn looked to David, half wondering if he'd picked up on the fact that she'd already agreed to Dean and Jesse's plan.

Jesse waved a hand. "They can't access the account because we've changed the security questions."

"But if we disappear with the cash, Stephanie will think we're leaving for good. She'll be forced to follow. That will show her we've split up, and it'll convince her that she needs to strike now." David warmed to the idea. "Dean and Jesse can leave separately from us. We can make a big show of taking them to the marina and seeing them off. Then we go to the bank, drain the account, and head to the cabin for a romantic getaway."

Autumn eyed him with more than a little hint of irony. "Only I would be attracted to a man who thinks setting a trap for a serial killer is a romantic getaway."

"Oh, Sugar, you won't be with me." He turned to Dean. "How fast can Frankie get here? She's a little taller than Autumn, but if we dress her the same and put a wig on her, we can switch her out for Autumn at the marina. Autumn can go with you two while Frankie and I wait for psycho and company."

Autumn stood, looming over David with the full force of her Domina side. "I'm going to that cabin with you."

"Fine," he said. "If you give up the idea of working for SAFE Security. This is your final adventure. You will never again put yourself in a vulnerable position."

Motherfucker thought she was manipulative? Just wait— this conversation was far from over. For now, though, she acquiesced. "Fine." Her single word carried the full weight of an I'll-show-you challenge.

Dean cleared his throat. "There's just one fly in the ointment here. Frankie called. She needs backup. I'm heading out on the next flight." He nodded toward a lone suitcase sitting next to the exit door. "I'm already packed. That leaves Jesse as backup for you."

David nodded, his expression grim. "How bad off is Frankie? Does she need both of you?"

Dean shook his head. "Jesse will follow as soon as you're done here. If we need you as well, we'll let you know."

Autumn glanced at David. "As your new office manager, I could make all the travel arrangements."

Frowning, Dean leaned forward. "Office manager?"

Planting seeds meant she was one step closer. Maybe David wouldn't let her join the team in the way she wanted immediately, but she had faith in her ability to work her way from one position to another. She rested her fingertips on Dean's arm. "Jesse's idea. Think about it. Take your time."

Chapter Twenty-Three

The cottage was barely more than four walls, and it was half the size of her apartment. One wall featured a kitchenette, one had a door to the patio and a small table for two, one had a front door and two windows, and the last one had a double bed pushed against it.

"It's tiny," he said. "I can't believe we left a luxury hotel and paid a thousand bucks for this."

"It's cozy, perfect for a romantic getaway." She examined it closely, picking up everything that wasn't nailed down. She wandered onto the open-air porch overlooking the pristine beach. Waves crashed on the shore in a gentle lullaby that reminded her of lazy summer days. "It has a great patio, with furniture and a shower."

David joined her on the patio. He peeked around a weathered wooden fence on one end of the patio. "The bathroom is outside. If you have to go during a storm, you're shit out of luck."

"That would be a real shit storm," she agreed. This wasn't the first place she'd stayed at that had an outdoor toilet and shower. At least this one had a cover over the toilet, though that wouldn't be much shelter in a storm. "I need a pry bar, a hammer, and finishing nails."

"Why?"

How could he not know that the first order of business was to stow their valuables in safe locations? "So I can hide the money and the passports. Seriously, Sir. Did you think we should just leave it out in the middle of the room?"

"Yeah. In a neat pile to taunt our target into the open."

Autumn rolled her eyes. If an opportunist happened along, or somehow their targets got away with the money, then it was best to have most of it hidden safely away. "Are you going to help or not?"

"Yes, and I added that eye roll to the list of your transgressions. You may not sit comfortably for a week."

After that last spanking, she'd just now started sitting comfortably. Part of her couldn't stop goading him, though. She chalked it up to being a lifelong smartass. He went outside and scrounged around in a small closet near the outdoor latrine. While he did that, she grabbed a square plastic piece from her purse. It looked like nothing, but it was her laser alarm system. She angled it up to catch anyone approaching the cabin. Set in a remote area, they couldn't even park next to the house. The driveway ended at a path lined with thick foliage that led to the cabin. Lush tropical forest surrounded them on all sides. It was very secluded.

They'd dropped Dean and Jesse at the airport. While Dean had boarded the plane, Jesse had doubled back to the cabin. Jesse would approach from the southwest. If all had gone right with their plan, he would be in position by nightfall. He'd keep watch on the cabin while Autumn and David waited inside. Stephanie and "Bruce" didn't stand a chance.

On the way to the cabin, Autumn had made David stop at a grocery store. While he waited, she had run in to buy some food staples and several thousand meters of plastic wrap. After setting her alarm, she set to work wrapping bundles of money. The house sat on a crawl space, so she wouldn't need to pry up floor boards. Some of the money went in the obvious places—the machinery in the back of the refrigerator, the access panel of the hot tub, inside the lid of the toilet—but most would go in places few people would consider.

David returned with his offerings. "I raided the maintenance closet. It now has a busted lock. Here's a construction stapler, pry bar, and finishing hammer. No nails."

But the construction stapler was a nice alternative. "I'm going under the house. Can you pry the facing off the base of the lower cabinets? Be careful not to leave scratches." She changed into older clothes, shimmied under the house on her back, and got to work stapling the plastic-wrapped money to the underside of the floorboards. When she finished, she army-crawled out to find David waiting for her.

"I stowed as much as I could fit, and you'll be glad to know I only left one scratch. It's on the inside, though, so it's not noticeable."

She dusted the sand from her clothes. "Great. How much is left? We can pile it on the table like you wanted—so they can see it the moment they walk in. We'll backlight it so that it seems to glow. Maybe set out a nice bottle of wine, and some finger foods."

"And we'll be laying in wait while staring at the weirdly romantic tableau?"

"No. The wine and snacks are for us. We'll tie them up and make them watch while we sip wine, eat yummy treats, and mock them."

David frowned. "Mock them?"

"Sir, she tried to kill me. She came into my apartment, told me all the ways she violated my privacy, how she set me up, and then she threatened to kill my sister if I didn't swallow a handful of pills. I have earned the right to mock her."

At this, David merely inclined his head and nodded while frowning.

They'd hidden most of the money, and Autumn counted the rest as she arranged it into an artistic pyramid-shaped centerpiece. David called Jesse to update him on their progress, and Autumn decided to make dinner. She washed and sliced fresh fruits and vegetables, arranging them on plates that she placed around the centerpiece. Then she added diced cheeses, several kinds of crackers, dips, and spreads. When she finished, she stepped back and admired her handiwork.

Having wandered outside while on the phone, David came back in once he was finished speaking to Jesse. "Wow. That looks beautiful, Sugar." He hugged her from behind and peppered her neck with kisses.

"Thanks. What did Jesse have to say?"

"They took the bait. They set sail from the marina a half hour ago and are en route, sailing around the island. Jesse pinged their GPS, so he has a lock on their location. They're probably waiting to catch us unaware."

Autumn clapped. "I love when a plan comes together."

He laughed. "I thought you didn't really watch TV growing up?"

"We didn't."

"But the plan thing—that's Hannibal's line from The A-Team."

She leaned back to stare blankly. "My dad used to say it."

"When this is all over, I'm going to make you watch an episode with me."

She believed that her father would co-opt a line from a popular show. He used to watch TV sometimes in hotels while she and Summer played. Wiggling her ass against David, she added, "Naked. I want to do a lot of things with you naked." She turned and draped her arms around his neck. Part of her wanted to forget why they were there and enjoy the secluded, minimalist paradise. "Nobody will be here for at least a half hour. Let's grab some food, go down to the beach, and appear to mess around."

"We need to lie in wait."

"We will be, but we won't look like it. I set up my silent alarm system in case they circle around and come in from the street. I'll put my phone on vibrate, and it'll go off when they get here. In the meantime..." She gestured toward the open door leading to the patio. Beyond that, a pristine, private beach awaited them. "I made plenty of food. We can spread a blanket and look like we're absorbed in feeding each other. Having us in the open will draw them out and give us an advantage because we'll be able to see them coming. Besides, I'm hungry."

He ran a hand through his hair, messing it up in a very sexy way. "I'd rather hide in the woods and watch for them to approach. We don't have weapons, and I don't see you talking to any arms dealers you may or may not have screwed over, so we need some way to get the upper hand."

She went outside. He followed to find her ripping twigs from a fallen branch.

"What are you doing?"

"Weapon. And you're right—I don't know any arms dealers around here. We'd have to break into someone's house and hope they have an illegal gun that we could steal.

We could do that, but it would take time." She hefted a branch the size of her arm. "This'll hurt."

He took it from her and pointed it ominously. "Freeze, or I'll stab you."

She rolled her eyes.

"There's another one. Sugar, maybe I'll look for a switch while I'm out here. I see red birch, and you're definitely asking for it."

Well, yeah. The spanking he'd issued four days ago had been about his stress release. Besides the op, she had a lot of other things on her mind—Summer's health, an imminent move to a new city with a man she'd only known for a month, clearing her name, and—though she didn't want to think about it—the idea that she'd been kidnapped as a child and raised by her kidnapper. She could do with a cathartic release. "Sir, you're supposed to hit them with the stick. There's no warning, no threatening—just good, old-fashioned whacking them upside the head." She took it from him and swung hard at a nearby tree trunk. Rather than absorb the force, it bounced back.

David laughed and took the stick from her. "Watch out, or you may whack yourself in the head."

"It's still a good weapon. I'm bringing it with us on the picnic. I'll pretend it's my walking stick. I've always wanted to be one of those hikers who pokes the ground with a stick." If she wanted to sneak up on a cabin where some bitch she thought she'd killed was holed up with her money, she'd dock somewhere nearby but out of sight and sneak up on them.

"Pokes the ground? What are you looking for?"

"I don't know. Quicksand, maybe. Or a hornet's nest. It'd rather not step on one."

He laughed, a loud guffaw. "Because poking it with a stick won't agitate them at all."

She narrowed her eyes. "I'll show you agitation."

He caught her in his arms and kissed her cheek. "Let's get you fed." He led her inside, and she brought her big stick along. They gathered food and grabbed an extra blanket from the cupboard. David led her to a spot on the beach near where the waves lapped at the sand. She spread the blanket and positioned her stick within reach while he set out the food. It would have been terribly romantic if they weren't bait for a serial killer and her boyfriend.

David plopped down and patted the place next to him. Autumn joined him. She dragged a cracker through cheese spread. Before she finished chewing her first bite, she snagged a handful of grapes. It all tasted so good, and it had been many hours since the light lunch they'd scarfed earlier.

"I would have thought you'd be too nervous to eat." David casually popped a cube of pineapple into his mouth.

Autumn shook her head. "I'm ravenous." Okay, she might have been stress eating just a little.

They ate in silence, with David grazing from the many dishes and Autumn shoveling it down without tasting anything. He watched her the whole time. As he casually spread garlic butter on a wheat cracker, he said, "Want to talk about it?"

With the earpiece he wore, she knew Jesse was listening in, and yet that didn't make her feel self-conscious. David's friends understood discretion, they didn't judge, and they were fiercely loyal. She paused, a handful of fruit and nuts in her hand. "I guess I'm nervous about moving to a new city."

"Why?"

For the first time in her life, she was putting down roots. She had a good friend, many acquaintances who were primed to become friends, and her sister was finally on the mend. "I don't know anyone there. I've moved plenty, but never anywhere in the Midwest. Dad kept us in coastal states or in the Southwest. When Summer and I wanted out, we purposely chose a Midwestern state because we knew Dad avoided them."

David watched her carefully, with sympathy and caution mixed in his eyes. "Do you know why?"

"He said they were boring." She tossed another grape into her mouth.

"You never looked at that file Keith sent over. Do you want to know the real reason?" He closed his hand over hers.

Did she want to know the real reason? The better question would be if she wanted to keep pretending that her entire life hadn't been a lie. She hazarded a guess. "We were kidnapped from a Midwestern state?"

David nodded. "From a suburb outside of St. Paul. You have a brother who is an FBI agent stationed in Kansas City. He had an alert set up to notify him if anyone looked at your files, and he expedited the genetic testing."

All of a sudden, moving to Kansas City to be with David seemed like a dangerous proposition. She had a brother who worked in the same city where David wanted her and Summer to build a new life. The idea made phantom walls seem to close in around her, and she didn't know why. "I have friends in Michigan. I don't think I want to leave."

If her abrupt change in topic threw him for a loop, David hid it well. "The wonderful thing about friends is that they don't care where you live. They call, text, email, and visit. I'm asking you to move to KC because I want to build a life with you. I know I'm asking a lot, Sugar, but I think it'll be good for you. Think of it as a fresh start. After everything that's happened to you, you deserve a chance to hit the reset button."

"What if I don't want to see this brother or the parents who lost me?"

He caressed the side of her face, forcing her to meet his gaze. "Sugar, that's an entirely separate issue. However, I think you owe them one face-to-face meeting. Whatever you decide after that, I'll support."

She didn't want to give them one meeting. They'd lost her, and behind the anger at her dad, she found anger at the people who had allowed her to be taken. "They lost us, Summer and me, but they managed to keep their son. Maybe they didn't want girl children." She trembled as she said it. Whether it was anger or fear, she didn't know.

"Your brother is three years younger. You were three when you were taken. Summer was six. Your mother was pregnant at the time. She left you in the backyard while she went in to use the bathroom. She wasn't gone for more than five minutes, and when she returned, both you and your sister were gone." He spoke softly, as if his normal volume might spook her.

Waves of anguish washed through her, their sound combining with the surf in a way that made her want to cry. A tear slipped down her cheek, but she refused to try to figure out why. "Summer is only two years older than me, not three."

He chuckled. "Sugar, she was a petite child and you were tall. Brian Sullivan had no idea of your actual ages when he took you."

Autumn swallowed a lump in her throat. "So I'm a year younger than I thought, and Summer is a year older?"

"It looks that way." He moved empty plates out of the way and pulled her to him so that she snuggled against his side.

His fingertips played down her arm in a soothing rhythm. "I know it won't be easy, but I'll be by your side. You can lean on me, Sugar. Always."

She rested her head on his shoulder. "I love you, Sir. I'd like to say that you should also give your blood relative one more chance, but I'm still pissed at your dad for having me arrested."

He chuckled. "I told you he was an asshole."

Garbled sounds came over the earpiece in David's ear. No doubt he heard it clearly. Autumn remained in place as she waited for instructions. Next time, she was going to insist on an earpiece.

"Don't move."

Autumn leaned forward to peer around David. Stephanie and Bruce moved toward them, each armed with a handgun. She smiled brightly. "Hi, Stephanie. Guess what? The pills didn't work as expected, and I found a bank account with a balance of three million dollars. Isn't that amazing? It's like winning the lottery."

Bruce stopped a few feet in front of their picnic blanket. "I told you not to move."

She laughed. "I suck at following directions." Nodding to David, she continued. "He'll vouch for me in that department."

With his stoic gaze fixed on the pair with guns, David didn't join the conversation.

Autumn decided to ad lib for him. She narrowed her gaze and dropped the pitch of her voice. "You won't get away with this."

Stephanie let loose a blast that was maybe meant to be an evil chuckle. "We know you have the money somewhere. Give it to us, and we'll let you live. Put up a fight, and we'll kill you, then we'll take the money."

David gestured behind them. "It's on the kitchen table."

Bruce snorted. "We already looked. Only a few thousand was there."

Autumn rubbed her hands together. "I smell a scavenger hunt. The first item on the list is a paper clip. The second will be a stick, and the third can be a corkscrew." She stage-whispered to David, "For the wine."

"Stop talking," Stephanie growled. "The next word that comes out of your mouth, I will shoot you in the leg. Say anything more, and I'll shoot you in the other leg. Piss me off, and I'll aim for your head."

David put up a hand. "There's no need for anybody to die. I'm going to get to my feet so I can show you where the money is hidden."

Bruce motioned with the gun. While his aim wasn't trained on anyone, David lunged at the man. Inside twenty-five feet, a person with a gun had no real advantage, and Bruce stood only a few feet away. From the woods, a loud firecracker sound got Stephanie's attention. She screamed as she fell, but the sounds were swallowed by the pounding surf.

Jesse had shot Stephanie in the shoulder, but she hadn't dropped the gun. The trigger finger on her other hand still worked, and Stephanie struggled to switch hands. Meanwhile, Autumn seized her big stick and swung at Stephanie as if her head was the ball and her body was the tee. The woman dropped like a stone. Turning to survey David's situation, she found him with his foot on Bruce's neck. The gun was now in David's hands, and he aimed it at Bruce's head.

Autumn lifted an inquiring eyebrow. "Want me to take a swing at him?"

Jesse emerged from the woods and jogged toward them. "Nice job, Autumn. You kept your wits about you, and you kicked ass."

She couldn't take all the credit. "You shot her in the arm. That was a great distraction. We make a fantastic team."

With an uncomfortable chuckle, Jesse secured Bruce's wrists and ankles with zip ties.

David shook his head. "Office manager, Sugar. That's the job offer. Take it or leave it."

She grinned. *Step One accomplished.* "I'll take it."

Jesse secured the unconscious Stephanie next. He looked up at David. "You've got your hands full."

"No doubt. Let's get these two on the yacht. Did you see where they hid the dinghy?" He cleared their picnic materials off the blanket and rolled their captives onto it.

Autumn frowned. "Why are you putting them on the yacht? This island belongs to Great Britain. Just turn them over to the authorities. This isn't a death penalty case, so they're great about extradition."

Jesse ran his palm over the short dark hairs on his head. "Extradition is a pain in the ass process that sometimes takes years. It's better to sail them back to US soil and turn them over to the FBI." He jerked his head to indicate a location somewhere to the northeast. "They tied up about a half mile away. The yacht is anchored off shore."

David nodded, but he didn't take his attention from Bruce, who hadn't been knocked out. "Autumn, get everything packed up. We're shipping out ASAP."

She gazed wistfully at the cabin. It would have been a great spot for a romantic weekend, and now that things were good between her and David, she really wanted to spend some quality time alone.

Though he didn't look at her, he seemed to sense her reticence. "We'll come back another time, Sugar. I promise."

David and Jesse turned out to be excellent sailors. As they were also Doms, they tried to give her orders and treat her like crew. She did what they asked, shooting glares whenever either one became too bossy, and they taught her rudimentary seafaring skills. Two days on the high seas in a small yacht had given her an appreciation for life on the water. They'd encountered one brief squall in the early morning hours, but David and Jesse hadn't been impressed. They'd shouted orders at her—mostly telling her to get below deck and watch the prisoners—while navigating their way through it. Just now it was smooth sailing. Jesse manned the helm while David and Autumn took a break.

"What time it is?" Autumn slipped a grape past David's lips. She straddled his legs because he'd ordered her to sit on his lap, but he hadn't specified how.

"Almost two." David fed her a bite, letting her suck the juice from his fingertips.

Muffled sounds came from the direction of the door. Jesse and David had showed off their bondage skills by tying Stephanie and Bruce in ways that were slightly uncomfortable and very secure.

"I'm jealous, you know. I prefer to be the one you tie up." She turned and whipped a grape at Stephanie. It bounced from her cheek and rolled out the open door to the deck. "Wasteful, I tell you."

"Yeah, but when I tie you up, I don't let my girlfriend pelt you with cheese and fruit. Keep that up, and we're going to attract seagulls." He fed her another chunk of pineapple. "Rats of the sea."

"I think I'm doing a great job managing my anger." She smooched him loudly.

"I agree, Sugar. You haven't once tried to torture or kill our guests." He smoothed a hand along her back.

"Hey, you two." Jesse came into the stylish sitting room. He grabbed a bottle of water from the fridge. "We'll be in US waters in about ten minutes. The Coast Guard will meet us at the boundary and take these two off our hands. Agents Rossetti and Adair will meet them at the Miami port."

They planned to dock there as well. "Are we flying back to Detroit?"

"Yep. I've booked our tickets, which is technically your job." Jesse winked at Autumn as if he'd known all along that she'd get her way. "I'm so glad I won't have to do the office crap anymore. We're supposed to split it, but it never quite happens that way."

She looked around. Though the yacht was on the small side, it managed to be spacious and elegant. "What happens to the boat?"

David ran his palms over her bare thighs where her shorts didn't cover them. "It's evidence. It goes to a Federal impound lot. They'll probably end up auctioning it off once it's no longer needed."

"Oh." Disappointment accented the single syllable.

David pressed a kiss to her lips. "SAFE Security owns a yacht. We can take that one out, just the two of us, and spend lots of time naked. If you're very good, I'll even tie you up and not throw fruit at you."

She laughed and hugged him tightly. She was overcoming her anxiety where moving to Kansas City was concerned. As long as they were together, it didn't matter where they were. And Summer would be nearby. For now, that's all she needed.

Chapter Twenty-Four

Their plane arrived at Detroit Metro in the early afternoon, and David took Autumn straight to the hospital to visit Summer. Her sister was sitting up in a chair, which was a vast improvement from the last time they'd seen each other.

Summer brightened when she saw Autumn. She leaned into the hug and lifted one arm to rest on Autumn's back in an attempt show affection. "Sorry. Physical therapy will take months, if not years."

"That's okay. You're not in a coma anymore." Autumn sat in the other chair. "We're going to focus on the positives."

David brushed a chaste kiss on Summer's cheek. "It's good to see you up and about."

"Thanks," she said. "It's good to be up. Julianne was here this morning. She filled me in on a lot of stuff. Have they dropped the charges against Autumn yet?"

David nodded. "Agent Rossetti called yesterday. She's in the clear." He looked at Autumn. "Did you want some time alone?"

Just as Autumn was about to tell him how sweet he was and ask him to pick her up in a couple of hours, three people came into the room. She didn't need name tags to know who they were. The younger man had rich brown hair and green eyes. His features matched hers and Summer's in a familial sort of way. He had the same oval face, though his jaw was squared off. The woman had light brown hair with blonde highlights, but her green eyes were startlingly familiar. The older man sported a salt-and-pepper look. All three of them stared at her in silence.

She slipped her hand into David's and held on tightly. He squeezed his in a gesture of reassurance.

"Hi." Summer broke the awkwardness with her friendly greeting. "I figured the best way to do this was to rip off the bandage. Autumn, these are our birth parents, Sylvia and Warren Zinn of St. Paul, Minnesota. And that handsome young man with them is our little brother, Leon." She tried to lift a hand to gesture to Autumn, but the effort proved too exhausting. "This is Autumn."

So many emotions zinged through Autumn. Anger—at Summer for springing this on her. Shock—to actually be in the same room as her parents and brother. She'd known it was coming, but she'd thought she'd have time to prepare herself emotionally. And grief—because she didn't remember them at all. They looked familiar because she and Summer had features in common with them, not because she remembered anybody.

"And this is David, Autumn's boyfriend. He's the one who set all this in motion."

She wanted to run, but they blocked the exit. No words came to mind, and so she continued to stare.

David extended his other hand. He looked as if this meeting had caught him off guard as well. "Mr. and Mrs. Zinn, it's great to meet you. Leon." He shook hands with everybody. "Autumn wasn't expecting to see you today. Give her a little time to acclimate."

Tears cascaded down Sylvia's cheeks. Warren put his arm around her shoulder and pulled his wife closer, but he was shaking too. Leon looked like a stone statue. Somehow it made Autumn feel less pain and anger.

"Don't be mad," Summer said. "I know you, Autumn. I know that you would have put this off as long as you could."

Sylvia approached, and she dropped to her knees in front of Autumn. She clasped Autumn's hand in hers. "Breanna. My baby girl. I never thought I'd see you again." Her tears showed no signs of slowing down. She sobbed and buried her face in Autumn's lap.

Autumn let go of David. She put a tentative hand on this woman's head, lightly smoothing her hair. "I remember that name." It had apparently been one of her favorite aliases for a reason. Her subconscious had clung to it. She lifted her gaze to study Warren. His features tugged a cord in her memory. "I kind of remember your face, but it's vague, like a dream."

He closed the distance, but he didn't fall to his knees. Instead he fingered a strand of her hair. "I used to brush your hair every morning and night. You liked braids, and you made me learn how to French braid your hair."

Sylvia lifted her head and wiped the wetness coating her face on her sleeve. She sniffled. "For gymnastics. You liked to have your hair braided for your gymnastics class."

Her father had let her continue learning gymnastics. She remembered asking him to braid her hair. He would chuckle, tell her that he'd forgotten how, and put it in pigtails. Part of her felt horrible for these people who had lost their daughter. She could never be that person again, but that didn't mean they couldn't get to know one another. A knot of anger at Brian Sullivan twisted her gut. No matter what he'd done, he'd been her father. He'd raised her, and she loved him—but she also hated him. She hated feeling these complex and diametrically opposed emotions.

She looked up at Leon. He hadn't been born when she and Summer had been taken. His life had most likely been seriously impacted by living in the shadow of two siblings who had been kidnapped. Numb from the overload of stimulation, she flashed a smile she didn't feel in her heart. "It's nice to meet you, Leon."

He flashed a sad smile, shades of ghosts haunting the green depths of his eyes. "Yeah. You too."

"Okay," Summer said. "The therapist said it's going to be awkward for a while."

Sylvia got to her feet. "We couldn't wait. As soon as Leon told us that you might have possibly been located, we started hoping. And then, when he told us that the DNA tests were positive, we flew out here. I know we jumped the gun a little, but we've waited twenty-six years. We couldn't wait a moment longer. Please don't be upset about that."

Autumn looked at Summer, and an understanding passed between them. She wasn't angry with either of them for forcing this meeting. More than anything, it broke her heart. If Brian Sullivan hadn't come into her life, these parents would have raised her. She would have grown up in one neighborhood, and she might even have met David while visiting her brother in Kansas City.

"I'm not upset," she said at last. "Just overwhelmed."

"Everybody is," Summer said.

All of a sudden, the room became too small. She stood as close to David as she could get without crawling into his skin with him. "I need some air."

He took her into the hallway and led her to a waiting room. She sat down and put her head between her knees. David knelt next to her. "Are you going to throw up?"

She hoped not. "I'm going to need you to scene with me tonight."

"I know, Sugar." He gathered her hair into a ponytail. "But right now, just breathe. I'm not going anywhere."

With him by her side, she calmed. She didn't have to face anything alone anymore. "Are you going to marry me one day?"

"Yes. I was going to wait for a more romantic time to ask you, though. I'd envisioned having a ring on hand as well. You are a damned impatient woman."

She laughed, and all the tension she felt melted from her body. Sitting up, she cupped his face in her hands. "I'm not asking you, Sir. I'm just making sure that you plan to be with me always. I love you, and I need you."

He kissed her firmly on the mouth. "Always, Sugar. I love you, and I need you too."

Michele Zurlo

I'm Michele Zurlo, author of over 20 romance novels. During the day, I teach English, and in the evenings, romantic tales flow from my fingertips.

I'm not half as interesting as my characters. My childhood dreams tended to stretch no further than the next book in my to-be-read pile, and I aspired to be a librarian so I could read all day. I'm pretty impulsive when it comes to big decisions, especially when it's something I've never done before. Writing is just one in a long line of impulsive decisions that turned out to showcase my great instincts. Find out more at www.michelezurloauthor.com or @MZurloAuthor

Re/Leased
Lost Goddess Publishing

Visit www.michelezurloauthor.com for information about our other titles.

Lost Goddess Publishing Anthologies
BDSM Anthology/Club Alegria #1-3
New Adult Anthology/Lovin' U #1-4
Menage Anthology/Club Alegria #4-7

Lost Goddess Publishing Novels
Re/Bound (Doms of the FBI 1) by Michele Zurlo
Re/Paired (Doms of the FBI 2) by Michele Zurlo
Re/Claimed (Doms of the FBI 3) by Michele Zurlo
Re/Defined (Doms of the FBI 4) by Michele Zurlo
Re/Leased (Doms of the FBI 5) by Michele Zurlo
Blade's Ghost by Michele Zurlo
Nexus #1: Tristan's Lover by Nicoline Tiernan
Dragon Kisses 1 by Michele Zurlo
Dragon Kisses 2 by Michele Zurlo
Dragon Kisses 3 by Michele Zurlo

Coming Soon: Re/Viewed (Doms of the FBI 6)
And look for SAFE Security—a new BDSM series from Michele Zurlo launching in 2017

If you enjoyed this title, please consider leaving a review at your point of purchase.

33673789R00221

Made in the USA
Middletown, DE
22 July 2016